AF235302

# *Our*
# Extraordinary
# Summer

# ALSO BY LORI WILDE

**THE HOBBY ISLAND SERIES**
*The Summer That Shaped Us*

**THE MOONGLOW BAY SERIES**
*The Wedding at Moonglow Bay* • *The Lighthouse on Moonglow Bay*
*The Keepsake Sisters* • *The Moonglow Sisters*

**THE STARDUST, TEXAS SERIES**
*Love of the Game* • *Rules of the Game* • *Back in the Game*

**THE CUPID, TEXAS SERIES**
*To Tame a Wild Cowboy* • *How the Cowboy Was Won*
*Million Dollar Cowboy* • *Love with a Perfect Cowboy*
*Somebody to Love* • *All Out of Love*
*Love at First Sight* • *One True Love* (novella)

**THE JUBILEE, TEXAS SERIES**
*A Cowboy for Christmas* • *The Cowboy and the Princess*
*The Cowboy Takes a Bride*

**THE TWILIGHT, TEXAS SERIES**
*The Christmas Brides of Twilight* • *The Cowboy Cookie Challenge*
*Second Chance Christmas* • *The Christmas Backup Plan*
*The Christmas Dare* • *The Undercover Cowboy* (novella)
*The Christmas Key* • *Cowboy, It's Cold Outside*
*A Wedding for Christmas* • *I'll Be Home for Christmas*
*Christmas at Twilight* • *The Valentine's Day Disaster* (novella)
*The Christmas Cookie Collection*
*The Christmas Cookie Chronicles: Carrie; Raylene; Christine; Grace*
*The Welcome Home Garden Club* • *The First Love Cookie Club*
*The True Love Quilting Club* • *The Sweethearts' Knitting Club*

**AVAILABLE FROM HARLEQUIN**
**THE STOP THE WEDDING SERIES**
*Crash Landing* • *Smooth Sailing* • *Night Driving*

# *Our* Extraordinary Summer

*A Novel*

# LORI WILDE

AVON

*An Imprint of* HarperCollins*Publishers*

Without limiting the exclusive rights of any author, contributor or the publisher of this publication, any unauthorized use of this publication to train generative artificial intelligence (AI) technologies is expressly prohibited. HarperCollins also exercise their rights under Article 4(3) of the Digital Single Market Directive 2019/790 and expressly reserve this publication from the text and data mining exception.

This is a work of fiction. Names, characters, places, and incidents are products of the author's imagination or are used fictitiously and are not to be construed as real. Any resemblance to actual events, locales, organizations, or persons, living or dead, is entirely coincidental.

OUR EXTRAORDINARY SUMMER. Copyright © 2026 by Laurie Vanzura. All rights reserved. Printed in the United States of America. No part of this book may be used or reproduced in any manner whatsoever without written permission except in the case of brief quotations embodied in critical articles and reviews. For information, address HarperCollins Publishers, 195 Broadway, New York, NY 10007. In Europe, Harper-Collins Publishers, Macken House, 39/40 Mayor Street Upper, Dublin 1, D01 C9W8, Ireland.

HarperCollins books may be purchased for educational, business, or sales promotional use. For information, please email the Special Markets Department at SPsales@harpercollins.com.

Avon, Avon & logo, and Avon Books & logo are registered trademarks of HarperCollins Publishers in the United States of America and other countries.

hc.com

FIRST EDITION

Interior text design by Diahann Sturge-Campbell

Title page and chapter opener art © Danussa/Shutterstock.com

Library of Congress Cataloging-in-Publication Data has been applied for.

ISBN 978-0-06-335219-3

26 27 28 29 30  LBC  5 4 3 2 1

*To Cynthia Scott: I treasure our friendship. Thank you for being you.*

# *Our* Extraordinary Summer

# Chapter 1
## *Eloisa*

*"Grief is the price we pay for love."*

—*Eloisa Hobby*

*Hobby Island, June 2*

Bring my daughters to your magical island," Demetra Sarris said, her faded gray eyes beseeching. "I've failed them. Please help them heal, Ellie. You're their only hope."

"My dearest, I'm not Obi-Wan Kenobi." Eloisa Hobby patted her dear friend's cool, dry cheek, shooting for a dollop of levity even during this most solemn of times. Eloisa was, after all, a joyful person by and large.

"Oh, no, you're far more powerful than that because you're real." Demetra paused, wheezing.

Fat tears gathered on Eloisa's eyelashes and clung thick. *No, no.* She promised herself she wouldn't cry. She would stay strong for the woman she loved like blood kin, the woman who saved her life when—

*Stop it, this isn't about you.*

"Promise me . . ." Demetra's restless fingers rubbed the crisp cotton top sheet.

Resolute, Eloisa blinked away the tears. "I swear it."

"Heal them the way you healed me."

"We healed each other," Eloisa corrected, her heart cracking right in two.

"If only we had more time to plan . . ."

"No worries, my love, I'll find a way. Leave it to me."

"It won't be easy. My girls are so stubborn." Demetra's voice came out faint, losing strength.

"*Shh*, rest."

Demetra's lids drifted closed, a soft, grateful smile forming on her lips, slipping away before Eloisa's eyes.

Grief scrubbed her insides raw. Hard as it might be to reconcile her friend's estranged daughters with each other, she would find a way. For the last three days, ever since Demetra returned to Hobby Island, she lay nestled in this bedroom, covered in a handmade quilt, which carried the faint scent of roses and sunshine.

Eloisa's faithful calico, Felena, curled up at her feet while she slept in the lounger beside the bed, straying from the sick room only for brief breaks. Throughout the ordeal, Eloisa held Demetra's hand, bathed her face with a cool washcloth, and gave her sips of soothing chamomile tea to ease her transition. A sacred duty, these precious few last hours, filled with hushed confessions, shared memories, and absolute forgiveness. They'd been through so much together—knitting, quilting, crafting, leaving abusive husbands . . .

Hobby Island was a sanctuary. A refuge for healing, where creativity flourished, and friendships deepened throughout the years. They'd created a haven for women like themselves, a space where crafting wasn't just a hobby but therapy as well.

Demetra's breathing slowed, and she dozed off again.

Eloisa sank her face into her palms, drawing in slow, deep

breaths to contain her tumultuous emotions, and then, a weak tug on her sleeve startled Eloisa upright.

"Ellie . . ."

"Yes?" Eloisa leaned forward to catch every word, her pulse quickening.

"Without you, I wouldn't have—" A hacking cough rolled through Demetra, shaking her entire body.

"No need to say more. I understand. Save your strength." Eloisa took the washcloth from Demetra's forehead, refreshed it in the white porcelain bowl of cool water sitting on the bedside table, and bathed her fevered face.

"No one ever treated me with such kindness or loved me the way you have. You never judged me for losing custody of my girls . . ."

"Oh, dear friend, who am I to judge anyone when I—" Eloisa gulped past the lump in her throat.

Demetra's hand dropped, and her eyes drifted shut once more, her breath growing fainter with each passing second.

"Demi?" Eloisa's voice quivered.

Demetra's lips moved. Her words came so faintly Eloisa had to press her ear close to catch them. "Until we meet again."

She took one final shuddering breath and her face went still, peaceful at last; her suffering ended.

With an anguished yelp, Eloisa gathered her friend to her chest and wept for everything Demetra had lost, for all the sorrow she'd been through and the heartache that weighed down her soul—the fate of her two daughters.

"I'll heal them, Demi, and I'll make sure your girls understand how much you loved them. I vow to reunite them if it's the last thing I ever do." She laid Demetra's lifeless body back onto the mattress, smoothed her friend's hair, and straightened the covers.

Wiping away tears with the back of her hand, she stiffened her shoulders, took in a resolute breath, and left the room, Felena at her heels.

Eloisa stepped from her cottage by the sea. The garden welcomed her with the heady scent of jacaranda blossoms, their purple petals spilling like confetti onto the flagstone path. As she strolled past, she brushed her fingers along the edges of tall, colorful gladiolas standing above the other flowers, grounding herself in their soothing textures. Each bud and sprout reflected the years of care and hope poured into this place, a reminder of how healing could flourish even in the hardest times.

At the patio table graced with Demetra's favorite tea set and breakfast foods, Eloisa's closest remaining friends, Dot, Clare, and Vivian, waited for her, their faces etched with sorrow and sympathy. They'd been in one another's lives for so long, quilted baby blankets and dropped stitches together, that she could hardly remember a time when these women weren't in her life.

"It's over." Eloisa dabbed at her eyes with a honeysuckle-scented, hand-sewn hankie pulled from her pocket.

Her friends rose to their feet and opened their arms. Grateful for their support, she fell into the group's embrace. Without a word, they held one another close. Eloisa wasn't alone because she had her lifelong friends, her chosen family, to lean on. Serenity filled her heart, calming the grief as the four of them mourned Demetra together.

*This.*

Difficult as her task might be, this was the beautiful gift she must give Demetra's daughters—love, peace, and community. She would carry out her friend's wishes down to the last detail.

She owed it to Calista and Athena.

She owed it to Demetra.

But most of all, she owed it to herself because helping others through their troubles was the only way for Eloisa to keep walking the path to everlasting light, to find meaning and purpose in the face of life's losses and heartaches.

With a deep sigh, Eloisa stepped from the group hug. "Let's get started. We have much work ahead of us."

# Chapter 2
## *Calista*

*"Without pain, we can't appreciate pleasure."*

—*Eloisa Hobby*

When Calista Dempsey was nine years old, her father, along with the support of the American judicial system, stole her and her older sister, Athena, away from their mother.

Dallas, Texas, courthouse steps at high noon. The bright August sun blinded her as sweat trickled down the armholes of her new blue sea-silk dress.

A smirking, mustachioed lawyer in a tailored pin-striped suit pumped Benjamin Dempsey's hand, offering congratulations in a too-loud voice that made Calista want to press her hands over her ears. Her father stood tall, his shadow falling over her. His face wasn't angry—it was something worse. He smirked the way he always did when he crushed his adversaries.

Stiff-shouldered grandparents waited nearby, their dour mouths and narrowed eyes disapproving of everything. Cantu, their longtime chauffeur, waited at the back door of the shiny black stretch limo parked at the curb.

*Full custody to the father. No visitation rights.*

The words the robed judge spoke just minutes before he banged down his gavel echoed in Calista's head. Courtroom spectators had risen from their seats while their mother let out a keening wail and collapsed to the floor.

Calista tried to rush to Mamá, but a refrigerator-size bald man with a silver name badge clamped a viselike grip on her shoulder and dragged her back. She darted a glance at Athena, but her sister inched closer to their father, slipped her hand into his, and did not meet Calista's gaze. He patted Athena's head, tugged her close, and glowered at Calista.

Alone, she stood stiff as a toy soldier, scared, trembling, and out of her mind with grief.

Four concerned-looking older women swept her whimpering mother away through a side door. She wanted to scream *no* and run after Mamá but feared Father's strict punishment. Instead, she popped her thumb into her mouth and cried silent tears as snot dribbled from her nose.

"God!" Her father's voice barked, sharp and loud. Calista flinched, his tone twisting her stomach in knots. He yanked her thumb from her mouth so hard her wrist hurt. She knew better than to talk back. He was bigger, stronger, and she never knew what he might do when he got that look in his eyes—the one that made her feel small and breakable. "You're disgusting. Wipe your face."

Once outside, in the broiling sun, she curled her hands into fists. No sympathy from him, no loving kindness, no comfort. She could count only on herself.

"Let's go." Her father waved them all toward the limo.

Everyone jumped to do his high-handed bidding, with Grand-mother and Grandfather Dempsey leading the way, noses in the air, chins granite. No soft hugs from these two, ever.

Cantu swung open the door, and her grandparents slid inside

along with Athena, but Calista balked. Fear gobbled her up. She did not want to go.

"Calista, get in the limo," Father said through drawn lips and clenched teeth as the sun glinted off the gold cuff link of his initials, blinding her.

*BD.*

Short for "bad" in Calista's childish mind, and she shook her head.

Her father loomed over her, grabbed her by the shoulder, and dug his sausage fingers into her collarbone with force meant to hurt. "Get in the car."

She wrenched away.

"Calista!"

They both turned to see her mother running down the courthouse steps. The four older women who'd helped Demetra from the courtroom rushed behind her, urging her to stop.

"Mamá!" She broke free and raced toward her mother, who held her arms outstretched.

"Calista, get back here!" Father's voice smacked her ears.

She flung herself into her mother's arms, and Mamá held her close, showering her face with kisses. "I love you, Calista. I love you, love you, love you, forever and always."

"Don't let him take me," she begged her mother. "Please, please . . ."

"The court says you must go with him." Tears streamed down both their cheeks, mingling together, the taste of salt overwhelming Calista.

"I don't want to."

"I know, I know. I don't want you to go, but you have to," Mamá said.

"Please take me with you!"

Mamá, smelling of peppermint and sweet flowers, squeezed her hard and whispered close to her ear, "I can't."

"I'll run away, and I'll come find you."

"No, no, please, *moro mou*, don't make this harder on yourself. He'll take it out on you. Behave, do what he says."

"I hate him." Calista spat out the words.

"Listen to me." Mamá rubbed her fingers over Calista's heart. "You are stronger than you know. You will survive this. You'll bloom into a beautiful young woman, and you'll make your own way in the world, but I will always be with you in spirit. Always loving you."

With trembling hands, her mother took off the gold locket from around her neck, the locket that held a picture of Calista and Athena when they were little, and pressed it into Calista's sweating palm.

"When you're eighteen, come find me. I'll wait for you and Athena, always. I'll send you cards and letters, and I'll call—"

"You'll do nothing of the kind, Demetra." Her father's voice was as hard as the Italian marble in his cold, glossy kitchen. "You'll obey the court order, and you'll stay away from my children, or I'll have you thrown in prison. You know I will." He grasped Calista's arm, wrenched her away from her mother, and dragged her back to the limo.

"Mamá!" she screamed, reaching out, desperate, yearning, pleading for this to be different.

Her mother sank to her knees on the courthouse steps, and her friends surrounded her.

And that was that.

The memory of that awful separation flashed through Calista's mind as she stood on the loading dock in Everly, Texas, waiting for the ferry to Hobby Island.

Three days had passed since Calista received word of her mother's death. Now, it was Friday midmorning and in her hand, she fiddled with the golden ticket—which had arrived via express mail the night before—bending it between her fingers, folding the stiff cardboard back and forth.

How was she supposed to feel about her mother's death? Sad? Check. Remorseful? Check. Hurt? Check. Numb as hell? Check and double check.

On this day, June 5, a perfect seventy-two-degree breeze ruffled the hem of Calista's sage-green paisley-print midi skirt and sent a strand of long, dark curly hair tickling across her nose. She brushed it back and scanned the area.

Behind her, the souvenir shops, nautical-themed restaurants, and vendor kiosks lined the weathered boardwalk bustling with happy tourists. Families with excited children, couples arm in arm, all eager for a beach getaway. Calista felt like an outsider among them, a dark cloud in their bright, carefree world.

She spied a palm reader's sandwich board, and the woo-woo side of her wanted to cross the street to visit the fortune teller just for fun.

Or for stalling.

Yes, well, she wasn't looking forward to her stay on Hobby Island. This visit would be difficult, but then nothing came easy to Calista, well, except for golf, her one natural talent.

The edges of the golden ticket bit into her palm, and she glanced down to see her fist clutched around it. She welcomed the discomfort, a distraction from the hollow ache in her chest, and turned the ticket over, her gaze snagging on the small handwritten note on the back she'd read a hundred times since yesterday.

*Your mother's last wish was for you and your sister to reconcile. Please come in remembrance of your beloved Demetra and let our island magic soothe your soul.*

A bitter, humorless laugh escaped her lips. Peace, what a farce. Peace was an ill-afforded luxury while her mother's ghost still haunted every corner of her mind, when she and her sister hadn't spoken to each other in five years.

She tucked the showy ticket into her shoulder bag. The breeze picked up, carrying with it the briny sea scent. Fingering the locket around her neck, the jewelry she never took off, Calista lowered her lashes and counted to ten, steadying herself. She had faced much worse, and she could handle a few days on an island paradise, even if it meant confronting the history she fought so hard to escape.

The ferry bobbed toward the landing, the inevitable countdown. Time to face the past, although she refused to linger there. She would deal with the details of their mother's estate and then leave as soon as possible.

Someone tugged on her skirt.

Calista glanced down into the tearful blue-eyed gaze of a sweet young girl in a blue jean jumper and puffy-sleeved white blouse who looked to be about five. The child clung to a worn stuffed bunny, missing a button eye and with patches of fur worn thin. She drew in a deep, shuddering breath that shook her little body all the way to her Grogu Crocs.

"I can't find my mommy!"

Empathy flooded Calista's aching heart. She understood what losing your mother felt like and knelt to the child's level, giving her a gentle smile.

"It's okay," she said, "we'll find her. Where did you see her last?"

"Over there." The child pointed to a refreshment kiosk. "She was getting lemonade, but I assadenally dropped BunBun, and when I looked up, Mommy was gone." The girl hugged her stuffed bunny as fresh tears watered her eyes.

Calista's heart clutched, grief both old and new squashing her chest. "What's your name?"

"Emily."

"Emily, I'm Calista. Let's go sit on that bench, and we'll look to spot your mommy."

"Okay." Emily bobbed her head.

The girl's mother must be frantic. Calista scanned the crowd, on the lookout for a distraught mom. The child reached for Calista's hand, and her heart melted. They settled onto the bench, Emily leaning back, clutching the bedraggled bunny in her arms.

"Is BunBun your favorite stuffed animal?" Calista asked.

Emily's head bobbed. "Uh-huh. He's my bestest friend."

"You're a brave kid, you know. Staying here and waiting for your mommy is the best thing you can do."

The girl smiled through her tears. "Thank you, lady."

A strange sensation came over Calista. She dissociated from her body, pulled down a long tunnel, and witnessed herself—not just as a child, but as the person she had become—still searching for something, still terrified of losing what little remained. She brushed a tear from her cheek, surprised by the surge of emotion.

"Emily!" A frantic woman rushed toward them. "There you are!"

Emily's face lit up, and she hopped off the bench. "Mommy!"

Calista got to her feet as the mom scooped up her daughter and rained kisses on her precious face. "You scared me half to death, pumpkin doodle. Please never wander off like that again."

Emily buried her face against her mother's neck and clung on for dear life.

The mother's eyes met Calista's. "Thank you so much," she said, her voice choked with relief. "I turned around and poof, she was gone."

"It's okay." Calista sent her a soft smile. "She's safe."

"Thank heavens for kind souls like you!"

"Anyone else would have done the same," Calista said.

The mother set Emily on the ground and took her hand. "Tell the nice lady goodbye."

"Bye!" Emily beamed, her traumatic moment forgotten, waving as she and her mother walked away.

Calista exhaled. That minor blip had distracted her from her problems for a few minutes, a welcome respite.

"Bang-up job with that kid. You're a natural mother," a masculine voice said.

Calista startled. She didn't even want kids. Kids made you far too vulnerable. Plus, that voice sounded familiar, and it wasn't a good recognition.

Pulse bumping, she turned to find a drop-dead handsome man her age standing there, and her stomach sank to the soles of her ankle boots. No forgetting that smug, gorgeous mug. Her most egregious nemesis . . . and onetime lover.

Reid Thornton. It had been five years since he turned her world upside down, and even longer since he'd broken her heart as a teenager. He'd always had a knack for showing up at the worst possible times. First love, first heartbreak, and the one person who had told her the truth about her father's ultimate betrayal. She'd thought she'd buried all those memories deep, but now they were bubbling up like a geyser.

Reid. The YouTube sports vlogger who covered her infamous meltdown at the Chevron Championship, writing about the humiliating incident that ended her career and shot her older sister to stardom. Oh, and with nary a mention that *he* caused said meltdown.

He'd been relentless after she left the LPGA, texting and sending emails she never answered, spurring him to show up at her condo. She hadn't answered the door, either, and finally he'd gone away.

At the time, she thought he was just chasing a story—a way to milk her fall from grace for clicks and views. Now, seeing him here, she wasn't so sure. Could there have been something more to his persistence? Either way, it was no coincidence he was here on the event of her mother's death.

But why?

"I thought that was you!" Reid said, shifting his weight as if uncertain of his welcome. "Are you headed to Hobby Island for the golf tournament honoring your mother?" He glanced at her suitcase, then back to her face with what looked like genuine concern. "Did you bring your clubs?"

"Golf tournament?" Calista blinked.

What was he yammering about? No one had mentioned a golf tournament to her, and it wasn't on the travel itinerary Eloisa Hobby sent her. She read through the paperwork a dozen times because, hey, yes, anxiety was her middle name.

Did they even have a golf course on Hobby Island? From what she'd learned when she googled the place, the location seemed restricted, with outsiders allowed to visit only if they'd received a golden ticket from the island's owner.

Could he be right? Was she expected to play in a memorial golf tournament? Her mouth went chalky, and the old wounds split wide open. Calista loosened her jaw to respond, but the words stuck in her throat like a thick jam. She'd spent so much energy running from her greatest shame on that green in the Woodlands five years ago. The last thing she wanted was a memory lane frolic.

Her ugly past stared her in the face in the guise of those familiar blue eyes that once made her feel like she could conquer the world.

"Is Athena with you?" he asked, hesitation in his voice. Something flickered across his face—was that guilt?

Calista refused to engage. She waved at the docking ferry, ducked her head, picked up her luggage, and started around him. "Excuse me."

Reid moved to block her way. His dark eyes sparked, but gently, not aggressively as they had when he'd dogged her after she left the LPGA. "Wait, please. I know I handled everything wrong back then. Your fans—the real ones—they've missed you. Not because of the drama, but because of who you are."

How could he say that straight-faced? As if he hadn't toppled the dominoes that day in the clubhouse . . . well, she would not dignify that memory with a response.

"Your fans—"

"My *fans*?" A hot flash of anger passed through her like a blowtorch set on scorch. "Are you talking about the same people who kicked me when I was down?"

Reid flinched, genuine remorse crossing his features. When she moved left, he stepped aside but spoke quickly. "People make mistakes, Calista. God knows I did. It's not the fall that counts. It's how you bounce back that defines you, and you . . . you've always been stronger than anyone I've known."

He stared at her with an intensity that made her uncomfortable, as if trying to convey something beyond his words, but Calista wasn't ready to hear it. She had spent too long letting others define her, letting their opinions and judgments shape the way she saw herself.

"Your sister bulleted to the top of the LPGA in your absence," he said, filling in the silent pause for her.

"That's life." She shrugged as if she didn't care.

"You're a better golfer than Athena." Something in his expression reminded her of younger days, of shared dreams and stolen kisses behind the clubhouse. "I never understood what really happened that day. I should have tried harder to . . ."

Stunned, she stared at him. Did the man honestly not remember what he did to dismantle her entire world? Or had he convinced himself that he wasn't behind her downfall?

"You know what, Reid?" She kept her voice steady, even as memories overwhelmed her. "I don't owe you or anyone else an explanation. What happened back then is between me, Athena, and our father. Right now, the only thing that matters is honoring my mother's memory."

"So you *are* planning to play in the memorial tournament." He pulled out his phone as if to record her but stopped himself.

"Out of my way. I have a ferry to catch." She brushed past him, nudging him aside with her shoulder.

"Calista," he called after her, his voice carrying a note of desperation she'd never heard before. "Please. You could inspire so many people—but that's not the only reason I'm here. I want to make things right between us."

She halted, then spun around, and he was following so closely he almost plowed into her. She shooed him back with both hands. "You just don't get it, do you?"

His eyes softened with concern. "I know you're working as an event planner now. Seems like you're good at it, from what I saw on the internet."

She gritted her teeth. "This isn't about some feel-good story or inspirational message. This trip is about a daughter grieving her mother, struggling to say goodbye to a complicated history. Please respect that if nothing else."

"Calista, I . . ." Raw remorse etched his features. "I never meant to hurt you. Back then, I was young and stupid, trying to prove myself in the industry, and I lost sight of what really mattered. *Who* really mattered."

"What you meant is of no consequence. What matters is what you did."

The ferry tooted, and a surge of passengers streamed around them to board the boat. Calista took a step closer, shoved her face in his, and locked eyes.

He stared right back, but this time without the old arrogance, just a complicated mix of regret and something else she couldn't name.

Oh, little did he know she was the master of the stare-down. Just ask Athena.

"Why don't you do us both a favor and leave me alone? Go find your story for your little vlog somewhere else." Okay, she knew he had over two million subscribers, but she didn't want him to know she knew.

"That's not what this is about, but if you prefer I talk to Athena . . ."

Just then, as if on cue, a white limousine pulled up to the pier, and Calista didn't have to ask who it was. Besides Benjamin Dempsey, she knew only one other person who traveled in limos to make a grand entrance.

*Athena.*

# Chapter 3
## *Athena*

*"Just a spoonful of sugar . . . well, you know the rest."*
—*Eloisa Hobby*

Final round. Eighteenth green. All eyes focused on the Dempsey sisters, each three under par, squaring off in the biggest sibling rivalry since Venus and Serena Williams. One putt could decide the Chevron Championship and a place in LPGA history.

If Calista sank the shot, she would win. Game over.

A solemn hush fell over the crowd. Which sister would snag the coveted Chevron Championship? Who would emerge as the victor?

*This* moment felt like that nerve-racking incident. A mental replay of the event that sealed Athena's reputation as the undisputed queen of women's golf and caused the irrevocable final split between her and her sister.

Not just the tournament caused hurt feelings but rather a lifetime of their father pitting them against each other. Athena, the golden child, and Calista, the scapegoat, the roles he'd assigned decades ago, trapping them in an endless sand bunker neither could chip shot their way out of.

Thirty-one years of guilt settled in Athena's stomach, thick as silt in a water trap. She smoothed her white pencil skirt down to the hem at her tanned knees. To the world, she was the picture of poise and confidence—a successful woman at the top of her game—but beneath the polished veneer, she was a bundle of insecurity.

Over the years, she searched for Calista online, heartened to see her sister had found a new path as an event planner specializing in unique children's parties. That was Calista—creative, unique, expressive. The novel path looked as if it suited her sister more than golf ever had, even though Calista possessed a natural talent for the sport.

More than Athena, if she were honest, but Athena was competitive. Once she set her mind on something, she achieved her goal, no matter what.

Her motto? *Win or die trying.*

Even if it meant throwing her younger sister hard underneath an oncoming Greyhound.

She leaned forward, peering through the limo's tinted window at the busy harbor. Somewhere among the tourist throng and locals was the one person she had both longed for and feared seeing for the past five years.

Now, as she prepared to face her sister again, uncertainty gnawed at her. So many complex emotions. What if Calista couldn't forgive her? What if the damage was too deep to repair? She hoped something as monumental as Demetra's death would change things, and they could build a bridge back to each other, no matter how shaky the beginning.

Athena crossed her fingers against her thigh. *Please.*

After the mess at Chevron, Athena tried to reach out to her sister in the months that followed, but Calista shut her out, blocking her calls, texts, and emails, leaving all social media. Total ghostville.

Athena didn't blame her. She deserved it.

After several failed attempts, Athena stopped trying, telling herself her sister needed space to heal. Still, the truth was, she'd been terrified of facing the role she'd played in Calista's downfall, petrified of acknowledging what their father had done to her sister.

Now, with their ostracized mother gone, Athena felt a renewed sense of purpose. She would be the one to bring their family back together, heal the wounds of the past, and build a brighter future. She would be the perfect daughter and sister, the one who had everything under control.

She spotted Calista near the ferry landing, and her heart jumped.

God, her sister was even more beautiful at twenty-nine than she'd been at twenty-four, her long dark hair whipping in the breeze. The last time she'd seen her, Calista had kept her hair cut shorter than Athena's stylish bob, but the loose flowing curls suited her far better.

When they were kids, Dad forced Calista to wear her hair in a pixie that she hated while he encouraged Athena to grow her hair to her butt. Benjamin said the short style was easier since Calista's hair was so thick and curly, but it was the absolute wrong cut for her sister's sweet, rounded face.

Athena winced at the cruel memory and bit down on her tongue. Dad had just been pushing her to do her best, and Calista's hair got in the way. She could just hear her father in her head. *Your sister looks like Cousin It with all that hair.*

Tears burned her eyes, and Athena slumped back against the seat. This reunion was already much more complicated than she ever thought, and she'd imagined a damned bumpy road, chock-full of potholes.

She took another look. Her sister wasn't alone. A handsome man stood beside Calista, and even from this fifty-yard distance, Athena saw tension running through her younger sister's stiff posture.

Who was he?

Athena put her hand on the chrome door handle and hesitated. Part of her wanted to rush out and intervene, but another part held her in check, afraid of peeling back the years and slicing open the wounds.

"We've arrived," said Cantu, her father's longtime chauffeur, stating the obvious.

"Yes, thank you."

"I'll retrieve your luggage, Miss Athena." Cantu popped the trunk, but before he could get out, his cell phone rang. He glanced down at the screen.

In the rearview mirror, Athena saw him wince.

"Excuse me a moment, Miss Athena, but I need to take this," Cantu said, remorse in his voice. Her father would have scolded him for even looking at his phone while on the job.

"Of course, please, take your call." Athena gave him a kind smile.

"Thank you, miss." He bobbed his head and answered.

She tried not to eavesdrop as she gathered her things, but she couldn't help noticing the strain in his voice, his staccato answers to the person on the other end.

"Yes . . . No . . . I don't know." Cantu ended the call and stuffed the phone in his pocket, his shoulders stiffened.

"I don't mean to pry," Athena said, leaning forward, "but you're upset. I've known you a long time, Cantu. Is there anything I can do to help?"

He gave an abrupt nod. "No, but thank you."

"Family?"

A deep sigh escaped him, shaking his entire body. "Your father would skin my hide if I unburdened to you."

"My father isn't here," she said, injecting a soothing tone into her voice. "Cone of silence."

She hadn't always been so cautious. When she was younger, she'd been a tattletale, running to Benjamin to spill her guts whenever she had the goods on anyone—almost always Calista. Damn, but she'd been a terrible sister. A fresh round of remorse dug into her.

"It's my son," Cantu said.

"Mateo?" Cantu's young adult son had once been Athena's caddie before he injured his back in a waterskiing accident.

Cantu bobbed his head. "He's in trouble again."

"Oh dear."

"He got arrested last night for shoplifting. His mother and I had such hopes that he would kick his opioid habit, but he just can't seem to do it on his own. We just don't have the money to send him to one of those expensive facilities—" He broke off and straightened his spine as if suddenly realizing he'd said too much to the boss's daughter. "I'm sorry. I shouldn't have said anything to you."

"No," she said. "I'm glad you told me. I can help."

He turned and looked her in the face, gratitude shining in his eyes. "Really?"

"I have a friend who runs a rehab facility. Here . . ." She opened her purse, dug through her business cards, and took out the one for the recovery center where her friend worked. "Call him and tell him I'll cover everything. You should be able to get Mateo into inpatient treatment after his release from jail."

"No, no, I can't let you do that. If your father found out—"

"What Dad doesn't know won't hurt him. Please, Cantu, let me help."

With trembling fingers, Cantu took the card. "I can't thank you enough, Miss Athena."

"Helping Mateo get better is all the thanks I need. He was an exceptional caddie."

Cantu nodded, tears brimming in his eyes as he pocketed the card. "You are an angel."

Calista would have a contradictory opinion. "You're so welcome," she said.

"How kind you are to worry about me when you have just lost your mother." Cantu swiped at his eyes with the back of a hand.

"I'm not grief-stricken. I hadn't seen my mother in twenty years. That was when I did all my grieving."

"It was wrong of your father to eradicate her from your lives."

"He tells a different story."

"Doesn't he always?" Cantu asked, and it was the first time she'd ever heard him say a negative word about her dad.

"I know Mateo can beat his addiction," she said. "He has a loving family on his side."

"Good luck on your voyage," Cantu said, fingering the Saint Christopher medal at his throat. "I'll be praying for you and Calista."

"Thank you."

Cantu got out and hurried to the trunk.

Exhaling, Athena stepped from the vehicle. A thousand-mile journey begins with a single step, right?

And she took that step toward her sister.

She ironed a perfect smile onto her face that belied the turmoil churning in her belly. Cantu deposited her luggage at the curb, pulled a fifty-dollar bill from his jacket pocket—cash her father gave him to cover her travel expenses—and motioned for a dock-worker to load her suitcases onto the ferry.

*Chin up, shoulders straight. You got this.*

She headed toward her sister, preparing herself for the moment Calista looked up and met her gaze. Would she smile in return? Would she come toward her? Would she back away?

Drawing nearer, Athena recognized the man with her sister, and dread closed in. Reid Thornton, the sports vlogger who'd been relentless in his coverage of Calista's breakdown at the Chevron Championship.

What was that son of a bitch doing here? He must have learned about Demetra's passing and come to ambush them. Athena groaned. She hadn't even considered media vultures. She widened her smile to show her teeth and quickened her stride.

"Calista!" she called with a cheery wave, as if their five years of radio silence wasn't a thing.

The wary look on her sister's face said she wasn't buying her forced effervescence. She should have known. Calista possessed a finely tuned BS meter.

"Did you know about the memorial golf tournament for Mamá?" Calista asked without preamble.

Disoriented, Athena stammered, "Wh-what? Where did you hear that?"

Calista jerked a thumb at Thornton.

Athena shifted her attention to the man. "Explain. Our mother's passing is a private affair. Why would Hobby Island host a golf tournament in her memory?"

"It's by invitation only," he said.

"And *you* were invited?" Athena shot him a tart glare.

Reid Thornton slid her a cocky grin. "Not exactly."

"How did you find out about it?" Athena tossed her head and narrowed her eyes. "No one told me."

Reid lifted his shoulders in a charming half shrug. "Gavin put it on his social. He's attending."

Gavin Gonzales.

Their father's lifelong archenemy and fierce rival on the golf course before both men retired from the PGA. Thornton had caddied for Gavin when he was a teenager, and at the same time, Calista had caddied for Dad.

Athena froze, stunned. She pressed a palm to her forehead, struggling to process the information. She shot a glance at Calista to see how she was taking it. Her sister looked as bowled over as Athena.

"Is he bothering you?" Athena asked.

"He was just leaving." Calista glared at Thornton.

"Shoo, go." Athena waved her hands at the sports vlogger. "Be gone."

"It's good to see you two together again." Reid Thornton's grin spread. "Working against a common enemy."

"Enemy?" Athena scowled. What was he talking about?

"All aboard!" the ferry driver announced.

"We've got to go," Calista said. "This is the last ferry to Hobby Island today."

"I can take a hint." Thornton turned but stopped and swiveled back. "Calista, remember what I said. Your story would inspire many people if you decide to challenge your sister and make a comeback."

"Our mother just died," Calista said. "Don't be a jerk."

Athena waited until he was out of earshot. "I'm sorry about him," she murmured. "I know how persistent he can be. He pestered me for a good six months after . . ."

Calista shrugged, her expression unreadable. "It's not as if I'm unaccustomed to it."

Athena flinched at the hurt in her sister's voice. She wanted to apologize for all that happened, but it was an enormous mountain of regret to climb, and nothing she could say would ease the pain. Words. Far too little, far too late.

"All aboard," the ferry driver repeated. "Last call for Hobby Island."

"Well . . ." Athena exhaled with a whoosh. "You ready?"

"No," Calista said. "It's gonna be wretched."

Athena knew her sister didn't mean it as a personal attack, but she marinated in the sting of the words. She felt judged, because she'd been on the wrong side of this whole thing. In the wake of Calista's shattered dreams and the ensuing fallout, Athena sought solace in the one thing she could count on—golf.

She poured herself into her career with a fervor that left little room for anything else. Now, as she confronted the prospect of reuniting with her sister, the weight of unresolved emotions and unanswered questions pressed upon her, an insistent reminder of the high price she paid for success.

If they both gave it a shot, maybe they could find reconciliation during their mournful stay on Hobby Island. Praying it could be so but dreading the alternative, Athena followed her sister.

Calista carried a forest-green shoulder bag and pulled a matching wheeled suitcase behind her. Dockworkers had already loaded Athena's bags, and she could see them in the boat's luggage cage.

"Here," she said, reaching for Calista's wheeled baggage. "Let me help."

Calista shied away. "I've got it."

"You sure?"

"Where are your bags?" her sister asked.

Athena blushed. "I—"

"What am I saying? Of course, the Dempsey strings already loaded your bags." There was no missing the disdain dripping from her tongue.

*Ouch. Okay, baby steps. Pace yourself. Long weekend.*

They crossed the threshold from the wharf to the passenger ferry, and Athena suppressed an irresistible urge to take her sister's hand the way she had when they were kids crossing the street.

The ticket agent, who wore a flat-brimmed boater's hat with a red carnation tucked into the band, stamped the golden tickets they presented and handed them back with a wink. "Your souvenir. Welcome to the Hobby Island ferry. The trip is about forty minutes. Help yourself to a cold drink." He gestured to a wooden barrel filled with ice and various nonalcoholic beverages. "Enjoy the ride."

Forty minutes in claustrophobic proximity without distractions? Terrific. How would they fill that much time?

"You want a drink?" Athena stopped beside the barrel filled with drinks.

"Sure."

A positive answer. Yay! "Pink lemonade?" Athena wriggled her eyebrows. "Your favorite."

"I'm not five anymore."

Feeling chastised, Athena forced an unconcerned laugh. "What do you drink these days?"

"Unsweet tea if they've got it."

Athena dug around in the barrel and found two bottles of tea. "Here we go."

"You don't have to do that."

"Do what?" Athena handed her a dazzling smile along with the ice-cold tea bottle.

Calista twisted off the lid and took a long swallow. "Try so hard."

Athena started to object, but she *was* trying too hard. "How about we sit in the bow?" She gestured toward the seating at the front of the boat. "I know you prefer seeing what's ahead instead of what's behind you."

Calista gave her an odd look but nodded.

Athena waited while her sister parked her luggage in the suitcase bin. She wanted to call her Lissy like before but feared crossing a boundary. She hadn't yet earned back the right to such familiarity.

"Look, there's an empty spot." Athena led the way to the casual box seating.

There were no cars on this ferry, so plenty of space for passengers to sit. Athena was about to ask Calista if she wanted to be next to the railing but worried that she was trying too hard, so she took the spot herself. Calista sat down in the seat beside her, leaving a good two feet of space between them.

"Well," Athena said. "This is pleasant. How have you been?"

"Over the last five years?" Calista's tone was dry, but underneath, a hint of wry humor. Encouraging.

"Can I give you a hug?" Athena could have kicked herself for asking.

Calista shook her head and leaned away. "I—"

"Our mother just died."

"A mother we hadn't heard from in twenty years." Calista pressed her lips together in a firm line and got a faraway look in her eyes.

Athena ached to hug her sister, but Calista was entitled to set her boundaries, and she needed to respect them, no matter how much it hurt. Okey dokey, bygones were not bygones. She must earn Calista's forgiveness. All right. She'd respect it.

Silence fell between them, even as excited conversations from the other travelers buzzed the air, and seagulls cawed overhead. The ferry pulled away from the dock.

"This is awkward." The tea bottle dripped condensation onto

Athena's bare knee, the icy cold a sharp contrast to the warm afternoon sun.

"Sit with it."

"Huh?" Athena blinked at her.

"Sit with your feelings."

Athena lifted one corner of her mouth. "You've been to therapy."

"It was that or end up in a gutter with a heroin needle in my arm."

"Calista!" Athena pressed a palm to her heart, horrified.

"Just speaking my truth." Calista stabbed her with a hard stare.

"Was it that bad?" Her gut wrenched, thinking how much her sister had suffered.

"You have no idea." Calista's chestnut-brown eyes were matter-of-fact, unflinching.

Athena steeled herself. "I'd like to know about it . . . if you feel comfortable sharing."

"I don't."

"Okay." Athena hauled in a deep breath. "But I'm here if you do want to talk."

"Noted."

Fresh silence.

Trying not to be obvious, Athena pulled her phone from her purse to check the time. They were five minutes into the forty-minute ferry ride, and Calista did not try to stir the conversation. The boat's engine rumbled beneath them, a subdued thrum that echoed Athena's restless thoughts. She watched Calista, waiting for a sign that forgiveness wasn't as distant as it seemed.

"Hey, do you remember that time Mom brought us to Hobby Island?"

Calista stared at her as if she'd sprouted horns and wings and started breathing fire. "What are you talking about?"

"We've been here before."

"When?"

Athena lifted her shoulders, then dropped them hard. "I was six or seven. That would make you four or five. It was maybe the first time she left Dad. He was on tour in England if I recall correctly."

"I don't remember that at all." Stone-carved face. No expression, emotionless.

Athena thought about shutting up but soldiered on. "We built a mermaid sandcastle at the mouth of a hidden cove while baby turtles swam everywhere in the surf."

"Oh." Calista blinked and her eyes rounded. "I do remember the turtles. I had a bright blue sand pail with yellow starfish on it. I caught one of the turtles and put it in the bucket, but Mamá made me put it back. That was on Hobby Island?"

"I'm sure it was, but I was little, too, so I could have misremembered."

"Huh." Calista gazed off across the bow, but her slender shoulders seemed to relax a little. "What do you know."

A tiny crack formed in her sister's granite facade. Calista bent forward, hiding her face. She'd lost weight, Athena noted. Calista had been stockier when she played golf. Their father kept her on a regimented, high-protein diet, telling her she needed bulk for power. He'd been less strict with Athena, as usual.

Calista hugged herself and curled away from the railing.

"Are you chilly? We could move back out of the wind."

"No."

What was she supposed to do with that? Feeling the heaviness of their history pressing down, Athena cleared her throat. "I-I'm sorry for what happened. I know that's not enough, but I just need to put that out there."

Calista's jaw clenched, but she nodded. That was a positive sign, right?

"Can we . . . I mean, you don't have to if you don't want to, but maybe we could . . . if . . . um . . ." Athena set her now tepid tea in the cupholder. "Do you think there's any chance we could repair things?"

"To tell the truth, Athena"—her sister's voice came out husky—"I have no idea."

"I'm willing to try if you are." Athena held her breath, waiting. The ball rested on her sister's green. It was up to Calista to sink the putt. "I know it won't be easy. I know sorrow and heartache will fill our time here. I know—"

"We'll see," Calista said, cutting her off. Then she got up and walked away, leaving Athena with no clue what to think.

# Chapter 4
## *Calista*

*"Grief is a funny thing. Sometimes it smacks you in the face, other times it whispers gently in your ear . . . it's okay to let go."*
—*Eloisa Hobby*

The ferry headed straight for Marshmallow Landing, and the lavender glow of numerous jacaranda trees in full bloom snatched Calista's breath away.

The vibrant purple blossoms created a sheltering canopy that stretched across the entire island. The sweet floral scent reminded her of her mother's fragrance, and sudden grief tugged at her like an anchor. A salty lump clogged her throat.

She supposed there would be many such emotional moments throughout the weekend. Calista fingered the locket around her neck to soothe herself and took in the surrounding ocean, sparkling with an intense crystalline brilliance. She shielded her eyes with her palm and marveled at the way the sunlight danced across the lapping waves like endless diamonds.

"Wow, it's like something from a fantasy dreamscape," Athena said.

They stepped off the boat and the dockworker, a teenage girl with short, spiky hair the color of the jacaranda blooms and an Indigo Girls T-shirt, asked to see their tickets.

"Hello, my name is Orion," she said. "Welcome to Hobby Island. Just as a reminder, there are no cars on the island. We get around via golf carts, scooters, bicycles, or our own two feet."

Another teen, this one a brunette in French braids, jean shorts, and Doc Marten boots, handed out island maps. "Hi, I'm Artemis. Please remember that cell service is quite spotty on the island. If you need a reliable way to communicate with family and friends, you can check out walkie-talkies from the Visitor Center in Crafters' Corner. Also, we don't have wi-fi. Island orientation is held this afternoon at four p.m."

The whimsy of Artemis and Orion appealed to Calista since she and Athena also had Greek names.

Orion led the way down the dock to an awaiting safari-style golf cart that accommodated eight. "Finnegan family, party of seven," Orion called out as she hopped behind the wheel. "All aboard!"

The Finnegans, two parents, three kids, and an older couple that Calista presumed were grandparents, climbed into the battery-powered vehicle. What would that be like—to have a close-knit family who vacationed together? Must be nice. Were they here to celebrate Demetra's life, or were they only regular tourists?

"Another cart will be along wiki-quickie. Artie will bring your luggage." With a laugh, Orion set off with her passengers.

Artie was busy accepting suitcases from the ferryman and stacking them on the dock. Other guests from the ferry milled around, taking in the island and snapping photos with their phones.

Edgy and overwhelmed, Calista stepped away from the others to collect her thoughts, her feet sinking into the soft, sugar-white sand. She closed her eyes and inhaled deeply, filling her lungs with tropical scents and sea air, trying to block out the world around her.

Okay, she needed a game plan.

First, she must find out about this ridiculous golf tournament Reid Thornton mentioned and make it clear to Eloisa Hobby that she had no intention of playing in it. She'd hung up her golf clubs five years ago. Golf offered nothing but pain and sorrow.

Unrealistic for Eloisa to spring this on her and Athena. In all honesty, Calista resented it. The past was past, and she resolved to keep it there. Well, as much as she could under the circumstances. She opened her eyes and slanted a glance over at Athena.

Her gregarious sister had struck up a conversation with Artemis, and she was helping the girl carry the suitcases to a golf cart with a small flatbed trailer attached. Her sister looked somewhat incongruous in her designer pencil skirt and spike heels.

Who was she trying to impress?

*That's uncharitable, Calista Grace. Get over there and help them.*

Calista grabbed the nearest suitcase and hefted it up. Gosh, the thing was heavy. The latch broke, spilling the contents onto the dock. A half-set of seven golf clubs—irons, woods, and putter— clattered as they hit the weathered boards. Terrific. What disrespectful lunatic packed their clubs loose in a suitcase instead of a golf bag?

All gazes swung to Calista.

"Sorry." She ducked her head and, cheeks burning, bent to retrieve the scattered clubs.

"Those are mine," a masculine voice said.

Reid Thornton.

Huh, where had he come from? She hadn't seen him on the ferry. She glanced up. Thornton was tying a motorized skiff to the dock. He'd gotten a golden ticket too? Ugh, her stomach soured. She did not have the mental bandwidth for this guy.

He squatted beside Calista as she stuffed his pitiful clubs back into the suitcase. She guessed he wasn't shooting anywhere close to par with this ragtag half set that looked as if he'd snagged them at a pawnshop. When they were teenagers, Thornton had been a decent enough golfer—so why the crappy clubs? What was up?

She didn't trust the guy any farther than she could heave him. She also didn't like being this close to him. Rising to her feet, Calista dusted her palms together and stepped back.

He closed the suitcase up and stood to meet her gaze with a nervous smile, which surprised her. He'd always been so cocksure of himself. "Thanks for the help."

Hand outstretched, Artemis hustled over. "Ticket?"

Thornton upped the wattage on his grin. "Hi there."

"Ticket." Artemis held her ground, her tone friendly but firm.

"I'm here for the golf tournament." Reid gave a head tilt and half-lowered lashes to make himself look even more endearing. Some things never changed. The man milked his charm like a dairy farmer.

Calista suppressed a snort.

"That's not until Fourth of July weekend," Artemis said. "You're a month early."

Wait, what? The golf tournament wouldn't be until the Fourth of July? Relief flooded Calista. She was only here through the weekend. She'd gotten herself worked up over nothing.

"If you don't have a golden ticket, you'll have to leave." Artemis pointed at his boat.

The guests remaining on the dock watched them with interest. Calista admired Artie's chutzpah. At that young age, Calista hadn't possessed the audacity to speak to an adult with such confidence.

What would Thornton do?

Calista held her breath. While the man was persistent, she'd never seen him angry when thwarted. She'd known the guy since they were fourteen, when he started caddying for Gavin Gonzales at PGA tournaments. He used that beguiling grin, believing he could persuade anyone of anything.

Two eight-passenger golf carts showed up, one driven by an older woman with steel-gray hair, basketball player height, and a crisp British accent. She wore sensible shoes and a frilly gingham dress.

"I'm Dot," she proclaimed and read the names of her passengers off a clipboard. The guests boarded, and Dot took off, belting out an off-key rendition of "Under the Sea" and urging her passengers to sing along.

After Dot left, the second golf cart, piloted by a vivacious blonde dressed head to toe in vibrant pink like a senior citizen Barbie, pulled up. Her Southern drawl dripped honey as she introduced herself as Vivian and invited the people on her list to climb aboard. Once Vivian's bunch left, only Calista, Athena, Artemis, and Reid remained on the dock.

Calista and Athena exchanged glances. What now?

At that moment, a steady clicking noise drew their attention to the cobblestone path leading into the heart of the island.

*Clack, clack, clack.*

From the thicket of jacaranda trees, another older woman appeared riding a unicycle as she knitted, her silver hair a striking contrast to the lush purple blossoms. Amazing coordination. She wore a dashing red bucket hat, looking as if she were a refugee from a flapper-era speakeasy. A stark white lily peeked from the hatband, and her layered clothing was a bold blend of crimson, scarlet, and ruby.

Even though twenty years had passed since Calista last saw this unusual woman on the courthouse steps soothing Demetra, she recognized her at once.

Eloisa's face broke into a smile as warm as a hug. She pocketed her knitting and hopped off the unicycle in an adroit move—leaving it standing upright by some miracle—and flew straight toward them, a joyous flame.

She hugged first Calista and then Athena. "Welcome, welcome to Hobby Island. I'm so sorry about your mother."

There were many things Calista wanted to ask her, but she didn't know where to start. Besides, this wasn't the time. Not in front of Reid Thornton.

"I'm sure you have questions," Eloisa said, reading Calista's mind. "But we'll have plenty of opportunity over the next month to sort things out. We have so many extraordinary events planned!"

A month? Numerous events? What was the woman babbling about? Calista had one goal—deal with her mother's passing as fast as possible and get back to her life. She had a job, obligations. Although her boss was understanding and he had told her to take as much time as she needed, a month away was not what he meant. At least, she didn't think so.

"Like what?" Athena asked.

"So many things! We're starting construction on a memorial garden for Demetra. There will be the golf tournament, of course, named in your mother's honor. We're planning on making it an annual charity event with all proceeds going to cancer research."

Calista met her sister's bewildered gaze. Athena was as much in the dark about this as she was.

"Auntie Eloisa," Artemis said, waving at Reid. "I don't want to interrupt, but this guy here doesn't have a golden ticket."

"That's okay," Eloisa said. "Mr. Thornton called and requested an invitation. I didn't have time to send him a ticket. Please have Orion escort him to bungalow ten when she returns."

Reid would be staying on the island too? Well, so what?

Calista would only be here long enough to bring closure to her mother's life, and then she was vapor. When she got Eloisa alone, she would make it 100 percent clear she would not be involved in any events beyond a small memorial service for Demetra over the weekend.

If Athena wanted to stay, that was her business. However, Calista had no idea how that was workable with Athena's LPGA commitments. Time to assert herself. If she'd learned one thing in therapy, it was that boundaries were important.

Orion pulled up and called out, "All aboard."

Reid strolled over to the golf cart, along with Athena, while Calista stayed rooted.

"You coming, sis?" Athena asked.

She did not want to ride with Reid, and she needed to set things straight with Eloisa. "You go on ahead. I think I'll walk. I need to clear my head."

"It's three miles to Crafters' Corner," Orion said.

"I run five miles a day." Calista forced a perky smile.

"Oh, well then." Orion waved and put the golf cart in gear. Artemis followed her in the smaller golf cart, pulling the trailer filled with luggage.

Leaving Calista alone with Eloisa. She turned to face the quirky island owner.

"Something is troubling you," Eloisa said.

She knotted her hands into fists, the breeze blowing her skirt against her bare legs. "Yes."

"You're allowed to speak without censure, Calista. Say whatever you like."

Eloisa's phrasing startled her. Whenever Benjamin Dempsey told her to express her mind growing up, and she'd done so, a vicious verbal berating always followed, and she'd learned to keep her mouth shut.

Hesitating, she fingered her bottom lip. Eloisa was not her father, but the ingrained fear lingered. Would she ever shed the wounds of abuse?

"Go on," Eloisa said, an encouraging tone curling into her comforting voice. "On Hobby Island, everyone may express their needs without judgment or pressure to conform."

Calista narrowed her eyes. Eloisa appeared genuine, and she had fond memories of the woman, but still, she didn't really know her.

*Your mother trusted her.*

The kindness in Eloisa's eyes deepened. "It's also okay if you're not ready to talk."

Calista studied the woman plumed in scarlet. "Mom's favorite color was red."

"I know." Eloisa stood arrow straight, her smile never wavering. "That's why I dressed in the color to greet you."

Wow. The island owner was that calculating? Her kooky demeanor cloaked a sharp mind.

Exhaling, Calista dropped her shoulders. "I don't know what you're expecting of me."

"Why, sweetheart, I expect you to be yourself."

Be herself? Even at twenty-nine, she was unsure of who she was. For twenty-four years, Benjamin Dempsey had drilled into her what she was—worthless, stupid, ugly, incompetent.

In the five years since she'd walked away from her family and golf career, she'd made sense of the world outside her controlling father and cobbled together a life of her own. Not an easy undertaking. Calista required a therapist's help, and she worked on improving herself every single day, but in times of stress, she still withdrew and blocked out the world. Right now, she ached to jump into Reid's skiff, motor back to Everly, and catch the first plane home to Denver.

Instead, she summoned her courage. "Having these events sprung on us, especially the golf tournament, seems manipulative to me."

Eloisa nodded. "I feel the same way."

Caught off guard, Calista blinked. "Then why are you doing it?"

Eloisa's smile faded, and her eyes clouded, as if seeing into the past. "It was your mother's wish."

That pulled Calista's head up higher. "Why didn't you tell me that when you called to say she'd passed?"

Eloisa winced. "Demetra asked me not to reveal her plans until you got here."

"Why would she do that?"

The slightest tremble shook Eloisa's bottom lip. "She was afraid you wouldn't come if you knew about the tournament."

Calista squeezed her hands into fists. "I've come to the island to say goodbye, but I'm not playing in the tournament. I no longer golf. *Ever.*"

"Understood." There was no judgment on Eloisa's face.

"I'm glad you accept it."

"But of course." Eloisa hesitated. "Do you mind if I ask how long you intend to stay? Just for housekeeping reasons, nothing else."

"I booked a flight home for Monday."

"That will work. We've scheduled the official ceremony for Sunday morning in our little island chapel."

"Athena and I don't get a say in the events?"

"I prepared things based on your mother's wishes. Would you like to see the letter she dictated to me?"

Did she? Calista considered the question and then shook her head. It was so engulfing. She was grateful to have her mother's wishes spelled out; after all, she'd had zero contact from Demetra in twenty years, well, except for . . .

No, she wasn't ready for this. "Not right now."

"Just let me know. I have a trunk full of Demetra's correspondence and journals—"

"When you phoned, you said she'd already prepaid for cremation. Has that been carried out?" Calista asked as matter-of-factly as possible.

"Yes." Eloisa bobbed her head. "The funeral home cremated her body in Everly, and her ashes are now in a beautiful urn in the Hobby Island chapel with visitation hours for the people who knew Demetra. We loved her very much, my dear."

That image was a visceral punch to the gut. Calista sucked in a deep breath, gulping in sea air and regret. "I wish I could have been there with her in her last hours . . ."

"She didn't want you to see her like that. She carried so much guilt and remorse, and it happened so quickly. She came to the island to ask for my help in preparing for the end, and within three short days, she was gone."

Too much to absorb. Again, the urge to flee sank talons into Calista's heart. *Go. Leave. Your mother never tried to contact you. Never tried to get you back. She let BD take you away from her.*

A hollow sensation carved into her body, whittling her to nothing. She was numb again, empty, the feeling that haunted her life.

"Calista." Eloisa laid a soft hand on her shoulder. "Where did you go?"

"Back in time," Calista mumbled.

The stark white lily in Eloisa's festive flapper hat bobbed when she nodded her head. "Your mother loved you so much. She was an imperfect person, as are we all, but her love for you girls never wavered."

Calista couldn't stop the scoffing snort that shot from her, and Eloisa looked sad, but she didn't try to make things better, which Calista appreciated. There was no making this better.

"I'll call Orion back with the golf cart," Eloisa said, taking a walkie-talkie from the deep pocket of her skirt.

"No," Calista said, the word coming out harsher than she intended. She lowered her voice. "I don't want to be around people right now."

"Are you sure that's not just a defense mechanism?"

"Oh, it totally is." Hell, she was self-aware. She didn't need this flamboyant senior citizen telling her about her messed-up emotional responses. "Please, just let me be."

Eloisa looked as if she wanted to give Calista a massive hug, but if the woman tried to embrace her, she'd come unraveled.

She raised her arms and backed away. "Please."

"As you wish. Have a peaceful walk. Take the path east for three miles, it's a straight shot." Then Eloisa mounted her unicycle, took out her knitting, and pedaled away, needles clicking.

# Chapter 5
## *Athena*

*"As long as your heart is beating, there's hope."*
—*Eloisa Hobby*

More than anything in the world, Athena wanted her sister back in her life, but mending their relationship wouldn't be easy. She understood why Calista walked away from everything. The stress and humiliation her sister suffered at the hands of their father became untenable on that horrible day at Chevron.

How could Athena ever hope to span the cavernous gap between them?

The problem? She was here, and Calista was back at the dock with Eloisa. She shouldn't have gone ahead in the golf cart with Thornton and Orion. She should have walked back with her sister, but she wore these damned high heels. Her image-conscious ego pushed her to dress her best even when traveling because she never knew when she'd run into a fan or the media.

But now? Silly how her adherence to a fashion code drubbed into her by her father prevented her from hanging back with her sister.

Maybe it wasn't just about the shoes, though. Perhaps it was that old habit of putting appearances first, meeting family expectations. Daddy said a true professional looked the part at all times.

Benjamin claimed he was hard on them because he wanted the best for them. "It's because I love you, Sugar Baby," he would say, and she believed him because what else could she do?

Still, a layer of uncertainty peeled off the onion as she wondered how much of her father's influence had kept her hog-tied to a life she wasn't even sure she still wanted. Speaking of, she needed to decide if she cared to stay on Hobby Island for a month. If so, she needed to cancel tournaments, and that was a whole mess with lasting repercussions, but if Calista stayed and they could work through their rift, then by gosh, she'd do it.

"This is B&B row." Orion drove up the cobblestone path to a row of stately replica Victorian houses, each painted a different pastel color. Cheerful as Easter eggs, the whimsical houses stood proudly in their ruffled gingerbread finery. "The guests stay here . . ." Orion turned in her seat to look at Reid. "Except for you, Mr. Thornton. Eloisa is putting you up in a vacant employee bungalow on the bluff above the north beach."

"Sounds like I got lucky," Reid said.

"You did. We have zero summer vacancies. If the employees' cottage hadn't been empty, you'd be bunking in a tent on the beach." Orion shot a look that said he shouldn't be here.

Athena exchanged glances with Reid, who looked amused by Orion's sass. Why was the man really here? Was a memorial tournament for the mother of a top LPGA golfer worth the time of a popular YouTube sports vlogger? Unless . . . he had another goal besides content creation.

Was he hoping to reconcile with Calista too?

"Here's where you'll be staying, Athena." Orion steered the laboring golf cart up the steep incline. "The Lavender Lark."

With its pale purple facade, decorative shingles swirling dreamlike as buttercream frosting, and turrets reaching for the sky like candles on an elaborate birthday cake, the stately house built in a Queen Anne Revival style projected warmth and welcome. Wisteria draped over the Lavender Lark's wraparound porch, the lilac-colored blooms beckoning visitors inside. Verdant honeysuckle vines twisted up trellises, perfuming the air with an intoxicating fragrance. It possessed the kind of fanciful charm Calista loved.

Or rather, it was the kind of thing her sister had once loved. Athena had no idea where Calista's passions lay these days.

Reid crossed one ankle over his opposite knee and leaned back, taking up more room in his man sprawl. "This island feels straight out of a storybook."

"What a welcoming veranda," Athena said as Orion halted the golf cart.

"They serve tea out here every afternoon at four, except on Fridays when there's orientation and a welcome reception at Crafters' Corner."

Maybe she and Calista could have tea out here tomorrow. Unless her sister had other plans . . .

A wave of melancholia washed over Athena despite the beautiful landscape and peaceful chirping of local birds. She hoped coming to this island and honoring their mother here would help repair the rift, but her sister was keeping her at a distance.

*Can you blame her?*

Sighing, she climbed from the golf cart, waved goodbye to Orion and Reid, and walked up the stairs to the Lavender Lark.

At check-in, a brunette in her early forties with twinkling eyes and a mischievous grin greeted her. She wore a multicolored painting smock, lavender leggings, and supercute ankle boots. Her hair was piled into a haphazard bun and anchored in place with two thin paintbrushes. Soft music played over speakers and Athena identified the song from *The Little Mermaid* soundtrack. The playful tune put a smile on her face.

"Hi, I'm Luna Chance. Welcome to the Lavender Lark." The woman beamed at her. "You must be Athena."

That took her aback. She pressed a hand to her hair, smoothing it down from the golf cart ride. "How did you know?"

Luna gave a giggle that sounded so carefree and girlish that it stirred jealousy inside Athena. When had she last been that lighthearted? Had she *ever* been that lighthearted? She racked her brain and couldn't recall such a time.

"Blond Greek goddess," Luna said. "You look just as Demetra described you."

That stopped Athena in her tracks. "You knew my mother?"

"Oh, yes. Your mom was a lovely woman."

"Um . . ." Lovely was not how she thought of the mother who didn't fight for her and her sister. Athena did not know what to say to the innkeeper, who appeared heartbroken over Demetra's passing.

For the first time since Athena entered the B&B, Luna's smile disappeared, and her eyes glimmered with unshed tears. "I'm so deeply sorry for your loss."

"Thanks."

Luna pushed the box of tissues on the check-in desk toward Athena. "Help yourself."

Not knowing what else to do with Luna looking at her as if she wanted to cradle her to her chest and encourage her to sob it all out, Athena took a few tissues from the box and stuffed them in her purse.

"Anything you need, you just holler," Luna invited.

"I will." She wouldn't.

"Demi spoke of you often. In her last hours, you and your sister were all she talked about."

*Demi?* Luna was so chummy with Athena's mom that she called her by a nickname Athena knew nothing about. Why would she know, though? She hadn't seen or heard from Demetra since she was eleven.

"We took turns sitting with her," Luna said.

"We?"

"There's fifteen of us who live year-round on Hobby Island. We've formed a little family. Of course, I do have my own family as well. My mother, Jeanie; my husband, Paul; our two daughters, Artie and Orion; and my son, Beck. I'm very blessed."

"How wonderful," Athena said, struggling to mask her sarcasm.

"It is." Luna didn't act as if she picked up on the mockery, and Athena felt terrible for her attitude.

Athena cleared her throat. "While you were sitting with my mother, none of you thought to reach out and give me or my sister a call?"

Why was she being so prickly? Luna was a kind, warmhearted woman who helped Demetra as she lay dying. She should be grateful, not angry and resentful.

Luna's face shadowed, and a brokenhearted expression came into her eyes. "She asked us not to."

"Could you direct me to my room, please," Athena asked before she needed the tissues in her purse.

"Oh, I can do much better than that. Let me show you the way." Luna's exuberant smile lit up her face again. She grabbed a key from the pegboard behind the desk and led Athena up the stairs.

Luna bounced up the steps, her paintbrush-adorned bun bobbing with each step. The foyer featured a stunning seascape that continued across the upstairs walls. Gentle waves in various shades of blue and green lapped at a golden shore dotted with tiny, perfectly rendered seashells.

As they ascended, the scene shifted to depict the island's lush landscape, with towering jacaranda trees in full bloom, their purple flowers cascading down the verdant hillsides. Athena trailed her fingers along the railing, her eyes widening as she took in the walls. She stopped dead in her tracks.

"Holy mackerel . . . are those walls actually moving?"

Luna glanced back, a grin spreading across her face. "Only if you've had too much of Dot's special punch, but I'll take that as a compliment."

"It's incredible." Athena stared at the seascape giving the illusion of ripples. Schools of fish darted between coral reefs, and was that . . . "Is that Sebastian from *The Little Mermaid* hiding behind that anemone?"

Luna's laugh echoed through the stairwell as she motioned Athena forward. "Good eye! The muralist likes to throw in Easter eggs."

Athena spun slowly, taking in the 360-degree view of an underwater paradise. "Whoever painted this is an absolute genius. It's like being inside a snow globe, but instead of snow, it's . . . ocean?"

"An ocean globe? Fantastic idea! I'll pitch that to the gift shop." Luna winked. "And thanks, by the way. It's always nice to be called a genius."

Athena's jaw dropped. "Wait, you're the muralist? You did all this? By yourself?"

"Well, the fish helped a little. They're excellent color consultants, but yeah, painting's my thing. I love running the inn, but art is my passion, and sometimes you just need to cover a wall in bioluminescent jellyfish, you know?"

"Oh, totally. I do that at least once a week," Athena deadpanned, then burst into genuine laughter for the first time in what felt like years. "Seriously, though, this is amazing. You're the Michelangelo of marine life."

Luna beamed, leading Athena down the hallway. "Just wait

until you see your room. I gave it the full Poseidon's-palace treatment. I hope you like seahorses because there may or may not be an entire seahorse rodeo happening on your ceiling." She swung open the door with a flourish. "Ta-da! Welcome to your underwater boudoir!"

Athena stepped inside and opened her eyes wide to take it all in. The room was lush with blues and greens, colors that caught the light like fish scales in the sun. A four-poster bed draped in diaphanous sea-foam-colored curtains dominated one wall, while a writing desk that looked made from driftwood sat beneath a porthole-shaped window.

"Wow." Athena exhaled, craning her neck. "It's like sleeping in a mermaid's guest room."

"Well, I'll let you settle in." Luna left the room key on the bedside table and slipped out, closing the door softly behind her.

Athena stood motionless, overwhelmed by the room. She wandered to the window and pushed it open wider. The scent of salt and jasmine wafted in, along with the distant sound of waves lapping at the shore.

How peaceful.

Then she remembered her mother's memorial. The estranged mother lost to her long ago. She thought of Demetra and Calista. How had it come to this? Five years of silence, and now they were supposed to what? Mourn together? Heal together? The task felt as impossible as breathing underwater without scuba gear.

With a deep sigh, Athena sank onto the bed, flopped back, and stared at the ceiling. True to Luna's word, a whimsical scene of seahorses engaged in an underwater rodeo. It must have taken the innkeeper forever to paint it.

Athena fingered the delicate gold bracelet at her wrist. From it dangled a tiny golf club charm—a gift from her father after her first junior championship win. She'd worn it every day since, a talisman of sorts. Now it felt heavy, like an anchor dragging her down.

Memories flooded in, unbidden and unwelcome.

Calista, age twelve, eyes bright with unshed tears as their father berated her for a missed shot on their backyard putting green.

"You're an embarrassment." He yelled it loud enough for Athena to hear from the golfing cage where she was improving her driving skills.

Calista, four years later, at her first major junior tournament win. Their father's gloating smile as he draped an arm around Athena's shoulders. "You see that? That's why I push her so hard. She's finally living up to her potential."

Athena had nodded then, ignoring the twist in her gut. Why didn't he push her the same way he pushed Calista? Did he not want Athena to be as good? She always told herself that Dad knew what he was doing, that he was just being fair, but old guilt wrapped around her now like a suffocating, weighted blanket.

Calista on the eighteenth green at Chevron. The sudden hush, the weight of expectation heavy in the air. Athena watching, heart in her throat . . .

And then . . .

*No.* Athena squeezed her eyes shut, willing the memories away. She *had* tried to reach out after that, she really had, but Calista vanished, cutting off all contact—with her, with their father, with the entire golfing world.

And Athena . . . well, she just let her go. She didn't try harder, didn't push back. Daddy had told her that Calista needed to learn a lesson, and Athena believed him because, well, wasn't he always right? It was easier that way, more manageable than facing the truth.

The shrill ring of the seashell-shaped landline phone on the bedside table jerked her upright, heart racing. Who could that be?

*Don't be so hypervigilant.* Most likely, it was Luna with some cheery bit of information she neglected to deliver.

For a moment, Athena considered ignoring it, pretending she'd left the room. But curiosity—and years of conditioning to always answer when called—won out. She curled her fist around the receiver. "Hello?"

"What the hell?" Her father's grumpy voice rankled the phone line. "You don't have cell service on that godforsaken island?"

"Hey, Daddy." She sank back down on the mattress, held her breath, and glanced at the door as if he might come busting through it at any moment.

*He's a thousand miles away. Relax.*

"Have you seen her?" Brusque. Overbearing.

Athena held the receiver away from her ear as a knot fisted in her belly, a Pavlovian response to his tone. "I just got to my room, I haven't—"

"But you've seen her? Talked to her?" The questions came rapid-fire, leaving no room for complete answers.

"Well, yes, but—"

"How does she look? Is she still in shape?" He was the one who'd driven Calista away, yet he seemed obsessed with her younger sister.

"Why do you care, Daddy?" She brushed a piece of lint from her skirt.

"Just answer my questions, Athena."

She shifted, uncomfortable. Her father had always been intense about their golfing careers, but this felt different, more wrong than usual, somehow. "She looks . . . fine. Good . . ."

"Has she mentioned golf at all?"

"What? No, we didn't talk for long." Athena got up to pace the room. Her bare feet sank into the plush rug, which she now realized looked like a sandy ocean floor, complete with tiny seashells.

"Guess who else is on the island," she said, deflecting. "Reid Thornton."

"What's *he* doing there?" Her father's tone darkened.

"They're holding a charity golf tournament in Demetra's honor." Around her father, she never referred to Demetra as Mom, or Mother, or the Greek version *Mamá* as Calista did.

"Focus, Athena," he snapped, the sound like a whipcrack through the phone. "I need you to convince Calista to come home."

Athena's stomach dropped, and she stopped pacing. "What? Why?"

"Can't a father be concerned about his daughters?" Now his voice softened, taking on a wounded quality Athena knew all too well. "I worry about her, you know . . . about both of you."

Sighing, she pinched the bridge of her nose. "I know, Daddy, but we're here to remember Demetra, that's all."

"Of course, of course. It's just . . . well, I've been thinking."

The knot in Athena's stomach hardened to concrete. "About what?"

"Family and second chances." He paused.

What was he getting at? He hadn't tried to get Calista back when she left. In fact, he seemed happy she was gone and threw all his efforts into promoting Athena's career.

Yet when Athena thought back to the days right after Calista's departure, she could still hear him rampaging around the house, cursing Demetra and Calista as if he could scare them back into his clutches.

And for what? To tear them down again?

*No. He just wants his family back. That's all it was. He's not a bad guy. He just . . . He just gets angry sometimes.* Expression of emotions trumped suppressing them, right?

"Hear me out," he wheedled. "You two were strongest together. Think of the publicity if you two reunited."

Ah, there it was. The man's true motivation. She didn't know the story behind it, but she knew how he operated, and Benjamin Dempsey always had an ulterior motive.

"What's up?"

"Nothing, nothing. Demetra's death has got me thinking about the importance of family, that's all."

That was not all, and Athena knew it, but she ignored the gnawing suspicion and clung to the hope that he really did care. "And . . . ?"

He sighed, a sound filled with exaggerated patience. "I'm just saying, there are opportunities out there. Big ones. For you both."

Athena gripped the phone hard. "What are you up to?"

"Nothing concrete yet, but people are interested in Calista's comeback."

"What people?"

"Just feel her out, would you? See if she's open to returning."

"Daddy, no," Athena said, firmer than she felt. "We're here to mourn our mother, not to . . . to what? Plan some kind of reunion tour?"

"Don't be dramatic. I'm thinking of your future, both of you. Just talk to your sister, Athena. You've always been able to get through to her when no one else could."

Athena closed her eyes, recognizing the manipulation for what it was. The same tactic he used for years, pitting them against each other while simultaneously forcing them together. A toxic dance that left them both scarred, but could this time be different? Perhaps he meant it. Maybe he really wanted them to heal.

"Dad—"

"Come on, Sugar Baby, do it for your aged father. It tears me up to see you two at odds. I'm counting on you," he said and then, without another word, hung up.

Hands shaking, she set the receiver back in its cradle. For a long moment, she just stood there, staring at the whimsical phone as if it might bite her. What game was her father playing now? And, more importantly, how could she keep Calista from getting caught in his cross fire again?

The cheerful underwater decor she'd appreciated before now felt stifling. The painted fish on the walls watched Athena with accusing eyes. How was she supposed to reconnect with Calista with their father playing puppet master from afar?

She sank her face into her palms. She came here with such hope that she and Calista could mend the chasm between them, that in mourning their mother, they might find a way back to being sisters again.

But now? Now she was a pawn in whatever game their father was playing, same as always.

What could she do? If she told Calista about their father's scheme, it would only drive her further away, but keeping it quiet would just add to the pile of secrets they'd kept from each other.

And what about this memorial golf tournament their mother had requested? Was that somehow tied to their father? It seemed impossible their mother had asked for such a thing. Demetra hated golf, but then again, Athena realized with a pang that she knew nothing about who their mother had become in the last twenty years.

She caught sight of her reflection in the mirror above the dresser. The woman who stared back looked tired and conflicted. She barely recognized herself without the polished veneer she usually presented to the world.

A soft knock at the door startled her.

"Athena?"

Athena took a deep breath, forcing a cheerfulness she didn't feel. She opened the door and found Luna standing there holding an old golf bag filled with clubs. She recognized the set at once, and an overwhelming urge to vomit pushed bile up her throat, but she fought it back.

"Wh-where did you get those?"

"Demetra wanted you to have them for the tournament." Luna extended the clubs.

Mom had kept Athena's first set of golf clubs? Hands trembling, she took the golf bag. "Thank you."

Luna turned to go.

"Wait."

Luna paused. "Yes?"

"Has Calista arrived yet?"

"She hasn't." Luna shook her head.

"Can you tell her . . ."

"Yes?" Luna leaned forward with her head cocked.

"No, never mind." Athena forced a smile, thanked the innkeeper again, and closed her door.

Alone with the clubs, Athena took out the putter, nicked with use and time. She wrapped her hands around the grip, the familiar weight comforting in her hands. Almost without thinking, she pulled a pocked orange Titleist from the bag, dropped the ball onto the plush rug, and lined up a putt, aiming for the shoes she'd kicked off.

The soft thump of the ball hitting its mark was satisfying in a way she hadn't felt in a long time. Golf had become so wrapped up in expectations and pressure that she'd almost forgotten the simple joy of a well-executed shot.

She bent to pick up the ball, and with her head upside down, boom, Athena tumbled into a disturbing childhood flashback.

Shouts. Shrieks. Slammed doors. Daddy grabbing Athena's putter from her golf bag, smashing it into walls and knocking holes in the Sheetrock as he screamed Demetra's name.

Athena's heart rammed into her chest as icy heat suffused her body. She saw herself at seven snatching hold of Calista's hand, dragging her to their bedroom, locking the door, and scooting under the bed. She held her sister close as they sobbed and waited for the worst.

And just like that, Athena, in the present day, passed out cold, surrounded by a corral of seahorses.

# Chapter 6
## *Calista*

*"In order to survive, a cycle breaker must fight the gravitational pull yanking them back into the heart of darkness."*
—*Eloisa Hobby*

Calista fled the dock, jacaranda petals swirling around her, their sweet scent a stark contrast to the bitterness rising in her throat.

Mindlessly, she ran. Her pounding pulse strummed over her eardrums, a rhythmic accompaniment to her anguish. Her mother was dead. No chance to repair what ruptured so long ago. It was over.

The finality struck her like a blow.

To outrun her grief, she picked up the pace.

The resort's cobblestone path gave way to wilder terrain. The feral, thick, verdant grass brushed against her shins as she plunged through it into a copse of trees. The jacaranda along the path merged into other vegetation—live oak, pecan, sugarberry, cedar elms, and mulberry. Branches snatched at her face and arms, and she welcomed the sting, a physical pain to distract from the overwhelming emotional turmoil.

Calista had no idea where she was going. Away. That was all she knew. Away from Athena's concerned looks and curated words. Away from the ghost of her mother. Away from the stifling burden of regrets.

The forest swallowed her whole. Shadows deepened as the canopy closed overhead. Shafts of sunlight pierced through in places, creating a dappled pattern on the forest floor that shifted and swayed with the breeze. The rich scent of lichen, rotting leaves, and damp earth filled her nose as her lungs heaved, gasping for air. But she ran on.

Ran and ran and ran . . .

Until her foot caught a protruding tree root.

Calista stumbled, instinctively thrusting her hands out to brace herself, and crashed into a white oak. Rough bark bit into her palm. Pain lanced through her ankle. She bit back a curse and slumped against the tree. Panting, she paused and glanced around, taking in her surroundings.

Gone was the charm of the dock, the gorgeous flowers, the quaint cobblestones, and the imperial jacaranda trees. Here, raw nature reigned supreme, dense and untamed. Forest sounds enveloped her—the rustle of leaves, birdcalls, the skittering of some small creature through the underbrush. Gradually, her racing heart slowed.

That's when she heard it.

Faint, melodic tinkling carried on the breeze. The sound danced just at the edge of her hearing, beckoning her forward. Calista cocked her head, listening intently.

There it was again, clearer this time.

Curiosity tugged at her, pushing aside the storm of emotions that had driven her into the forest. Without thinking, she moved toward the sound, favoring her injured ankle. She couldn't put full weight on it, but she could hobble.

The path—if it could be called that—narrowed. Moss cushioned her steps. The light filtering through the canopy took on an ethereal quality, fracturing through leaves in ways that seemed to defy the laws of physics. Shadows moved strangely, always just at the corner of her vision.

More than once, Calista could have sworn she saw figures darting between the trees, but when she turned to look, there was nothing but foliage and dappled sunlight.

A shiver ran down her spine. Her rational mind insisted it was tricks of the light, her imagination working overtime, but there was something about this place that made her question what was real and what wasn't.

The tinkling grew louder with each step, building from a whisper to a symphony.

Calista pushed through a curtain of hanging vines, their leaves cool against her flushed skin. She parted the overgrowth and stretched out in front of her was a clearing, unlike anything she'd ever seen.

Thousands—no, tens of thousands—of wind chimes hung from branch after branch. The chimes ranged from delicate crystalline things, pinkie-size, to massive tubes with bone-deep tones. Metal gleamed alongside driftwood and glass, creating an audiovisual cacophony that should have been overwhelming but was not.

Calista stepped into the clearing, and it seemed as if the chimes responded to her arrival. Their song swelled, a melody into her very soul that plucked at tender heartstrings she didn't know existed. Each note carried with it a fragment of emotion—joy, sorrow, hope, regret—as if the chimes were giving voice to all the feelings she'd gulped down for years.

Awestruck, she stood rooted to the spot, tears welling in her eyes.

The music washed over her, through her, leaving her feeling lost and empty. All the pain she'd been running from caught up with her in a rush, but here, surrounded by this otherworldly chorus, it felt bearable somehow.

Cathartic, even.

In the center of the clearing stood an ancient oak, its trunk gnarled and twisted with age. It towered over the other trees, branches reaching toward the sky like grasping fingers.

Drawn to it, Calista approached with tentative steps.

The tree branches creaked, like a murmured secret in the middle of the night. Getting closer, she noticed something odd about the base of the trunk. Nestled between two massive roots was a hollow, covered by a transparent lid that shimmered iridescence.

What was this?

Calista knelt. Pain shot through her ankle. She winced and repositioned her leg and inspected the ship-portal-shaped lid with a gold handle in the center.

She slid her fingers over the cool, smooth surface, but when she touched the handle, a warm sensation spread up her arm and settled in her chest. A rational person would have argued the sensation came from the sun as the clouds parted overhead, but the heat was too warm for that simple explanation.

Compelled, Calista turned the handle and lifted the lid.

Inside the small space, she found an old book and, for a moment, thought it was a grimoire. A spell book would explain a lot.

The leather cover, soft and supple from years of handling, was the color of rich bourbon. Its edges were worn smooth, the corners gently rounded, with tooled vines wrapping around the spine, leaves and flowers intricately detailed.

A brass clasp, tarnished with age, held the book closed.

She pushed down on the center of the clasp, and it released

with a satisfying click, revealing fanned pages warped from humidity. The paper was thick and creamy, with a smooth tooth that caught the light and shone off gilt edges, flaking in places.

Calista opened the book, and a soothing scent wafted up—a mixture of old paper, leather, and something else, something earthy and green. It smelled of secrets and memories, hopes and dreams poured onto the pages.

A journal.

But whose?

She shifted, sat against the oak, and settled in. The chimes quieted as the wind calmed, giving her space to read.

The first page bore an inscription in deep blue ink, the handwriting elegant and flowing. Tiny flecks of sand clung to some of the letters as if the writer had been sitting on a beach. In the top right corner, a pressed flower—a tiny purple blossom Calista didn't recognize—had been affixed to the page.

*To those who find solace in these pages, may you leave a piece of your journey and take with you the strength of those who came before. –EH*

EH—Eloisa Hobby?

Had the island's owner created this repository of confession and healing? Calista turned the page. The first entry was dated fifteen years earlier:

I came to this island broken, convinced my life was over. My husband's betrayal shattered everything I knew about myself and my future, but in this place, surrounded by the whispers of the wind, the wisdom of nature, and the kindness of strangers, I found a peace

*I never thought possible. The pain isn't gone, but it no longer defines me. I leave this clearing lighter than I arrived, ready to face whatever comes next. Thank you, Hobby Island, for showing me that endings can also be beginnings. —Much love to other seekers, Vivian*

Was this the same woman who'd shown up at the dock dressed in pink to escort guests to the resort? Vivian's words touched her heart. How many others had come here seeking connection and hope?

Calista flipped through the pages, skimming entries from people of all ages, genders, religions, and backgrounds. Some wrote of loss, others of fear or confusion, but running through them all was a thread of transformation, of finding strength they didn't know they possessed.

The anger and hurt that drove Calista into the forest receded, replaced by unexpected calmness. These strangers, separated by time and circumstance, had sat where she now sat, pouring their hearts onto these pages.

Toying with her locket, Calista read on, seeking more comfort. She was so engrossed in her thoughts she almost missed it . . . but the handwriting stopped her.

The loose script, the deep forward slant.

A scrawl she recognized instantly, even though it had been twenty years since she'd last seen it.

Her mother's handwriting.

The entry was unsigned, but she *knew* to the depths of her soul that Demetra had written this entry.

Calista's heart pounded as she stared at the page, torn between the desperate need to know and the fear of what she might discover. The chimes went silent, seeming to hold their breath, waiting.

*The island's magic works in mysterious ways.*
*I came here to escape, but instead, I confronted*
*the truth. My greatest regret and my deepest*
*love are two sides of the same coin, one light and*
*one dark. To my lost stars: If you ever find your*
*way here, know that the night sky doesn't rule*
*forever. Look for the light. It's always been there,*
*even when you can't see it.*

Lost stars? Was Demetra speaking of her and Athena? Calista wrapped a twirl of her long dark hair around her index finger and almost popped her thumb into her mouth the way she had as a nine-year-old torn from her mother, back before her father cropped her hair.

Blurred tears spilled onto the page. She clutched the journal to her chest, body shaking with silent sobs. The wind chimes sang around her, their melody now more mournful than magical.

Slowly, her sobs subsided as grief moved through her. An ink pen lay in the box's bottom. Should she leave an entry? Did she dare?

But what would she say? She had no wisdom to offer anyone. No palliative advice. With tears rolling down her cheeks and staining the pages, she began to write. She wrote and wrote, pouring her anguish onto the paper, and when she finished, she hiccuped, dried her eyes, and closed the book.

With care, Calista returned the journal to its resting place, making sure the resin lid was securely in place. She stood, favoring her injured ankle, and for the first time noticed a narrow path leading away from the clearing—one that looked far easier to navigate than the way she arrived.

Bidding the wind chime sanctuary goodbye, Calista found a tree branch to use as a cane and braced herself to shuffle down the path. With each step, a wince of pain gripped her ankle, but it wasn't unbearable. A light sprain. Nothing more. She was tough. She'd endured much worse.

The tinkling of the wind chimes faded behind her. Calista continued, leaving the forest and making her way into a sunlit meadow filled with a sea of beautiful wildflowers stretching out before her.

Poppies blazed crimson in the grass. Bluebonnets stood in proud clusters, their flowered spires reaching skyward. The lupines were spring flowers. Odd that they were still in full bloom in June. Bees buzzed from flower to flower, their bodies heavy with pollen. Hundreds of butterflies flitted on the breeze, their delicate wings fluttering.

At the meadow's edge, three deer grazed, almost invisible among the taller stalks. The meadow was atop a rolling hillside that led to a cliff overlooking the sea. The waves a soft lull lapping against the shore.

The sun warmed Calista's skin. She breathed deeply, inhaling the mingled scents of earth and blooms. Athena claimed their mother had brought them here as children, but Calista had no memory of this whimsical oasis. If she'd been here, wouldn't she have recalled such a place as this, even if she had been little more than a toddler?

Balancing against her makeshift cane, she tilted her face up, absorbing the mild heat, and gave thanks to the heavens, the universe, nature, whatever created this serene moment. Her panicked flight brought her here, but tranquility rooted her to this spot.

No wonder her mother escaped to Hobby Island. Calista wished for the millionth time that Mamá could have taken them with her. How different life would have been!

A hard knot of sorrow wadded in her throat. She closed her

eyes, fighting off melancholy tears. She couldn't start bawling every time she thought of her mother and the tsunami of regrets. Fingers curled around the tree branch cane, she gulped past the fresh round of grief, waiting for the pain to ebb. She had to control her emotions or she would dissolve entirely.

Then she felt something odd.

Vibrations. Thundering across the earth. Faint but growing stronger, faster. She opened her eyes and spied nothing at first, but then something huge parted the sea of blooms, heading straight for her.

An ostrich.

Actually, an enormous ostrich charging straight toward her, its powerful legs propelling forward. The bird's black eyes fixed on her, its razor-sharp beak open as if it intended to eat her for an afternoon snack.

*Eek!*

Calista blinked, unable to believe her eyes. Ostriches on Hobby Island? It made no sense, and yet this genuine threat bore down on her. She couldn't run. Her injured ankle made that impossible. Flight wasn't an option, so fight it was.

Gripping the tree branch, Calista raised it like a Louisville Slugger. Her palms sweated, and her breath shot out rapid and shallow. The thundering of the ostrich's feet escalated her pounding pulse.

"Stay back!" she screamed.

The ostrich showed no signs of slowing, coming within fifty feet. Forty. Thirty. It was almost upon Calista!

She steeled herself, timed her move, and just as the bird came within striking distance, she swung the branch with all her might, aiming for its head.

The ostrich's reflexes were quick. It veered at the last second, the branch whistling through the air where the creature's head had been a second before, but the sudden movement threw the bird off balance. Unable to alter its course, the ostrich's large wing clipped Calista hard as it zoomed past.

The impact sent her spinning, the tree branch flying in the air.

The world tilted. Wildflowers and sky blurred together as Calista toppled and tumbled down the slope above the ocean.

She rolled, desperately trying to dig her heels into the ground and slow her momentum. But the slope was too steep, the soil too loose, her injured ankle too weak.

Her fingers clawed at the earth, seeking any handhold but finding only flowers and grass that tore away in her grasp.

The edge rushed up to meet her. A fleeting glimpse of the sheer drop beyond, waves crashing against rocks far below.

Calista absorbed the danger, gritted her teeth, and braced for a fall. No sweat. She'd danced on the razor's slicing edge for most of her life.

She'd either survive or not.

Just like always.

# Chapter 7

## *Athena*

*"Family are the people who stand by you when the rest of the world turns its back."*

—*Eloisa Hobby*

Athena's eyes snapped open, her mind a hazy mush. The ornate ceiling of her room at the Lavender Lark swam into focus, its painted seahorses galloping across her vision. She blinked, disoriented.

Why was she on the floor?

Her gaze landed on the putter lying beside her, and suddenly, like a wave crashing over her, the memories flooded back. She was no longer in the Lavender Lark. She was back in that room, back with *him* . . .

Benjamin stormed into their bedroom, yanking Calista from Athena's desperate grip. Her father hauled Calista over his knee, his hand coming down with a sickening thud.

"This." *Smack.* "Is." *Smack.* "How." *Smack.* "A." *Smack.* "Good." *Smack.* "Father." *Smack.* "Shows." *Smack.* "His." *Smack.* "Love."

Each strike a brutal punctuation, each cry from Calista cutting deeper into Athena's paralyzed heart. Why hadn't he ever hit *her*? Didn't he love her too?

Bitter bile rose in her throat now. She pressed a hand to her mouth, forcing the nausea back. No wonder she'd buried the memory so deep.

Athena scrambled to her feet, urgency coursing through her. She had to find Calista. Had to tell her . . . What? That she remembered? That she was sorry? Words felt woefully inadequate, but she had to do something.

In the bathroom, she splashed cold water on her face. The mirror reflected wide, haunted eyes that bore no resemblance to the polished, professional golfer the world knew. Here, stripped of her cultivated image, she was just a scared little girl again, desperate to make things right.

She slipped into her shoes and rushed from her room, nearly colliding with Luna on the landing.

"Whoa there!" Luna's laughter rang out, her paintbrush-adorned bun bobbing. "Is everything okay? You look like you've seen a ghost."

"Calista?" Athena's voice came out rough. "Has she arrived yet?"

"Hmm, no. Your sister hasn't checked in, but maybe she went straight to Crafters' Corner. Orientation starts at four, and it's . . ." Luna glanced at her watch. "Three forty-five."

"I'll try there. Thank you. When Calista shows up, can you tell her I'm looking for her?"

"Will do." Luna's smile faltered as she studied Athena. "Are you sure you're okay?"

*Not in the least.* Athena forced a smile anyway. "I'm fine."

"Do you need a scooter?" Luna asked, leading the way down the staircase. "Or do you prefer to walk?"

Athena glanced down at her high heels—utterly impractical. Luna followed her gaze.

"We sell flip-flops." Luna pulled a cellophane-wrapped pair from behind the desk. "Would you like a pair?"

Athena considered the alternative footwear, but they wouldn't go with her outfit. "Do you know when my luggage will arrive?"

"Artie should be here soon, but I'd hate for you to miss orientation. Tell you what . . ." Luna fished in her pocket for a key. "You can take the Lavender Lark's golf cart parked out front."

"You won't need it?"

"Nah." She waved her off with a grin. "Go ahead."

"That's very kind of you." Athena took the key and walked out the front door into the late-afternoon sun. Its warmth pressed down on her skin, but it did nothing to thaw the chill that had settled deep within her bones.

She found the purple golf cart wrapped with Lavender Lark branding, hopped inside, and took off toward Crafters' Corner. She motored past the row of stately B&Bs built in various replica Victorian styles, their flower gardens a riot of blooms. The breeze carried the grape soda scent of jacaranda blossoms and sea salt. On any other day, Athena might have found the scene idyllic, but now it felt like a facade hiding darker truths.

She rounded a bend, and Crafters' Corner came into view. The place was so darn cute that Athena almost laughed. Calista would say it looked like Pinterest exploded and birthed a town square.

The thought made her long for her sister and the close relationship they once had before their father pitted them against each other.

A yeasty perfume wafted from Breaking Bread, the bakery that looked as if plucked straight from a Hallmark movie. Across the way, an outdoor bistro flaunted colorful umbrellas. Its chalkboard menu promised interesting seafood dishes.

Flowers spilled from planters, painting the cobblestones with splashes of color that shouted *Summer!* Overhead, string lights crisscrossed the village in a layout that suggested either artistic genius or a spider on caffeine.

In the quad, a temporary stage had been set up, with people already seated in neat rows of folding chairs facing the stage. This gathering must be orientation.

Athena parked the golf cart alongside scooters, bikes, and skateboards. Music drifted from hidden speakers, the kind of soft, breezy tunes that belonged in an old seaside movie. She canted her head, identifying the familiar croon—Frank Sinatra's "Sand and Sea." The charm of the town distracted her for a moment, but she couldn't forget why she was there. She had to find Calista. She swept her gaze around the quadrangle, searching.

No little sister.

She pulled her purse off her shoulder, went for her cell phone, and realized the island's poor service. She sent Calista a text, anyway.

Hey! Orientation is about to start. I'll save you a seat.

Immediately, her phone informed her that the message had gone unsent. *Well, shoot.*

Not knowing what else to do, she stood in the middle of the quad. Eloisa appeared beside the stage. The woman had changed into a rainbow-colored island-print muumuu with a tangerine bird-of-paradise plume tucked into a yellow pillbox hat.

Eloisa spied Athena and waved her over.

Athena pressed a palm to her chest. *Me?* she mouthed silently.

Eyes and smile beaming, Eloisa nodded and motioned her forward.

What was the woman up to? Athena didn't want to go onstage, but perhaps the older woman had seen her sister.

Heads turned as Athena threaded her way up the aisle. Despite her career in the public eye, she felt self-conscious, ducking her head and letting a sheaf of hair fall over her face as murmurs ran throughout the crowd. She caught snatches of conversations as she passed by—not gossip, but definitely attention.

"*That's Demetra's girl.*"

"*The oldest.*"

"*The champion golfer.*"

"*Isn't she beautiful? Like a Greek goddess.*"

At the stage, Eloisa motioned for Athena to bend down. Athena leaned over and she got another unfortunate blast from the past.

Her father, whenever he triangulated her against Calista, would pull her aside, lean down, and whisper in her ear, "You're much, much better than she is. Never forget, you're the princess. She's just sooty Cinderella."

The image flashing through her brain shot her head up. Not since Calista walked away had Athena felt her father's papery, ice-cold fingers plucking at her shirtsleeve or his bourbon-soaked breath brushing hot against her ear.

"Dear?" Eloisa's voice jolted Athena back into the present.

"Huh?" Athena flipped her sunglasses up on her head to get a better look at the woman.

"Where did you go?" Eloisa asked, her tone gentle.

Athena shook her head, clearing it. "Sorry, woolgathering. Have you seen Calista?"

"Why, no, my dear, not since I left her at the dock." Concern creased Eloisa's brow. "She should have arrived by now. I certainly hope she just took a brief detour to see the island, and nothing untoward has happened."

"I'm sure she's fine," Athena said, trying to convince herself. She darted her gaze around, a rising sense of urgency gnawing at her.

"Introverts need time to ourselves." Eloisa rubbed a palm along Athena's upper arm. "Give her space."

Hell, she'd given Calista five years. When did space become estrangement?

"Would you mind coming to the mic when I introduce you?" Eloisa waved at the gathered crowd. "Our community would like the opportunity to know Demetra's daughters. Your mother was much beloved here on Hobby Island, and we'd like to acknowledge you and your sister."

Athena glanced at the audience, who were studying her with curious gazes. She did not want to do this, but Benjamin Dempsey, who was all about "the Brand," had raised her. "Success is 99 percent appearance," he was fond of saying. "It's why you rise, and Calista sinks. She doesn't get the importance of the public mask."

"It's all right. I've asked at an inconvenient time." Eloisa gave a gentle smile. "No worries."

Eloisa had done so much for her mother. What would it hurt to give the woman a few minutes of her time?

"I'll do it," Athena said.

"Are you sure?" Eloisa's voice softened, her eyes narrowing as if she could see the cracks forming beneath Athena's polished surface.

Athena pasted her mask back in place and glued it down with a forced smile. Was she sure about anything anymore? "Yes."

"That's lovely. Thank you." Eloisa's eyes were as kind as Mrs. Santa Claus's, then she turned and climbed the stage to the podium.

"Good afternoon, dear friends," Eloisa said into the microphone, her voice spreading throughout the quadrangle. "We've gathered not only for our usual orientation but to begin our summerlong journey in honoring our beloved Demetra Sarris. Every single one of you received a gold ticket to the island for this purpose. If you're here, Demetra changed your life in some significant way."

Athena stood off to the side, one hand clasped around the handle of her purse, the other fisted against her thigh. Indeed, Demetra's absence in their lives had changed her and Calista's destinies in immeasurable ways.

"Demetra is an inspiration to us all. Despite facing many challenges, all she ever wanted was to help those who were suffering. After her healing journey, she became a registered nurse, driven by a passion to make the world a better place. Her work with the Peace Corps took her to remote villages, where she battled disease and championed education."

Athena couldn't catch her breath. She tried to draw in air, but an invisible band squeezed her rib cage like a vise. She had no idea Demetra went to nursing school and joined the Peace Corps.

But why would she know? She'd had zero contact with her mother since she was eleven years old, and her father forbade them from ever bringing up her name. Once or twice, when she was old enough, she thought about searching for Demetra and reuniting, but Benjamin clarified that if she made such a move, he'd completely cut her off.

"After her stint in the Peace Corps, Demetra joined Doctors Without Borders, risking her safety in war-torn regions to bring medical care to those most in need. Her courage and compassion knew no bounds," Eloisa said.

A wave of admiration rippled through the audience. Athena felt disconnected, as if watching a movie about a stranger's life.

"And now," Eloisa said, turning toward her, "we're honored to have Demetra's oldest daughter with us. A few of you will remember Athena from when she visited Hobby Island with her mother and sister, back when the resort was just a gleam in my eye. Athena, would you like to say a few words?"

On leaden legs, Athena approached the microphone. The faces before her blurred into a sea of expectation. She gripped the podium, steadying herself.

"Thank you all for coming here to honor my mother," she said. "And for remembering her. I'm . . . I'm learning about her, too, it seems."

A mild murmur spread through the crowd. Everyone peered at Athena with gentle, caring eyes. Overwhelmed, she stepped back and nodded for Eloisa to continue.

Back at the microphone, Eloisa outlined the monthlong celebration of Demetra's life—a groundbreaking on the projected Demetra Sarris Remembrance Garden, craft-oriented fundraisers for the medical causes Demetra championed, and to cap it all off a charity golf tournament on the Fourth of July weekend.

"Demetra's ashes currently rest in the island chapel," Eloisa said. "We've arranged visitation hours for those wishing to pay their respects in quiet contemplation today, and afterward, we'll have a short tribute." She paused, letting everyone absorb the information. "Now, we'll proceed with the normal housekeeping announcements and general orientation. After this, all the craft shops are holding receptions, so please drop by and visit. Since Demetra was an avid knitter, items she made over the years are for sale in The Yarnery. One hundred percent of the proceeds go to cancer research."

As the crowd dispersed, Athena remained rooted in place. The urge to see her mother's urn, to connect with the woman who was a mystery to her, warred with a more urgent need to find Calista.

Uneasiness tugged at her. Something wasn't right.

The quadrangle speakers played Weezer's "Island in the Sun," an odd contrast to her tumultuous emotions. She headed toward the golf cart, but an older woman with gray curls piled so high atop her head it rivaled Marge Simpson called out to her. "Athena, wait."

Stuffing down her impatience, she turned to face the woman. "Hi, hello, how are you?"

Without the hair, the woman stood around five foot four, but with it, she was almost as tall as Athena at five eight. She wore a navy-and-white-striped scoop neck blouse and beige cargo shorts; the pockets were stretched and stuffed with items—scissor handles protruded from one pocket, a ruler from another, and a seam ripper from a third. She had a thimble on her right thumb and tortoiseshell glasses perched on the end of her nose.

"I'm Clare." She extended her hand, and Athena took it. "I run the quilting store, A Stitch in Time." She pointed in the direction of the quaint shop with an orange tabby sitting in the window, licking its paw. "I loved your mother madly."

"Thank you for saying that. It's nice to meet you, Clare. I'm sorry I don't have long to talk. I need to find my sister." She let go of Clare's hand and stepped back.

"So you two have repaired things?" Clare clapped her hands together. "That's wonderful!"

Athena shot Clare a look, an odd feeling winnowing through her. How did the woman know about her rift with her sister?

Seeing Athena's look, Clare said, "We share everything on Hobby Island—our sorrows, our difficulties, our joys. Your mother spoke of you often."

Athena's heart skipped a beat. "What did my mother say about us?"

Clare studied her for a moment too long before responding. "While we share our troubles and our celebrations, we try not to gossip."

"How is this gossiping? You'd just be telling me what my mother said."

"Your mother isn't here to defend herself."

"So you won't tell me?" Frustrated, Athena frowned.

"It's best to let things unfold as Demetra planned."

"What's that supposed to mean?"

Clare put an index finger to her lips and giggled. "You'll see. If you'd like to quilt a little, stop by the shop. We're making a memorial quilt for your mom, and we would love to include a square hand-quilted by you and your sister. But only if that's something you want to take part in. Grief is funny and joining us might be too painful. I understand. Simply come and hang out. We've got cookies and fresh-squeezed lemonade, and we'll tell stories of Demetra and how she enriched all our lives."

The Hobby Island community was sewing a quilt for Demetra. They loved her that much.

Right then, Athena identified the disturbing feeling simmering in the back of her mind ever since she arrived.

*Jealousy.*

She was jealous that these people loved her mother, and apparently, Demetra loved them right back. Yes, yes, Sainted Demetra, the healer of children in faraway places.

Athena's big question?

If Demetra was so damned incredible, why hadn't she loved her daughters enough to fight for them? And why, after all these years, was Athena still so desperate to find pieces of a mother who chose to be a stranger?

Of course, Athena could have reached out when she came of age. In fact, she'd tried. Sort of . . .

She remembered sitting in the luxury hotel suite on tour the month she turned pro at eighteen, the smell of leather and Benjamin's cologne thick in the air. Her laptop sat open on the desk, the search bar blinking at her, daring her.

It would be so easy. To see if her mother's name brought up anything—a picture, an address, a clue to where she might be now. Slowly, she'd typed each letter: *D-E-M-E-T-R-A-S-A-R-R-I-S*.

She hovered her index finger over the enter key, heart pounding. Then, with a deep breath, she pressed it.

The page loaded slowly, the sluggish hotel internet spinning its wheel endlessly. She stared at the screen, her nerves jangling with what might appear. Would Demetra look the same? What if there was nothing? What if . . .

The door opened behind her.

She slammed the laptop shut, flew out of her chair, pulse roaring in her ears, and spun around.

Benjamin stepped into the room, his phone in hand, his expression inscrutable.

"Athena." He leaned against the doorframe, scanning the room before locking his gaze on her. "You should be resting. Big day tomorrow. I'd hate to see you lose focus."

Her stomach flipped, guilt knotting inside her, terrified he'd known what she was up to. Yet, how could he? He couldn't see through walls. But her father did possess an uncanny sixth sense when she was doing something he disapproved of.

"I-I was just checking tomorrow's schedule." Not a complete lie. She *had* checked her schedule before the unexpected impulse to search for her mother gripped her. She was old enough now, to find Demetra . . . *if* she wanted.

"Hmm." His gaze flicked to the laptop for a brief moment before meeting hers again. "That's my girl. Always planning ahead."

The praise sent warmth rushing through her, easing the guilty knot in her chest. He believed in her, always had. He was the one who saw her potential, who worked so hard to make her successful. The thought of disappointing him burned her cheeks.

Benjamin crossed the room. He sat down on the end of her bed and patted the spot beside him. Slowly, she eased down next to her father. He leaned forward, studying her face. "Do you know why I've always been so proud of you, Athena?"

Her breath hitched. "Why?"

"Because you're everything a champion should be. You're not just talented—you understand the work, the sacrifice. You don't let emotions or distractions get in the way of what matters. You're not sentimental. You know how to put the past behind you and move forward."

She nodded. "I won't let you down, Dad."

"I know you won't." He lowered his voice. "That's why I trust you." He hesitated, his gaze sharpening. "You're not like Calista."

Athena frowned. She didn't like it when he talked bad about her sister. "Calista works hard, too—"

"Calista works when it suits her. She's too emotional. Impulsive. She doesn't have your discipline, or your focus. That's why she'll never go as far as you will." He smiled, patting her hand. "You've always been the one who understands what it takes to win."

The words filled her with a quiet pride, then she thought of the search engine and how she'd been on the verge of betraying his trust by looking up her mother. "Thank you, Daddy."

"Dinner's in an hour." He stood and adjusted his cuff links. "Wear the blue dress. The sponsors will love you in it."

After the door clicked shut behind him, she opened the laptop again but couldn't bring herself to look at the results. Instead, she shut down her computer and shoved it into her bag.

Later, when she was older, Athena thought again about searching for Demetra, but she didn't. Her mother had never sent a card, never called, never even tried to keep in contact. And hadn't Benjamin always said their mother was unstable, dangerous? Back then, she'd believed him without question, clinging to his every word.

But now, standing here in the shadow of her past, Athena could see how he'd twisted everything. It was so much easier to believe him than to face the painful truth. Her father's love had always been a cage that kept her in and her mother out.

# Chapter 8
## *Calista*

*"Authenticity lives in imperfection. Don't worry if your art isn't perfect, it's not supposed to be."*

—*Eloisa Hobby*

Some would have panicked. Many would have scrambled, grabbing at whatever their frantic hands encountered. Most would have done both.

Calista did neither.

She barely registered the blur of feathers and beady eyes—the ostrich's unexpected assault—before the ground vanished beneath her feet. Whether by instinct, years of black-belt-level practice, or a wide self-destructive streak, she went limp. The tried-and-true defense mechanism of the opossum. Tonic immobility. Playing dead.

Her body relaxed, absorbing the impact as she tumbled down the hill.

Tall grass slapped against her skin, angry bees buzzed as she disturbed their wildflowers, and her stomach lurched with the uneven terrain. Nausea coiled in her throat. Fantastic, they'd find her dead and covered in vomit.

She squeezed her eyes shut, surrendering to the fall. If it was her time to die, well, at least she'd see Mamá again.

Images and sensations careened through her mind, blending past with present—Demetra pushing her on a playground swing, her mother's laughter warm and sunlit in the Texas air. The scent of jasmine and sea salt.

Athena's stoic face on those courthouse steps, while Calista's own was tear-streaked. Athena's tentative smile on the ferry to Marshmallow Landing. Calista could use a marshmallow landing right about now.

The satisfying thwack of a perfect drive, the ball arcing against an azure sky. Eloisa's kind eyes offering a lifeline she wasn't ready to grasp. The acrid taste of anger propelling her away from that green at Chevron. Children's joyful shouts at a fantastical birthday party Calista had planned, filled with surprises and unique twists. The weight of the locket at her throat was a constant reminder of everything she'd lost. Her therapist's gentle voice. *You are more than your past, Calista.*

Each memory flickered in a heartbeat as her life distilled into fragments. This was it, the end of her life. She braced herself, expecting pain or oblivion.

But instead . . . stillness.

Calista lay on her back, eyes clenched shut, ankle throbbing, heart hammering. Slowly, she cracked one eye open and then the other, staring up at an endless sky dotted with fluff-bunny clouds drifting by.

Music reached her ears, faint at first but growing louder. Was it a heavenly chorus? Pearly gates beckoning?

*Dearly beloved . . .*

No, no. It was Prince. "Let's Go Crazy."

Huh?

She propped herself up on her elbows, looked to her left, and let out a soft gasp. She had stopped inches from the cliff where the ground mysteriously cupped upward like a curling wave. Just beyond, a hundred feet below, the shimmering blue ocean lapped against the shore. The salty air stung her eyes, and she exhaled slowly, releasing a long-held breath. Dropping her shoulder blades back to the earth, she let the tension seep from her limbs.

The music grew louder, and the iconic guitar riff carried on the island breeze. Calista sat up, cross-legged in her long skirt, and swiveled her head, searching for the source.

A golf cart sped toward her as fast as it could go, mowing down wildflowers as it bounced along the uneven terrain and stirred the silence with rock music.

*Aww, the poor flowers.*

She hoped they'd spring back. Shading her eyes with her palm, she squinted, trying to identify who was behind the wheel. Unmistakable, even from a distance. The man's poufy Elvis-esque hair ruffled in the wind.

Reid Thornton.

Calista groaned and fell back onto the grass, legs still crossed. Of course it would be *him*, of all people, to come upon her. She cocked one eye at the sky. "Really?"

The cart halted a few feet from her.

Reid killed the engine, cutting off the music and leaving Prince hanging mid-note. The golf cart had a pretty sweet sound system—Bose if she wasn't mistaken. Calista knew her audio because her work assistant, Skylar, shared his passion with anyone who would listen.

"Calista?" Reid rushed over. Concern etched his face. "I saw you take a tumble, and I thought . . ." He shook his head, the rest of the sentence hanging in the air between them. "Well, never mind that. You didn't go over the cliff, and I, for one, am thrilled you're okay. You are okay . . . right?"

Since when did he care about her well-being? She wanted to ignore him. To pretend she was invisible among the camouflaging wildflowers, but her throbbing ankle had other ideas.

"Hunky-dory." *Damn, her stupid voice quiver.*

"Yeah, because people who are 'hunky-dory' lie spread-eagle on cliff edges."

Despite herself, Calista twitched her mouth upward. She'd forgotten his knack for dry humor, the way he could disarm her with a single line.

"I'm not spread-eagle."

"No?" He loomed over her, blocking out the sun, a big grin on his stupidly handsome face. "Oh, I see. You folded your legs underneath your skirt."

"Stop staring at my nether regions." He'd lost that right thirteen years ago, but she wasn't about to churn *that* up again. She shifted slightly, trying to maintain some dignity despite her position.

"Is something wrong with your limbs that you can't straighten them?" he asked.

He crouched beside her, concern returning to those striking blue eyes as he searched her face. "Seriously, Cal, are you hurt?"

The old nickname she'd once forbidden him to use punched her in the gut. She moistened her bottom lip. "My ankle. I twisted it, running away from a deranged ostrich."

Reid blinked. "I'm sorry, did you say ostrich?"

"You heard me."

A beat passed, and then Reid burst out laughing. "Only you could come to an idyllic island and end up in an altercation with Big Bird."

Calista tried to hang on to her scowl, but she felt it crumple at the edges. "It's not funny."

"It's kind of funny, but you're right, I'm sorry. Near-death experiences are serious business."

"I could have tumbled into the ocean."

"Not really." He eyed the way the ground curved upward at the cliff's edge. "You didn't have enough momentum."

"Maybe not, but I crossed my legs to sit up when I heard your music, and now I'm afraid to move since, for the moment, my ankle doesn't hurt."

"Are you cutting off your blood supply?" He reached to lift her skirt.

"What are you doing!" She slapped both hands on the ground, pinning her skirt down, her heart skipping a beat.

Grinning, he stepped back and held out a hand. "You ready to get up?"

She exhaled. "Okay, let's do it."

"I'm here. I got your back." Oh, he'd said that before, and he had not, in fact, had her back. He seemed to realize that as his face flushed. "I promise."

"We'll see." She grasped his outstretched hand, and he hauled her to a standing position. She hissed through clenched teeth. "Ouch, ouch, ouch."

"Here, lean into me." He wrapped an arm around her waist, and she caught a whiff of his cologne—sandalwood, palo santo, and citrus. He still used the same fragrance he had at sixteen.

*Then, boom!*

Memory engulfed her, spinning images of things she thought she had buried thirteen years ago after Reid broke her heart.

The musty smell of the clubhouse locker room, the cool metal against her back, her eager sixteen-year-old self, raging with hormones and need.

The feel of Reid's calloused hands on her bare skin, eager yet gentle. Hushed giggles and whispered promises.

In the distance, outside, the *thwack* of late-night golfers hitting balls on the driving range. His warm mouth against her neck. The rough texture of the towel they'd spread on the bench, moonlight filtering through the tall windows, casting shadows. The tang of their nervous sweat mixed with the aroma of his cologne.

Her heart had pounded so loudly she was sure he could hear it. The way he nicknamed her *Cal* with such reverence. Fumbling fingers and awkward angles. Bumping chins and grinding hips. Escalating desire and . . . a moment of discomfort, then his body was inside hers as they rocked together. Afterward, the comfort of his arms around her as they lay panting, skin to skin.

"Cal?" Reid asked, dragging her back to the present.

"Uh-huh." She shook her head, dislodging the memory's cobweb sticking to her brain.

"Does it hurt?"

"Hell, yes," she said, talking about the memory, not her ankle.

"Can you move it?"

Calista rotated her foot, wincing.

Reid nodded. "Probably just a sprain, but we should get some ice on it. Come on, I'll give you a ride to Crafters' Corner."

Calista hesitated. Getting in a golf cart with him felt dangerous in a way that tumbling down a cliff hadn't.

"I can walk." She raised her chin.

Reid arched an eyebrow. "Cal, it's almost five miles. On uneven terrain. With a sprained ankle."

"I could crawl." Okay, yes, she was being ridiculous.

"Stubborn as always." There was a fondness in his tone that clipped her chest. "Look, I know you're not thrilled to see me, but can we call a truce? Just until we get you some medical attention?"

Calista studied him, searching for any hint of the boy he'd

been. Something that reminded her of stolen moments behind the caddie shack, of nervous laughter and the taste of his lemon ChapStick.

She sighed, relenting. "Fine, but only because the alternative is death by ostrich, and I refuse to give that feathered maniac the satisfaction."

Reid's grin rebounded. "That's the spirit. Now, let's get you to the golf cart."

He tucked her closer to him, and Calista tried to ignore the warmth of his body heat. With his support, she hobbled to the golf cart and sank into the passenger seat. Fine, she was grateful for him. There, she admitted it.

He settled behind the wheel and started the golf cart with an ease that sent her back to their caddie days, recalling a time when he wasn't so graceful, tripping as he hustled after his guardian and spilling Gavin's expensive clubs all over the green.

Calista recalled cringing and waiting for Gavin to explode on Reid the way her father would have detonated on her. But Gavin had not. As Reid scrambled to gather the clubs, Gavin made a self-deprecating joke about his bad habit of club hoarding and overloading his bag, put a reassuring hand on Reid's shoulder, and helped him pick up the irons and woods.

Meanwhile, Benjamin, as part of the foursome they'd been caddying for, snapped his fingers for Calista to follow him to the next fairway, muttering, "Clumsy putz."

At that moment, Calista had wished with a desperate yearning that Gavin was her father or at least her guardian.

Unbidden, her gaze now went to Reid's profile. His wavy brown hair tousled from the wind, and his plain white T-shirt stretched across shoulders that were broader than she remembered.

"So . . ." He winked at her. Oh, that dangerous wink! "Ostriches, huh? And here I thought the wildest thing on this island was Eloisa's hat collection."

Calista snorted. "Trust me, I was just as surprised. One minute I'm having a walk through nature, the next I'm living out a real-life simulation of Angry Birds."

Chuckling, Reid navigated the cart down the hill, slowing over dips and bumps in the road. She appreciated his consideration. "If it makes you feel any better, I almost got taken out by an aggressive seagull who was after my breakfast muffin in Everly this morning."

"Oh, the horror."

They lapsed into silence, underscored by the sound system playing Jack Johnson's "I Got You."

The soothing, beachy stylings sent the sweet lyrics straight to her heart. Calista stole glances at Reid's profile, noting the faint lines at the corners of his eyes that hadn't been there when she'd last seen him five years ago.

"Cal?"

"Yeah?"

"I'm sorry."

Calista's brain short-circuited. "For what? The ostrich incident? I'm fairly sure that's not on you."

"I meant Chevron and what I said at the clubhouse that day. The relentless way I reported on your leaving."

"You didn't just drop the story after I left golf. You kept chasing me. You even came to my condo. Why? Was it just a slow news cycle, or did you enjoy kicking me while I was down?"

He winced. "I wasn't chasing a story. I was chasing *you*. I thought if I got you mad enough, you'd pick up a club and start swinging again."

"So you decided to 'help' by harassing me? Great strategy."

"I was an idiot, okay? I thought you'd realize how much the sport needed you. I didn't think you'd hate me for it."

"Hmm." She eyeballed him, scared to trust this man.

He fixed his gaze on her. "The way I turned into human spam afterward? It wasn't cool, and I'm sorry."

The apology blindsided Calista harder than that rogue Frisbee at last year's company picnic. She'd spent so long pretending that chapter of her life didn't exist, and here was Reid, reminding her it did.

"Sorry?" She raised an eyebrow. "What? Did you trip and *accidentally* write those vlogs about me?"

Reid's face crumpled. "I know it fixes nothing, but I want to make amends if you'll let me."

Calista suddenly found the passing trees fascinating. Anything to avoid those puppy eyes that made her want to forgive him and then kick herself for even considering it. "Leaving the tour was the smartest thing I ever did, but that doesn't mean it didn't hurt like hell. You made me feel unhinged."

The golf cart puttered along. The two of them were alone out here, and what felt like every poor decision Calista had ever made all lined up to watch the show.

Reid clutched the steering wheel like a life preserver. "If I could go back and knock some sense into past me, I would. Hard. Repeatedly. With a one wood."

Calista's heart fluttered. Dammit. His voice did that thing—that soft, sincere thing that made her want to believe him, but the part of her brain that got third-degree burns screamed *danger*.

"Words are just words, Reid. Even pretty ones."

He glanced at her. A look so loaded it should've come with a warning label. "I'm here, aren't I? That's not nothing."

Calista's mind felt like a browser with too many tabs open.

One part wanted to believe in this apologetic Reid, who was all grown up and sorry. The other part was frantically googling "how to tell if someone's actually changed or if you're just being a sucker again."

"Being here is . . . *something*," she said, softer than she intended. "But it doesn't undo how hard it was to rebuild, to find any scrap of normalcy. I don't trust you. How do I know you're not just here for a scoop?"

Reid stopped the cart and turned to her with an intensity reserved for people about to confess love or admit to murder. "Let me help. Let me be part of that normal, even if I have to earn it one painfully awkward conversation at a time."

Contrition looked good on him.

Calista felt poised on the high dive above a deep pool of trust issues. The water below could be refreshing—or filled with sharks wearing party hats. The real question? Did she still remember how to swim?

"You were just doing your job," she said, aiming for nonchalance and missing by a mile.

"No, it wasn't just about the job. I thought you deserved to know the truth, but I didn't think about how it would hurt you—or what it would cost you. When you walked away from golf, I blamed myself. I didn't want you to give up the thing you loved most because of something I told you." He hesitated, running a hand through his hair. "But I see now that it wasn't about you, not really. It was about me, trying to fix what I broke, trying to make myself feel better. I didn't think about what you needed, and for that, I'll never stop being sorry."

For the first time, Calista saw something new in Reid—not just regret, but a vulnerability that felt genuine. Maybe he really had been trying to save her all along, in his own messy way.

The cart bumped over a large tree root, jostling Calista's ankle. She winced, using the pain to gather her thoughts.

"Why are you telling me this now?"

"Well, we are on this island together." Reid paused, and when he spoke again, his low voice almost got lost in the island breeze. "Because I've regretted what I did every day for the past five years."

Calista turned to look at him, taking in the set of his jaw and the way his eyes darted to her for just a second before focusing back on the path.

"Reid—"

"You don't have to say anything. I'm not expecting forgiveness or . . . anything, really. I just needed you to know."

Calista nodded, not trusting herself. The walls she'd constructed wobbled, and she wasn't sure if she wanted to shore them up or let them fall, especially with this guy.

He gave her his best dashing grin and changed the topic. "So, other than your thrilling ornithological adventures, how are you finding Hobby Island?"

Grateful for the lifeline of a topic change, Calista latched onto it. "It's . . . not what I expected. Everything's so quaint and colorful . . . whimsical. It's like stepping into a storybook."

"I know, right? I half expect to see woodland creatures helping with the laundry."

"Please," Calista scoffed. "As if Eloisa would trust a bunch of squirrels with the linens."

They laughed together, and for a moment, it felt like no time had passed at all, as if they were still those two teenagers, sharing jokes and stolen kisses between rounds of golf. Back before he dumped her and broke her heart. Back before he went off to college at Columbia. Back before she turned pro.

But they weren't those kids anymore.

"I've missed this. Talking to you. Making you laugh." Sadness watered down his grin.

Calista's heart did a complicated somersault. "Reid . . ."

"I know, I know." He held up a hand in surrender. "We're not here to rehash the past. I just . . . I'm glad to see you again. Even if it's under these circumstances."

Calista nodded, not quite able to echo the sentiment but not wanting to dismiss it either. Instead, she focused on the path ahead, watching as Crafters' Corner came into view. The quaint village square bustled with activity. Vibrant banners fluttered in the breeze, and mingled scents surfed the air—freshly baked bread, sunscreen, coconuts, saltwater taffy.

"Looks like orientation is wrapping up." Reid maneuvered the cart around clusters of chatting guests.

She scanned the crowd. "Do you see Athena?"

"Not right off the bat. Want me to help you look for your sister? It's annoying that you can't just text her."

"Yeah, it is, but I'm fine. I don't need you. I can find Athena myself," Calista said.

"Huh?" A flash of hurt in Reid's eyes.

Ouch, okay, that was curt. "I mean, I'm sure my sister is around somewhere. Perhaps headed back to the Lavender Lark. I can manage on my own."

"Not with that ankle. We're getting you some help." He drove to the golf cart parking area and glanced around. "Where's medical triage?"

"I dunno. I missed orientation." She let out a giggle.

"Be right back." He hopped from the cart and headed toward a kiosk underneath a Visitors Center sign.

She watched him go, and felt a strange tugging in her stomach. What was that all about? He spoke to the couple operating the kiosk. A brisk-looking woman in blue scrubs appeared. Reid and the woman turned toward her. Bystanders stared. Feeling sheepish, Calista lifted a hand. She hated that she'd gotten hurt and drawn attention to herself.

Reid hurried to her side. "The nurse practitioner said to bring you on to the clinic."

She swung her injured ankle out of the cart, and he wrapped his arm around her waist again. She didn't much like it, but she was glad he was there for her to lean on, just for a moment. Then her foolish mind wondered what might have happened if . . .

*Nope. Stop it.* Things had played out the way they'd played out. Not daydreaming of mystical what-ifs.

They made their way across the quad, and the nurse practitioner motioned them into the small clinic tucked between the bookstore and the metalwork shop.

"This way." The efficient-looking woman with gunmetal-gray curls and a stethoscope around her neck led them into an exam room. She looked to Reid. "Can you help her onto the table?"

"I've got this," Calista said to the nurse. To Reid, she said, "You can go now."

He ignored her, guiding her to sit on the exam table covered in crisp white paper that crinkled beneath her.

"I'm Belinda," the nurse said. "Can you tell me what happened?"

"Don't you need my insurance or something?" Calista winced and thought about her deductible.

"No charge. You're Eloisa's guest. She pays the medical bills for anything that happens on the island."

"Really?"

Belinda's smile widened. "Really. Well, she *is* a billionaire and generous to a fault. Now, just relax and let me check out that ankle. What happened?"

"Bulldozed by an ostrich."

"That's Shushu." Belinda slid the sandal off Calista's foot and prodded her ankle with gentle fingers. "She's a naughty girl, but she loves to race. Eloisa rescued her from ostrich racing after she injured a wing."

Calista arched her eyebrows. "Ostrich racing is a thing?"

"Sadly, yes." Belinda scowled. "Which is why Eloisa gave Shushu a forever home. But the bird never lost her love for racing."

Interested, Calista asked, "How did Eloisa find out about Shushu?"

Belinda shook her head. "That's not my place to say. We try not to gossip on Hobby Island."

Reid leaned forward, his nose twitching as if smelling a story. That's when the clinic door burst open, and Athena stalked in. Her sister took one look at Calista on the table and Reid standing beside her.

Immediately, Athena rounded on him. "What did you do to my little sister, you unethical muckraker!"

# Chapter 9

## *Athena*

*"The hardest person to forgive is often yourself."*
—*Eloisa Hobby*

The sight of her younger sister perched on an examination table, an elastic bandage wrapped around her ankle as Reid Thornton hovered, triggered Athena's protective instincts. She didn't trust that guy.

Reid's palms flew up and pushed out through the air toward her. "Whoa, easy there, champ. I—"

"He did nothing wrong," Calista said. "Reid found me after I twisted my ankle and brought me here. That's all, Athena."

Her rage deflated like a punctured carnival balloon. "Oh."

Heat spread across her nape, and in her mind's eye, she saw her golf coach shaking his head and scowling. *And how does jumping to conclusions serve you, Athena?* Her coach had been talking about golf, but the criticism applied here as well.

The nurse practitioner, a no-nonsense woman with the build of a weight lifter, cleared her throat. "Now that we've established Mr. Thornton's innocence, perhaps we could focus on the patient?"

"Right, of course," Athena mumbled, trying to regain her dignity. She smoothed her skirt, a nervous habit left over from childhood. "Lissy, are you okay? What happened?"

*Lissy.*

She hadn't called her sister that since . . . well, since Demetra abandoned them. It had been their mother's nickname for Calista, and their father had forbidden Athena from using it just as he'd forbidden Calista from calling her Attie.

Calista's head shot up, and she locked gazes with her sister. Her face softened, and she let out a heavy sigh. "I had a run-in with an ostrich, don't ask."

Athena blinked. "I'm sorry, did you say ostrich? As in, the giant flightless bird?"

"No, I meant the tiny flying ones that wave magic wands and grant wishes," Calista said.

"It was quite the sight." Reid chuckled. "I found her at the edge of a cliff, looking as if she'd gone ten rounds with Big Bird."

Athena's anger flared again, and she narrowed her eyes at the interloper. "I'm sure you were thrilled to find her in distress. What a scoop, right? 'Former LPGA star attacked by exotic bird on quirky island.' I can see your YouTube thumbnail now."

Reid's easygoing demeanor cracked like a dropped egg. "Look, Athena, I know we have a complicated history, but I was just trying to help."

"Help?" Athena scoffed, her sarcasm thick enough to pour over pancakes. "Like you 'helped' when you dumped her at sixteen? Or hounded her after Chevron?"

As the words left her mouth, a small, rational part of Athena's brain whispered, *Oh no!* It was like watching a train wreck in slow motion, except she was both the train *and* the wreck.

"That's enough." Calista's voice, quiet but sharp, cut through Athena's rant. "Reid, thank you. I appreciate the ride into town, but you can go now."

Reid nodded. His jaw clenched strong enough to crack walnuts. "I hope your ankle feels better soon, Cal." He paused at the door, turning back to face them. "For what it's worth, I really am sorry . . . for everything."

And then he was gone, closing the door behind him.

Athena crossed her arms over her chest and sagged against the wall. She felt as winded as if she had run a marathon in her designer heels. "I'm so sorry, Calista. I shouldn't have lost my temper like that."

Her sister stared, hard-eyed. "No, you shouldn't have. Reid was just trying to help. Your outburst complicated things."

A wave crashed over Athena. She'd come here to make amends, and instead, she made them worse. Story of her life, really.

"I know. I'm sorry. I just . . . I saw you hurt and him there, and I jumped to conclusions. My brain short-circuited."

"Some things never change," Calista said. "But I no longer need your protection. I haven't needed you in years."

Athena gulped, hurt to the quick.

The nurse practitioner, who'd observed their drama with saintly patience, stepped forward. "All right, ladies. Family therapy is two doors down. Right now, let's focus on this ankle." She helped Calista off the table, supporting her as she tested her weight. "How's that feel?"

Calista winced. "Hurts a little, but I'll live."

"I'll give you an anti-inflammatory pill and a cane to use but try to stay off it for today and keep it elevated whenever you can. Avoid activities that cause pain or swelling. Use an ice pack for twenty minutes every three hours for the next two days while you're awake. After that, switch to heat until the swelling is gone."

"Thanks," Calista said.

The nurse practitioner unlocked a cabinet, removed a pill bottle, opened the lid, shook out two blue pills, filled a paper cup with water from the faucet, and handed the tablets to Calista. She washed them down and handed the cup back to the woman. The nurse then opened a small closet and took out a cane carved in the shape and color of a giraffe. "You can return the cane later."

"Thank you."

Athena offered her arm to Calista. "Let me help you."

Calista leaned on the cane and away from Athena. "I've got this."

"Suit yourself." Athena shrugged and dropped her hand. *Don't get your feelings hurt.* But she did. "I'm headed to the chapel for Mom's visitation. Did you want to come along?"

Calista nodded, thanked the nurse practitioner again, and hobbled for the door.

Athena's mind raced, trying to find the right words to bridge the Grand Canyon–size chasm between them, but every time she opened her mouth, the words died on her tongue. Finally, in white-flag surrender, she returned to the topic they'd already exhausted. "So, an ostrich, huh."

"It *is* a quirky island."

"*Quirky* is one word for it," Athena said. "I feel like we've stepped into a Wes Anderson movie, but nobody gave us the script."

A genuine laugh from Calista and Athena's hope surged. "God, yes. I half expect Bill Murray to pop out from behind a tree."

For a brief, shining moment, it felt like old times. Before golf and fame and their father's cruel machinations drove a wedge between them.

Across the quad, Eloisa stood at the entrance to the chapel. Her hat, adorned with an entire flower shop, wobbled as she waved them over.

"Welcome, my dears." Eloisa enveloped them both in a gardenia-scented hug. "I'm so glad you're here. Demetra would be thrilled to see her girls together again." She stepped back and eyed Calista. "Oh dear, what happened to your ankle?"

Calista relayed the details of her run-in with the ostrich.

"I am so sorry about our mischievous Shushu. I'll have the ostrich wrangler give her a stern talking to when she comes back to the barn tonight."

"There's an ostrich wrangler?" Athena asked.

"Oh, yes." Eloisa nodded. "He also handles the flamingo flock and the peacock pride, but that's a story for another time. Come on in and get settled."

Eloisa ushered them over the threshold, the heavy chapel door closing behind them with a soft thud. It shut out the direct sunshine and left them in muted shadows filtering through the stained glass windows, casting rainbow patterns across the polished wooden pews. Wood carvings brought the walls to life—birds flew by the windows, fish swam along the beams, and bits of shell and coral nestled in the corners. The whole place felt like a slice of the island itself, with sunshine, salty air, and birdsong drifting in from outside.

The air smelled of Stargazer lilies and roses. Soft music played in the background, a melody Athena recognized as "Supermarket Flowers" by Ed Sheeran, and unwanted tears pressed at her eyes. At the front of the chapel sat the urn, along with a portrait-size photograph of their mother propped on an easel.

Gutted, Athena put a hand to her mouth and willed herself not to throw up. Her stomach clamped down hard as Ed sang of his angelic mother.

The urn was beautiful, a ceramic piece decorated with intricate floral patterns in shades of red and gold. It was so perfectly Demetra that for a startling second, Athena felt like she was eight years old again, watching her mother arrange flowers in their kitchen while Benjamin was on tour, and the house was peaceful for once.

Beside her, Calista drew in a sharp breath. "I can't believe she's really gone, even though she's been out of our lives for twenty years. I always hoped that one day . . ."

Athena nodded, not trusting herself to speak without bursting into tears. She wanted to reach out, to take Calista's hand and offer some kind of comfort, but the gulf between them felt wider than ever, a chasm she didn't know how to bridge.

"Ladies," Eloisa said from behind them, gentle but firm. "If you're ready, we can begin."

Athena turned to see that the chapel had filled behind them. People sat in the pews, wearing expressions of sympathy and grief. It was surreal, seeing all these strangers mourning a woman Athena hardly remembered.

"Please, be seated." Eloisa guided them to the front row.

Once they settled in, Eloisa moved to the front of the chapel, her scarlet ensemble a stark contrast to the somber atmosphere. She cleared her throat. "Friends, family, welcome. We're here to celebrate the life of our dear Demetra. Now is the time for sharing memories, for laughter through tears, for honoring a woman who touched all our lives in unique ways."

Athena glanced around the chapel, taking in the faces of strangers who somehow knew her mother better than she did, and a coppery taste filled her mouth.

"I invite anyone who wishes to share a memory, a poem, a song—anything that reminds you of Demetra—to come forward."

For a moment, the chapel fell silent, and then a woman with silver hair and a paint-stained smock stood up. "I remember the first time Demetra joined our art class," she said, her voice heavy with emotion. "She claimed she couldn't draw a straight line with a ruler, but oh, the joy on her face when she finished her first watercolor!"

A ripple of soft laughter moved through the gathering.

Next, a man in his forties with a guitar slung across his shoulder approached the front. "Demetra loved this song," he said. "She said it reminded her of her girls." As the first chords of "Landslide" by Fleetwood Mac filled the chapel, Athena couldn't hold back the tears any longer. She recalled her mother humming this tune as she braided Athena's hair for school.

One by one, people stood up to share. A retired teacher spoke of Demetra's volunteer work. A young woman, her eyes brimming with tears, recounted how Demetra sat with her through a long night when she thought she might lose her baby. Each story painted a picture of a woman Athena didn't recognize—kind, brave, and involved in her community. The mother she remembered was a faded photograph in comparison, a ghost haunting the edges of her childhood memories, and in her father's narrative, a villain who'd ruined his life.

"Would either of you like to share something?" Eloisa asked, her gentle eyes meeting Athena's.

Athena felt panic rise in her throat. What could she say? That her strongest memory of her mother was the sound of her sobs? For years, she blamed Demetra for abandoning them even as she knew her father was the one who took them away from her.

She peeked at Calista, hoping her sister might offer her comfort, but Calista's face was a mask, her eyes fixed on some distant point.

Athena was the oldest. It was up to her. She got to her feet and turned to the crowd. "I-I . . ." Athena began, her voice faltering. "I wish I had known her the way you all did."

The words hung in the air, raw and honest. Athena felt exposed and vulnerable in a way she hadn't allowed herself to be in years.

Eloisa's eyes filled with understanding. "Demetra wished that, too, my dear. She spoke of you both often, always with love and hope."

Then Eloisa moved on, inviting others to share. Someone got up to read the Mary Oliver poem "When Death Comes." Athena felt Calista's hand slip into hers. She looked over at her sister, surprised.

Calista's eyes were wet with unshed tears, and she whispered, "Life is so unfair."

At that moment, surrounded by the memories of strangers and the weight of lost time, Athena squeezed her sister's hand. It wasn't forgiveness, not yet, but it was a start.

Eloisa took over again, painting a picture of a woman who was kind, brave, and loving. Athena felt a growing sense of loss. Not just for the mother who had died, but for the relationship they'd never had, for all the years wasted in separation caused by their father. He wouldn't allow any contact between them and their mother. The courts had ruled in his favor, declaring Demetra an unfit mother, and that had been that.

But why hadn't Demetra reached out to them once they were grown and less under Benjamin's sway?

When the ceremony ended, Eloisa announced a welcome party going on all evening in the quad, and the other attendees began to file out, offering quiet condolences as they passed. Athena touched Calista's hand. "Lissy, can we hang back and talk for a moment?"

"Okay." Her expression was guarded but not hostile.

Once the chapel emptied, leaving them alone with their mother's urn, Athena took a deep breath and turned to her sister.

It was now or never.

"I'm so sorry, Lissy," she said. "Not just for today, but for everything. For not standing up for you more when we were kids.

For letting Dad pit us against each other." She took a tissue that Luna had given her from her pocket and wiped away her tears. "I've made so many mistakes, and I don't expect you to forgive me right away, but I want you to know that I'm here now, and I want to make things right between us."

Calista listened but her face was unreadable. "I appreciate you saying that, Athena. I really do, but it's not that simple. We can't just erase years of hurt with one apology."

"I know it will take time, but I'm willing to put in the work if you are. We're all we have left now, Lissy. I don't want to lose you too."

A ghost of a smile flickered across Calista's face, but it was gone so fast Athena thought she might have imagined it. "We'll see . . . Attie."

*Attie.*

The forbidden nickname passed her sister's lips for the first time in twenty years. It wasn't forgiveness. It wasn't even in the same zip code, but it was something. A tiny green shoot in the wasteland of their tattered relationship.

# Chapter 10
## *Eloisa*

*"Deep down in our anger lies the source of grief."*

—*Eloisa Hobby*

I hope you know what you're doing." Eloisa fixed her gaze on Demetra's portrait that rested on an easel directly beneath the bell tower.

After everyone had left the visitation, Eloisa returned to tidy up. The sweet, cloying scent of funeral flowers hung heavy in the air, a reminder of endings and beginnings intertwined.

This picture was Eloisa's favorite photograph of her friend. Taken five years ago, when Demetra was still vibrant in her early fifties, her smile pouring out pure joy. Unsettling, really, how happy she looked when she'd seen so much darkness, so much heartache. Though slow and painstaking, her miraculous healing helped Demetra to heal others.

The only thing that hadn't healed was the forever hole in her heart from losing her children. In quieter moments, Demetra would trace their names in the sand at low tide, letting the waves wash them away as tears tracked down her cheeks.

So the sacred task of reuniting Demetra's daughters fell to Eloisa. The weight of this responsibility pressed down on her shoulders like the thick summer air of Hobby Island.

"They'll get furious at me, but I will bear their anger gratefully for you, my friend, because of all you did for me." Eloisa let out a soft sigh. "I just pray this turns out the way you hoped."

Light from the setting sun filtered through the stained glass windows, casting rainbow shadows across Demetra's face, making her appear almost ethereal.

The creak of the chapel door broke the stillness. Eloisa turned to see Calista framed in the doorway, her dark hair tumbling over her shoulders, looking so much like Demetra's that it took Eloisa's breath away.

The resemblance went beyond mere features—it was in the way she held herself, the subtle lift of her chin, the careful way she surveyed a room before entering. Overwhelmed, Eloisa hiccuped and pressed two fingers—which smelled of the Stargazer lilies she'd arranged—to her mouth.

"I left my cane in here somewhere." Calista's voice echoed in the empty chapel, bouncing off the wooden beams above. "Have you seen it?"

Eloisa tacked on a bright smile, though her heart ached at the wariness in Calista's eyes. "Let's look for it together, shall we?"

Calista moved with a lithe grace that belied her injury. She had a dancer's build, willowy and lean but muscular, just like Demetra. Even her movements echoed her mother's—deliberate yet fluid—as if she were moving through water rather than air.

"There." Eloisa pointed. "I see Germaine's head poking out."

"Huh? Germaine?"

"That's what we call your cane. Germaine the Giraffe." Eloisa let out a giggle, her natural effervescence bubbling through the sadness. "We are a tad whimsical on Hobby Island."

"I've noticed," Calista said with a dryness that indicated maybe she did not bend toward whimsy.

Eloisa didn't judge. She could appreciate that not everyone enjoyed flights of fancy.

Calista leaned down to retrieve Germaine the Giraffe from beneath the pew and let out a little gasp. "Oh!"

"Is it your ankle?" Eloisa rushed closer, joining Calista in the pew. The wood creaked beneath them.

"No, the cane is stuck on something."

Eloisa reached down to help, her hand brushing Calista's as they both grasped the cane and tugged it free—together. For a moment, neither let go of the cane, and Eloisa felt Demetra stretch between them like an invisible thread of yearning.

Calista met Eloisa's gaze, her eyes filled with unanswered questions, each one a weight she'd carried for two decades. "I miss her."

"I miss her too." Eloisa released her grip on the cane.

"At least you got to know her a lot longer. I only had her for nine years." Calista set down the cane and leaned against it.

"I'm sorry about that." The words felt hollow, insufficient against the vastness of lost time.

"Me too."

In unison, they turned in the pew to stare at the portrait of Demetra. The silence between them grew thick with unspoken words and buried memories.

Eloisa knew the entire story, and eventually, she would dole it out to the girls just as her dear friend planned, but she understood how badly Calista and Athena were hurting. The pain radiated from Calista like heat from summer pavement.

Unfortunately, feeling the pain was part of the healing process. The young women were in the thick of sorrow, and there was no rushing grief. It had its own timeline, as unpredictable as island weather.

"You know," Eloisa said, "your mother planted a fig tree next to the cottage where she once lived. It's the same cottage where Reid Thornton is bunking."

"I see." Calista's expression was neutral, revealing nothing.

"The fig was a spindly little thing." Eloisa forged on with the story, praying Calista would pick up on the underlying message. "Little more than a twig, really. Our soil here isn't ideal for figs, you see. Too sandy and too close to the sea."

Calista's fingers tightened on her cane, and she canted her head, listening. A muscle worked in her jaw, betraying the emotion she tried to hide.

Grief.

"For years, that tree just stood there, no fruit, just a few leaves. Dormant. Not dead, but not fully alive, either. My grounds-keeper, Paul Chance, wanted to dig it up and transport the tree to his in-laws' house in Everly and give it a fighting chance, but Demetra wouldn't hear of it."

"The patron saint of lost causes, huh?" Calista asked, bitterness edging her words.

"I think that's Saint Jude, but I see your point. Your mother spent hours nurturing that tree, talking to it, singing to it. She got compost from Paul and mixed it into the soil. I'd find her out there, checking the leaves for signs of growth. Sometimes in the rain, sometimes under the scorching sun."

Calista's breathing slowed, and her eyes fixed on some distant point as if she were struggling not to tear up. The late-afternoon light caught the moisture in her eyes, turning them into melted chocolate.

Eloisa pulled a clean monogrammed hankie from her pocket and passed it to Calista, who took it and wadded it in her fist. The delicate embroidery disappeared into her grip.

"One day, your mother came to me, excited about something she'd read about grafting. She found a cutting from a hardier fig tree on the mainland and said she would join it to her fig, make it strong enough to survive on Hobby Island."

"She was stubborn, huh?" A faint smile played at Calista's lips, gone as quickly as it appeared.

"I remember thinking she was fighting a losing battle, but she was so determined. It took two more years before the fig bore fruit. Two years of constant care. Of protecting it from storms. Of talking and singing to it. But then, one spring morning, there it was. A single, perfect fig."

Calista sucked in an audible breath. The sound reverberated sharply in the quiet chapel.

"I'd only seen your mother cry like that one other time and that was the day Benjamin took you girls away, but this time it was tears of joy. She cradled that fig like it was the most precious thing on earth. She said it was proof that with enough love and patience, anything was possible."

"Wh-when was this?" Calista's voice wavered, barely above a whisper.

"She first planted that fig the day after she returned from the mental hospital." Eloisa hesitated, feeling the weight of the next words. "The first time."

Calista's lips parted, a storm of emotions in her eyes. "She was in a mental hospital . . . more than once?"

"She was devastated over losing you, Calista. It broke her in ways that never fully healed. And when she got out, she tried to contact you. She called, she wrote, she sent gifts. But Benjamin sent them all back, blocked her on social media and blocked her phone too. That sent her back to the hospital again."

"Oh, no." Calista let out a soft cry.

"Because your mother grew up in foster care, she never knew what it was to fully feel safe, to be loved unconditionally. Benjamin knew exactly how to use that against her. He'd grown so skilled at manipulating her fears, her trauma." Eloisa clamped down on her tongue to keep from telling Calista the worst of it—that Benjamin had threatened to take it out on the girls if Demetra kept trying to contact them.

Demetra knew what he was capable of—she'd lived with that fear for years. Her depression was like a thick fog that would roll in and out of her life. Some days she could barely get out of bed. She'd sit by that fig tree for hours, lost in her own darkness. Even after years of therapy, after she'd done so much healing work, that terror of what Benjamin might do to her daughters never fully went away.

Even when they were grown, Demetra was afraid to contact them. Terrified of Benjamin and what her daughters would think of her cowardice. She was so ashamed she wasn't strong enough to confront him.

Although Demetra had tried once more. Five years ago. At Chevron.

Calista's eyes misted, and in the softening, Eloisa spied a hint of the little girl who once chased baby turtles across the beach, but the look was gone in an instant, replaced by a guarded wariness that had become her armor.

"Calista, there's so much you don't know about your mother."

"So tell me." Anger flushed Calista's face, bringing spots of color to her cheeks. "Make me understand."

"First, you need to be in the headspace where you can accept what you hear."

Calista scowled. "What does that even mean?"

"You're in too much emotional turmoil right now. That's

the point of spending the summer here. It's what your mother wanted." Eloisa's voice took on a pleading note.

"Yeah? Well, I wanted a mother who fought to keep us!" Calista hopped up fast and gave a little yelp as she put too much weight on her ankle.

Despair wrapped around Eloisa's heart like morning fog on the island. "What if this summer could help you heal? Help you and Athena find your way back to each other?"

"Heal? How does time on an island erase twenty years of silence? Twenty years of wondering why she didn't love us?" The pain in Calista's voice was a living thing, raw and intense, echoing off the chapel walls.

"Stop that!" Eloisa said in a harsher tone than she intended. "Demetra loved you with every cell in her body. Her dying thoughts were only of you and Athena."

"Why didn't she come to us?"

"She was too sick by then, both in body and spirit." Eloisa's voice cracked. "The cancer came on fast, but the depression . . . that had been her constant companion for years. Even when she was doing better, helping others heal, she couldn't quite heal that part of herself."

"Not even at the end? Not even when she needed us most?"

"She . . ." Eloisa swallowed hard. "She convinced herself you were better off without her. That she'd only hurt you more by coming back into your lives at this late stage of the game. I disagreed with her, fought her on it. But the depression twisted everything, made her believe she didn't deserve your love." Eloisa longed to offer more comfort, but she knew some wounds must reopen before they could truly heal. "But now she's giving you this chance—an opportunity to understand the whole truth, to forgive—not just her and Athena, but yourself."

"Excuse me." Calista hunched against the giraffe-shaped cane, skirted past Eloisa, and headed for the door. Her footsteps echoed against the wooden floors, each step a reminder of distance yet to be crossed.

The door closed behind her.

Eloisa sat alone in the chapel, the silence pressing in around her like a physical presence.

Dust motes danced in the remaining shafts of sunlight, reminding her of all the particles of truth still suspended, waiting to settle. She glanced back at Demetra's portrait, seeing both a challenge and a plea in her frozen smile.

The portrait caught the last rays of sunset, giving her friend's face an almost otherworldly glow, as if she were trying to reach through time itself to heal this breach.

"Well, old friend. I've done what I can. The rest is up to them now." She exhaled through pursed lips, her gaze fixed on Demi's. "Let's just pray it's enough."

# Chapter 11

## *Athena*

*"In every stitch, there is a story. In every craft, a piece of the soul."*
—*Eloisa Hobby*

After Calista returned to the chapel for her cane, Athena lingered on the church steps, standing at the edge of the Crafters' Corner welcome party, feeling as out of place as a cat at a dog show despite the warm glow of the twinkle lights strung overhead.

She tugged at the restrictive hem of her pencil skirt, feeling overdressed and underprepared. She could go back to the Lavender Lark and change. Her luggage should have arrived by now, but she couldn't summon the energy for even that minor task, especially when Demetra's friends continued to offer their heartfelt condolences.

Athena stapled a glossy smile to her face, the manufactured mask she perfected over years of press conferences and award ceremonies. But this was different. This gathering wasn't a crowd of golf enthusiasts, adoring fans, or eager reporters. These people knew her mother and loved her in a way Athena never had the chance to.

"Oh my stars, you're Athena Dempsey! I can't believe it!" A fortysomething woman rushed over to Athena. She beamed like a lighthouse, her hands glee-clenched into fists that she shook like maracas.

"Nice to meet you," Athena said. *Chill, relax your jaw, act human.*

"My daughter will not believe this! She's hoping for the LPGA, ya know. She's sixteen with an *eight* handicap, and you're her absolute idol. She's gonna hate that she didn't come on this trip, but she's at golf camp this summer. Could I get a selfie, please, please? And maybe a video shout-out to Tatiana?"

"Um, if you can make it quick. I'm waiting for my sister." Athena's facial muscles ached from forcing a smile.

Tatiana's mom's eyes widened. "Is this the sister who walked away from Chevron on the eighteenth green without sinking the putt?"

"That'd be the one." Her right eye twitched.

"What happened? Why would she do that?" The woman shook her chin like a bobblehead.

"Let's video that message to Tatiana, okay?"

The woman whipped out her phone and hit record. Athena made the short video, giving the young woman a rah-rah speech about perseverance and dedication to craft.

"Thank you so much. You are so nice. How kind!" The woman clutched her phone to her chest. "Well, I won't keep you. Hope to see you around!"

"Bye." Athena wriggled her fingers and wondered what was keeping Calista.

"Athena!" A cheerful voice cut through her worry like a machete through jungle foliage. "Come, come, you simply must join us!"

She turned to find Clare from the quilt shop approaching her, eyes twinkling brighter than the string lights overhead. Behind her trailed Dot, who had stepped out of the local apothecary, and Vivian, who had emerged from A New Chapter, the Crafters'

Corner bookstore, looking for all the world like a jolly gang of fairy godmothers.

"Great, all I need now is a pumpkin, some mice, and glass slippers, and we've got ourselves a Cinderella ball," Athena muttered under her breath.

Except she wasn't Cinderella. That role went to Calista. In this scenario, Athena was most likely a wicked stepsister. A fresh pang of guilt drove a spike through her heart. Yeah, well, the truth hurts.

"Hello, Clare, lovely party." *Amazingly banal, Dempsey.*

"Oh, it's just getting started! Wait until the conga line! It'll snake all around Crafters' Corner. Demetra loved conga lines, you understand."

No, she did not.

Clare linked her arm through Athena's as if they were old friends and not virtual strangers connected by the gossamer thread of a dead mother's memory. "This way. Everyone's dying to meet you!"

"Um, I'm waiting for Calista."

"She can catch up. We're just going across the quad." Clare steered her toward a group of eager-looking women. Dot flanked Athena's other side.

"We're so excited to have you and your sister here." Vivian hurried along after Dot's long-legged strides. She wore pink kitten heels. Her eyes peered at Athena from behind glittery cat-eye glasses. "How are you finding the island?"

*Oh, you know. Nothing like a family reunion slash memorial service on Willy Wonka's summer getaway to really lift the spirits.*

"It's . . . unique." Athena settled on diplomacy. "Very colorful."

"Oh, yes!" Clare made a cooing noise and put a hand to her ample cleavage. "Eloisa believes color is food for the soul. Speaking of food, have you tried the crab puffs?" She gestured to the lavish buffet. "They're divine!"

Before Athena could politely decline (or less politely flee), she found herself swept into a whirlwind of introductions. Every shopkeeper, craft enthusiast, and long-lost third cousin twice removed was eager to meet her, each armed with a story about Demetra.

*"Your mother's laugh was like music . . ."*

*"I'll never forget the time Demetra organized that beach cleanup . . ."*

*"She always said her girls were her greatest joy . . ."*

These people spoke of a Demetra she'd never known. The mother Athena remembered was a faded photograph, a meek mouse in drab clothes, a ghost that haunted the edges of her childhood memories.

Just as Athena considered faking a sudden and highly contagious case of island fever, she spotted Calista leaving the chapel.

Her sister looked . . . different, softer somehow, despite the clear fatigue in her posture and the way she favored her injured ankle, her face drawn, almost gaunt, her eyes haunted. She paused on the steps, looking lost in the crowd pulsing between them.

"Calista!" Clare waved Athena's sister over. "Come join us!"

A shadow passed over her sister's face, and for a moment Athena thought she might walk away. Instead, she smiled warmly and approached them.

Athena moved toward Calista, mouth open, ready to ask about her injury and say something, anything, to bridge the Grand Canyon gap. Still, before she got the words out, Vivian grabbed her arm and tugged her backward.

"Tell us more about your mother's influence and how she made you who you are today." Vivian batted eyelash extensions as long and thick as paintbrushes. She looked good in them.

How? By not putting up a fight and letting Benjamin take them away from her. That was how. Demetra's absence made Athena driven, trying her best to prove she was worth something.

"Demi was the most incredible person." Vivian let out a wistful sigh.

What could Athena say? That her most explicit memory of her mother was as a cowed and subservient woman? For years, she blamed Demetra for abandoning them and for choosing fear over her own daughters.

She searched for Calista, hoping for rescue, but her sister was deep in conversation with Artie and Orion. Then Calista laughed at something one of the teens said, the sound carrying across the quad, open and unguarded.

How had they drifted so far apart? Oh, right, Calista walked away from her just as Demetra had.

*Stop wallowing. Fix it.*

But could she? Would Calista allow it? Her sister gave Reid a second chance. Why not her?

Trapped in a conversational merry-go-round, Athena spun from one group to another as people sought her attention, always just missing Calista, who seemed caught in a loop too. A cosmic game of keep-away, with the universe dangling her sister just out of reach.

After what felt like hours of smiling so hard her cheeks hurt, Athena spotted her chance. Calista headed toward the buffet, her limp more pronounced as she braced against the cane. She needed to get ice on that ankle.

Zeroing her gaze on her sister, Athena broke free from her latest conversation, but just as she neared, Calista stumbled. One minute, her sister was upright. The next, she was falling, her arms pinwheeling, cane flying as she struggled to catch herself.

A chorus of concerned "Ohs!" rang out across the quad. Athena's heart jumped as she pushed through the gathered throng.

"Let me through," Athena said, injecting power into her voice and rushing forward. Still, Calista was already being helped to her feet by a couple of burly lumberjack-size men. Someone handed Calista her cane.

"I'm fine," Calista said, face flushed as she brushed off the hands reaching to steady her. "I need some space, please."

Wasn't that just like her younger sister? Pushing people away when all they wanted was to help. Calista turned and limped away, the crowd parting before her like the Red Sea.

And just like that, their moment vanished. The chance to connect, to explain, to ask what had been burning inside her for five long years.

*Why did you leave?*

Athena stood rooted to the spot, the jovial party swirling around her. The twinkling lights shone too bright, the laughter too loud. She felt exposed, raw, like a nerve ending left open to the air.

"Are you all right, dear?" Dot's concerned voice cut through Athena's foggy thoughts.

She blinked, realizing she had been staring after Calista's back for who knows how long. When was the last time she answered that question honestly instead of with *I'm fine*?

"I . . . I'm not sure."

Dot patted her arm. "Family can be complicated, especially when there's toxic behavior involved."

Athena whipped her head around and stared up at the tall woman. "What do you know?"

Dot's eyes looked black in the shadows. "Demetra told us everything."

Everything? That encompassed a lot of territory.

"Well . . ." Dot's straightforward voice seemed older than the island itself. "Sometimes the best way to move forward is to stop trying to fix the past."

"Huh?"

Dot reached into her apron pocket and pulled out a small round tin that she pressed into Athena's palm. "You look like you could use this."

Athena glanced down at the container. "What is it?"

"Lavender-orange ointment," Dot said. "I call it Self-Empowerment Salve."

Athena raised an eyebrow. "Self-empowerment? From lavender and oranges?"

"Oh my, yes! Sometimes we understand the next step we need to take, but we hold ourselves back out of fear or self-doubt, and that's where this little wonder comes in."

"I'm not sure I follow." Athena looked down at the cute label featuring a cartoon version of Dot's beaming face.

"It's simple, really. When you're feeling stuck or unsure, just rub a bit of this on your temples or your wrists. As you do, repeat the following, 'The only things I can control are my own thoughts and actions,' and watch what happens."

"Seriously?"

"Don't knock it till you've tried it." Dot winked. "By saying those words, you're reminding yourself that you have all the power you need. There's no reason to procrastinate any longer."

"I'm not sure mantras and salves will solve my problems."

"Maybe not, but they might just give you the push to solve them yourself. Remember, this is your one wild and precious life. If you want to succeed, take responsibility."

What? No one had ever criticized Athena's ability to achieve her goal; achievement was Athena's middle name (not literally, of course, but close enough), and the woman's words gave her pause. What did Dot see in her that others did not?

Athena glanced down at the tin and then back at Dot. "I . . . Thank you. I'll try it."

"Who knows? You might just surprise yourself with what you can accomplish when you believe."

With that, Dot patted Athena's arm once more and melted back into the crowd, leaving Athena alone with her thoughts and a tin of lavender-orange Self-Empowerment Salve.

She opened the tin, the soothing scent of lavender and citrus wafted out, and she dabbed a bit on her wrist. "The only things I can control are my thoughts and actions, not anyone else's."

Feeling like a giant dork, she capped the tin and stuck it in her purse.

"Athena?"

She turned to see Luna.

"There's a call for you. It's your father. He said it was urgent, so I had him call my satellite cell. He's on hold." She held the phone out to Athena.

Athena's stomach dropped like a broken elevator. She reached for the phone, fingers trembling. "Th-thank you, Luna."

Moving to the shadows of the chapel for a quieter place to take the call, she steeled herself and unmuted the phone. "Hello, Daddy."

"Where have you been?" His commanding voice jumped through the airwaves. No "hello," not "how are you?" Just straight to the interrogation. Classic Benjamin Dempsey.

"I'm sorry. I told you the island was remote—"

"Never mind the excuses; listen, catch the next flight home and bring Calista with you."

Athena's free hand clenched into a fist, nails digging into her palm. "But we just got here. We're here to honor—"

"Your mother is gone, Athena," Benjamin said, his tone cold enough to frost a cake. "What matters now is the living. Family reputation. Your career."

Athena's stomach churned. Of course. It always came back to the Dempsey brand, the family legacy. "I don't think—"

"Leave the thinking to me. It's never been your strong suit. Why do you think I still take care of your finances? You have no head for math. You never did. Now, you've got to do what's best for the family. For your future. You've always understood that."

Had she? Or had she just been too afraid to question it?

Athena's mind raced, a whirlwind of conflicting emotions. The little girl who craved her father's approval warred with the woman who came to this island seeking . . . what? Closure? Connection? A chance to rewrite the ending of a story that went so terribly off-script?

"I'll . . . I'll talk to Calista," Athena said, the words ash in her mouth. "But you've got to give me time."

"Tick tock. In case you've forgotten, your next tournament is this coming weekend in Scotland. You need to get home and rest up."

"Dad, I have to go." Defiance flared in her chest. "I will call you when I've made progress with Calista."

"Athena, listen up—"

"Goodbye, Daddy. Luna needs her phone back." Before Benjamin could get in another word, Athena ended the call, her heart pounding.

She stood panting as if she had just run a three-mile race, sprinting dead out, the phone heavy in her hand. Had she really just hung up on the great and powerful Benjamin Dempsey, the man who had micromanaged every aspect of her life since she was old enough to hold a putter?

"Athena?" Luna's voice pulled her from her jumbled thoughts. "Are you okay?"

She nodded, forcing a smile that felt as brittle as spun sugar. "I'm fine. Thank you for bringing me the phone."

Luna didn't look convinced, but she took the phone back with a gentle smile. "If you need anything, a listening ear, a cup of tea, or maybe just a quiet place to hide for a while, my door's always open. Well, not literally, but you know."

"Thank you. I appreciate your kindness."

"Anything for Demetra's daughters." Luna gave a wave and melted back into the crowd.

Athena took a deep breath, trying to center herself. The festive atmosphere felt at odds with the turmoil churning inside her. She glanced around, feeling exposed, as if everyone could see the truth about her.

She was nothing but her father's puppet.

# Chapter 12

## *Calista*

*"Secrets shared is a burden halved."*

—*Eloisa Hobby*

Calista perched on the chapel steps, her butt numb from the cool stone beneath her, foot propped on a planter, an ice pack Artie brought her resting on her sore ankle.

Boisterous partygoer laughter mingled with chirping crickets and singing frogs, creating a sweet island melody that should have soothed. Instead, the sound grated like the world's most annoying white noise machine, unable to mask her mental chatter.

She'd planned to head for the Lavender Lark instead of hanging around this shindig, but the thought of scaling Mount B&B with her bum ankle made her whimper. She did the next best thing, plopped down and tried to summon the willpower to move.

Closing her eyes, she leaned her head back and did deep breathing exercises. In through the nose, out through the mouth. *Don't think about the fact your long-lost sister is here. Or that your dead mom had a secret island life, or that—*

"Hello, Daddy." Athena's voice cut through the temperate night like a hot knife through Calista's feeble Zen. Her eyes snapped open as goose bumps carpeted her entire body.

*Daddy.*

Weird how that word still got to her, the way Athena used the term of endearment like it wasn't spring-loaded with years of manipulation and deceit.

Calista stopped calling Benjamin "Dad" ages ago, and as for "Daddy"? Please. She'd sooner call a cactus cuddly. She peered into the darkness, spotting Athena pacing beside an azalea bush a few feet away, clutching the phone to her ear like a lifeline.

Great. Now Calista was stuck in an accidental game of "Spy on Your Sister." Should she announce her presence? Crawl away on her hands and knees? Freeze like a statue and hope Attie didn't spot her?

Athena's voice drifted over again. "I'm sorry. I told you the island was remote. . . ."

There was a pause, and Calista could practically hear Benjamin's voice, sharp enough to draw blood. Her body tensed, muscle memory from years of bracing for impact.

Nope. Not doing this. Calista was a grown-ass woman, safe from Daddy Dearest's reach. Time for a strategic retreat.

She stood, and oops, yes, her ankle was garbage. She stumbled against the chapel wall, unwieldy as a newborn foal. Fantastic.

Using the Germaine the Giraffe cane, Calista shuffled down the steps and cursed whoever made ankles so flimsy, catching snippets of Athena's conversation. Benjamin must have a new manipulative scheme cooking with Athena, his unwilling sous chef.

"Goodbye, Daddy. Luna needs her phone back."

*Wait, what?*

Calista froze, peering through the shrubbery separating her from this alternate universe where Athena had grown a spine. She watched, slack-jawed. Her sister ended the call, her face set in stone, and she handed the phone back to an awaiting woman who Calista presumed was this Luna person.

Seriously? Had Athena just hung up on Benjamin Dempsey, manipulator extraordinaire and professional dream crusher? A tiny spark of something dangerously close to hope flickered in Calista's chest.

Maybe this island was magic, after all.

A distant pop drew her attention skyward. The first fireworks of the night exploded in a shower of gold, illuminating the world in white, fiery light.

For a moment, Calista could see everything—the weathered wood of the chapel door, the delicate flowers lining the path, the partygoers moving toward the beach en masse.

Athena turned, her gaze sweeping the area, and their eyes met. A brief hesitation. A flicker of something . . . surprise? guilt? . . . crossed Athena's face.

They stared at each other.

Calista's pulse pounded. Part of her wanted to flee, to avoid this confrontation, but she was tired of running, tired of hiding, and besides, the ankle wasn't up for a footrace. Time to face this head-on and let the chips fall.

"Mind if I join you?" Athena asked, tone neutral.

Calista shrugged. "Free country. Or free island, I guess."

"Golf cart ride?" Athena pointed to the golf carts parked in a row.

"Can we just take one?"

"I brought one from the Lavender Lark earlier."

"Oh."

"Did you ever get checked in?"

"No. I came straight from my bout with Big Bird to the clinic."

"You don't want to watch the fireworks?" Athena inclined her head toward the beach.

"I've seen fireworks for a lifetime," Calista said, and they both knew she wasn't talking about the rockets lighting up the sky above the ocean.

"Hang there. I'll get the cart and pick you up." Athena dashed across the quad, procured a cart, and zoomed up beside Calista. "Do you need help to get in?"

"I can manage." Taking care of where she placed her foot, she climbed aboard. Calista sneaked glances at her sister's profile as they headed toward the B&B, trying to read her expression in the intermittent flashes of light.

Athena looked . . . different.

Older, yes, but there was something else. A weariness Calista had never noticed before. Had it always been there, hidden behind the perfect facade their father demanded from her, or was this new?

Another firework exploded, bathing them in red light. Athena turned to Calista, her face cast in shadows again.

"Why did you walk away on the eighteenth green five years ago?"

*Wow, okay. No more pussyfooting around.* The question hung in the air like a solid thing.

Memories of that day flooded back—the suffocating pressure, the weight of expectations, the moment it became too much to bear.

Calista smelled again the freshly cut grass, felt the sun beating down on her neck, and heard the murmur of the crowd. The sensations were so vivid she half expected to look down and see grass stains on her knees, remnants of her old life spent chasing perfection.

The past had a way of sneaking up on her, wrapping around

her legs like clinging vines, threatening to pull her under. She exhaled, willing the stiffness from her lungs. "I . . ."

"Yes?"

She couldn't force out more words, old instincts kicking in. How many times had Athena turned tattletale, running to their father with Calista's secrets and her vulnerabilities? And yet, Athena had been a kid too.

In fresh light from another round of rockets, she saw something in Athena's eyes that gave her pause. Was that honest concern? Or just another trap?

Did she dare risk it?

Athena guided the golf cart up the long driveway to the Lavender Lark. The grounds lay quiet and empty, but the welcoming porch light was on. Calista assumed most of the guests were at the fireworks show.

Her sister parked, shutting off the cart, and turned to look at her. "You don't have to tell me why you walked away, but you *were* winning. I've wondered for five years why you pulled the plug and handed me the glory. It made no sense."

"Not glory to me. Poison."

Athena blinked. "What do you mean?"

Calista cleared her throat, trying to locate the words locked away. "There's . . ." She paused and moistened her lips. "Something you don't know."

"I figured."

The cool breeze against her skin raised goose bumps, and Calista hugged herself for warmth and comfort the way she had as a kid hiding in the laundry hamper from their father's tirades. The half-moon hung high in the sky above the lavender Victorian.

"Never mind. I can see this is hard for you. In the end, it doesn't really matter. You left, and now I'm the Queen of the LPGA." Her sister's laugh was rough, humorless.

"You got what you wanted, and I'm happy for you," Calista said and meant it.

"It's what *he* wanted." Bitterness crept into Athena's voice.

"Oh no, it isn't." She shook her head.

Athena's mouth dropped open. "W-what?"

Calista fisted her hands against her knees, really too weary for this conversation this late at night after a long day of trouble, but she was leaving on Monday, and they wouldn't have much time together. Might as well dive into the deep end.

"All right. Here goes. I'm placing my trust in you, Attie. Please don't betray me."

Hurt flashed across her sister's face. "I know I haven't been a safe person in the past, but I want to change that if you'll allow it."

The admission hung between them. Calista nodded, acknowledging the olive branch. "I don't blame you. We both did what we had to do to survive him."

Silence.

Had she overstepped already?

Athena met Calista's gaze, and a world of understanding passed between them. Both shaped by Benjamin's expectations, molded and bent until they hardly recognized themselves.

Another firework streaked across the stars, this one a vibrant blue that lingered in the air. Calista steeled herself. This was it. The moment she'd both dreaded and longed for, the secret she'd carried for five long years pressing against her like a physical weight. How nice to set her burden down, but how weird it would feel to no longer carry it.

"Before gameplay started on Sunday, the last day of the tournament, Reid came to see me in the clubhouse."

"Thornton?"

"Uh-huh. Reid found out something about our father, and he wanted to let me know."

"What was that something?" Athena asked, dread in her eyes.

"Benjamin had placed a wager with a bookie. A *huge* bet."

"How huge?" Athena's voice lowered.

"One million dollars."

"Wh-what . . . kind of wager?"

"He bet against *you*, Athena. A million bucks that his golden girl would fail."

All the color drained from Athena's face. "Da-Da-Daddy bet on you to win the tournament?"

"Yeppers."

"*Why?*" The word came out plaintive, keening.

Empathy for her sister pushed through Calista.

"No," Athena said. "Reid was wrong. Daddy would never bet against me."

"That's what I told myself. Benjamin *never* sided with me. Why would he wager so much money on me beating *you*?"

Athena slumped forward, bonking her forehead against the steering wheel. "Because you're the better golfer. Because he knew you would win."

"But he was wrong. I didn't have the killer instinct. I couldn't beat you. Not when I knew he'd make a mint off me if I did."

Athena lifted her head. "I didn't want to win like that, Lissy. I wanted to beat you fair and square."

"I know. You care about golf. I just don't, and that's what made Benjamin so mad."

"You have more natural talent than I do."

Calista shook her head and bit down on her bottom lip. "Don't sell yourself short. You've stayed at the top of the leaderboard for five years. We both know how rare that is."

"If Reid told you this before gameplay, why didn't you drop out then? Why play eighteen holes before you walked away?"

"I'm not proud of myself, but I wanted to keep Benjamin on

tenterhooks. I wanted him to think he would make bank off me. I wanted an epic fireworks show, petty as it sounds."

"Lissy, I get it. I truly do, but why did you leave completely? Why didn't you stick around to watch him dissolve into a puddle of rage? Which was a spectacular meltdown, by the way. He never even congratulated me on winning. He was too busy ranting about you."

"I can just imagine. I'm sorry you had to sit through my blowback." Calista paused. "I hadn't planned to walk away. I'd actually planned to keep hitting horrible putts so you would easily beat me, but then . . ."

"But then?" Athena echoed, hanging on her every word.

"I looked out at the crowd, and that's when I saw *her.*"

"Her who?"

"Mom."

"What?" Athena looked at her as if she were speaking a foreign language. "You saw Mom?"

"Demetra was watching us play, and I just dropped my club and went toward her."

"Why didn't you tell me?" Athena touched her cheek as if Calista had reached out and slapped her.

She looked away, unable to bear the accusation in Athena's eyes. "I made my choice to leave everything behind, and that included you. I'm sorry to say it, but you were too enmeshed with him. The messages you left on my voicemail. The texts. Begging me to come back and making excuses for our father. You wouldn't have understood where I was coming from, and I knew that. Plus, I wanted to spare you the pain of knowing he bet against you."

"What about Mom? What happened to her? I'm so very jealous you got to see her."

"But I didn't." Calista heard the abject sadness in Athena's voice. "That's what jettisoned me away from the LPGA. I went looking for her. I spent months trying to find her and nothing. She had no social media presence and no family. Finally, I convinced myself that I'd seen a mirage. A ghostly Mamá sending me the message to strike out on my own."

"I wish you'd told me. We could have searched for Demetra together."

Calista met her sister's gaze. "I thought about it, but I knew you would have told *him*. I couldn't risk it."

Shamefaced, Athena lowered her gaze, a misting of tears in her eyes. "I admire your strength. I could never walk away from golf. It's my identity."

Calista quirked a smile. "Remember Mamá's favorite quote?"

"Never say never." Athena let out a sad half laugh.

"You were on the phone with Benjamin back in Crafters' Corner," Calista said.

"How did you know?"

"Who else would insist on contacting you while you were mourning your mother?"

"Touché."

"Do you remember the time Dad made me practice putting for six hours straight because I'd missed an easy shot in a junior tournament?" Calista asked.

Athena made a noise of despair. "You were what, twelve? Your poor blistered hands!"

"Thirteen, and yeah, they were, but you know what I remember most about that day? You sneaking me Band-Aids and Gatorade when Dad wasn't looking."

A wan smile touched Athena's lips. "I'd forgotten that part. I felt so bad for you."

"I didn't," Calista said. "It was one of the few times I felt like . . . like we were on the same team, you know?"

"We should have been on the same team all along. I'm sorry I didn't protect you."

Calista shook her head. "You were just a kid, too, Attie. We were both just trying to survive. I didn't blame you."

"He wants me to come home right away and bring you with me," Athena blurted.

Calista held her gaze. "That's not happening."

"I know."

"I'm sorry you're still under his control, but I get it. Leaving was the hardest thing I've ever done. There were so many lonely days and nights, and I wasn't always sure I'd get through it."

"But you did, and you're thriving!" Athena dabbed at the tear rolling down her cheek. "I am so proud of you."

Her sister's kind words touched Calista's heart. "Thank you for saying that."

Athena reached across the seat of the golf cart and touched her hand. "I love you."

"I love you too." This time Calista was the one who choked up. They sat there looking at each other, united in their pain. "He's never going to change, you know. His patterns are too ingrained."

"I know." A soft whimper escaped Athena.

"As long as you're within his sphere of influence, you won't be able to change either."

Athena's jaw clenched. "I know that too."

"So, are you leaving tomorrow at his behest?"

"I told him Monday."

"He's probably already sent Cantu to pick you up."

"I hope not." Athena groaned. "What about you? Are you still leaving on Monday?"

"I was . . . but you know what? If you're willing to stay and help me work on uncovering and healing our past, then so am I."

"I . . . I . . ."

Calista studied her sister, really looked at her, in a new light. She saw the worry lines around Athena's eyes, the tension in her shoulders, the hope and fear warring in her expression. She saw not the perfect golden child their father had always portrayed but a woman as scared and scarred as Calista herself.

"You're too afraid to go against him." Calista tried not to let disappointment creep into her voice, but she feared she failed.

"It's all I know."

"Sister, there's a whole wide world out there of kind, loving, generous people you know nothing about. I know it's hard to imagine from where you're sitting, but it's true."

The expression on Athena's face said she wished more than anything to believe that. "You have a good life in Denver?"

"Oh yes, and so many wonderful friends."

"We didn't have friends growing up. He ruined every friendship we tried to make."

Reid crossed Calista's mind, and she nodded. "Yes, he did."

The fireworks reached their finale. The sky erupted in a kaleidoscope of colors. But the real fireworks were happening right here in this golf cart parked outside the Lavender Lark. Years of hurt and misunderstanding were finally being addressed, and while it wasn't comfortable, it felt . . . necessary, like lancing a wound to let the poison out.

"I'll help you any way I can," Calista said. "But I understand if you're not ready."

There was a long pause, and then Athena whispered in the tiniest voice, "I think I'm ready."

Calista held out her pinkie finger. "We stay for the golf tournament on the Fourth of July?"

Athena hooked her pinkie around Calista's and echoed, "Pinkie swear."

"Already, you're officially committed to this. I'll call my boss in the morning and tell him I'm staying until after the Fourth of July to wrap up Mamá's affairs."

"Do it," Athena said.

And for once in their life, they were united against Benjamin Dempsey.

# Chapter 13

## *Athena*

*"Forgiveness is a journey, not a destination."*

—*Eloisa Hobby*

After what seemed like the longest day in the history of days, Athena fell asleep in a bed so comfy she didn't stir once during the night and dreamed happy dreams of sandcastles and baby turtles and long walks on the beach.

But the second she awoke that Saturday morning, her agitated mind was back at it, fretting and restless.

The vow Athena made to her sister the previous evening prowled like a caged cougar. Before the mirror in the seahorse-palooza bathroom, Athena stared at her reflection as she ironed her hair flat and considered her options.

Yes, she wanted to spend the summer on Hobby Island, reconnecting with Calista and memorializing their mother. Yes, she desired a much-needed break from the LPGA. She hadn't had a proper vacation since . . . well, she never had a vacation once she became a professional golfer. Not once did she miss a scheduled tournament, not even when sick. She powered through.

Always.

But now, two daunting tasks stretched before her like a long par five—canceling her appearances and breaking the news to her father that she was leaving the tour.

Her hand trembled and not from the weight of her iron as she pulled a strand of hair through the heated ceramic plate. How would Daddy react? Her stomach roiling, hot bile rose in her throat as she imagined his fury.

She spent her life catering to his wishes and polishing her golden child image. What would happen when she defied him? Would he berate and shame her the way he did with Calista?

A cold shaft of fear shot through her body.

Calista put up with Benjamin's anger and ridicule for twenty-four years. Okay, Athena could take his inevitable harangue if it meant having one extraordinary summer with her sister.

Also, what would this time off do to her career?

Athena stared at herself in the mirror. Tendrils of steam drifted up from her damp hair. "You can do it."

Yes, and she would call her father . . . Athena glanced at her smartwatch that tracked her life down to the last detail . . . well, he was on the golf course right now. She couldn't interrupt his game. Later. In the evening after he'd had dinner and a few mood-mellowing nightcaps.

*Don't put it off. Do it now.*

In her mind's eye, she saw him on the green, pulling the phone from his pocket, glowering at the inconvenience.

No, no, tonight was better.

*Coward.*

Okay, she'd do it now, Daddy's temper be damned. She was Athena Dempsey. She faced down the world's best golfers on the most challenging courses. She could handle one phone call to her father without shanking it into the metaphorical rough, right?

Then she remembered the fit he'd thrown when Calista left.

He'd been apoplectic. At the time, it hurt that he hadn't acknowledged Athena's winning Chevron, the pinnacle of her career. Now she understood his rage stemmed from a million-dollar gambling loss and not from losing Calista as she believed.

*Put down the flat iron and call him right this minute.*

Yes. Before Athena's nerve faltered, she switched off her flat iron, perched it on the edge of the bathroom sink to cool, and picked up her cell phone.

No bars. No service. Right. Landline.

She padded into the bedroom, picked up the whimsical conch shell phone cordless receiver, and dialed her father's number. As it rang, Athena cringed, then braced herself and rehearsed what she would say. *Hi, Daddy, I'm taking a break.*

No, no, she needed to ease into the bad news. Ask her father how he was. If his back was acting up again. Praise him for his patience—

*Click.*

"You have reached the mailbox of Benjamin Dempsey . . ."

*Oh, thank God.* Athena slumped against the wall, relief washing over her like a cool breeze on a sweltering day. Relief sweat pearled on her upper lip.

The voicemail beeped. *Leave a message.* She primed her tongue to drop the bomb on her father, but a sudden knock at the door startled her, and she hung up the phone without saying a word.

"Coming!" she called out, sounding far cheerier than she felt.

Luna stood in the hallway, her smile as bright as a polished trophy. "Good morning! I didn't wake you, did I?"

"No, no. I get up before dawn every morning to work out." Her ingrained athlete's discipline.

"Eloisa asked me to give you today's itinerary." Luna handed her a printout.

Athena frowned down at the paper. "I have an itinerary?" The concept of a schedule she hadn't crafted herself was as foreign as using a pool noodle to putt.

"No, no. You're free to spend your day however you see fit." Luna's smile offered high-beam sunshine. "Eloisa thought you might like to be aware of the day's activities."

"Um, thanks . . ." Athena scanned the offerings.

First on the list, after breakfast, a ceremony near the Prism Pavilion—whatever that was—for the groundbreaking on the remembrance garden honoring Demetra. Someone had hand drawn a star next to the entry in red Sharpie.

Was she expected to go?

Luna reached out and touched Athena's wrist with featherlight fingertips. "Just remember, no matter how tough things feel right now, they won't stay that way forever. Be in the moment. That's the solution."

Huh? Athena frowned.

But then the innkeeper was gone, leaving behind her cinnamon-scented fragrance and a deepening air of mystery.

Five minutes later, Athena entered the Lavender Lark's dining room and spotted her sister sitting by the window, but Calista wasn't alone.

A man in his early forties sat across from her, his tanned fore-arms resting on the table as he leaned in, smiling. Did everyone on this island smile like they drank from the Elixir of Immortality? Honestly, kind of creepy.

Calista glanced up and caught Athena's eye. Grinning, she waved her over, looking a little too smiley herself. Was there something in the water? Naturally occurring lithium, perhaps?

"Athena! Come meet Paul."

Paul stood up and offered his hand. "I'm Luna's husband and Eloisa's nephew by marriage."

"Nice to meet you." Athena shook his calloused hand.

His eyes flicked to Athena's hair, a hint of amusement crossing his face. Feeling self-conscious, she patted her head and realized one side of her hair lay ironed straight, the other side was still wavy. Oh, good grief. What was wrong with her? In her anxiety over her father, she neglected to finish her hairstyle.

Calista pulled out a chair. "Have a seat. Paul designed a blueprint for the remembrance garden based on a quilt Mamá made called the Labyrinth. It's gorgeous. Take a look."

Athena sat next to her sister.

Paul pulled a rolled blueprint from his back pocket and passed it to Athena. "Demetra won a quilting competition with the Labyrinth."

Calista gave a soft, melancholy sigh and propped her chin in her upturned palm.

Athena studied the design, her throat constricting like she swallowed a golf ball. The central motif presented a complex labyrinth, its paths winding and intersecting in a mesmerizing pattern that dizzied her head. Around the edges, stylized waves crashed against rocky shores, their foamy crests rendered in such delicate detail. In each corner, a different season unfurled like a time-lapse nature documentary.

Spring flowers bloomed in one quarter, summer sun blazed in another, autumn leaves drifted in the third, and winter snow blanketed the fourth. These seasonal vignettes flowed into the labyrinth, as if time itself lived in the maze, trapped in an endless loop of renewal and decay. The overall effect was both beautiful and unsettling, like stumbling upon perfectly preserved ruins in the middle of a desert. It was an invitation to lose oneself in contemplation, and the longer Athena looked at it, the more details emerged.

She could almost feel her mother's sorrow rising from the

fabric, wrapping around her own heart like a cold, damp fog. The sense of loss, the struggle to find a path forward, and perhaps hope in the beauty of the surrounding island. It was all there, stitched into every seam.

"It's . . . intricate." She handed the blueprint back to Paul, fighting off sorrow. "Translating this into a garden will be challenging."

"We might have to deconstruct a bit, yes, but we're shooting to catch the spirit of the quilt more than a replica. You're coming to the groundbreaking with Calista?" There was no expectation in his voice or his eyes, so why did she feel she would disappoint him if she said no?

"Eloisa said we're the guests of honor," Calista added.

"Indeed you are," Paul said. "We've got a little groundbreaking ceremony planned and were hoping you could dig a shovelful of dirt to get us started, but no pressure. You don't have to do anything that makes you uncomfortable."

Athena gulped. The idea of participating in a ceremony, digging into soil that represented her mother's pain and absence, made her want to bolt, but Calista looked at her with such hope, and Paul's kind eyes held no judgment.

"I . . ." She cleared her throat. "I'm not sure I'm ready for that."

Calista's face fell, but she hid it with a fast smile. "That's okay, Athena. I can represent us both."

She thought of the intricate paths of the labyrinth. Wasn't that exactly how she felt right now? Lost in a maze of emotions, trying to find her way out? Athena's fingers curled into fists beneath the table. She wanted to say no, to retreat to her room and hide from the memories and the guilt. Trapped between her desire to mend things with her sister and her need to avoid pain, Athena nodded, never mind the mental quicksand sucking her down.

"All right," she said. "I'll go."

* * *

Twenty minutes later, they arrived at the site of the planned remembrance garden in a golf cart with Athena behind the wheel.

Calista wore high-topped sneakers for support and brought along the giraffe cane. It was all Athena could do not to rush to her sister's side and help her from the golf cart. "The swelling is much better, Attie, I promise, and I took an anti-inflammatory, so it hardly hurts."

"Okay, if you're sure." Athena worried her bottom lip with her teeth.

Reid broke from the crowd and rushed over to offer Calista his arm. To Athena's surprise, Calista took it. His smile was as lively as the tropical shirt he wore, which featured a pattern of dancing flamingos.

Athena raised an eyebrow. Hmm, was something cooking beneath the surface between these two? Interesting.

Reid guided Calista toward the gathering. A twinge of something—protectiveness? jealousy?—tugged at Athena's heart. She pushed the feeling aside and followed them, her shoes sinking into the lush grass.

The breeze off the Gulf of Mexico did little to cool her flushed skin or settle the butterflies in her stomach. She tugged at the collar of her polo shirt, wishing she'd worn something more island-appropriate than professional golf attire. Beside her, Calista looked effortless and cool in a breezy light-blue sundress, her curls pulled up into a messy bun atop her head.

Their eyes met.

"You ready for this?" Calista asked.

Athena nodded, not trusting her voice.

Ready? Ha. Nothing had prepared her for this island dreamscape, but here she was, about to take part in a garden groundbreaking for a mother she scarcely remembered, surrounded by people who seemed to know Demetra better than her own daughters ever had.

Life had a twisted sense of humor sometimes.

Reid and Calista moved ahead, and Athena took a moment to look around. The bare plot of earth, soon to be transformed into a garden, stood in stark contrast to meticulously groomed golf courses.

"Athena, Calista," Paul greeted them, somehow making their names sound like Greek poetry. "Are you ready to see your mother's vision come to life?"

"We can't wait." Calista rubbed her palms together, full of glee Athena couldn't quite muster.

Paul led them to a table where the quilt lay spread out, its intricate pattern a maze of colors and shapes.

Athena blinked, trying to make sense of the design. In person, it was even more compelling than the blueprint. The quilt looked as if someone had taken a map, a kaleidoscope, and a geometry textbook, thrown them in a blender, and somehow created this beautiful quilt. She knew nothing about sewing, but she could tell a quilting master had created this.

Eloisa paraded over. Today she wore a straw Panama hat with a single red rose tucked into the band and a wide-legged turquoise pantsuit. "Your mother called the quilt Life's Labyrinth. We had such fun working on it with her during our quilting bees."

Behind Eloisa, Dot, Clare, and Vivian nodded in unison.

Athena's hand hovered above the quilt. She could almost feel the hours of work, the love poured into every stitch. Had her mother thought of her daughters as she sewed? Had she imagined them standing here one day, marveling at her creation?

She swallowed hard, pushing down emotions threatening to overflow. Now wasn't the time for a breakdown. She had one goal. Get through this ceremony without making a fool of herself or disappointing Calista.

Simple, right?

Why did it feel so impossible?

Paul talked about the garden layout, his animated hands gesturing as he pointed out different sections of the blueprint.

Athena tried to focus, she really did, but her mind kept wandering to her mother and what Demetra's life had been like on this island paradise while Benjamin raised her daughters. She caught phrases like "Zen rock garden" and "yoga gazebo," but they floated past her like soap bubbles.

"And here in the cool shade"—Paul's voice cut through Athena's mental fog—"we're including String of Tears plants."

"No," Calista said, her voice sharp enough to cut glass. "Not those."

Everyone in the gathering turned to stare at Calista. Paul leaned in, quiet curiosity in his blue eyes.

Athena blinked, surprised by her sister's vehemence. "What? Why not? Mom *loved* String of Tears plants."

Calista turned to her, disbelief etched on her face. For a moment, Athena felt like she was looking in a fun-house mirror, seeing a distorted version of herself reflected in her sister's eyes.

"Are you serious right now?"

Athena frowned, confused. "What do you mean? Remember when Dad let Mom pick one out at that nursery near our house? She was so happy."

The memory floated to the surface of Athena's mind, soft-focused and golden-hued, like an old photograph. Benjamin's indulgent smile as Demetra cooed over the sweet teardrop-shaped leaves. The rare sound of their mother's laughter. A typical, happy family for once.

But Calista was looking at her as if she'd just announced she was quitting golf to become a professional yodeler. "You honestly don't remember, do you?"

Then Calista turned and walked away, leaving Athena standing alone, feeling like she missed a crucial step and tumbled down the rabbit hole into some bizarre alternate reality.

"Calista, wait!"

Athena hurried after her sister, but she stumbled on the uneven terrain, catching herself before she face-planted in front of the entire community. *Smooth, Dempsey, real smooth.* She caught up to Calista at the edge of the proposed garden site.

"What did I say wrong?"

Calista had her arms folded over her chest, hugging herself as she had as a child self-soothing.

"Lissy?"

Calista turned, her eyes flashing with emotion. Was it anger? Disappointment? "Just leave it, Athena. You don't understand."

"What?" Athena raised both arms, confused.

Paul approached with two Sharpshooter spades in his hands and an Eagle Scout smile gracing his face. "Ready to break ground?"

*No, right now, she was trying to connect with her sister. Be gone, Handsome Garden Man.*

Calista grabbed one of the spades and marched back to where the crowd waited.

Paul gave Athena an empathic smile and passed her the other tool and Athena followed her sister.

Side by side, the Dempsey women faced the crowd. A red satin sash proclaiming "The Demetra Sarris Remembrance Garden" stretched across the two stone pillars positioned at the entrance of where the garden would be.

Paul guided them to their positions behind the pillars as people fixed them in the viewfinders of their cell phones. Eloisa appeared with a pair of giant scissors. She gave a heartfelt speech about Demetra to the crowd and then moved to cut the ribbon.

"Now," Eloisa announced as the ribbon fell away, and she turned to Athena and Calista. "Your turn."

"On the count of three, dig earth," Paul said, perky as a sports coach. "One . . . two . . . three!"

In unison, Athena and Calista plunged their spades into the ground. The initial resistance of the soil, the give as it yielded to their force—it seemed significant somehow, as if they were breaking more than just ground.

As her shovel hit the dirt, something inside Athena's brain shifted.

The world tilted on its axis, colors bleeding away until she was somewhere else entirely.

She was small again, peering around a doorframe into the living room of their childhood home. The String of Tears plant sat on a side table, its delicate leaves cascading down like a leafy waterfall. Delicate and tender.

Just like their mother.

Demetra sat on the couch, her shoulders shaking with silent sobs. Benjamin loomed over her, his face a mask of contempt. He reached out and plucked a leaf from the plant with deliberate slowness.

"Every tear," he said, his voice low and menacing, "costs you. Remember that."

And then he ate the leaf, chewing exaggeratedly and making smacking noises like it was the most delicious thing he ever ate.

The scene shifted, blurred, and re-formed. In different instances, again and again, Athena watched as her father used the plant as a weapon, stripping away leaves for every show of emotion, every perceived weakness her mother presented. The plant growing barer with each passing day.

Athena saw herself, small hands covered in dirt, digging a hole in the backyard, the plant now nothing more than naked stems. Demetra crouched beside her, silent tears falling as they buried the remnants of the once beautiful plant.

How had she forgotten this? How had she twisted this memory into something benign, even pleasant?

The spade slipped from Athena's grasp and clattered to the ground. She staggered backward, her legs suddenly unable to support her weight. The world spun, faces blurring around her.

"Athena?" Calista's voice cut through the fog, sharp with worry. "What's wrong?"

Athena opened her mouth, but no sound came out. How to explain? How could she put into words the horror of what she remembered and the guilt for having forgotten in the first place?

She looked at Calista, really looked at her, and saw not the sister she'd lost touch with but the little girl who endured so much abuse. The sister who'd seen the truth, while Athena buried her head in the sand.

"I remember," Athena said, her voice a ragged whisper. "The plant. Dad, he . . . oh god, Calista. How could I have forgotten?"

Understanding dawned in Calista's eyes, followed by relief and then sorrow. "You finally see it."

It wasn't a question, but Athena nodded anyway. "I'm so sorry." Tears spilled down her cheeks. "I didn't want to believe it . . ."

She trailed off, unable to finish. How could she explain that she rewrote their history, painted over the dark parts with a veneer of normalcy? That she'd chosen the comfort of denial over the harsh truth because she was his golden child and enjoyed the perks?

Calista's face softened, the angry hurt from earlier melting away. She stepped forward, closing the gap between them. For a moment, Athena thought her sister might hug her, but Calista stopped just short, uncertainty written in the lines of her body.

"It's a lot to take in," Calista said. "Believe me, I know."

Athena nodded, swiping at her tears with her fingers. Someone reached out a hand with a wad of tissues. Blinking, she thanked whomever it was, her vision too blurry to see, and pressed the tissues against her eyes.

Her body tensed, aware of the surrounding people, of the concerned murmurs and curious stares. This fear wasn't how a professional acted. This breakdown wasn't how Athena Dempsey, golf prodigy and media darling, behaved in public.

But maybe it was okay not to be brave right now. Maybe, on this weird, fantastical island, she could just be Athena—messy, confused, and finally facing the truth.

"I don't know what to do," Athena said, the words foreign on her tongue. When was the last time she allowed herself to be this vulnerable?

Calista's lips quirked in a small, sad smile. "Join the club, sis. I've been feeling that way my whole life."

A laugh bubbled up in Athena, surprising her. It wasn't funny, but something about Calista's dry delivery, about the absurdity of their situation, struck a chord. Before she knew it, she was giggling, the sound high and slightly hysterical.

Calista's eyebrows shot up, but then she laughed too. They stood there in the middle of what was supposed to be a solemn ceremony, laughing like loons. It wasn't elegant or dignified, but it felt authentic in a way nothing had in years.

# Chapter 14

## *Calista*

*"When the past comes knocking, answer with grace, but never forget to lock the door behind it."*

—*Eloisa Hobby*

Their crazed laughter faded, leaving behind a charged silence. Calista studied Athena, noting her red-rimmed eyes and the quiver in her usually steady hands. The crowd's expectant gazes prickled Calista's skin and reminded her of the public setting.

"Excuse me," Athena mumbled and headed toward the outdoor restrooms. Calista had a feeling her sister's exit was just an excuse for breathing room.

Calista scanned the crowd, gauging the audience, and spied Reid, leaning against a palm tree, a wicker picnic basket resting on the ground beside him. He had one foot planted flat against the trunk with his knee bent up. His eyes met hers, beckoning her.

Calista sucked in a hot breath. She pressed her lips into a grim line and shook her head despite the rush of excitement scurrying down her spine.

In one smooth move, he pushed off from the tree, bent down, scooped up the picnic basket, and headed toward her.

Calista's stomach somersaulted.

Reid's confident stride belied the way he clutched the picnic basket like a shield. He flashed a grin that was two parts charm, one part nerves. "I convinced Eloisa to let me borrow one of her sailboats for the day. Wanna come?"

Calista hesitated, glancing in the direction Athena had disappeared. Should she go after her sister or leave her to sort herself out? "My ankle's better, but it's still wobbly."

"I'll handle everything. You just sit back, relax, and enjoy."

"Not sure going off with you is such a great idea."

His grin softened into something more genuine. "Come on, Cal. Where's your sense of adventure? Besides, I promise to be on my best behavior. Scout's honor."

"You were never a Boy Scout."

"No, but I did learn how to tie a mean bowline knot in sailing class. Could come in handy if you decide to throw me overboard."

"Hmm . . ." She canted her head, sizing him up. "That last part sounds tempting."

"Sailing is where all the cool kids air out their emotional baggage. Up for a little maritime therapy session?"

Calista arched an eyebrow. "Maritime therapy? Is that what we're calling it these days?"

"Well, I considered 'Picnic of Past Mistakes' but thought that might be a bit too on the proboscis." Reid held up the picnic basket and looked at her as if she were something special, and dang it, she fell for his charm.

"Oh, like maritime therapy is subtle?" Okay, she liked him. Probably not wise, but he was extra handsome when he groveled.

Reid laughed and shrugged, a casual gesture that didn't quite hide the tension in his shoulders. "Subtlety's overrated. Besides, I've got sandwiches and approximately thirteen years to atone for. Wouldn't want to undersell it."

Calista's thoughts pinballed between *absolutely not* to *well, maybe*. On the one hand, alone time with Reid promised all the comfort of a cactus massage. On the other, the promise of getting answers to long-ago questions dangled—tempting, probably ill-advised, but oh-so-alluring.

"Please," he coaxed.

"All right, fine. One sailing trip. But if you get squirrelly, I *will* throw you overboard."

Reid's face lit up. "Deal!"

Calista found Eloisa and asked her to tell Athena where they went, and they took off in Reid's golf cart. But on the drive to the docks, she couldn't help wondering if she was making a mistake. They'd be all alone in the ocean. She didn't fear him, far from it. Rather, she didn't trust herself. Too many old, unresolved feelings reared their heads.

She glanced over to find Reid studying her intently, his hair tousled by the sea breeze, looking for all the world like he just stepped out of a J.Crew catalog. "I never knew you could sail."

"I've been taking lessons. Turns out, you *can* teach an aged dog new tricks."

"You're hardly old. We're practically the same age."

"Why, Calista Grace Dempsey, was that a compliment?" Mischief twinkled in his eyes.

"An observation, and don't full-name me. You lost that right a long time ago."

The playfulness in his eyes vanished, replaced by something more earnest. "I know, and I'm sorry about that."

He guided her toward the small catamaran bobbing at the dock and helped her into the boat with a light hand, his touch sending a bittersweet jolt up her arm. She tried to ignore it, focusing instead on settling herself onto the seat.

"So, Captain Thornton, where are you taking us on this grand adventure?" she asked, keeping it light.

"Paul mentioned something about Mermaid Cove. He said few tourists know about it and it's a great picnic spot."

Mermaid Cove. The place where, as children, she and Athena built sandcastles and chased baby sea turtles under their mother's watchful eye.

"Cal?" Reid's voice was soft, concerned. "Is something wrong?"

"Mamá took us there when we were little. Or at least that's what Athena says. I only remember the turtles, not the location."

"We don't have to go there if you don't want to."

She shook her head, blinking back the memories. "No, it's fine. I'd like to see it again."

With expert skill, Reid maneuvered the boat away from the dock, adjusting the sails with practiced ease. Thick, puffy clouds floated above them.

"I should warn you," she said, "I don't know the first thing about sailing. I'll be pretty useless if you need help."

"No worries. I got you."

*I got you.*

Yeah, she'd heard that from him before and it hadn't been true. The boat rocked gently on the waves, and seeking to hide her feelings in case they showed on her face, Calista stretched out, closed her eyes, and savored the feel of the wind flowing over her skin.

Several long minutes passed with nothing but the clang of sailing gear and the cries of seagulls.

"Cal?"

She opened her eyes to find Reid watching her with a curious expression. His soulful eyes were tinged with regret.

"Yes?"

"Thank you for agreeing to spend time with me."

His words stirred weird feelings inside her. Feelings she liked too much. "Hey, I just wanted to catch some rays, and you were the one with a boat."

He chuckled and lapsed into fresh silence. Calista's eyes drifted closed again, and she almost dozed off.

"Mermaid Cove up ahead," Reid murmured a few minutes later.

Blinking, she sat up and watched their destination come into view. The secluded beach boasted pristine white sand and crystal-clear turquoise water.

"It's magical." An unexpected tear slipped down her cheek.

"Beautiful," he said, looking at her and not the cove.

She wiped away the tear and met his steady gaze. He once meant so very much to her, back when they were young, before he cavalierly broke her heart.

"Nice place for our picnic," he said.

"It's perfect."

He dropped anchor in the calm cove waters, scooped up the picnic basket, got out, and offered his arm to help her from the catamaran.

A sweet warmth bloomed in her chest as she took his arm and stepped off onto the soft sand. She helped him spread out a blanket on the shore, and Reid unpacked the picnic basket. "You know, I used to dream about this place without even realizing it was Hobby Island I was dreaming of," she murmured.

Reid looked up, surprise flickering across his face. "Yeah?"

Calista nodded. "After Chevron . . . I'd close my eyes and see this view. It was like some part of me remembered the time my mother brought us here, even though I didn't consciously recall we'd ever visited."

"That's interesting. Something about this place called to your soul."

She eyed him. "You're much more poetic than you used to be."

"Older and hopefully wiser." He chuckled.

Calista leaned back on her elbows and lifted her face to the sky. The clouds clumped thicker, the breeze cooler. "Tell me about your life. I know you're a globe-trotting sports vlogger, but that's it. What else have you been up to?"

"Not much," he said. "Running a YouTube channel is an eighty-hours-a-week job."

"And yet, you've come to Hobby Island for a full month. Why?"

He shrugged. "I haven't taken a vacation since I started the vlog, and I worked overtime prerecording interviews and Q&As for my team to upload while I'm gone. And I can film on location too."

"You'll be covering the charity tournament?"

He nodded, his gaze hooked on her face. "Would that bother you?"

She shrugged, trying to shake off her distaste for the idea. "I don't get why your viewers would care."

"Human interest. The reuniting of two sisters who are the best golfers ever to play in the LPGA. There will be plenty of interest."

"I haven't agreed to play in the tournament. I don't even own golf clubs."

"Hey, you saw what I brought. I don't golf anymore either. I got those from Gavin's storage shed. But you? I can't imagine you giving up your clubs."

She shrugged. "I sold them when I quit the circuit. Honestly, I sold everything."

"Wow, hardcore. You torched those bridges, huh?"

"I didn't want any temptations to return lying around the house." She moved her achy ankle back and forth, stimulating blood flow. "But this morning, Luna Chance brought my first set of golf clubs to me. My mother apparently saved both mine and

Athena's first set and asked for us to use them during the tournament, so I guess I'm committed."

"How do you feel about that?"

"Weird. Conflicted." She made a face, not wanting to talk about it anymore.

"How'd you end up in Denver?" he asked, picking up on her vibes and abandoning that line of conversation.

"A love interest," she said, keeping it simple. The man didn't need to know the details of her sex life.

Reid lowered his eyelids and an odd expression plucked at his lips. "Hmm, how's that relationship going?"

"It didn't work out, but I fell in love with Colorado, and I stayed."

"What happened with the love interest, if you don't mind me asking?"

Calista winced. "He turned out to be too much like my father."

"Ouch. How about now? Anyone else in your life?"

"Not at the moment." She spoke casually, but his question stirred unexpected goose bumps on her arms, or maybe it was just the breeze blowing in off the water. "How about you? Do you have a significant other?"

"No."

"Why not? You're a good-looking guy."

"I work too much. No time to cultivate anything meaningful." Reid shrugged and raised his gaze to meet hers.

Calista felt a spark of the old intimacy they once shared. They were both single and without romantic commitments. *Stop thinking like that.* "Ah, the grind. I remember how all-consuming that is."

"Do you miss it?" he asked.

"Touring? Oh, hell no." She let out a humorless laugh. "Once in a while, I miss golf itself, but not enough to pick up a club again."

"Until now."

"Yeah, well, I never said that I would play in the tournament."

"But you are staying through the Fourth of July even if you don't end up playing?" he asked.

"For Athena's sake, yes."

"You two are making progress mending fences?"

"Looks that way."

"I'm glad you're in a forgiving frame of mind. Bodes well for me." His gaze was intense and too challenging to hold.

"Why don't we eat," she said. "I'm starving."

"Sure, sure." He opened the picnic basket. "We've got chicken salad sandwiches on buttery croissants because I'm nothing if not a cliché."

"That's wonderful. I love chicken salad."

"I know." He produced two packages wrapped neatly in wax paper. "Got potato chips, the ruffly kind you like." He tossed out two packages of Ruffles. "Some fresh fruit, because scurvy is so last century, and . . ." He paused for dramatic effect before pulling out a bottle. "Sparkling cider. I considered wine but decided day drinking might not be the best start to our heart-to-heart."

"How responsible of you. I'm impressed. The Reid I knew would have brought a six-pack of Mountain Dew, convenience store hot dogs, and called it a day."

"The Reid you knew was an idiot," he said, his tone light but his eyes serious. "The current model comes with slightly better judgment and a heaping side of regret for how I ended things when we were teenagers before you turned pro and I went off to college."

And there it was, the elephant in the cove acknowledged.

"Regret," she said. "That's a therapisty way of saying 'I screwed up,' isn't it?"

Reid nodded, his affable grin replaced by a somber expression.

"Yeah. I've made a lot of mistakes, Cal. Letting you go was the biggest one of all."

The raw honesty in his voice made Calista really look at him for the first time since they'd set sail.

The years had been kind to Reid. The boyish good looks of his youth had matured into rugged handsomeness. She glanced away and took a bite of her sandwich to buy time. The chicken was tangy with tarragon and dill aioli, a soothing counterpoint to the turmoil in her stomach. He waited while she chewed and swallowed.

"You gonna leave me hanging?" he asked.

She met his gaze and held it. "Why now, Reid? After all these years?"

He toyed with his glass, condensation beading on its surface like tiny glistening doubts. "I recently learned some things that cast our past in a new light."

Calista narrowed her eyes. "What could you have learned that changes anything?"

Reid couldn't hold her gaze and instead glanced out across the cove, his profile etched against the backdrop of sky and sea. "Back then . . ." He paused, cleared his throat. "Someone pressured me to break up with you."

"Who?" She frowned, a sinking feeling in her gut.

He paused and winced. "Someone who had power over me. This person convinced me that breaking things off with you was for the best, although I didn't understand why at the time."

"But now you do?" She searched his face, willing him to come clean.

"It's . . . complicated." Reid dropped his gaze, and he stared at the rippling water as if searching for the right words beneath its surface. "There were circumstances I didn't fully understand back then."

The words hung in the air, heavy with implication. Her pulse quickened, a staccato beat of loss and heartache. "Was it my father?"

He flinched. "Calista . . . I can't—"

"Just say it, Reid! If it was Benjamin, just admit it!" She pushed aside her half-eaten sandwich, and her appetite vanished. She shouldn't have been shocked, but stupidly, she was. Benjamin hated to see her happy. No wonder he destroyed her relationship with Reid. Sick to her stomach, she put a hand to her mouth.

Reid rubbed his chin, a habit he used when he was conflicted. "It's not that simple."

"Not that simple? What could be simpler than telling the truth? You owe me that much, don't you? Why can't you just tell me? What did my father do? Bribe you?"

"I'm sorry," he apologized again. "I was a kid and in over my head."

"So you let someone else decide our fate? Why didn't you trust me enough to tell me the truth?"

Reid ran a hand through his hair, mussing it in a way that tugged at Calista's heartstrings. "I was young, stupid, and scared. I thought I was protecting you, but I was really just protecting myself. Getting out of our relationship before I got in too deep."

"And yet you want to make amends with me?" She folded her arms over her chest.

He winced. "I do and I wish I could tell you everything, but it's not just about us. There are other people involved. Other consequences. I can't just—"

"What aren't you telling me?"

"Please, just trust me on this." His pleading gaze asked her to drop it. "I'm not hiding this to hurt you. Quite the opposite. There are things in motion that you're better off not knowing, at least for now."

The sting of tears pricked her eyes, but she blinked them back. "You don't get to decide what I should know, Reid. Not anymore."

He sighed, clearly torn. "You're right, but can you trust me enough to let this play out? I promise, when the time is right, I'll tell you everything. Just not yet."

Calista turned her head, unable to look at him any longer. "I don't know if I can trust you, Reid. Not after the breakup. Not after what you told me at Chevron. Not after the way you hounded me for weeks afterward."

"I understand." His pupils narrowed and he pulled a palm down his mouth. "But I'm asking you to try. For old times' sake, if nothing else."

"Fine, I forgive you, but don't think for a second that I'll forget."

"I wouldn't expect you to," Reid said, relief tinged with regret in his voice. "I'll make this right, Calista. I swear."

Unnerved, she glanced at the sky again and saw the fluffy white clouds that sailed them to Mermaid Cove darkening, thickening. The wind picked up, disturbing the once-calm waters of the cove and sending the sandwich and chip wrappers flying across the beach. Reid hopped up to retrieve their litter.

"We should head back," Reid said, stuffing the wrappers into the picnic basket along with the cider bottle and glasses. "I checked the weather this morning, and there was no rain in the forecast, but it looks like they were wrong."

Once on board, Reid hurried to raise the anchor and adjust the sails to catch the wind. A few minutes later, the boat lurched as the first oversize wave hit, nearly knocking Calista off her seat. Fat raindrops splattered the deck around them.

"Uh-oh." Reid maneuvered the sails, attempting to speed up the catamaran, but they couldn't outrun the storm.

The raindrops quickened, pelting down, obscuring their vision. She shook herself, hair flinging water. "Reid! What can I do to help?"

He fought with the tiller, his jaw set in grim determination. "Just hold on tight! I'll get us through this!"

Calista gripped the sides of the boat. She felt utterly useless, watching Reid struggle against the elements. Waves crashed over the side, drenching them both.

"I can't see the shore!" she cried.

"It's okay," he said. "I've sailed through storms before. We'll make it."

But the bad weather intensified. Through the curtains of rain, Calista caught glimpses of jagged rocks looming dangerously close.

"Reid!" She shouted over the storm and gestured. "We're being pushed toward the rocky shoals!"

He nodded, muscles straining as he battled to keep the catamaran upright. "I'm tacking away. Whatever you do, don't let go!"

# Chapter 15
## *Athena*

*"Sometimes the bravest thing you can do is admit you're lost."*
—*Eloisa Hobby*

Dirt under her nails. Wouldn't come off. Her thoughts were disjointed, floaty. Athena scrubbed and scrubbed in that tiny bathroom sink. Soap that smelled like fake lemons. Mom had hated fake lemon smell. Said it reminded her of hospitals.

She washed again and got most of it out, but she still felt like it was there.

With a heavy sigh, she left the bathroom. People were getting in golf carts, drifting away. She looked around for Calista. Where was her sister?

Eloisa's voice. "Athena."

She turned.

The diminutive woman strolled over, smiling like she didn't know how to stop. "Calista wanted me to tell you, she went sailing with Reid."

Sailing? Calista hated Reid. No, used to hate Reid. Things changed. People changed. Except for Benjamin. Except for her.

But maybe she was changing too.

Athena nodded at Eloisa. Should she say something? Words stuck in her throat. She nodded again.

"Are you all right, dear?"

No, but she didn't want to talk about it. She felt the corner of her mouth lift, mirroring Eloisa's, pointed toward the golf cart and said one word. "Go."

"All right." Concern knit Eloisa's brow. "Are you—"

"Later." Two words. That was good, right?

Athena hopped in the golf cart and peeled away from the memorial garden as fast as she could in the slow-moving vehicle. So this was what an emotional blender felt like. Not a fan.

Calista tried to warn her, for sure, but Athena had been unable or unwilling to hear it.

*There are none so blind as those who will not see.*

The lush greenery of Hobby Island rushed past, all cheery, verdant, and oblivious to the fact that her entire world was crumbling faster than a sandcastle at high tide.

Her mind raced, replaying the bomb her vicious flashback exploded. Her father, the man she'd spent her entire life trying to please, the architect of her golfing career, the man who ran her life and managed her money—was a grade-A, certified shithead.

*Don't sugarcoat it, Attie. He's a monster.* Calista's voice in her head. Sharp and clear.

"Congratulations, Universe." Athena rolled her eyes at the sky. "You've outplotted M. Night Shyamalan. What a twist!"

She whizzed along, leaving the coastline for the interior of the island, having no idea where she was going. The destination didn't matter. Outrunning her mental demons was impossible, but she was sure gonna try.

The golf cart, as if sensing her existential crisis and reveling in it, decided this was the perfect moment to quit. It slowed, whirred, and then gave up. The battery drained, and the charge lost.

Rats! Why hadn't she checked the gauge?

"Perfect." With a groan, she cast a glance at her unfamiliar surroundings. Okay, where was she?

Athena got out. Her legs were as steady as a newborn giraffe on roller skates. She needed help, but more than that, she needed . . . what? A time machine? A lobotomy to erase the last twenty-four hours? A trained psychiatrist specializing in daddy issues?

Seriously, this part of the island looked like *Hansel and Gretel*. In the distance, a few cottages. Roofs all wrong. Tilted. Crooked. Her head spun. Her high school geometry teacher would've had a fit. Paths. Winding. Twisting. Going nowhere and everywhere. Flowers along the sides. Wild. Untamed.

Where did they lead? Nowhere, probably. Everywhere maybe.

What was happening to her brain?

Couldn't make sense of paths. Tried to follow one. She caught another path. Then another. Too many choices. No straight lines. Nothing made sense here. Colors and angles and paths. All jumbled up. Like her thoughts.

"Right," Athena said, "because clearly what this day needs is a dash of surrealism. What's next? Talking flowers? Doc and a DeLorean?"

The trees thickened until she was in a forest. How would she find her way out of here? Forcing her brain to engage logically, she spotted a sign that read Dot's Apothecary.

The vine-covered cottage with board and batten shutters, and a slate roof that looked straight from Stratford-upon-Avon. Athena raised an eyebrow. Dot had an apothecary out here too? Or was this the mothership for the apothecary in Crafters' Corner? The place where the older woman compounded potions and spells?

Lacking any better options (and secretly wishing Dot had the Ramones on her playlist and a tonic labeled "I Wanna Be Sedated"), Athena made her way to the door and knocked. Dot had been at the remembrance garden. What were the odds she was at home?

Fingers crossed . . .

She knocked again, and the door swung open to reveal the towering British woman with a smile so enthusiastic, Athena wished she'd worn sunglasses.

"Athena!" Dot's face lit up like she just won a lifetime supply of tea cakes, and calories don't count on Saturdays. "Darling, you look like you've been hit by a runaway lorry. Come in, come in!"

Before Athena could dredge up a believable excuse involving alien abductions, she got swept into a cottage that looked as if Mary Poppins opened an herb shop after a wild night out with Macbeth witches.

Dried plants hung from every available surface, shelves groaned under the weight of colorful bottles, and various animals lounged about as if they were paying rent. A sage-looking black cat gave Athena a once-over that said, *Honey, you think you've got problems? Try coughing up hairballs.*

"My golf cart ran out of juice," she said.

"Your buggy needs a bit of a pick-me-up, does it?" Dot pushed against the lace curtain to peer out the window. "Let's get it sorted."

They ventured back outside and walked to the path where the cart had died. Together, they pushed the golf cart back to Dot's and a small charging station hidden behind a honeysuckle bush. Athena noticed the strange contraption next to the charger—a bicycle connected to what looked like an old-fashioned butter churn, with an old Vitamix attached to the handlebars and a small wind turbine affixed to the back.

Dot followed her gaze. "Oh, that's my pedal-powered potion mixer. Combines exercise with herbal brewing and smoothie making, and on windy days, it charges my satellite phone. Efficient, don't you think?"

Athena blinked, wondering if Dot was kidding or if she herself accidentally stepped into an alternate universe where logic took an extended vacation to Narnia. "Sure, because who doesn't want their kale smoothie with a hint of lavender and a dash of static electricity?"

"Exactly! Now, this will take a little while. Why don't you come inside and have some tea while you wait? I promise it won't turn you into a frog. Well, probably not. There was that one time with Mr. Ribbit, but he's much happier now, I assure you."

Athena wasn't sure whether that was a joke or not, but she gave a forced laugh out of politeness. Either way, reality left the station some time ago.

Back inside the cottage, Dot guided Athena to a small table by a window overlooking a garden. Flowers of wildly vivid colors grew next to vegetables, showing off like they were in a county fair competition.

"Now then." Whistling a jaunty tune that sounded like "Don't Worry, Be Happy," Dot busied herself with a kettle.

The irony was not lost on Athena, who hadn't been this far from happy since she found out Santa wasn't real. (Which, incidentally, had also involved her father lying, now that she thought about it. Red flag, much?)

Dot set a steaming cup of tea in front of Athena. The liquid was a deep, rich purple that didn't occur in nature and probably glowed in the dark. "What's on your mind, dear? You've been through the emotional wringer and then some."

Athena stared at the rough-hewn table, tracing a knot in the wood with her finger. How could she explain the tornado whirling inside her? Where would she even start? *Previously on Athena's Life: Everything You Thought You Knew Was a Lie?*

"I . . ." she began, then faltered.

Dot sat across from her, cupping the delicate teacup in giant palms and sending Athena a look of large-hearted sympathy. "Mm-hmm."

"I don't know who I am anymore. It's like I showed up to life's costume party, and I've been wearing the wrong outfit this whole time."

Dot arched an erudite eyebrow. "Ah, an identity crisis. Tricky business that, but also an opportunity."

Athena snorted. "An opportunity? For what? A complete mental breakdown? Because let me tell you, it's happening."

"For reinvention, dear." Dot stirred her tea, which was changing colors from purple to blue. Athena wondered if she was hallucinating or if this was just another day on Hobby Island. "When we lose our sense of self, we have the chance to rebuild. To choose who we want to be, rather than accepting who we've been told we are. It's like redecorating your soul. Pitch out the old and in with the new self-actualization!"

The words hit Athena like a well-aimed golf ball to the forehead, leaving her surprisingly clear-eyed. What false story did she believe about herself? The golden child. The golf prodigy. Daddy's little champion. But were any of those things really her? Or were they just roles she'd been cast in without ever seeing the script?

Mind boggled.

"Everything I thought I knew about my childhood, my father . . . it's all a lie," she said in a soft voice. "I feel like I can't trust my memories. It's like my entire identity is crumbling faster than my resolve in front of a plate of hot fudge brownies."

"You know, Athena, memories are like garden herbs. Some are sweet and healing, like chamomile or mint. Others are bitter and can hurt if mishandled, like that time I accidentally used ghost peppers instead of peperoncini in my 'Soothe Your Soul Soup.' But let me tell you, it cleared everyone's sinuses!"

Athena couldn't help laughing at the woman's deadpan delivery, the sound coming out somewhere between amusement and despair. "So . . . um . . . what are you saying? I just need to make a memory salad and pick out the bad bits?"

"Something like that." Dot's eyes twinkled. "It's never too late to start tending to your garden of memories, to nurture what's good and weed out what's not. Think of it as extreme mental landscaping."

The metaphor was about as subtle as a neon exit sign in a dark theater, but Athena considered it.

Could it really be that simple? Just . . . choose which memories to keep? It sounded like something out of a cheesy self-help book. 7 *Habits of Highly Effective Emotional Gardeners* or *The Life-Changing Magic of Tidying Up Your Trauma*.

"But how do I even begin?" Athena asked, feeling a tiny spark of hope for the first time since Calista brought up Benjamin's wager against her at Chevron. It was small, a faint flicker, but it was there, like the little engine that could. "How do I move on from all this pain? Is there a *'Get Over Your Dad Being a Jerk' for Dummies* book I missed?"

Dot smiled gently. "You start by letting go of what harms you. Sometimes that means distancing yourself from those who've hurt you, even if they're blood, and sometimes, it means forgiving yourself for not seeing the truth sooner. It's like cleaning out your closet. You might love that sparkly Stars and Stripes halter top from college, but if it doesn't fit anymore and makes you feel bad, it's time to let it go."

Forgive herself? Athena hadn't even considered that. She'd been so focused on her anger, at the unfairness of it all, that she hadn't stopped to think about her role in perpetuating the lies.

She'd been wearing designer blinders, custom-made to match her golf outfits.

"I don't know if I can," she said, her voice small. "Forgiving myself seems about as likely as me developing a passion for underwater basket weaving."

"Of course you can," Dot said with such conviction that Athena almost believed her. "You're stronger than you know, dear. You just need to give yourself the chance to prove it. And hey, don't knock underwater basket weaving until you've tried it. It's surprisingly therapeutic."

Athena sipped her tea, surprised by its complex flavor (it tasted like a breezy summer day and a cozy flannel blanket got married in her mouth, with notes of sunshine and maybe a hint of fairy dust), much tastier than she expected.

Dot leaned forward, her eyes glowing in the light. "Now then, would you like me to read your tea leaves? Sometimes the leaves have a way of showing us what we need to see. Like a Magic 8 Ball, but with more antioxidants."

Athena raised an eyebrow. "Tea leaf reading? Really? What's next, tarot cards? Crystal balls? A Ouija board to ask my mother for advice?"

Dot shrugged, a mischievous smile playing on her lips. "This is Hobby Island, dear. We specialize in the whimsical and unexpected. Besides, what have you got to lose? Other than your skepticism and last shred of sanity."

Put that way, Athena couldn't argue. Her sanity had already packed its bags and left a Gone Fishing sign, anyway. She finished the tea and handed over the cup. Dot peered into it with the concentration of a bomb disposal expert defusing a tricky explosive.

"Hmm." Dot turned the cup this way and that as she stared into the leaves.

"What does that mean?" Athena clutched the arms of her chair and leaned in.

"Interesting. Remarkably interesting indeed. Either you're about to embark on a journey of self-discovery, or you're going to be attacked by a flock of angry seagulls. Tea leaves can be vague sometimes."

"Huh? What do you see? And please tell me it's the self-discovery thing. I don't think my insurance covers seagull attacks."

Dot looked up, her eyes going serious. "I see a path leading away from darkness and into light. It's a complicated path—there are obstacles and challenges along the way, but at the end, there's a brightness that outshines everything else. Oh, and there's something that looks like a golf club. Or perhaps a snake. Hard to tell with these things."

Before Athena could respond with another sarcastic quip (she had several lined up), a soft chime rang out, sounding like wind through crystal. Or the timer on an extrafancy oven finished baking an enlightenment soufflé.

"Ah, perfect timing," Dot said. "Cart's ready. Unless the local squirrels have staged another protest against electric vehicles; they're very environmentally conscious, you know, and believe everyone should walk or use bicycles."

"Um, okay."

They stepped outside, the late-afternoon sun painting everything in soft golden hues that made the world look honey dipped. Dot unplugged the cart, and Athena found herself reluctant to leave. For all its strangeness, the apothecary felt like a haven, a bubble of whimsy in a sea of harsh reality.

"Remember, Athena," Dot said, handing her a small pouch of tea leaves that sparkled purple in the sunlight. "You're not alone. You have people who care about you and want to help you find your way. Don't be afraid to lean on them, and if all else fails, you can always take up an obscure hobby. Origami is quite soothing."

Athena clutched the pouch, feeling the weight of the leaves and Dot's words. "Thank you. I feel like I should pay you or something. Do you take credit cards? Or maybe just my firstborn child?"

Dot waved her hand. "Oh, pish posh. Consider it a free sample of joy. Just promise me you'll water your garden. Speaking in metaphors, that is. Unless you actually decide to take up gardening, in which case, literal watering is also important."

Athena climbed into the golf cart.

"Oh, and Athena? Don't forget to enjoy the journey. Life's too short for boring self-discovery montages!" Laughing, Dot waved goodbye.

The drive back to the Lavender Lark felt like a fever dream—surreal, slightly nauseating, but with the vague promise of clarity once it was over.

Athena's mind raced, replaying her conversation with Dot, trying to make sense of the swirling emotions inside her. The island seemed different now, as if her shifting perspective had altered the very landscape around her. Was that topiary always shaped like a life-size chess piece, or was her brain just playing tricks on her?

Parking the golf cart, Athena took a deep breath before heading inside. She caught sight of her reflection in the golf cart's side mirror. She looked different, somehow. Older, maybe. Or just . . . altered. The woman staring back at her wasn't the polished golf pro she'd been just days ago. This woman had cracks in her facade, but there was something else there too. A flicker of something that might have been hope or just glitter from Dot's tea making its way through her system.

The Lavender Lark was quiet, the guests out enjoying the

island's attractions, unaware and uncaring of her world-tilting revelations. She felt alone.

She spoke to Luna, asking if she'd seen Calista. She couldn't wait to tell her sister about meeting with Dot and her ensuing epiphany, but Luna said Calista had yet to return.

In her room, Athena paced. She'd made dozens of calls to her father over the years—updates on tournaments, strategy sessions, postgame analyses, but this . . . this was different. This call? The most crucial of her life. She felt as if she were standing on the edge of a cliff, knowing she must jump but unsure if her parachute would open.

Inspired, she dug in her purse for the salve Dot had given her the previous night, uncapped the tin, applied some Empowerment Salve on her wrists, and chanted Dot's mantra.

Then, before she could talk sense into herself, she picked up the landline receiver and dialed her tour manager.

# Chapter 16
## *Calista*

*"In the storm's eye, we often find the strength we never knew we had."*

—*Eloisa Hobby*

Calista gripped the edge of the fiberglass catamaran. The tranquil waters of Mermaid Cove turned treacherous, and waves crashed, dark clouds roiled overhead, ominous thunder rumbled, and lightning flashed.

"Hold on tight!" The howling wind snatched Reid's voice away. His hands steadied on the tiller. His hair was plastered to his forehead, rivulets running down his face.

A rough wave crashed over the boat and drenched her to the bone as panic bloomed. Her pulse galloped, and her breath shot out shallow and quick.

The terrifying storm dredged up dark memories she spent years trying to release. A violent gust rocked the catamaran. Suddenly, Calista was no longer on a boat in Mermaid Cove.

She was twelve years old again, cowering on the balcony outside her childhood home as her father's voice boomed louder than the thunder through the locked French doors of her upstairs bedroom.

"You think you can come home with a second-place trophy and expect praise?" His words, slurred from too many whiskeys, cut more profoundly than the icy rain pelting her skin. That's when he was most dangerous. When he'd been drinking. "Winners don't make excuses. Winners don't fail. You're a loser. You disgust me."

"Please." She hated begging, but her clothes were soaked through. "It's storming. Let me inside . . . Daddy."

Unmoved by her pleas, her father's silhouette visible through the sheer curtains, the door stayed shut.

She huddled in the dark for hours, shivering and alone, until Athena got home from a party and let her in.

"Calista!" Reid's voice cut through the memory, yanking her back to the present. "I need your help with the mainsail. Can you do that?"

"Y-yes. Tell me what to do." She blinked hard to clear the water from her eyes and focused on Reid's face and saw dread.

Fresh fear squeezed her stomach.

Reid gave her instructions, and Calista pushed away the echoes of her father's voice and followed Reid's commands. She wasn't that helpless girl anymore, and yet, as she fumbled with the ropes, the memory persisted.

*Snap out of it.* Gritting her teeth, Calista forced her frozen fingers to cooperate. She worked in tandem with Reid to adjust the sail.

"You've got this, Cal, you're doing great."

Their efforts paid off. The catamaran steadied a bit, pitching less, settling and lulling them into false security. They spared a brief grin for each other.

Then another monstrous wave loomed over them like a liquid green mountain. Calista let out a shriek.

The wave smacked the sailboat hard.

She was thrown backward and lost her balance. For one heart-stopping moment, she was airborne. The world blurred into just gray sky and turbulent waves. She hit the water with a painful *smack* as the cold shocked her lungs.

Frantic, she struggled to orient herself. The waves tossed her like a Raggedy Ann doll. Which way was up? Where was the boat? Where was Reid?

She flailed. Her lungs burned. Salt stung her chapped lips. A stark reminder of how close she was to drowning. Spots danced at the edges of her vision. Bad news.

A brawny arm wrapped around her waist and hauled her upward. Calista broke the surface, coughing and sputtering.

"You're safe. I got you." Reid was in the water with her. The sailboat bobbed a few feet ahead of them. He nodded at her, and they swam against the current. Reid never let go of her.

After what felt like hours but was, in actuality, mere minutes of Herculean effort, they reached the bucking catamaran. With a grunt, Reid heaved her onto the deck and then pulled himself up beside her. They lay on their backs for a moment, chests heaving, staring up at the furious sky.

No time to rest.

The storm raged on, and they were still in grave danger. Reid scrambled to his feet, braced himself against the mast, and extended a hand to Calista.

Over the noise, he raised his voice. "We have to get control of the boat. Can you stand?"

Calista nodded, took his hand, and let him haul her to her feet. Her legs wobbled like jelly, and her sodden clothes clung to her body, but she was alive.

For now.

Together, they fought to regain control of the catamaran. Another memory tripped from Calista's mind. This time, it wasn't her father's angry face she saw, but a much younger Reid, catching her eye at the tee box as they caddied for her father and Gavin.

*Don't let him get you down*, Reid mouthed behind Benjamin's back after her father gave her a harsh dressing-down for handing him the wrong wood.

The years fell away, and she saw the boy who had been her best friend, her fiercest competitor, and her first love. The boy who had believed in her when no one else did. The guy who recognized her strength long before she did.

Another wave hit. Huge. The boat rocked, and Calista stumbled. Something tugged at her neck. Her hand flew to her throat. Nothing there but bare skin. Gone. Where was her locket? Mom's locket. Her greatest comfort for so many years?

Doom settled over her. Lost. Everything slipped away. She couldn't think over the howling. A battering ram of rain stung her face. The boat creaked and groaned. Would it fly apart?

Locket gone. Mom gone. Everything gone.

The storm didn't care. The ocean didn't care. Did anyone care? Calista cared. Too much. Always too much.

"Calista, listen to me." Reid's arm went around her waist. "You're okay. We're going to be all right. Hang in there."

They battled on, fighting against the storm. The waves sloshed their boat up and down. Endless.

Then, almost as abruptly as it had whipped up, the wind started dying down.

Calista clung to the mast, her arms trembling from exertion. One moment, the gale shrieked in her ears, drowning out everything but the thunder of her heartbeat in her ears. The next, it was just . . . gone.

Just like her locket.

The sudden quiet was as disorienting as the storm.

"Reid?" Her voice sounded small in the newfound calm. She met his gaze across the boat. "You okay?"

"Right here, right beside you, doing fine. We made it." Reid grinned at her. "You?"

"I lost my locket."

"The one your mother gave you?"

She bobbed her head, too grieved to speak.

Sadness and sympathy tinged his gaze. "I'm sorry."

"It's okay." She didn't want to talk about it. She'd cry.

He pulled her close and held her against his chest. She listened to the comforting beat of his heart. "How's your ankle?"

"To tell the truth, I forgot all about it, but Belinda's giraffe cane washed overboard."

"Don't worry, you can lean on me." He paused. "We make a pretty good team, Cal."

Despite everything—the lingering fear, the bone-deep exhaustion, the salt crusting her eyelashes, losing her locket—Calista returned his smile. "Don't get cocky, Thornton. We're not out of this yet."

But even as she said it, she realized it wasn't entirely true. The waves, while still choppy, no longer threatened to swallow them whole. The sky, which had been an apocalyptic slate gray, gave way to streaks of gold and pink peeking through the parting clouds.

They made it. They survived. Battered, tattered, but still here.

Calista let out a sigh. Her legs, deciding they'd done their job, gave out. She slid down the mast and landed on the deck on her butt. *Thump.*

"Whoa, hey." Reid was at her side in an instant, his hand warm on her shoulder. "You sure you're okay?"

She studied him up close. His hair was a mess, molded to his forehead in some places and sticking up in others. He looked ridiculous. He looked spectacular.

"Just processing, I guess."

Reid nodded and sank beside her, their shoulders almost touching. For a long moment, they sat in silence, watching the sea settle.

"So, that was . . ."

"Intense."

"Yeah. It really was."

She waited for him to say more, to fill the silence with jokes or questions or plans for getting back to Crafters' Corner.

But he didn't. He was just there, a solid, steady presence at her side. Like when they were kids. Those years when only golf mattered.

The thought of golf brought a montage of fresh memories. Her father's rage. The numerous trophies that were never enough. The constant, crushing pressure to be perfect. But this time, the memories didn't paralyze her. They didn't send her spiraling into panic or self-doubt. Instead, she felt safe. Strong.

"I thought we were gonna die," Calista said.

Reid tensed beside her. "Cal—"

"No, let me finish. I thought we were gonna die, and you know what scared me the most? It wasn't the dying part. It was the thought I'd die scared and small and still living in *his* shadow." She didn't have to specify who she meant. Reid knew. "When that enormous wave smacked us and I flew overboard, for a second, I was back *there*. Reliving my father's abuse. Except this time, I didn't beg. I fought back. I was saving myself."

Reid's eyes were soft, filled with an emotion she couldn't identify. His hand found hers. He intertwined their fingers as if it were the most natural thing. Like no time had passed.

"You did save yourself, Cal. I just wish you could see yourself the way I see you." There was something in his voice, something raw and honest, that touched her heart.

"And how's that?"

Reid's free hand came up to cup her cheek, his thumb brushing away a stray droplet—of seawater or tears, she wasn't sure which. "You're the strongest person I've ever known. Your resilience is astounding."

Calista stared at him, this guy she'd known since she was stupid young but felt as if she were seeing him for the first time. Her heart fluttered. It had zero to do with their near-death experience. It was how he studied her.

"Reid," she said, her voice husky. "I think I want you to kiss me now."

His eyebrows shot up. "You think?"

"Well, I'm about 90 percent sure," Calista said. Apparently, a near-drowning turned her into a rambling idiot. "Maybe 95. There's still a slight chance I might chicken out. Or fall overboard again or—"

Reid cut her off, pressing his lips to hers.

Oh.

*OH.*

She shut her eyes. It wasn't fireworks or sparks or any of those cliché romance descriptions. Reid's kiss was far better. Like finally breathing again after being underwater. Or the first sip of morning coffee after a restless night. Or collapsing into a soft thick mattress following a strenuous workday.

It was coming home.

When they finally broke apart, Calista kept her eyes closed for a moment, savoring the feeling, tracing her lips with a finger. She opened them to find Reid watching her with a mix of wonder and amusement.

"So, was it everything you'd hoped for?"

Calista pretended to consider. "Hmm, I don't know. I need another sample to be sure."

She smothered Reid's laugh with more kisses. It wasn't graceful. Their noses bumped, their teeth clacked together, and he tasted of salt, anxiety, and adrenaline, but oh, was it perfect.

Reid's hand slid from her cheek to the back of her neck, drawing her closer. Calista's fingers tangled in his damp hair, holding on like he was a lifeline. Which, she supposed, he kind of was.

The kiss deepened, years of unspoken feelings pouring out all at once. It was an apology and a promise, a question and an answer. Both the eye of the storm and the calm rolled into one.

Afterward, Calista kept her eyes closed again. Part of her was afraid that if she opened them, she'd find out this was a dream and that she still would be in the water, still drowning, still lost.

"Cal." Reid pressed his forehead against hers. "Look at me. Please."

Taking her time, she opened her eyes. There Reid sat. Just inches away, looking at her as if she were the sun breaking through storm clouds. Her eyes crossed, staring at him, and she giggled.

"I never stopped thinking about you," he said.

For years, she'd believed Reid's pursuit after Chevron had been about sensationalism, about turning her heartbreak into headlines. But now she saw the truth. He hadn't been trying to hurt her. He'd been trying to save her. In his own clumsy, misguided way, he'd thought pushing her back to golf was the answer. And maybe it would've been, if she'd still loved the game the way she once had.

He lowered his voice and his eyes. "Or wanting you."

*Huh?*

Gobsmacked, she stared at him as his words hit her like another wave, but this time, Calista didn't feel as if she was drowning. Instead, she was free-falling.

"Reid, I—"

He shook his head. "You don't have to say anything. I know we have a lot to talk about, a lot to figure out. I just . . . I needed you to know. After today, after almost losing you, I couldn't go another minute without telling you how I feel. It's always been you, Calista. Always."

# Chapter 17

## *Athena*

*"True strength lies not in facing the tempest alone, but in finding the courage to lean on others and dance through the rain."*

—*Eloisa Hobby*

Athena paced her room at the Lavender Lark, her mind racing faster than a golf ball off a pro's driver.

She'd done it. Canceled her LPGA tour for the rest of the year. Her fingers twitched, muscle memory reaching for a golf club that wasn't there. The weight of her decision pressed down on her, heavier than any golf bag she'd ever carried.

The thought made her want to laugh hysterically, vomit, or both, which would not be a pretty sight and definitely not cover material for *Golf Digest*.

*Okay, Athena, you've decided. Now what? A new hobby? A vision board? Mental breakdown?*

That last option seemed likely. Better choice? *Find Calista and share this monumental news because canceling your entire career wasn't quite enough drama for one day.* Too bad she couldn't just text.

Athena stopped at the front desk to see if Calista had returned, but Luna hadn't seen her. Not knowing what else to do, she borrowed a scooter and set out for Crafters' Corner and arrived to find a small crowd gathering at the boat dock.

What was up? Curiosity piqued, Athena followed the group.

The murmuring grew louder as she neared. People sounded concerned or shocked. Anxiety rippled through Athena. Although she had no explanation for her fears, she pushed through the collective to uncover the source of the commotion.

At the pier, being helped off a battered sailboat that looked as if it had gone ten rounds with the Kraken, were a stumbling Calista and Reid.

Athena let out a gasp and rushed forward. Clearly, her sister and Reid had been through hell and back—clothes sodden, hair wild, exhaustion etched into their faces. Relief and fear collided, and she quickened her pace. People stepped aside, letting her through.

"Calista!" Athena hurried down the pier.

Her sister, soaked, shivering, gave her a weak smile. "Hey."

"Oh my god, are you okay? What happened?"

"Long story."

Athena didn't even think. She just scooped her sister into her arms. The scent of sea clung to Calista, mingling with the faint trace of the perfume she wore. The same perfume Demetra once used when they were little. It was a jarring combination of the familiar and the unknown, much like their current relationship.

Calista hugged her back with surprising strength for someone who looked like a drowned rat (a cute drowned rat, but still).

"I'm okay. We're fine. Just had an unexpected swimming lesson."

Reid appeared beside them, looking far too attractive for someone who'd nearly become fish food. It was downright inconsiderate, really. His windswept hair and the way his wet shirt clung to his body showed off his hard abs.

"What happened?" Athena asked him.

"A freak storm hit," he said, his voice rougher than the sandpaper Athena used to smooth her golf grips. "One minute calm, next minute . . . well, let's just say we now know what it feels like to be inside a washing machine on spin cycle."

Athena could almost hear the tumbling of waves and the creak of the boat, imagining the terror they must have felt. It trivialized her own worries.

Vivian hustled aside the crowd with blankets clutched in her arms. She rushed up in her pink feathered mules to wrap first Calista and then Reid up like burritos as she shook her head and clicked her tongue. "You went to Mermaid Cove, didn't you?"

"How did you know?" Reid asked.

"In June, Mermaid Cove has the most peculiar weather patterns. It's unsafe to sail there." She gestured toward the bookstore. "Come on, let's get you two warmed up. I've got hot chocolate and snickerdoodles that'll make you forget all about your aquatic adventure."

The mention of Mermaid Cove sent a shiver down Athena's spine. There was still so much about this island she didn't understand, so many secrets lurking beneath its quaint exterior.

Calista leaned into Reid like he was her personal support beam. Something had shifted between them out there on the water. Athena wasn't sure if she wanted to hug Reid for keeping her sister safe or push him off the dock for putting Calista in danger. Maybe both things in quick succession.

"Come, come." Vivian motioned for them to follow her into A New Chapter.

Athena felt a pang of something she couldn't quite name. Envy? Longing? Whatever it was, the feeling settled in her chest like a weight and reminded her of all the experiences she'd missed while endlessly chasing eagles.

The aroma of books and fresh-baked cookies welcomed them inside. The scent wrapped around them, a stark contrast to the briny air outside. Calista and Reid dropped into big squishy side-by-side armchairs.

Vivian bustled into the back room and reemerged, carrying a tray with four steaming mugs of hot chocolate and a plate of snickerdoodles piled high as a fortress. Athena eyed the cookie tower. Is that what ordinary people did in times of crisis? Comfort food? In her world, it was protein shakes and intensive training sessions.

"Okay." Vivian perched beside Athena, who'd settled on the couch across from the chairs Calista and Reid were in. "Spill it . . . and I don't mean the hot chocolate."

Reid recounted their seafaring tale. Calista's eyes never left his face, a soft smile playing on her lips as they held hands.

It was a look Athena had never seen before on her sister—part admiration, part something deeper she couldn't quite identify. Had *she* ever looked at anyone that way, or had her life been too full of golf clubs and her father's expectations to leave room for intimate connections?

"But we survived," Reid said, finishing up the story. "And we made it back in one piece, so all is well."

"I was so worried," Athena said. "When I saw you, I thought . . . Well, it doesn't matter what I thought. You're safe now."

Calista reached out with her free hand to touch Athena's shoulder, and she felt suddenly joyous at the sisterly contact. The warmth of Calista's hand grounded her, a lifeline in this sea of unexpected emotions. For a moment, Athena could almost remember what it was like being sisters before golf and their father's ambitious manipulations drove a wedge between them.

"Can't get rid of me that easily, sis." Calista grinned and leaned back in her chair. "Besides, we've got too much to sort out still, right?"

"Actually," Athena said, "there's something I need to tell you. Big news."

Calista set down her mug and gave Athena her full attention. "Yes?"

"Are you up to hearing it? You just had an earthshaking experience." Athena darted a glance at Reid, unsure if she wanted to reveal all in front of him.

"Hot chocolate, warm blankets, and cookies made it better." Calista flexed a bicep. "I'm all ears."

The normalcy of the moment—sitting in a cozy bookshop, sharing cookies and secrets—felt surreal after the drama of the day. Vivian beamed and hustled to refill their mugs with more hot chocolate.

Everyone's gaze rested on Athena. She took a deep breath. *Here goes nothing.* Or everything. Maybe both.

"I canceled my LPGA events for the rest of the year."

The words hung in the air like the Magnus effect, the perfect spin on a golf ball causing it to achieve maximum lift. Time stretched, each second feeling like an eternity as Athena waited for her sister's reaction. She'd faced less pressure on the eighteenth hole of a major.

Calista blinked, absorbing her words, and then her eyes widened. If she were a cartoon, her jaw would have hit the floor with an audible *thunk.* "Athena! That's . . . wow! Are you sure? I mean, your career—"

"My career will still be there if I decide to return," Athena said, surprised by the strength of her conviction. Where had that come from? "But this—us, you and me, figuring out who *we* are without dear old Daddy's influence—that's the most important right now. I want to stay here, on the island, honoring Mom and getting to know you again, Calista. To be the sisters we should have been all along."

The words tumbled out, years of unspoken feelings and regrets pouring forth. It was terrifying and liberating all at once, like stepping off the edge of a cliff and realizing she had wings.

Tears misted Calista's eyes, and for a heart-stopping moment, Athena thought she'd messed up. Maybe Calista didn't want to know her. Perhaps she burned that bridge so thoroughly that not even the magic of Hobby Island could rebuild it. Panic rose in Athena's throat. She'd faced down the world's best golfers without breaking a sweat, but the thought of her sister rejecting her made her feel like a scared little girl.

But then Calista was up out of her chair and hugging Athena so hard they nearly toppled backward off the couch, a tangle of limbs, emotions, and the lingering scent of sea salt.

The force of Calista's embrace knocked the breath out of Athena. She couldn't remember the last time someone had hugged her like this—not for a photo op or a congratulatory moment, but just because they wanted to be close.

"I'm so proud of you," Calista said. The words wrapped around Athena, soothing hurts she hadn't even known were there.

Before Athena could respond (probably with something sappy and embarrassing that would ruin her cultivated image of cool detachment), the bookshop door chimed. The four of them—Vivian, Reid, Calista, and Athena—turned to see who entered.

The interruption felt like a record scratch, jolting them out of the moment. Athena resisted the urge to groan.

It was Luna, holding her satellite phone and wearing an expression that screamed *I'm about to ruin this beautiful moment.* "Sorry to interrupt, but Athena, it's your dad, and he's insisting on speaking with you. FYI, I've got him muted."

Luna extended the phone and just like that, reality crashed in as if a rom-com director yelled *Plot twist!* in the middle of the movie and switched to a psychological thriller.

Athena half expected dramatic music to rise in the background, perhaps something like "The Imperial March." How did her father constantly intrude on the most critical moments of her life?

Athena's stomach dropped. Benjamin must have learned she quit the tour. She stood, ready to face her father's wrath, to weather the storm of disappointment and manipulation she knew lay ahead. Sucking in a deep breath, she held out a palm for Luna to pass her the phone. Years of conditioning kicked in. Spine straight, chin up, game face on. It was the same routine she'd followed before every tournament, every interview, but this time, it felt hollow.

"Wait," Calista said, her eyes blazing with a protective fury that Athena had never seen before. "Before you talk to him, you need to know something."

The steel in her sister's voice gave Athena pause.

"What is it? I need to assert my independence. Maybe throw in a few choice words that definitely weren't in the Dempsey Family Approved Vocabulary."

Calista shook her head and looked deadly serious. "Athena, listen to me. Our father is most likely a malignant narcissist. According to my therapist, his behavior ticks off all nine traits needed for a diagnosis of narcissistic personality disorder."

"Huh?"

"I know you've rarely experienced his dark triad as the golden child, but he'll deny his destructive behavior, attack you for bringing it up, and then he'll make himself out to be the victim. He'll turn everything around on you, and no matter what you say or do, you'll only get ensnared deeper in his trap. Trust me, I've been there. It's not pretty."

Athena's mind reeled. Not engaging with her father? The idea seemed impossible. He was Benjamin Dempsey. He got what he wanted. *Always.* Telling him no was about as likely as getting a hole in one on a par five.

Her world tilted. Everything she thought she knew about her family, about her father, was called into question. It was like discovering the golf course she'd been playing on for years was actually a minefield, but then again, hadn't she just taken the first step in breaking free from his influence? Wasn't that what canceling the tour was all about?

Luna hovered, looking uncertain.

"I . . . I don't know if I can ignore his call," Athena said, hating how small her voice sounded. Where was Athena Dempsey, golf prodigy and media darling now? "And besides, I can't just leave Luna to deal with him. It's not fair. He'll probably threaten to sue her or something equally dramatic."

Luna's face softened. "Don't worry about me. I can handle Benjamin. My own father had emotional problems, and I get how complicated that kind of relationship is. Let me do this for you. You've made a big step today, and you deserve some peace."

Athena looked from Luna to Vivian to Calista to Reid, seeing nothing but support and encouragement in their faces. It was so different from the expectations and judgment she was used to.

So terrifyingly different.

Athena squared her shoulders and nodded. "Okay. Okay, you're right. Luna, would you mind . . . ?"

"Consider it done." Luna turned to leave. "Enjoy your hot chocolate and cookies."

Athena did it. She refused to engage with her father's coercive control. It was a small step, maybe, but it felt like winning Chevron. She looked to Calista. "So, what now? Start a support group for recovering golf prodigies?"

The question hung in the air, half joking, half serious. Because really, what did one do after upending their entire life?

Calista grinned, a mischievous glint in her eye. "Well, I was thinking maybe plan a heist to steal all Dad's trophies and melt them down into a giant middle finger sculpture. You know, normal sister bonding stuff."

For a moment, Athena imagined it—her and Calista, partners in cookie-fueled crime, giving a big metallic *screw you* to their past. It was ridiculous. It was juvenile. It was absolutely perfect.

The mental image was so absurd, so utterly at odds with the curated world she'd lived in for so long, Athena couldn't help but laugh. Laughter bubbled up from somewhere deep inside her, years of repressed emotion finding release.

"Count me in," Athena said, feeling lighter than she had in years. "But fair warning, my lock-picking skills are rusty. Turns out, country clubs frown on breaking and entering. Who knew?"

"Do you think interpretive dance will help work through trauma?" Vivian giggled. "That might be a healthier alternative to trophy heists."

The idea of herself—stoic, serious Athena Dempsey—doing interpretive dance was so absurd it set off another round of laughter. It felt good to be silly, to let go of the weight she carried for so long.

"Why not start now?" Vivian said and went to the controls of the sound system piped through the store. She fiddled around and soon the store filled with the music of Sara Bareilles, "Brave."

The first notes of the song filled the air, carrying with them a sense of possibility and hope. It was cheesy, sure, but maybe that's what Athena needed right now.

Vivian came back and held out a hand to Athena. "May I have this dance?"

Reid hopped up and bowed toward Calista as Vivian and Athena bopped around the store. Grinning, Calista let Reid pull her up from her seat.

And for those precious few minutes, life was absolutely beautiful.

# Chapter 18
## *Calista*

*"Healing means learning when to hold on and when to let go."*
—*Eloisa Hobby*

Calista's heart did that thing again—the same erratic flutter as when they were on the catamaran. It made her wonder if she should've paid more attention in biology class. Or anatomy. Or maybe cardiac arrhythmia 101. Whatever.

The last notes of music faded into the bookstore.

Somehow they'd bounced and bopped their way from the front of the shop all the way to the back. Calista found herself breathless, grinning like an idiot at Reid in the Self-Help section.

The irony wasn't lost on her. For sure, she could use some help right about now. Maybe *Dating Your Ex for Dummies* or *How to Not Combust When He Looks at You Like That: A Beginner's Guide.*

Their impromptu dance party left her face flushed, and her skin tingling where Reid's hands had been. In their little bubble of history and unresolved tension, the air felt charged, like the moment before lightning strikes.

"So," Reid said, running a hand through his hair in that endearing way of his. The way that made her want to reach out and smooth it back down. Or maybe mess it up further.

*Get it together, Calista.*

"Hungry?" he asked, his voice a touch husky.

The question hung between them, weighted. Hungry for food? For conversation? For a chance to explore whatever this crackling energy between them was?

Yes to all of the above.

She glanced at Athena, who was pretending to be fascinated by a display of inspirational journals. Her sister's eyes held that raw, exposed look Calista knew too well, like someone had stripped away a layer of skin she didn't know she could live without.

"I—" Calista started, then stopped. What she wanted to say was *Yes, I'm starving, and not just for food.* But what came out was "Rain check?"

Reid's smile dimmed a fraction, but he nodded. "Sure. I hear the food is excellent at the Someday Café."

"Someday Café?" Calista arched her eyebrows, then realized belatedly he was joking.

"Yeah, you know. It's that place where all the 'maybe laters' and 'rain checks' go to feast on what-ifs and almost-weres." He gave a half-hearted chuckle. "I hear their specialty is a bittersweet blended with missed opportunities and lingering hope."

Calista's cheeks heated. Trust Reid to turn rejection into wordplay. It was both infuriating and charming, like most things about him. "Save me a seat?"

"Always," he said with a wink and then just walked away.

Calista felt a pang of . . . something. Regret? Relief? Both? It was like standing on the edge of a diving board, simultaneously terrified of the plunge but exhilarated by the potential. Part of her wanted to call him back, to hell with responsibility. The other part knew that sometimes, the bravest thing she could do was wait.

She watched him disappear around the corner, taking with him the tantalizing aroma of what-could-be, leaving behind the comforting scent of books and sisterly duty. To Athena, she said,

"Hey, wanna go back to the Lavender Lark for takeout and a movie marathon?"

"Really?" Athena's grateful look said more than words ever could.

Calista slipped her arm around her older sister. "I only have one request."

"What's that?"

"For one night, no talking about the past. We just have fun. Deal?"

"Deal," Athena said.

"Pizza?"

"I'm buying."

"Not gonna argue, but no anchovies, please." Calista laughed.

They waved goodbye to Vivian, thanked her for the hot chocolate and cookies, and headed out the door toward the Lavender Lark.

Calista felt lighter than she had in ages. Sure, she just rainchecked a date with Mr. Dreamboat for a carb-laden movie night with her big sis, but they were slowly forging the kind of connection Calista never dreamed could happen.

Reid Thornton and his declaration of undying love would just have to wait.

* * *

The next morning, after a double feature of *When Harry Met Sally* and *Forget Paris* borrowed from the Lavender Lark's extensive DVD collection and scarfing down an entire large pizza with pepperoni and black olives, Calista and Athena woke up next to each other in Calista's king-size bed.

She and her sister hadn't slept in the same bed since . . . well, before Demetra lost custody of them. It brought back old memories.

So much for their temporary moratorium on talking about the past. Today, Calista needed to dig in and truly prepare her sister for what lay ahead when their father took his revenge on Athena for canceling her tour and refusing to take his call.

"Maybe he won't do anything," Athena said.

"Huh? You read my mind." Calista blinked at her. "I was just thinking about Dad."

"I've been awake for half an hour. I haven't been able to think of anything else. Plus, I needed to pee and couldn't fall back to sleep."

"Why didn't you just go?"

"I didn't want to wake you." Athena was on the side next to the wall, and she would have to climb over Calista to get to the bathroom.

"Good grief, woman!" Calista had forgotten how ingrained not rocking the boat was as an essential part of living with Benjamin Dempsey. "It's okay to have needs." She threw back the covers and jumped up. "Go pee!"

Athena launched herself off the bed and into the bathroom. Laughing, Calista straightened the covers and made the bed.

A few minutes later, Athena returned. "What do you want to do today?"

"It's Sunday. They're having an official memorial service for Mamá at nine at the chapel, according to the itinerary Luna gave me."

"Is it really only Sunday? It feels like we've been here for a month already."

"So breakfast and then the memorial?"

"Can we skip the memorial? I'm all memorial'd out. With the visitation on the day we got here and the groundbreaking of the memorial garden . . ." Athena shrugged. "I need to pace myself."

Calista hesitated, torn between honoring her mother and bonding with her sister. Mamá was gone, but Athena was still here. She chose the living.

"Sure." Calista tacked on a smile.

They changed into shorts and T-shirts, slathered on sunscreen, and headed out. The day was picture-perfect, all blue skies and fluffy white clouds that looked arranged by an ambitious set designer. They grabbed a golf cart and went to Crafters' Corner to collect supplies for their picnic.

"You okay?" Athena asked as they left the bakery, a bag of still-warm banana nut muffins scenting the air. "You look far away."

"Just thinking about Mamá."

Athena stopped walking. "You sure you don't want to go to the memorial service?"

"I want to be with you."

"Really?" Athena sounded so vulnerable.

"Absolutely."

They shared a small, sad smile. It was a tiny moment, insignificant in the grand scheme of things, but it still felt like a victory.

"Where shall we go?" Calista asked.

"The lighthouse?" Athena pointed to the regal structure visible over the town's rooftops.

The golf cart ride to the lighthouse was pleasant, but the walk up the stairs was more challenging than Calista expected, and they took several breaks. By the time they reached the top, Calista's achy ankle reminded her it wasn't 100 percent.

But the panoramic view was breathtaking—endless blue ocean stretching to the horizon, the lush green of the island spread out below them like a patchwork quilt, flushed purple with the jacaranda trees.

"Jeez," Athena said, panting. "I thought I was in shape, but apparently, my cardio game needs work."

"Hey, try planning elaborate children's birthday parties. It's basically CrossFit with glitter." Calista paused. "So, how are you *really* doing? With everything, I mean."

Athena was quiet for so long that Calista thought she might not answer. When she finally spoke, her voice was soft, almost lost in the sound of cawing seagulls circling overhead. "To tell the truth, I have no idea. It's like, you know, in cartoons, when a character runs off a cliff but doesn't fall until they look down? I feel like I'm suspended in that moment, waiting for gravity to kick in."

"Yeah, I get that. When I first left, I felt like that for months. Kept waiting for the other shoe to drop, you know?"

"Did it? Drop, I mean?"

A question loaded with more than just curiosity. Calista could hear the fear behind it, the desperate hope that maybe there was a way out that didn't end in complete disaster.

"Eventually, but by then, I'd built a parachute. I found people who supported me, who helped me see that there was life beyond golf and Dad's expectations. It wasn't easy, but it was worth it."

"I'm scared." Athena brushed her hair back. "Of what comes next. Who am I without golf? Without *him*. What if I disappoint everyone?"

The admission hit Calista like a punch. How many times had she experienced those exact fears? How many sleepless nights spent wondering if she'd made the biggest mistake of her life?

"Do you even like golf? Once I quit, I discovered I didn't," Calista said.

"Honestly?" Athena shook her head. "I have no idea. It's all I've ever known."

"I understand." She reached out to squeeze her sister's hand. "But you're not alone, okay? Whatever happens, whatever the dragon throws at us, we'll face it together."

Athena turned to her, eyes shining with unshed tears. "Promise?"

"Promise."

They hugged then, awkwardly at first and then with growing intensity, as if trying to make up for five years of missed hugs all at once.

"Come on," Calista said, forcing cheer into her voice. "I don't know about you, but all this emotional growth is making me hungry. Time for that picnic?"

They left the lighthouse and found a grassy spot nearby, spreading out the blanket. Calista thought about the picnic in Mermaid Cove with Reid and yesterday's wild event at sea. She wondered what he was doing today.

"So." She bit into a plump ripe strawberry they got at the fruit kiosk next to the bakery. "Tell me about your wildest fan encounter. I bet you've got some stories."

Athena laughed, the sound carrying on the breeze. "Oh man, where do I even start? There was this one time in Japan . . ."

"Japan? Do tell." Calista leaned in, intrigued.

"Picture this." Athena swept her palm out, painting a picture. "I'm at this superfancy sponsorship dinner in Tokyo. I'm jet-lagged, barely keeping my eyes open, when suddenly this guy starts shouting at me in rapid-fire Japanese."

Calista raised an eyebrow. "What'd you do?"

"What could I do? I smiled, nodded, and hoped I wasn't agreeing to sell my soul or something. Turns out, he was challenging me to a putting contest right there in the restaurant."

"No way! Did you do it?"

Athena grinned. "You bet I did. Beat him using a soup ladle as a putter."

They burst out laughing.

"Okay, your turn." Athena pulled a muffin from the bag. "Any wild party-planning stories?"

Calista thought for a moment. "Once, I wrangled a herd of escaped petting zoo animals at a farm-themed birthday party. Picture a dozen third graders hopped up on cotton candy, chasing chickens across a suburban backyard. Meanwhile, I'm trying to lure a very stubborn goat off the trampoline with a head of lettuce."

"Please tell me you have photos!"

"God, no. I was too busy keeping the rabbits from digging up the neighbor's prize petunias." Calista shook her head, grinning. "But I did get a five-star review and three more bookings from that chaos, so I guess it worked out."

"Sounds like you found your calling."

Calista met Athena's gaze. "Yeah, I guess I did. It's not professional golf, but . . ."

"It makes you happy. That's what matters." A comfortable silence fell between them, and then Athena spoke again, her voice quieter. "You know, sometimes I envy you."

"Me?" Calista pressed a hand to her chest. "Why?"

"Because you dared to walk away, to find something that truly fulfills you. Meanwhile, I'm in an unfamiliar hotel room every week, staring at the ceiling and wondering if this is all there is to life."

"It's never too late to make a change, you know."

Athena nodded, and then a mischievous glint lit her eyes. "Speaking of changes, what's going on with you and Reid? I saw the way he looked at you in the bookstore yesterday. And how close you two were dancing."

Calista ducked her head to hide the flush of her cheeks. "Oh, that's . . . it's nothing. Hey, did I tell you about the time I had to make an emergency piñata out of an Amazon box and leftover Easter candy?"

"Nice deflection, but fine, I'll let it slide . . . for now. Tell me about this MacGyver piñata situation."

Calista launched into her story, thanking the party-planning gods for providing her with an arsenal of distracting anecdotes. The Reid situation was definitely not something she was ready to unpack just yet.

"You know," Athena said, "I can't remember the last time I laughed like this. Certainly not around Dad."

The mention of their father sobered Calista. She took a deep breath to steel herself. "Attie, speaking of Dad, we need to talk about him."

Athena's smile faded, replaced by wariness. "Do we have to?"

"I know you're hoping he won't retaliate for you canceling the tour and refusing to take his call, but you need to prepare yourself. He won't take this lying down. His prime source of narcissistic supply is balking."

Athena's jaw clenched, a familiar stubbornness settling over her patrician features. "He's our father, Cal. Surely he wouldn't—"

"He *would* and he *has*. Whenever anyone challenges his control, he lashes out, and you canceled your tour without his permission. That's a *major* challenge."

"But I'm his 'little angel.'" Her words shot out bitter and twisted. "His perfect golf prodigy. He wouldn't risk ruining that, would he?"

Calista sighed, wishing she could shield her sister from harsh reality. "You're only the favorite as long as you're doing what he wants. The minute you step out of line, well, let's just say I've been there and it's ugly."

Athena sat quiet for a long moment, methodically shredding

a blade of grass. When she spoke, her voice was small, almost childlike. "What do you think he'll do?"

"Honestly? I'm not sure, but knowing Dad, it'll be calculated. He'll find a way to make it seem like he's the victim and you're the one being unreasonable. He might try to cut you off financially or use his connections to make it hard for you to find sponsors when you return to golf."

"How do you know all this about his motivations?"

"For one thing, I've had a lot of therapy." Calista winced. "For another, Daddy Dearest sued me."

"What!" Athena gave a vigorous shake of her head. "He *sued* you? For what?"

"Breach of contract."

"You signed a contract with him?"

"No." A soft sigh escaped her, and the old sadness filled her body. "He claimed we had a verbal agreement that he would provide financial support in exchange for a percentage of my earnings. By walking away, I breached the verbal contract."

"You're kidding!"

"Sadly, I am not."

"So what happened?"

"My lawyer demanded a forensic accounting of my earnings dating back to when I first turned pro and our father became administrator of my finances. I was so focused on my career, and he paid for everything and gave me an allowance, I never questioned how the rest of the money was spent."

Athena made a soft mewling sound.

"That is until I walked away. Athena, he embezzled *thousands* from me for years. When presented with the evidence, he dropped the lawsuit under the condition I didn't pursue legal action against him for stealing *my* money."

Athena gasped. "No!"

Calista met her gaze. "Is he still managing your finances?"

Her sister's face turned beet red. It was answer enough. "He wouldn't do that."

"Because you're the golden child?"

"No, I didn't mean it the way it sounds."

"He did it to me." Calista shrugged, tension tightening her muscles. "Just saying you might want to take a look at your bank account."

"No." Athena rapidly shook her head. "Yeah?"

"Yes."

"Good god." Athena flopped back onto the blanket. "How did we end up with such a manipulative asshat for a father?"

"Bad luck? Or maybe the universe's idea of a cosmic joke. 'Let's take two sisters with incredible athletic ability and saddle them with a dad who makes Darth Vader look like a contender for Father of the Year.'"

That startled a laugh from Athena. "You know, when you put it that way, it almost sounds impressive. Like, congrats, Universe! You really outdid yourself this time."

They giggled together, the sound slightly hysterical but genuine. When the laughter faded, Athena sat up, a serious expression in her eyes. "So what do we do? How do we . . . I don't know, protect us from him?"

"I'm already on the outs, so I'm pretty safe. You're the one who's in the crosshairs now." Calista took Athena's hand in hers. "We get through it by sticking together. We make ourselves triangulation-proof. Remember that his opinion isn't the one that matters, and you build a life outside his shadow."

"Is that what you did?" Athena asked.

"Eventually, yeah. It wasn't easy, and there were definitely times I wanted to give up and crawl back to the familiarity of golf and my desperate attempts to gain his approval, but I found my path. You can, too, Attie."

"Well, I guess we better head back." Athena gently pulled her hand away. "I wanted to try a woodworking class in Crafters' Corner. Maybe I'll make birdhouses for a living."

"Why not?" Calista teased. "Follow your dreams."

They packed up their picnic and took the golf cart back to Crafters' Corner. Calista imagined a future where this—spending time with her sister, laughing and sharing and just being together—was a regular occurrence.

But the moment they pulled up to the Lavender Lark, Calista understood they were already in trouble.

Cantu sat in a rocking chair on the wide veranda, sticking out like a corporate penguin at a luau, all crisp lines and polished shoes amid the B&B's whimsical charm.

"Oh, holy hole in one. Darth Vader is one step ahead of us." Calista put a restraining arm on Athena's shoulder.

Beside her, Athena froze statue-still, as if Cantu were a *T. rex* with movement-based vision. Around clenched teeth, she mumbled, "Lissy, I can't—"

Cantu was already gliding toward them, his face expressionless.

Here was the thing about having a narcissistic, near-billionaire father. He never just texted. No, Benjamin Dempsey's preferred method of ruining a perfectly good day was to dispatch his most loyal employee, complete with vintage chauffeur cap and crushing guilt, to deliver a gilded cream-colored envelope.

"Miss Athena," Cantu said, removing his cap with the solemnity of a man delivering last rites. "Your father requests your immediate return home."

Calista swallowed a laugh that tasted like battery acid. Of course he did. Heaven forbid Benjamin Dempsey go twenty-four whole hours without micromanaging someone's life into submission.

"Cantu?" Athena's voice held the kind of worry that ached in Calista's chest. "I thought Mateo needed you."

The man's gaze dropped to his polished shoes. "He did, but your father summoned me back to Dallas." The embossed, golden Dempsey crest on the envelope caught the late-morning light like a warning flare. "He instructed me to give you this."

Athena's hands shook as she accepted the envelope. Her fingers fumbled with the red wax seal, and it took her several attempts to open it and unfold the letter. Silently, she read the note and then passed it to Calista.

*Athena,*

*End this childish rebellion, now. Return home immediately. If you persist in this spectacle, I will be forced to reconsider Cantu's role as my chauffeur. His family's security rests in your hands. You have until the end of the day to make the correct decision, or Cantu will find himself standing in the unemployment line without a reference. Oh, and as for Mateo, I'll cut off your credit card that's funding his rehab.*

*—Benjamin Conrad Dempsey*

Calista wasn't sure what that last part about Mateo meant, but she met her sister's troubled gaze. Athena gnawed her bottom lip and knotted her fingers together. Gone was the competent golf pro and in her place was the anxiety-riddled eldest child always trying to keep the peace and make things right.

"This is what he does." Calista crumpled the paper in her fist as if doing so could crush its poison. "He finds the weakest point and presses until people collapse and bend to his will. You can fight back, Attie. You don't have to let him win."

But she already knew what Athena would do. It was written in her posture—the rigid shoulders, and the downward tilt of her chin. The stance of someone preparing to sacrifice themselves for the sake of others.

"He's bluffing," Calista said, her voice harsher now, trying to break through. "Cantu's worked for him for over two decades. No one else would put up with Benjamin's crap and he knows it."

"And if he's not bluffing?" Athena's voice cracked, the raw edge slicing the sea air. "What happens to Cantu? To his family? Am I supposed to gamble with their lives?"

"That's not your responsibility!" The words burst out of Calista before she could stop them. "You've spent your whole life letting him pull the strings. When does it stop?"

"When someone else doesn't have to pay the price for my insurrection!" Athena shot back.

And there it was. The truth that had shaped Athena's entire existence, laid bare between them like an exposed nerve.

"You've always had a choice," Calista whispered. "You just have to be brave enough now to make the one that's right for you."

For a moment, Athena's stony mask cracked, and doubt flashed over her face. Calista crossed her fingers. *Please.*

But then the moment was gone. Athena's expression hardened. "Like Mom's choice? The woman who let him take us away from her?"

Her words punched hard, and before Calista could respond, Athena turned toward the house.

Cantu lingered, his cap still clutched in his hands. His solemn gaze met hers. "I'm so sorry, Miss Calista."

"Me too," she murmured. "Me too."

# Chapter 19
## *Eloisa*

*"True freedom comes not just from breaking chains, but from discovering the strength within never to let them bind you again."*
—*Eloisa Hobby*

Eloisa Hobby believed in magic, but not the mystical kind found in dusty spell books or wand-waving theatrics.

Her practical magic was the stuff of everyday miracles. The perfect cup of tea on a rainy afternoon. The way a stranger's smile could brighten her whole day. Or how a well-timed pun could diffuse a tense situation. The magic of human connection, of finding joy in life's footnotes rather than headlines.

This belief in everyday enchantment was why she stood in her living room, attempting to juggle silk scarves. The scarves—marigold yellow, sea-foam green, lavender, purple—seemed determined to obey gravity rather than her will.

"Come on, Eloisa, if you can create an island paradise, you can do this."

But her heart wasn't in it this morning after Demetra's memorial service that Athena and Calista chose not to attend. She tossed the scarves higher, letting them float down like colorful rain. Her dear friend's last wish echoed in her head, a melancholy refrain that became the soundtrack to her days.

*Bring my daughters to your magical island. Please heal them, Eloisa. You're their only hope.*

The yellow scarf escaped and drifted to the floor. The other scarves followed suit, surrounding Eloisa in a sea of silk and sadness.

"Oh, Demetra." She bent to gather the scarves. "I'm trying, my friend. But your girls . . . they've got walls higher than Clare's hairstyle, and trust me, that's saying something."

She collected the slippery scarves, cool against her palm, and fretted uncharacteristically. Was she really the right person for this solemn task? Her own life was less a well-plotted novel and more of a choose-your-own-adventure book where half the pages were stuck together with jam. Who was she to guide two wounded souls toward healing?

But then she remembered Demetra's unwavering faith in her.

Her friend had seen something in Eloisa that she sometimes struggled to see in herself. A strength that went beyond her ability to ride a unicycle and knit at the same time, a wisdom that wasn't limited to knowing which ice cream paired best with ugly crying. (For the record, it was Chunky Monkey, although Rocky Road was certainly a contender.)

"All rightee, Universe. I hear you. No more juggling acts. Time to face the judge and jury. Or, in this case, two golf prodigies who seem to think 'fun' is a four-letter word. So intense, both of Demetra's girls, but each differently."

Eloisa folded the scarves and settled them into a special box she bought on her travels to Morocco. A frantic knock on her front door interrupted her. *Rap-rap-rap-rappity-rap.*

Hmm, something urgent afoot?

She opened the door to find Luna on her doorstep, holding her side and panting as if she'd run the entire way from the Lavender Lark. "We . . . you . . . problems."

"Come in, come in." Eloisa ushered her inside. "Now, slow down, catch your breath. Let's have a seat in the living room."

"No time." Luna gave her head a vigorous shake and clutched the doorframe like it was the only thing keeping her vertical. "It's Athena. Benjamin Dempsey's chauffeur showed up at the Lavender Lark. He's here to take her home!"

Eloisa's heart plummeted. "What? She can't leave now. We're so close to . . . well, I'm not entirely sure where, but I know we're close! It's that feeling when you're sure you've forgotten something but can't remember what. Except this forgotten thing might heal years of family trauma and fulfill a dying woman's last wish. So, you know, no pressure."

"Athena is in her room packing." Luna's words tumble out like a waterfall. "I tried to stall. I told her about our world-famous Sunday night bingo game—which we don't actually have, but I was improvising. Did you know I can name the capitals of all fifty states in alphabetical order while standing on one foot? Because apparently, I can, and Athena now knows this useless fact about me."

Oh goodness. These days, Eloisa rarely became flustered about anything, but she'd promised Demetra she'd set her daughters on the path to healing, and she couldn't accomplish her goal if one of them left the island. Not that she would try to hold anyone hostage, but it was time to deploy her persuasive powers.

"Here, dear." She placed a hand on Luna's shoulder and guided her to a comfy chair in the living room, where her calico rested on the plush, wide arm. "Sit down and rest with Felena. I'll handle this situation."

"What will you do?" Luna asked.

"Implement part of Demetra's plan a little sooner than expected." She hurried to a small wooden chest beside the fireplace, its surface covered in enough seashells and glitter to decorate a mermaid's boudoir. Demi and her girls had such fun when they'd made this box together on that long-ago visit. Kneeling, she drew in a deep breath to center herself before flipping back the lid.

"Are you sure?" Luna didn't sit in the chair with Felena as Eloisa instructed but instead came closer to peer over her shoulder.

"Desperate times." Eloisa raised a hand and waved like a beauty pageant hopeful, all swivel and thrust. "Desperate measures. Ahh, here we go."

She unclasped the leather strap, pushed open the box, and looked down at journals, letters, scrapbooks, cards, and gifts, all addressed to either Athena, Calista, or both, most of them stamped with RETURN TO SENDER in red ink.

With her tongue pressed to the roof of her mouth, Eloisa removed a scrapbook with a letter inside addressed to Athena. In her hands rested the weight of years—of secrets kept, of love unexpressed, of a mother's desperate hope for her children.

Eloisa's mind churned a whirlwind of conflicting thoughts. Was this right? Was she about to cross a line that couldn't be uncrossed? Or was she coloring outside the lines in a way that mattered?

"Oh, botheration," she muttered, borrowing one of Dot's pet phrases. "What would Demetra do?"

But she knew the answer. Demetra would move heaven and earth for her girls, and now it was up to Eloisa to do the same, even if moving heaven and earth felt a lot like trying to parallel park a tank while blindfolded.

Eloisa turned to Luna. "I need you to do something for me."

"What do you need?" Luna said. "Anything. I mean, except skydiving. Or eating cilantro. Or—"

"Luna, focus. I need you to gather everyone. Dot, Vivian, Clare, Paul, Orion, Artie—the whole Hobby Island gang—and tell them . . ." Eloisa paused, savoring the moment like the last bite of a yummy cheese slice. "It's time for Operation Prodigal Daughters."

Luna's eyes widened, her face lighting up like she discovered the secret to turning water into wine. "You mean . . . ?"

"Yes." Eloisa nodded. "It's time to bring out the big guns."

"On it!" Luna took off to complete her tasks.

"Well, Demetra," Eloisa said to the empty room, "here goes nothing. Or everything. Possibly both. Your girls are about to get a crackerjack course in Hobby Island magic, whether they like it or not. Let's just hope they're better students than I was in my brief stint as a fire-eating apprentice."

Clutching the scrapbook to her chest, she strode from her cottage, her azure maxi skirt swishing around her ankles in a way that she thought looked dramatic and purposeful.

Her heart pounded with equal parts terror and exhilaration, a feeling she associated with trying new hair colors or experimenting with fusion cuisine, but this was neither. Far more was at stake here than a messed-up dye job or a ruined Swedish paella.

Eloisa did not like to think ill of anyone, but Benjamin Dempsey sorely tested her goodness. Gritting her teeth, she quickened her pace. The Lavender Lark loomed before her, its purple paint a royal beacon in the early-afternoon sun.

On the wide veranda, rocking gently in a wicker chair that had probably seen more drama than a soap opera marathon, sat Cantu. She hadn't laid eyes on him in twenty years, but she instantly recognized the long-suffering man who did Dempsey's dirty work.

She straightened her back and channeled her inner Joan of Arc.

"Good afternoon, Cantu." She kept her voice warm but firm, like a hug wrapped in barbed wire. "Lovely day for dirty deeds done dirt cheap, isn't it? Though I hear the traffic on the road to emotional rescue is terrible this time of year."

Cantu stood, removing his cap with all the gravitas of a man disarming a bomb. "Ms. Hobby," he said, his tone respectful but guarded. "I'm here on Mr. Dempsey's orders."

"Of course you are." Eloisa's kindness was unwavering, though it might have a slightly maniacal edge. "And I'm sure Mr. Dempsey would want his daughter to have all the information before deciding, wouldn't he? After all, nothing says 'I respect your autonomy' like sending a chauffeur to whisk you away from an island paradise."

Cantu lifted his shoulders and looked embarrassed.

Eloisa sailed past him and into the Lavender Lark. Outside Athena's room, Eloisa paused and cocked her head. She heard movement inside—the rustle of clothes, the zip of a suitcase, the sound of dreams packed away.

"Demetra . . ." She looked heavenward. "If you're out there, now would be a great time for some ghostly intervention. I'm talking full Swayze in *Ghost*. Although maybe skip the pottery wheel part. That might be a bit much."

She knocked on the door. "Athena? It's Eloisa. May I come in? I promise I'm not here to stage an intervention."

There was a pause, then Athena's voice, strained and distant like she was speaking from the bottom of the ocean. "It's open."

Eloisa entered to find Athena standing over an open suitcase, folding a golf shirt with military precision that would have made Marie Kondo weep with joy.

"I suppose you're here to convince me to stay," Athena said without looking up, her voice as crisp as her starched collar.

Eloisa moved farther into the room. "I'm here to give you something."

Athena narrowed her eyes in a look that said she suspected a trap. "What do you mean?"

Eloisa held out the scrapbook. "This was your mother's. I thought you might want to take it with you."

Athena's hands stilled over her suitcase, hovering like hummingbirds unsure where to land. For a moment, she looked younger, more vulnerable. Like the little girl who once chased after baby sea turtles heading for the sea. Then the mask of cool detachment slipped back into place, fitting as snugly as a new golf glove.

"Why now? Why didn't you give it to me when I first arrived? Was there a minimum stay requirement I had to meet first?"

Eloisa let out a soft sigh and sank onto the love seat by the window, feeling every one of her years and possibly a few she hadn't lived yet. "Your mother had a plan, Athena. She wanted you and Calista to have time to reconnect, to heal, before you learned the whole truth."

"The truth?" Athena's voice cracked slightly like fine china developing a hairline fracture. "What truth is that?"

"About what really happened all those years ago. About why she lost custody of you. About why she didn't try to contact you once you were grown." Eloisa patted the seat beside her. "Sit with me, please? I promise the seat isn't booby-trapped."

Athena hesitated, her body half turned toward her suitcase as if it might sprout wings and fly her to safety at any moment. However, curiosity, that eternal cat killer, won out. She perched next to Eloisa, her posture so rigid it made Eloisa's back ache.

She passed the scrapbook to Athena.

Athena hesitated, her hand hovering over the cover. Her fingers curled inward, then stretched out again, like she couldn't quite decide whether to touch it.

Eloisa watched her carefully, sensing the hesitation but not pushing. "Your mother wanted you to have this. There's a lot in here. Photos, mementos, legal documents . . . and a letter."

Athena's eyes widened. "A letter?"

"Yes. For you," Eloisa said. "She poured her heart into it, Athena. She wanted you to know everything."

Athena dropped her hand to her side. "Why now?" she asked, her voice barely above a whisper. "Why didn't she try harder when we were kids? Or later, when we were grown?"

"Because your father made sure she couldn't."

Athena's head snapped up, her face a mask of disbelief. "What are you talking about?"

"Benjamin threatened her," Eloisa said. "He said if she ever tried to contact you after you turned eighteen, he'd cut you off. No money, no connections. He used your financial security as leverage. She was terrified of what he might do to you."

Athena blinked against the tears misting her eyes. "No. He wouldn't . . . he couldn't . . ." Her voice faltered, as if saying the words aloud might make them true.

"He would and he did. He filed restraining orders to keep her away. He had a company scrub her name from the internet so you couldn't find her if you searched. He hired private investigators to monitor her. He even returned the cards, letters, and gifts she sent to you, every single one." Eloisa tapped the scrapbook. "The evidence is all in here. This is what she kept, hoping that one day you'd see the truth."

Athena pored over the scrapbook, turning pages quickly, her

breathing ragged, like she'd just run a marathon in stilettos. "No, no, this can't be true."

"I'm so sorry, Athena," Eloisa said. "But your mother wanted you to understand why she couldn't be there, even though she desperately wanted to be. She was trapped. It's a lot to process, but know your mother never stopped loving you. She wanted you to have the truth so you could free yourself of his control."

Athena set aside the scrapbook and stood. "Why should I believe any of this? For all I know, you and my mother cooked this up together. A convenient story to absolve her of guilt."

Eloisa remained calm and kept her voice steady. "You're right to be skeptical. You don't know me, and you barely knew your mother, but ask yourself this. What do I have to gain by lying to you? Why would your mother go to such lengths if it wasn't true?"

Athena turned away from Eloisa. For a long moment, she was silent, her shoulders shaking. "If this is true . . . if Daddy really did all this, then everything I've believed, everything I've worked for, it's all been a lie."

"Not everything," Eloisa said. "Your talent, your dedication, your achievements. Those are real. Now you can reshape your story, to decide for yourself who you want to be. Think of it as a midlife crisis, but instead of buying a sports car, you redefine your sense of self. Much more cost-effective, really."

Athena turned back to Eloisa. Her eyes were red-rimmed but clear. "I don't know if I can do that. I don't know who I am without golf, without Daddy's approval. It's like trying to imagine a fish without water."

Hope bloomed in Eloisa like a stubborn dandelion through concrete. "That's why you're here, Athena. That's why your mother wanted you and Calista to come to Hobby Island. To figure that out together."

Outside, a commotion erupted.

*Whew!* Right on time.

Eloisa parted the curtains, and together, they peered out to see a crowd gathering in the backyard below, led by Luna and Paul and the sweet strains of a ukulele, accompanied by a kazoo orchestra. People carried balloons and banners, wore funny hats and flower leis.

"What in the world?" Athena leaned out the window.

"That, my dear, is Hobby Island magic in action. Looks like the cavalry has arrived. And by cavalry, I mean a bunch of loving folks who believe that there's no problem so big a luau and some positivity can't cure it."

Athena turned to her, a mix of emotions playing across her face—confusion, anger, hope, and something that looked suspiciously like the beginnings of a smile.

"So," Eloisa said, holding out her hand. "What do you say? Are you ready to give Hobby Island—and yourself—a chance?"

"It's not that simple. My father—"

"Forget him. Do *you* want to stay?"

Athena looked at Eloisa's outstretched hand, and then back at the suitcase on her bed. "I—"

"Or you could just go back and live the life you've been living. It's not an awful life. Top of the LPGA, living in a mansion with your father . . ."

Outside, Paul's voice rose above the gentle strum of his ukulele, singing about second chances and island dreams. It was melancholy and fantastic all at once, a perfect encapsulation of Hobby Island itself.

Athena shook her head. "He'll take it out on Cantu. He's already threatened me with firing him. I've got to go."

"Why don't you let Cantu take care of himself? You're not responsible for your father's actions."

Athena took a deep breath. "This won't turn out well."

"Or it could be the best thing that ever happened, although granted, not without some potholes. There's a party raging in the backyard just waiting for you to attend. Or you can walk out the door and go back to the way things were. It's all up to you."

# Chapter 20

## *Athena*

*"In the quiet unraveling of past shadows, we find the strength to step into the light of our true selves."*

—*Eloisa Hobby*

The door clicked closed behind the eccentric senior citizen, leaving Athena staring out at the effervescent group dancing in the backyard to the sounds of their own music. They seemed so joyous.

A deep longing seeped into her bones. She was not the melancholy sort, that mood belonged to Calista, but the bittersweet moment was too strong to ignore. Dispirited, she sank back down on the love seat and reached for the scrapbook, the weight of it far heavier than it should have been.

Demetra's scrapbook.

The woman who had been little more than a ghost in her life, a name whispered in hushed tones when her father was out of earshot. A maelstrom of emotions swirled within Athena—curiosity, anger, fear, and a longing she buried so deep she almost forgot it existed.

The musty scent of old paper wafted up, carrying with it the weight of history. She shifted through it again, heart clutching as she took in the newspaper clippings, photos, mementos of her career achievements preserved on each page.

She saw a little girl, swinging a golf club in the backyard until her hands were raw and blistered. The memory, long buried under years of pressure and expectation, surfaced with startling clarity.

Athena could almost feel the weight of the club in her hands, the ache in her muscles as she practiced swing after swing, determined to live up to her father's vision of her. Her father's stern face appeared in her mind's eye, watching her from the patio. She remembered the mixture of fear and grit that drove her, the desperate need to keep him from looking at her the way he looked at Calista. With disgust and disdain.

The taste of salty tears in her mouth, Athena picked up the envelope, broke the red wax seal in the shape of a heart, and read the letter inside penned in her mother's handwriting.

Her gaze moved across the page, drinking in every word as if they were water droplets in a desert. Her mother's voice, one she had longed to hear for years, whispered from the pages.

Delving deeper into the letter, Athena felt the world around her fade away. The half-packed suitcase, the seahorse-decorated room receded into the background as her mother's words painted vivid pictures of a past she barely recalled.

*Dearest Athena,*

*It's raining today. The soft patter against the window reminds me of that April morning when you were five. You'd just lost your first tooth and were convinced the tooth fairy wouldn't find our house because of the storm. We sat on the porch swing, counting raindrops and lightning flashes, your small hand in mine.*

*I wish so badly I could go back to that moment. There's so much I need to tell you, but words feel inadequate. How do I explain years of absence in a single letter?*

*You were always quietly stubborn. Remember when you decided to learn French because you overheard your father say it was a beautiful language? You spent that entire summer with your nose in textbooks, emerging triumphant in August with a flawless "Bonjour, Papa. Comment allez-vous aujourd'hui?" The stunned look on his face—I'll never forget it.*

*I saw that same determination when you picked up your first golf club. Hours in the backyard, day after day, until your swing was perfect. I'd watch from the kitchen, hands deep in dishwater, marveling at your focus. You were so small then, all knobby knees and untamed curls, but there was a fierceness in you that both thrilled and terrified me.*

*Your father noticed too. "She's got the eye," he'd say. "Like me." But there was something else there, too—his expectations. Demands.*

*I should have said something then. Should have told you that you were already enough, golf skills or not. But because I was afraid of him, I stayed silent, and that silence grew between us like a wall.*

*Athena, being separated from you and Calista was the hardest thing I've ever gone through. Your father . . . well, it's complicated. He wasn't always the man you knew. When we met, he was charming, ambitious, full of dreams. But success changed him, or maybe it just revealed who he truly was all along.*

*The first time he hit me, you were at school. I told myself it was a mistake, that I should have watched my mouth, that it wouldn't happen again. I was wrong.*

*It got worse. I tried to hide it from you girls, but kids always know more than we think. Remember that night you crawled into my bed, your little arms wrapping around me? "It's okay, Mamá," you whispered. "I'll protect you." You were nine.*

*I need you to understand—I never wanted to leave you and Calista. That day I packed our bags I thought we were starting a new life together. I thought I was protecting you both. I didn't count on your father's influence, his ruthlessness. Depression had been my unwelcome companion for years, a shadow I tried to hide from you girls. But Benjamin knew. He used it against me, twisted it into a weapon in the courtroom.*

*"Unfit mother," they declared. Two words that shattered my world forever.*

*I fought for you, Athena. With everything I had. But your father's money spoke louder than my love. In the end, all I could do was watch as he drove away with you and Calista in that limo. You were looking back at me, confusion and fear in your eyes. That image haunts me still. I've spent every day since then trying to get back to you, to explain. Your father's restraining orders, his legal threats, they've kept me at arm's length, but they never stopped me from loving you. He told me if I contacted you, he'd ruin your future and cut you off financially. I couldn't risk it, Athena. Not even when you were grown. Not when it meant jeopardizing the life you were building.*

*From afar I watched you, collecting pieces of your life. Every golf tournament win, every achievement. I'm so proud of you, Athena. Not because of your trophies or your grades, but because of who you are.*

*A strong, competent woman.*

*I know things with Calista are strained. You two were always oil and water, but there's a bond there, deeper than you might realize. She needs you, Athena. And I think you might need her too.*

*You are my brave, beautiful girl. I know the strength that runs in your veins. Trust that strength. Trust yourself.*

*It's okay to change direction. It's okay to choose a path that's uniquely yours, even if it's not what your father—or anyone else—expects.*

*You are loved, Athena. Completely and without conditions. Whatever you decide, wherever you go, hold on to that truth.*

*With my undying love, Mamá*

Athena's tears fell freely now, dotting the paper, smearing the ink. All these years, she had harbored a quiet resentment toward her mother for not trying to get them back. The realization that her mother had been watching from afar—collecting these mementos, following her journey—shook Athena to her core.

Her mind spun with her endless pursuit of perfection, the missed opportunities for fun and friendship, the longing looks at a casual world she felt she couldn't be part of—it was all there, laid bare in her mother's words.

She put a hand to her mouth, stifling a sob. How had her mother seen so clearly what Athena herself had barely acknowledged? The constant pressure, the fear of disappointing her father, the relentless drive for perfection—it had all come at a cost she was only now beginning to understand. She had spent so long trying to be perfect, to meet her father's impossibly high standards, that she had lost sight of who she truly was. The idea that she could be enough, just as she was, seemed revolutionary.

For several long moments, Athena sat in silence, the letter clutched to her chest. Tears streamed down her face, but she made no move to wipe them away. The perfect, composed facade she had maintained for so long cracked and fell away, leaving her raw and vulnerable.

She looked up, her gaze falling on the open suitcase.

For the first time, she allowed herself to really feel the pain of her mother's absence, the weight of her father's expectations, the love for her sister she had never fully expressed.

With shaky hands, she picked up the scrapbook and flipped again through the pages. Each clipping, each photo, each memento was a piece of the puzzle of her life viewed through her mother's loving eyes. Studying the carefully preserved memories, Athena felt a shift within herself. The need for perfection, the fear of failure that drove her for so long, loosened their grip. In their place, a new resolve formed, a determination not to be perfect, but to be authentic.

Athena took a deep breath, feeling as if she was truly filling her lungs for the first time in years, left her room, and walked out the front door to speak with Cantu.

# Chapter 21
## *Calista*

*"In releasing the grip of the past, we can fully embrace the future."*
—*Eloisa Hobby*

Unable to bear the thought of her sister returning to their father's clutches, Calista had left Cantu on the veranda and fled the Lavender Lark for the sanctuary of the chapel.

Inside the building packed with island flowers, desperate for solace, she sank to her knees in front of her mother's portrait, inhaling a scent cocktail, two parts beach vacation, one part Demetra's favorite perfume. The wooden floor bit into her knees, but hey, what was a little physical discomfort compared to the emotional trapeze act she had been performing since disembarking on Marshmallow Landing?

Okay, yes, sarcasm helped her deal with her grief. Healthy or unhealthy? She didn't know. She looked up and met her dead mother's smiling gaze. In the photograph, Demetra had so much love in her eyes Calista's heart skipped and sputtered.

"Hey, Mamá." From habit, her fingers went to her throat, searching for the locket that once provided so much comfort, but it was now gone. Lost at sea.

Tears misted her eyes. Calista cleared her throat, pressed her palms together in front of her heart, and tried again. "So, um, I don't know whether you're up there listening or I'm just audition-ing for the role of Crazy Chapel Chick, but I could use some motherly advice."

She paused, half expecting a beam of divine light or a talking seagull to swoop in with literal pearls of wisdom. It *could* happen, given the wacky nature of this place.

"Okay, I get it. You're just listening for now."

Wisecracking in a somber situation? Another defense mecha-nism. Dang, how many of them did she have?

"I am so sorry about Athena. I tried. Honest, I did. But Ben-jamin sent Cantu after her, and she jumped sky-high the way she always does when he snaps his fingers, and I . . . I don't know what to do. How do I make her stay? Or should I leave her be and hope she finds her way back to me?" Bitterness over-whelmed her then. "I mean, because that worked out so well for you, right?"

Okay, enough of that. The comment wasn't fair. Calista knew nothing about her mother's situation. A pang of shame and regret punched her in the chest. *Be less judgmental, okay.*

"Sorry, that was uncalled for. I just . . . I can't lose her again, Mamá. Not when we're finally starting to connect. It's like we've been playing emotional Marco Polo for years, and we've both just now got our heads above water at the same time." Calista closed her eyes, the weight of everything pressing down on her. "And then there's Reid."

The floorboards creaked and she snapped her eyes open, peer-ing into her mother's loving gaze. "I know you never met the guy, but we used to caddie together when we were kids. Also, he's the one who told me about Benjamin betting a million bucks on me to beat Athena at Chevron. Because of Reid, I found the courage to walk away. Well, him and seeing you in the gallery that day."

Calista inhaled, diving into the past again, but this time, she recognized it as a paper bag of regret with no way out except to push her way through the bottom of the sack.

"He broke my heart into more pieces than a thousand-piece jigsaw puzzle. Well, surprise! He's here for your memorial golf tourney, and he told me he still cares about me, and I just . . . How am I supposed to trust that? He hurt me so badly, and now he's here, disrupting my peace, making me feel things I thought I buried a long time ago."

She paused, waiting for what she did not know. "Mamá, here's the thing. I still care about him too!"

From the bell tower, the sound of movement drifted down into the chapel and then a voice, male and a little shaky, said, "Cal?"

Startled, Calista jumped to her feet and slapped a palm over her heart. Oh dear heavens, was Reid in the bell tower? She cocked her head and looked up.

*Reid.*

Peering down at her through the opening of the bell well, sporting a grin that should be illegal in at least twenty states.

Breathless and scared that she got caught admitting she had feelings for him, Calista fell back on humor. Defense mechanism number three.

"What are you doing up there? Auditioning for Quasimodo?"

"Meditating, actually," he said, smooth and glib. "Though eavesdropping on your soliloquy is a bonus. Wanna join me? The sunset's incredible from up here."

Calista hesitated, torn between embarrassed flight and the magnetic pull of Reid.

"C'mon, Calico," he coaxed, using the extra-special nickname that made her heart do the cha-cha and her defenses shoot up faster than her father's disapproval. "When's the last time you watched a sunset from a bell tower?"

"I've never watched a sunset from a bell tower."

"Well, here's your once-in-a-lifetime chance."

"Not unless it comes with commemorative T-shirts and liability waivers." But even as the quip left her lips, Calista moved toward the staircase to the left of the altar. Her legs made an executive decision and overruled logic.

Her footsteps echoed on the stone steps, and Calista couldn't shake the sensation she was ascending into another world. One where she might find some answers or at least a good enough view to distract her from the three-ring circus of her life. She took the stairs slowly, favoring her ankle, which was still a little dicey.

"So," she said, desperate to fill the silence of the stairwell. "You meditate now? That's unexpected."

Reid's laughter echoed down, hitting her squarely in the chest where her heart used to be before she'd locked it away in a vault labeled "Do Not Open: Contains Feelings and Other Dangerous Substances."

"People can change, Cal. Give me a chance to prove it."

She reached the landing and stopped to gape. The view knocked the breath right out of her, replacing oxygen with pure awe. The masterpiece of a sky would make Bob Ross jubilant, all "happy little clouds" set ablaze by the setting sun. The island stretched below, a patchwork of greens and colorful rooftops that led to the dark blue ocean shimmering in the distance.

But it wasn't just the view that overwhelmed her. Rather, it was sight of Reid Thornton sitting on a cushion in lotus pose, his hands resting on his thighs, palms upturned, index fingers touching thumbs.

"Wow," she said.

"Breathtaking, huh?"

"I'm stunned." Calista stared at his face, which possessed a peaceful sheen. Okay, so she was jealous. "You really are meditating."

"You seem shocked."

"I never would have pegged you for a Zen kind of guy."

"Zazen, actually."

She crinkled her nose. "Huh?"

"It's the style of meditation I trained in. Zazen."

"Um, okay. So you're a Buddhist now?"

"You don't have to be Buddhist to meditate. Join me."

Hey, why not. She sank beside him on the stone floor, cross-legged, and a quiet hush fell over them, the soft wind and gentle ocean waves a lullaby. Heat radiated off his body along with his familiar scent and salty sea air.

Suddenly, Calista was sixteen again. Same fluttery butterflies. Same floaty hope. Same surging chemistry. Except now, with added baggage and a healthy dose of cynicism.

"So," Reid said as the sun sank below the horizon and the lights of Crafters' Corner flickered on. "Wanna tell me what's really going on? Or should we pretend we're just two old friends enjoying a sunset, ignoring the elephant in the bell tower wearing a 'We Have Fraught History' T-shirt?"

"Er, I don't even know where to start. It's like trying to untangle Christmas decorations, except instead of garlands, it's my feelings, and instead of Christmas, it's a lifetime of daddy issues, motherly absence, and sisterly estrangement." Yikes, was she really going *there*?

"How about we start with the easiest thing first."

She turned to look at him. He was so close, mere inches from her, and she noticed how long his lashes were, how deep blue his eyes. "Which is?"

"Athena."

She eyed him.

He shrugged. "I overheard you and Athena with Cantu when I walked by the Lavender Lark on my way to the beach."

"Eavesdropped, you mean," Calista said, but there was no actual heat behind it, more a lukewarm attempt at maintaining her prickly exterior.

He grinned, unapologetic. "Potato, po-tah-to. The point is, I heard enough to know your father is yanking your sister's strings, and she's playing marionette."

"As always." Calista nodded. She fixed her gaze on the horizon where the last rays of sunlight dwindled. "Why am I so shocked she chose Benjamin?"

"Over you?" Reid turned on his cushion toward her, but she stayed looking straight ahead.

Calista swallowed hard and blinked back tears. Crying in front of Reid was *not* on her to-do list.

"Over herself, really. Athena was finally starting to break free, to see who she could be without his influence, and now, at the first sign of trouble, she just rolled over. It's like watching someone walk out of a prison cell only to see them turn right around and lock themselves back in."

"Maybe she's not giving up. Maybe she's just not ready yet. Change is scary, Calico. You know that better than anyone."

Calista turned to face him. They sat knee to knee. Shadows fell over his face as the sun slipped away. It was easier, talking in the dying light. "What do you mean?"

He gestured between them. "This. Us. That we're sitting here, having an amicable conversation after I blew up your world five years ago. That's change, Calista. Big, scary, 'oh god, what am I doing' change."

Calista's defenses rose, an instinctive reaction like a drawbridge closing, shoring up the castle, but instead of keeping invaders out, it tucked her feelings in. "Yeah, well, change isn't always good. Sometimes it's just another word for 'heartbreak waiting to happen.'"

The moment the words left her mouth, she regretted them.

Reid's face fell, hurt flashing across his features before he wrangled them back to neutral.

"Is that what you think this is? Just another heartbreak in the making?"

Calista opened her mouth, but no words came out. Truth? She didn't know what this was.

Part of her wanted to believe in second chances, in healing old wounds, while another part of her screamed, *Run!*

"I know nothing anymore. My life is messy."

Reid leaned closer, and it was like being pulled into the orbit of a handsome planet. "Everyone's life is messy, Cal. That's what makes it interesting."

She let out a shaky laugh. "Interesting? Is that what we're calling it now? Because from where I'm standing, it feels more like a tornado hit a train wreck."

Reid reached out to tuck a strand of hair behind her ear. His touch sent shivers down her spine. "Hey, it's okay, you know, not to have all the answers."

And the dam just broke.

Just cracked right in two and all the emotions Calista held back—fear, anger, loss—came crashing down at once Jenga-tower style. Tears spurted from her eyes, hot and fast, and a sob tore from her throat.

Reid's eyes widened. "Cal? Are you okay?"

"I-I can't keep doing this," she said, words muffled against her hands as she tried in vain to stem the flow. "I'm drowning."

Reid tugged her into his arms, and just like that, he was a safe harbor. Calista buried her face against his chest, inhaling his scent as years of pent-up emotions poured out. His hand rubbed soothing circles on her back.

"It's okay. Let it out. I'm here."

They sat there for what seemed like hours, Calista's sobs gradually subsiding into hiccups and sniffles. The sky turned deep purple and navy blue, the first stars twinkling above them, tiny beacons of hope in the vast darkness.

Calista pulled back. She must look a mess—red-eyed, tearstained, probably sporting mascara streaks that could double as a Halloween mask. But Reid peered at her as if she was the most beautiful thing he'd ever seen.

"Thank you." A whimper escaped her. "For being here."

"Always." The single word carried the weight of a thousand promises.

Maybe it was the lingering emotion, or the way starlight glinted off his eyes, or just the fact Calista was tired—so very tired—of fighting her feelings.

She kissed him.

Reid tightened his grip around her, pulling her as close as he could. The solid wall of his body stirred old memories and hopes for new ones. His lips moved against hers with a passion that matched her own, as if pouring five years of unspoken words and buried feelings into this one spectacular moment.

Calista tangled her fingers in the soft strands of his hair and deepened their kiss, desperate for more. She tasted the salt on his lips and breathed in the familiar scent of his cologne mixed with something uniquely Reid. Intoxicating and overwhelming in the best possible way.

The world around them faded away—the chapel, the island, the complications waiting outside the chapel doors—until there was nothing but this, the two of them *finally, finally, finally* giving in to the yearnings pulling them together.

When they broke apart, panting, Calista felt lighter than she had in years. The weight she'd been carrying for so long—the pain of their past, the fear of the future—lifted.

"Wow." Reid rested his forehead against Calista's.

"Yeah, I agree."

They peered into each other's eyes, the world beyond their cozy bell tower fading into the background, but as the initial rush of their kiss receded, reality crept back in—the doubts, the questions, the complications were all still there waiting.

"Reid," Calista said. "I'm tired of hurting. I'm tired of being afraid. I just want to feel good. Can you . . . can we . . . go back to your cottage?"

He pulled back, his eyes searching hers. "Are you sure? I don't want you to regret anything."

Calista nodded, more confident than she'd been about anything in a long time. "I'm sure. I need this. I need *you*."

Hand in hand, they made their way down the winding stone staircase. Each step felt like a countdown, a thrumming anticipation building between them for the night ahead. They pushed open the heavy chapel doors, ready to slip away into the night.

A wall of sound hit them. Music, laughter, and the unmistakable rhythm of a street party pulsed through the air.

"What in the world?" Calista squinted into the exuberant chaos that had overtaken Crafters' Corner while they got lost in their little world.

In the streets, people played musical instruments and danced, fairy lights strung between buildings like a web of stars brought down to Earth, and there, in the center of it all, leading a conga line that snaked through the village, was Athena.

"Is that your sister?" Reid asked. "I thought she left the island with your father's chauffeur."

Indeed.

Calista's jaw dropped because, yes, there was her sister, hips swaying, arms raised in triumph as she led the conga line, and right behind her, looking simultaneously uncomfortable and oddly pleased with himself, congaed Cantu.

"What is happening right now?" she whispered.

Before she could process the bizarre scene, Athena sighted them, and her face lit up with a grin equal parts mischievousness and glee.

"Lissy! Reid!" she shouted over the music. "Come join us!"

Pulled into the conga line, swept up in the infectious energy of the crowd, Calista found herself sandwiched between Reid and Clare, who'd teased her hair exceptionally high today.

Shimmying their way through Crafters' Corner, the back of the line met the front, and she passed Athena.

Her sister winked and mouthed, *I stayed!*

Joy exploded inside Calista like a whacked piñata. Not only had Athena stayed, but somehow, through what Calista assumed was some kind of island magic, she'd gotten Cantu to hang around as well.

The humid night air kissed Calista's skin as the music thrummed through her veins. Reid's hands were steady on her hips as they moved together and Calista felt truly, deliriously happy.

Minutes later, the conga line showing no signs of stopping, Calista tilted her head back to look at Reid. He grinned down at her, his eyes crinkled with laughter, his hair mussed from their bell tower rendezvous, and she was struck by how she'd missed him.

"So," she said, raising her voice to be heard over the music, "I guess your place is gonna have to wait?"

"I'm in no rush. Let's relish our reunion." He leaned forward and pressed his mouth to her ear and whispered, "We've got all the time in the world, Calico."

# Chapter 22

## *Athena*

*"Sometimes, the greatest act of love is letting go of the story you thought you knew."*

—*Eloisa Hobby*

*Sunday, June 28*

Three weeks had passed since Cantu returned to Benjamin and told him Athena wasn't coming back, and her world hadn't crumbled.

*Yet.*

Her father's silence hung in the air like the scent of an approaching thunderstorm—electric, unsettling, impending. Athena tried not to dwell on it but wondered if each day of quiet brought her closer to a storm.

Or if her father had finally decided to let her go.

Ha!

Despite their fears, she and her sister settled into a comfortable routine on Hobby Island, and it quelled her anxiety a bit. In the morning's cool, Athena and Calista worked with Paul, Reid, and eager volunteers on the memorial garden, laying the stones for the labyrinth and gardening.

In the afternoons, she and Calista got to know each other

all over again as they visited various attractions around the island, taking in Prism Pavilion, the butterfly hatchery, and Old Turtles Grotto and hiking Opportunity Ridge. They attended gatherings—joining the quilting circle one night, the knitting club another, and cross-stitch a third. They participated in an author event at the bookstore and took painting classes at the art store. Reid often joined them for meals and events, and later in the evenings, he and Calista would go off together, leaving Athena to pal around with Dot, Vivian, Luna, Clare, or Eloisa.

She noticed how Calista's eyes lit up whenever Reid appeared, but when she asked what was going on, her sister simply shrugged and smiled shyly. "We're taking things slow and just having fun."

Athena was happy for her sister but prayed she didn't get hurt. Reid had broken Calista's heart twice, and she didn't fully trust the guy. But since it was none of her business, she kept her opinion to herself. Who was she to comment on anyone's love life? She'd been too busy rising to the top of the LPGA to have any relationship more profound than a hot summer fling.

On this Sunday morning, exactly three weeks after Cantu left the island, Athena's anxiety honed its teeth on her bones. Today would have been their mother's fifty-eighth birthday if she'd lived, and Calista had planned a private celebration with just the two of them.

Before the B&B guests stirred, they headed out in the dark, climbing Opportunity Ridge to watch the sunrise and share stories of Demetra. As the sun broke the horizon in a spectacular display, they caught sight of the ferry chugging toward the island with shopworkers arriving from Everly.

Afterward, Calista suggested they walk to the beach and build a sandcastle to wish Demetra a happy heavenly birthday. As they mounded sand and shared stories, they laughed together and then cried.

Through the mist of tears, they released flowers they'd brought with them into the ocean and watched them slowly drift away on the tide. They hugged and sobbed and, in the catharsis, found a gentle peace.

But despite their lovely communion, Athena couldn't stop fretting about her father. "Three weeks of radio silence and I keep waiting for the other Gucci loafer to drop. It's unlike him not to retaliate when he feels wronged. I can't help feeling he's planning something Machiavellian."

"Dad's living rent free in your head," Calista said. "Can't you let him go, at least for today?"

"I'm trying, but it's not working. I feel like he's pouting and plotting his revenge."

"Ah, yes, the Benjamin Dempsey Blackout. The silent treatment. His favorite weapon of choice when throwing money at a problem doesn't work. Guaranteed to make you grovel if you believe his dark moods are your fault."

"I've never been on the receiving end of Dad's cold shoulder before," Athena said. "It's unsettling."

Calista quirked a sardonic grin. "Welcome to the dark side, darling."

Athena smiled despite her fears. The father she knew didn't give up, he just changed tactics, and he'd taught her to do the same. His silence wasn't surrender. It was reconnaissance.

"You know . . ." Athena said. "Part of me wishes he'd just blow up already so we can move on."

"And miss out on all this delightful friction?" Calista winked. "Where's your sense of drama?"

Athena snorted, but she felt a spark of something new. Not quite confidence, but possibility. For the first time, she was the author of her own story, not just a character in her father's narrative. Let Benjamin plot and scheme. Athena spent her entire life as a perfectly polished chess piece. Now? She was ready to flip the board.

But, what a challenge!

"Was this what it was like when you left?" Athena asked. "Were you this scared?"

"Attie, I was terrified. I intentionally lost him one million dollars."

From farther up the beach, a lone figure approached. A solo shadow backlit by a pinky-orange horizon behind the interloper.

"It's Reid!" Calista broke out in a wide grin and went running toward him.

Great. She'd wanted Calista all to herself and now she had to share her with him. She watched as Reid flung his arms wide and Calista launched herself into them. He spun her around, and they both threw their heads back, laughing.

Petty jealousy bit into her. Had her sister somehow gotten the manual on "How to Be a Normal Human Being" that she'd missed?

Reid set Calista down on the sand, and they wrapped their arms around each other's waist and came toward Athena. She waited, feeling irritated and jumpy, biting her lip and counting under her breath until they reached her.

"Hey, Athena," Reid said.

"What a coincidence. Here you are at the same time and place as us." She sent him a message with her eyes that said, *Mess with my little sister, buddy, and you're in for a world of pain.*

To his credit, Reid bobbed his head and met her gaze, steady and earnest. *Easy, big sister, I'm all in.* Athena narrowed her eyes. His trustworthiness remained to be proven.

"I walk the beach every morning," Reid said.

Hmm, that explained why Calista suggested heading to the beach after watching the sun come up. It had little to do with building a sandcastle in honor of Demetra's birthday and more a chance to run into Reid.

Calista smiled up at Reid and leaned her head against his shoulder. He drew her closer and grinned at Athena as if to say, *See, she forgave me.*

Yeah, well, Calista was far more forgiving than Athena and far less cutthroat. Probably why, while Lissy was the far better golfer, Athena was the one who came out on top.

*Either that or because you were Daddy's little sycophant.*

Okay, enough self-awareness for one day. Calista and Reid exchanged moony glances, and it was all Athena could do not to roll her eyes.

"I'm heading to the Lavender Lark to grab some breakfast before I head to the remembrance garden," Athena said. "You two enjoy yourselves."

"Oh!" Calista bounced on her toes. "We're coming too."

They walked back together, Athena slightly ahead, chin up, passing by the shuttered shops of Crafters' Corner, most of which wouldn't open until ten. She suspected Reid and Calista were sneaking kisses, but she didn't turn around to find out.

Athena sailed up the drive, an inexplicable tightness in her belly, but she stopped short at the hubbub on the veranda. Icy fear clutched her. Was it him? Had Benjamin arrived to drag her back home?

But no. It was Cantu and his wife, Julia, and son, Mateo; they were walking up the front steps carrying suitcases, followed by Artie and Orion, their arms stacked high with packing boxes.

"What's up?" Calista asked, coming to join Athena on the lawn.

"I don't know, but I intend to find out." She practically flew up the front steps, Calista and Reid at her heels.

Inside, Luna greeted Cantu, Julia, and Mateo at the reception desk.

Before Athena could ask what they were doing here, Eloisa emerged from behind the double French doors that opened out onto the backyard patio. Today, the island owner radiated sheer joy in a sunshine-yellow dress with a pleated accordion skirt, white espadrilles, and a white-and-yellow-striped cartwheel hat adorned with fresh daisies.

"Cantu," Athena said, her voice coming out strangely high. It looked so odd seeing her father's longtime employee without his chauffeur's cap and uniform. "Why are you and your family here? It looks like you are moving in."

"My dear girl." Eloisa giggled and clapped her hands. "They are! Meet the newest residents of Hobby Island!"

"Wh-what?" Confused, Athena shook her head.

Cantu's grin grew as wide as Eloisa's. He settled one arm around both Julia's and Mateo's shoulders and drew his wife and his son closer as they gave shy smiles of their own. "Thanks to you, I was free to leave your father's employment."

Athena stared at him open-mouthed. "I don't understand."

"I fulfilled my promise to your mother." Cantu's smile faded.

"What promise to our mother?" Calista scowled. "What are you talking about?"

"It is a long story." Cantu shifted his gaze to Eloisa. "Is now the time to tell it?"

"Absolutely!" Eloisa waved toward the backyard. "Over a meal. Brunch awaits!"

Brunch? The word felt wrong in Athena's mouth, like biting into something sour when she expected sweet. What was going on here? The smell of coffee and cinnamon wafted over her, at odds with the acid churning in her stomach.

"Come, come, everyone." Eloisa beckoned them forward.

The group followed Eloisa, who adroitly walked backward with both arms thrown wide in enthusiastic welcome.

The backyard space of the Lavender Lark lay transformed. A long table stretched before them, draped in white linen that gently stirred in the morning breeze. Matching straight-backed chairs issued an invitation—*come sit*. Wildflowers spilled from mason jars, with lavender sprigs peeking between the blooms. The air smelled of freshly mown grass and ripe peaches from the nearby fruit trees. The scents wafting from the laden table hit Athena next—rich coffee, yeasty bread, peppered bacon. For a moment, Athena was eight years old again, padding into the kitchen on tiptoe, drawn by the promise of her mother's special French toast.

She blinked hard, forcing the memory away. No time for ghosts.

"Eloisa," Calista asked. "What is all this?"

"A welcome for Cantu, Julia, and Mateo." Eloisa's eyes held sage wisdom. "And a time to reveal an old secret."

*Secret?* Athena frowned and bit her bottom lip. "What secret?"

"First, let's gather and share this lovely meal and the story will unfurl at its own pace."

"This is stunning," Calista said. "Absolutely beautiful, but I feel underdressed in shorts and a tee. Should I run upstairs and change?"

"Absolutely not. You look lovely just as you are." Eloisa waved them all to sit down.

It felt odd to be sitting down to a meal with Cantu and his wife and son, but good in the best possible way.

Eloisa settled at the head of the table. Paul near the foot, manning the French press and passing cups of hot coffee down the line. Luna sat to her husband's right, with Artie and Orion to his left. Calista took the spot next to Eloisa, and Reid filled in the remaining chair between Calista and Artie, leaving Athena to ease down next to Cantu, Julia, and Mateo.

Pleasant small talk, light and frothy as seafoam, went around the table, but Athena couldn't concentrate. What secret was Eloisa about to reveal, and why were Cantu and his family moving to the island? Were the two things connected? They seemed to be.

She tried to wait an acceptable amount of time to let everyone get comfortable and enjoy their meal, but after fifteen minutes of idle chitchat and noshing, she couldn't stand it any longer. She turned to Cantu beside her.

"What happened with Daddy? Why are you moving to Hobby Island? What is going on?"

From across the table, Calista shot her a pointed look that said, *Chill, Attie,* but Athena simply could not.

Cantu glanced down the table at Eloisa, who nodded. Giving him permission? How was the island owner involved in all this?

Then Cantu turned toward Athena, readjusting the linen napkin in his lap and clearing his throat. "When you didn't come back with me, I realized I had completed my obligation to your mother. I handed in my resignation and called Eloisa to tell her we were ready for the last phase of Demetra's plan."

"Phase? Plan? What are you talking about?" Athena heard her voice rise high, losing control of her anxiety.

Cantu spared a look for Calista, who smiled at him kindly. He sucked in a deep breath and then exhaled slowly. "I should start from the beginning."

"Yes," Athena said. "Please do."

"Your mother and I grew up in foster care together. We were as close as siblings."

Athena stared at him, her brain struggling to keep up with the words. They hit her ears like foreign syllables she couldn't decipher. Demetra's childhood had always been a blank space in the family story that one no one bothered to fill in.

"Wh-what?" Athena stammered.

Cantu repeated himself.

Athena blinked, her mind skimming over the words. She shot a look at Calista, who shook her head, eyes wide. "We knew she grew up in foster care, but she never talked about it. We didn't know *you* were part of that."

Calista shook her head, her brow furrowed. "She always kept it vague. She mentioned once she was in the system but didn't go into details. She said it wasn't important."

"It *was* important," Cantu murmured and dropped his gaze to the table. "Her past shaped everything about her—who she was, the choices she made. She didn't want you girls to carry that burden."

Calista pressed her lips together, looking stricken. "That sounds like her."

Athena's stomach twisted, guilt mingling with insatiable curiosity. "So you were in foster care together? What else didn't we know?"

He paused to take a sip of water. "Demetra's mother died in childbirth, and no one knew who her father was. She went into foster care as an infant. I arrived later when I was five after a carjacker killed my parents in a police chase."

"God, how awful for you both." Calista put a palm to her mouth.

Reid slid his arm around Calista's waist.

The air seemed to thicken around the table. Athena felt a dull ache in her chest as Cantu's words settled over her. She clenched her hands in her lap. "I'm so sorry."

"Don't feel sad. It was a good home, a safe home," Cantu said. "The couple who took us in loved us like their own. Demetra and

I stayed there together until we graduated from high school. We were the best of friends, Demi and I." His voice took on a dreamy quality.

Julia reached for her husband's hand, running her thumb along his knuckles to comfort him.

Athena startled, realizing Cantu was grieving Demetra as surely as everyone else on Hobby Island. Cantu wasn't just a messenger. He had loved her mother too. She pleated her linen napkin, unsure what to say or do.

No one spoke. Only the trill of a mockingbird from the peach trees rippled the silence. Athena's heart felt too heavy for her chest. Oh, Mom! What she must have gone through.

Calista broke the silence. "And after high school? Did you stay in touch?"

He nodded. "Demi got a scholarship to the University of Texas, and I went into the army. We didn't see each other for those long years, but we kept in touch with letters and occasional phone calls. When I left the military, I met Julia, and we married." He patted his wife's hand and gave her a soft smile. "In the meantime, Demetra met Benjamin when she was hired on as a communications coordinator for the PGA. He swept her off her feet, and she thought she'd found the love of her life."

Athena tightened her jaw at the mention of her father. Her mind reeled at the thought of her mother, young and full of hope, falling for the man who'd become a controlling tyrant.

"Thought she'd found the love of her life," Athena echoed, hearing the bitterness in her voice. She exchanged glances with her sister. How did Calista feel about all this?

"Julia and I fell on hard times. I won't go into our financial struggles, but when Demetra heard about our plight, she persuaded Benjamin to hire me as his chauffeur. His previous driver had just quit, and I was so grateful to have such a high-paying job, even if Benjamin was a demanding boss." Cantu looked from Athena to Calista and back again.

How had she not known that Cantu and her mother were so close? Had her father known?

"Why didn't she just leave him then?" Athena asked.

"Your mother didn't always see her own worth. She carried the scars of her childhood with her, no matter how much she tried to hide them. It made it hard for her to believe she deserved better. Benjamin exploited her vulnerability."

Athena's chest tightened, her guilt twisting with a new ache. *She stayed for me, but she also stayed because she thought she had no other choice.*

Memories rushed to the surface—her mother's subdued smiles, the quiet way she'd retreat during Benjamin's outbursts, the looks she gave her daughters that seemed to hold a thousand unspoken words. Each recollection shifted, taking on new meaning, reframed by the truth Athena had only just begun to uncover.

"She truly believed—or convinced herself—that having you would calm Benjamin down." Cantu's voice sagged heavy with sorrow. "She had seen enough children from broken homes in foster care to know how hard it was. She hoped that starting a family might bring out the better parts of him, that being a father might soften his edges."

"So Dad never knew about your past with Mamá?" Calista asked.

"No. Your mother feared he'd use our relationship as a tool for manipulation. Threatening to fire me to get her to comply with whatever he might want her to do. And she was right. He would have."

It made sense, but it hurt to think of Demetra forced into a life of secrets and lies. But it wasn't just Demetra. How many times had Athena lied and hid things to keep peace with her father? Far too many to count.

"After the divorce," Cantu went on, "after your father took you away from her and got legal custody, Demetra begged me to stay, to watch over you girls, to be her eyes and ears when she couldn't be there herself."

The revelation hit Athena like a badly shanked drive, leaving her off-balance and struggling for solid ground. Every car ride, every quiet moment, Cantu had been silently observing and reporting back to her mother. Did he tell Demetra about the times Athena had cried after losing a tournament? Or when she'd confided her doubts to Cantu about following in her father's footsteps?

"All those years," Calista said, "she kept in touch with us through you."

Cantu nodded, his face carved with the pain of over thirty years of silence and secrets kept. "When you left golf, Calista, I almost quit then." He shifted his gaze back to Athena. "But I couldn't leave your sister alone with him, unguarded and unprotected."

"And then, when Demetra died, you were set free," Athena said.

"No. Although it was kind of your mother to leave this B&B to me and Julia, so we would have a place to call our own for all my years of loyal service, I didn't feel free to leave until *you* decided not to return to your father." Cantu's gaze locked on Athena.

"But I thought the Lavender Lark belonged to Paul and Luna," Calista said.

"No." Luna shook her head with a kind smile. "We were just temporarily running the place for Demetra until Cantu, Julia, and Mateo could make their way to Hobby Island."

Athena jumped to her feet, her chair scraping against the flagstone. She needed to be alone. Needed space to process this bombshell.

"Dear?" Eloisa asked, concern twined through her voice. "Are you all right?"

Athena didn't respond. She couldn't. She simply walked away from the table and the people gathered around it, knowing she could not stay there one second longer.

# Chapter 23
## *Calista*

*"Some truths are only revealed when we're capable of facing them."*
—*Eloisa Hobby*

"Athena," Calista called, rising to her feet.

Eloisa reached across the table to touch her arm. "Let your sister have some time alone, my dear."

Calista hesitated, torn between the urge to follow Athena and the spiral of her own spinning thoughts. She sat back down stiffly, the chair creaking under her. The silence that followed felt charged, unspoken truths hanging heavier than any words.

Cantu cleared his throat, drawing her attention. His caring gaze settled on her, steady and unflinching. "You've always been the one who needed to run."

She frowned. "What's that supposed to mean?"

Cantu's lips twitched as if suppressing a smile. "You were always searching for something—something that wasn't in your father's world. Your mother saw that, you know. She admired it."

Calista blinked, startled. "She did?"

"She told me you'd be the one to leave first. She hated how much her banishment hurt you, but she was proud of you for making your own choices. She said you had the courage she never had."

Calista stared down at her hands. She thought about all the times she'd felt untethered after leaving golf, the nights she'd doubted her choices, the times she tried to find her mother but didn't know how.

"I was so in awe of you when you walked away at Chevron," Cantu said. "You were magnificent."

"Oh, Cantu." The words came out on a sob.

Everyone fell silent, giving Calista space to collect herself.

"Fresh coffee?" Eloisa asked the group, bringing her back to the moment.

That seemed to break the spell of Athena's exit, and everyone went back to eating.

The food was excellent, but Calista barely tasted it, her mind wrapped around her sister. Calista remembered how unmoored she felt when she walked away from professional golf—adrift, alone, anguished—and her heart went out to her sister.

"You okay?" Reid leaned close, his voice low and comforting.

She bobbed her head, unable to speak.

"How can I support you?"

It was a touching question, and she appreciated he asked it. Over the past three weeks, a genuine friendship had bloomed between them again, echoing their closeness when they were teens.

A highlight reel played through her mind from this most extraordinary summer so far. On one early morning beach walk, Reid appointed himself Chief Crustacean Namer. He christened a grumpy-looking crab "Sir Pinchy McScuttles," and he narrated Pinchy's life story in an accent that was less "British aristocrat" and more "guy who once watched *Downton Abbey* while tipsy."

Calista laughed so hard she almost fell into a pool of sea urchins.

They took a basket weaving class together, a day that would

live in infamy (or at least in the instructor's nightmares). Reid's fingers, so nimble when it came to golf clubs or a keyboard, staged a rebellion against all things wicker. Watching the teacher untangle Reid for the third time, a look of utter bewilderment on his face, Calista wondered if it was possible to pull a muscle from giggling.

The night of the astronomy club meeting was a revelation, though not in the way their star guide wanted. Reid pointed out constellations that existed solely in the vast universe of his imagination. "Ah yes, there's the Great Cosmic Pineapple, locked in an eternal battle with the Celestial Hedge Trimmer. A tragic tale of forbidden love and improper pruning."

That set the entire group into gales of laughter.

He filled each day with joy, and each night ended with hot kisses that tasted of sea salt, sunscreen, and tropical fruit drinks, although they never went beyond kisses. They were both savoring this in-between space, this rediscovery of each other, and building trust before taking the leap into the point of no return.

Now peeking at Reid through half-lowered lashes, Calista felt a surge of affection.

He caught her eye and raised an eyebrow, waiting.

She shrugged, shy and nervous.

It hit her with all the subtlety of a coconut to the head. Somewhere between naming cranky crustaceans and butchering constellations, she'd gone and fallen in love with him all over again.

The thought should have terrified her and sent her running for the hills (or at least the nearest golf cart). Instead, she felt as if she finally got the punch line to a joke that the universe had spent years setting up.

God help her, she was in love with Reid Thornton.

*Again.*

Still. Whatever. English really needed a word for falling in love with someone you used to love but then didn't, but now do again, but in a new way that's also kind of like the old way but different.

Conversation fizzled. Dishes cleared. Calista's brain felt like an overcooked noodle, limp and useless under the weight of the morning's revelations. She locked eyes with Reid. His lips quirked. At that moment, she swore he could read minds.

"Well," Reid said, stretching lazily, "I think it's time for a joyride in one of those glorified lawn mowers they call golf carts. Calista? You in?"

Relief and gratitude hit her. "Yes, please."

They said their goodbyes. Cantu gave her a big hug and whispered, "Your mother is up there in heaven, her heart busting with love for you. Know that. Believe it."

Calista thanked everyone for their patience and understanding during the Dempsey drama. Eloisa promised to check on Athena and encouraged Calista to enjoy her day guilt-free.

"Appreciate the meal." Reid waved goodbye. His arm locked around Calista's waist in a way that made her feel special.

"Try not to scandalize the entire resort," Luna called after them, her sly smirk implying that mild scandal was, in fact, the recommended course of action.

Away from the shelter of backyard trees, the sun assaulted their eyes, and Calista pulled sunglasses from her purse. A fleet of flower-festooned golf carts awaited, looking like the unholy offspring of a country club and a florist's shop.

Gosh, but she loved this wacky place. Now she understood why her mother sought refuge here.

Reid swept his arm toward the carts with all the gravitas of a game show host. "Pick your poison, buttercup. We've got 'Midlife Crisis White' or 'Lawsuit-Waiting-to-Happen Green.'"

Calista snorted, surprised by how good it felt to laugh. "Surprise me. Just promise you won't name this one."

"You wound me." Reid clutched his chest dramatically. "Sir Wheelie McZoomZoom is deeply offended."

He helped her into the cart, his hand lingering a beat too long and Calista's heart flip-flopped. They pulled away from the Lavender Lark, the breeze whipping through Calista's hair. For a moment, she let herself believe that they could outrun their problems. The golf cart zipped along on the straight parts of the road, but the electric motor protested every incline, slowing to a chug. Reid, ever the knight in shining polo shirt, pretended he'd slowed down on purpose on a steep hill.

"You know . . ." Calista giggled. "When you suggested a joyride, I pictured something a little more . . . joyful. Less potential for death by golf cart."

Reid gasped in mock offense. "I'll have you know this is a top-of-the-line model. Zero to sixty in, well, never, but that's not the point."

"And the point would be?"

"Adventure, Calico. Living on the edge. Feeling the wind in your hair and the imminent threat of mechanical failure in your heart."

Calista snorted. "Truly, you are a poet for our times."

Laughing, they finally crested the hill, and the landscape opened up before them. So much green, stretching out before her like some fever dream of Irish fields crossbred with country club aspirations. Sand traps and water hazards stretched throughout pockets of trouble, waiting to ruin someone's day. The nine-hole golf course hosting the charity event in her mother's honor on the Fourth of July.

They'd been all over this island, but it was their first time coming here because she'd wanted to avoid it. Calista's heart did a weird little stutter step like it momentarily forgot how the whole beating thing worked.

Reid drove down the hill. No one was playing the course. They were totally alone. He killed the engine and turned to her.

"You okay?"

Calista nodded, not trusting her voice. She climbed from the cart on tentative legs, half expecting the ground to pull a magic trick and disappear from beneath her, but it was solid, real. The grass tickled her ankles through her sandals, a gentle reminder that this wasn't some elaborate hallucination brought on by brunch mimosas.

"It's a beautiful little course." He came to stand beside her, his shoulder brushing hers. The warm point of contact anchored her.

The breeze ruffled their hair and carried the scent of freshly mown grass and the sound of the distant ocean. A humid dampness hung in the air despite the sunny skies. Calista scanned the course. It *was* beautiful. Painful. Perfect. Everything she ran from.

"Yeah, it really is."

"Wanna inspect it?" Reid gestured toward the first hole.

Did she? Maybe not, but if she decided to play in the charity tournament, smart money said to scope out the course before the competition.

"Okay."

They walked the first fairway, side by side, step by step.

In the distance, a faint haze crept in from the shoreline, barely noticeable against the bright sky. Her fingers twitched, muscle memory kicking in. She hadn't swung a club in years, but it all came rushing back—the weight of the iron in her hands, the satisfying *thwack* of a well-struck ball, the thrill of watching her Titleist soar toward the hole.

"Bet you wish we had clubs right now, huh?" Reid nudged her shoulder gently.

Calista snorted, the sound caught somewhere between amusement and disdain. "Please. I'd wipe the green with you, and you know it."

"Big talk from someone who's been out of the game for five years. For all I know, you've forgotten which end of the club to hold."

"Hey, I saw that mangy golf set you brought. You're at a serious disadvantage. And golf is like riding a bike, only with more opportunities to humiliate yourself in hideous plaid. I never forget how to crush dreams and look good doing it."

He laughed. "Touché."

They reached the first green, and Calista found herself reading the slope, calculating the break. Old habits die hard. Or they just went into hibernation, waiting for the right moment to pop up and remind you of who you used to be.

At the fourth hole, they took in the view. The ocean stretched out before them, waves crashing against the cliffs. A thin veil of mist clung to the water's surface, slowly inching its way toward land. She felt both small and expansive beyond measure.

Together, they gazed out at the water, letting the peace of the moment wash over them. Calista stole a glance at Reid's profile. The faint lines at the corners of his eyes crinkled when he smiled, softening his features and lightening her heart.

"So, Reid . . ."

"Yeah?" He turned to face her, that endearing quirk pulling up the corners of his full, angular mouth. A mouth she thoroughly enjoyed kissing.

"Why did you *really* come to Hobby Island?" she asked. "And don't say you're here just to vlog the tournament. If that were the case, you'd have arrived right before the Fourth like everyone else."

His step faltered.

She stopped and turned back. "Reid?"

When he spoke, his voice was neutral, the verbal equivalent of beige paint. "Oh, you know. Right place, right time. I needed a break from the rat race."

"Uh-huh." Calista wasn't buying it. If this were poker, Reid would be broke and owing his shirt to the house.

Reid's laugh was too loud, too forced, like a sitcom laugh track played at the wrong moment. "Look at this bunker! Isn't it something? The way the sand just sits there. Really makes you think about the fragility of human achievement in the face of nature's sandy wrath."

"C'mon, what's really going on here?" she asked. "Why did you come to Hobby Island so early?"

His expression sobered. "Because I wanted to make amends. I've regretted what I told you five years ago at Chevron at the most important moment of your career."

"That's it?"

"And I . . ." He paused, his gaze finding hers. "I missed you."

"Nothing more? No clandestine reasons?"

Reid looked at her for a long moment, distress in his eyes mingled with something else she couldn't pinpoint. "It's complicated. There's a lot of history here, a lot of things aren't what they seem."

Calista felt a chill run down her spine. It was cooler up here than down in the valley, but the shiver wasn't just about the temperature. "You're freaking me out. Is something wrong? Is it about my family? Because I've got to tell you, if there's a secret sibling or a long-lost uncle waiting in the wings, I'm gonna need a flowchart to keep track."

A sudden breeze swept across the course, carrying with it the first tendrils of a thickening mist, giving the course a mystical feel. "I promise everything will make sense soon. Just trust me on this, okay?"

The plea in his voice tugged at Calista. Something else *was* going on, but he was asking her to trust him.

The question was, should she?

# Chapter 24
## *Athena*

*"A caged bird thinks flying is an illness."*

—*Eloisa Hobby*

Desperate to understand her mother, Athena headed to the Hobby Island chapel while everyone else was enjoying Eloisa's brunch, but when she arrived, the propped-open doors invited a string of well-dressed churchgoers inside.

Oh yeah, it was Sunday, wasn't it?

She peered around the shoulders of attendees and scanned the front of the church where her mother's urn and portrait had sat for the past three weeks. But now they were gone. A hollow feeling settled into her stomach. Nothing for her here. Now what?

Return to the Lavender Lark and the welcome party for Cantu and his family? Ugh. That was a heavy lift.

She could go to the service, but she felt too restless for a sermon. Perhaps she'd just wander around Crafters' Corner.

Yet even that distraction soon rankled. The tourists who skipped worship service for a leisurely Sunday morning seemed off-the-chain happy—eating ice cream cones and saltwater taffy, taking selfies in front of the mermaid fountain, strolling hand in hand, carrying umbrellas and tote bags to the beach. A group of laughing middle-aged women knitted and sipped coffee at an outdoor café. On the beach, a flock of teens played volleyball while a troupe of square dancers commandeered the quad.

Far too cheerful for her melancholy mood.

She thought about ducking into a hobby shop, but nothing appealed to her. What was the point of a hobby anyway besides killing time? She honestly didn't get the purpose, but everyone on this island seemed over the moon thrilled, pursuing a craft simply for the fun of it. Why couldn't she do that?

Why? Because she'd spent thirty-one years honing her golf game, never sparing a moment to develop any other aspects of herself. She'd been single-minded and dedicated, but now she saw how unwise she'd been to close herself to everything but whacking a little white ball toward a faraway hole with a stick.

*You're lopsided, Dempsey.*

Okay, so that was the thing about earth-shattering revelations. They really should come with a warning label. Something like "Caution: Your entire worldview is about to be flipped upside down and shaken like a maraca."

But life didn't work that way.

Instead, Athena got the "Your mom's foster brother has been secretly watching over you for years" bomb, and the cherry on top of this revelation sundae? Demetra owned the Lavender Lark and gifted it to Cantu for his decades of loyal service to her daughters.

Not that she resented Cantu and his family their inheritance. Far from it. She didn't need a garish purple Victorian on a far-flung island. She was rich as all get-out. It was just the whole thing came out of nowhere.

All this startling information hung over her like an approaching thunderstorm—electric, unsettling, ominous. The calm before Hurricane Benjamin churned to Category Five force gales, and Athena couldn't shake the feeling that she was standing on the beach with nothing but a golf umbrella and a sand wedge for protection.

Any second now, she half expected to see her father's private jet streaking across the sky, ready to rain down guilt trips and ultimatums. Or worse, a lawsuit over the memorial garden and charity golf tournament, because heaven forbid anyone remember Demetra Sarris without her ex-husband's express written consent and a hefty licensing fee.

Hyperbole granted but not as far-fetched as it might sound. Benjamin was notoriously litigious.

Athena's mind raced faster than a golf cart barreling down a steep grade with no brakes. How many times had Cantu stood by, watching Benjamin push her beyond her limits? How often had he wanted to intervene but held back, knowing that open defiance would only result in his removal from her life? It was like finding out your favorite caddie had been an undercover CIA agent all along.

Memories flooded in, taking on new meaning.

The time when she was twelve, sitting in the back of the limo, exhausted from a tournament she'd lost, and Cantu had "accidentally" taken a wrong turn, giving her an extra fifteen minutes of much-needed composure time before facing her father.

Or when she was sixteen and Cantu had appeared with Icy Hot and ibuprofen for shoulder bursitis right before a big tournament, saving her from having to admit weakness to her father.

And just last year, when she went on a crying jag after a punishing practice session, and Cantu "forgot" to hit record on the camera, sparing her from Benjamin's scathing analysis.

Each memory was a breadcrumb, leading back to a truth. Demetra had been looking out for her daughters through Cantu. She couldn't be there for them, but she'd tried her best.

Grief tears clogged Athena's throat, but she battled back with flippant thoughts. Welcome to her life, where family secrets came out swinging and emotional baggage was always over the weight limit. Buckle up.

Athena snorted, earning a concerned look from a seagull pecking at a half-eaten cinnamon roll on the ground outside Breaking Bread. Great, even the wildlife thought she was cuckoo.

She needed peace, quiet, and possibly a lobotomy. The chapel had been her go-to spot for a bit of me time, but now?

Athena caught sight of her reflection in store windows. She hardly recognized herself. She'd stopped bothering to iron her hair somewhere over the past three weeks, and the humidity created a riot of curls fluffing around her face. She couldn't help but feel like she was starring in her own personal *Truman Show*. Any minute now, her father would appear, director's megaphone in hand, ready to yell "Cut!" and drag her back to the perfectly scripted world of professional golf.

"Get it together," she mumbled, earning the side-eye from a passing tourist. "You're not exactly blending in with the island vibe here."

Desperate to hide, she ducked into A New Chapter. Books. Yeah, she'd never been much of a reader, which was more Calista's bailiwick, but books seemed safe enough. Far safer than people and conversations.

The bookstore smelled like paper, ink, and poor life choices—although maybe that last one was just Athena. She disappeared into the stacks, trailing her fingers along the book spines, the tactile sensation grounding her. "Self-help, self-help, where are you? Help me help myself before I start a new career as a beachcomber."

And then, she found it.

The book she hadn't known she was searching for. *It's Not You: Identifying and Healing from Narcissistic People*. Well, if that wasn't a neon sign from the cosmos, Athena didn't know what was.

She cracked open the book and started reading, and suddenly *everything* made sense. There, in black and white, was her life story. Hmm, according to the author, a renowned expert on the topic, narcissists often use their children as extensions of themselves. They might appear supportive, even loving, but their affection was conditional on the child's performance. Their world was entirely transactional.

Well, slap her with a nine iron and call her Tiger Woods. If this book were any more on the nose, it'd be a pair of reading glasses.

All those years of strict training schedules, controlled diets, and limited social interactions—it was like her father had been following some twisted *How to Raise a Golfing Prodigy/Emotional Hostage* manual.

Calista tried to tell her, but Athena had made excuses and enabled her father's behavior. No wonder Calista had cut off ties with her as well when she left. Athena had been too enmeshed in the trauma bond to be a safe enough person for her sister.

Guilt grabbed her and gave her a good hard shake. She needed this book like she needed oxygen. Or an excellent therapist. Or a time machine to go back and hug the child she'd been. Clutching her newfound lifeline, Athena approached the counter.

The cashier smiled and said in a voice warm enough to toast marshmallows, "Find everything okay?"

Athena nodded, not trusting herself to speak without word-vomiting her life saga and handed over her credit card.

The cashier swiped the card. Frowned. Swiped again.

Athena's stomach dropped.

"I'm so sorry," the cashier said, her face a master class in sympathetic wincing. "It seems the bank declined your card."

"That can't be right. Could you try again?"

The woman tried again. "Perhaps you've been hacked, and your credit card company put a lock on this account. Do you have another way to pay?"

"Sure." Athena pulled out another card.

Declined.

"Try this one."

Card after card, all rejected. With each failed attempt, Athena's anxiety strengthened as a line formed behind her. She could hear the impatient huffs and feel the eye rolls burning into her back. Great, she was "that person" holding up the line. Add it to her list of achievements, right under most-likely-to-have-an-existential-crisis-in-a-bookstore.

"I don't understand," Athena said, more to herself than to the saintlike cashier.

"Perhaps you've been a victim of identity theft. Banks have really upped their fraud alert policies."

"But how? For the past three weeks, I've been on this island and—"

*Unless* . . .

Her father was playing financial hardball. His name was on her banking accounts. Had been since he opened them in her name when she was a minor. Calista had warned her, but she'd never imagined her father would freeze her bank accounts and suspend her credit cards.

The cashier, bless her heart, offered Athena the store's landline phone to call the bank. She stood off to one side, letting the other customers go ahead of her. After navigating a detailed AI bot-propelled services menu, Athena reached a human at last. She explained her situation, trying to sound less like a deranged person and more like a responsible adult who definitely had control of her life. Thank you very much.

"Ms. Dempsey," the bank rep said, his voice so neutral he could have been announcing the weather or the apocalypse. "If you want to access funds, you'll need to speak to your father. He's the one who requested we restrict all your accounts. I can't unlock them without his permission."

But of course he did because why *wouldn't* her father have the ability to kneecap her finances from hundreds of miles away?

Athena hung up, feeling like she'd just gone ten rounds with reality and lost by knockout. She turned back to the cashier, her cheeks burning hotter than the surface of the sun.

"I'm so sorry," she said, wondering if it was possible to die of embarrassment. "There's been a mix-up with my accounts. I won't be able to buy the book today."

The cashier's eyes softened with understanding, usually reserved for lost puppies and people who accidentally reply all to company-wide emails. "Don't you worry about it, dear." She lowered her voice, leaned in, and gave a conspiratorial wink. "Why don't you take the book, anyway? You can come back and pay for it when you get things sorted."

Athena blinked, sure that she'd misheard. In her experience, kindness usually came with strings attached and a hefty price tag. "I couldn't possibly—"

"I insist," the cashier said, bagging the book. "Everyone needs a little help sometimes. Just pay it forward when you can, all right?"

Throat tighter than her father's grip on her life, Athena nodded. She took the bag, gave a heartfelt "thank you" she hoped conveyed "you've restored my faith in humanity" rather than

"I'm two seconds away from ugly crying in your store," and made a beeline for the exit.

Outside, the cheerful bustle of Hobby Island felt like a personal affront. She clutched her book lifeline, feeling simultaneously lighter and heavier than she had in years. For the first time in her life, she had no idea what came next. No tournament schedule, no training regimen, no carefully planned future laid out like the world's most boring connect-the-dots.

It was terrifying. It was exhilarating. It was . . . freedom?

Athena Dempsey, golf prodigy and cognitive dissonant contortionist extraordinaire, was officially off-script. Maybe that wasn't such a bad thing. How could she unravel? She was free for the first time, and she had a huge safety net. *Calista*. Her sister had navigated this same path before her.

# Chapter 25

## *Calista*

*"Sometimes, you just have to let down your guard and trust that everything will turn out all right."*

—*Eloisa Hobby*

Calista squinted, searching for the ninth green. While they'd been talking, and she'd been staring into Reid's gorgeous blue eyes, a rolling sea of gray fog crept over the golf course, the flag and fairway evaporating into the mist.

"Uh, Reid? Did we somehow stumble onto a horror movie set?"

He jumped and glanced around. "Whoa, it came in fast. Huh. Well, this is . . ."

"The word you're looking for is 'apocalyptic.' Or 'Stephen King–esque.' Take your pick."

"I was gonna say 'suboptimal,' but your version is much more descriptive, if a tad dramatic."

"Wow, flexing your vlogger vocabulary. They teach you the art of understatement in journalism school?"

He rolled his eyes but grinned. Ridiculous how one tiny quirk still made her stomach flip. Her internal organs needed a stern talking-to about questionable responses to ex-boyfriends turned bosom buddies.

Unnerved, Calista shifted her gaze to her feet, which were now invisible, as if someone left a haunted house fog machine pumping on high. "This island has the wackiest weather patterns."

"All part of the magic." He mimicked Eloisa's speaking style and sent his voice up a couple of octaves.

Calista giggled. "Well, if we don't move, we might find ourselves sucked into a time-traveling portal and wind up in the Scottish Highlands in 1707."

"If I could time-travel, I would go back in time and change the way I treated you," he said, all levity leaving his face as mist curled around his jaw.

"We can discuss that later."

The fog kept rolling in, billowing clouds swallowing the landscape whole. Visibility dropped from "some squinting required" to "legally blind" in the span of a heartbeat. Yikes!

"It feels as if we're inside a giant cotton ball."

"Let's hump it." He reached for her hand.

They set off in the direction of what she hoped was the golf cart. The fog was so thick now Reid was little more than a shadow beside her. Every part of her was damp: her socks, her clothes, her hair.

"We're headed away from the cliffs, right?" she asked.

"Um, I think so, but don't hold me to it. I'm sightless as a mole."

Calista snorted. "We're in slasher film territory."

Reid's laugh cut through the shroud, warm and rich as sunlight. "That's my Calico, always the optimist. Inspiring, in a twisted way."

"It's a gift," she said.

He tightened his grip, understanding that she needed that extra reassurance, and she exhaled a relieved sigh.

"Whose brilliant idea was this adventure?" he asked. "Because I have a bone to pick about their decision-making skills."

"You need a mirror? Although, I suppose that's useless in this miasma."

"Um, if I'm not mistaken, you agreed to this quest."

"Remind me never to listen to Past Calista again. The woman is an idiot with delusions of grandeur and a questionable grasp on meteorology."

"I don't agree . . ." His voice took on a provocative quality. "I kind of like the woman."

A dark shape loomed from the mist.

Alarmed, she let out a yelp, dropped his hand, slapped her palm across her mouth, and stumbled back. She crashed into Reid's solid chest, and his arms wrapped around her waist.

"It's okay," he murmured against her ear. "Just a jacaranda tree. No worries. I got you."

"Right, of course, I was just testing your Johnny-on-the-spot reflexes. Gold star for you, Thornton. Your knight-in-shining-armor skills are top-notch."

"Sure, Cal. Whatever helps you sleep at night. You can admit your fear. No judgment. I won't laugh, and I promise your reputation for unflappable coolness is safe with me. Vault lock. Cone of silence. I won't tell a single soul the fearless Calista Dempsey trembled in the face of . . . shrubbery."

"Not scared, startled. Major difference."

"Uh-huh, and the difference is a few letters and a lot of stubborn pride."

She opened her mouth to retort, to deny, but something in his tone gave her pause. His voice held a gentleness, a touching undercurrent of affection. She gulped, grateful for the fog hiding her expression. "Should we keep moving?"

"Absolutely."

They set off again, holding hands once more. Calista told herself the hand-holding was for navigation purposes and had nothing to do with how each touch skittered sparks across her skin or how his familiar palo santo scent urged her to bury her face against his neck and inhale for days.

After what felt like an eternity of plodding through the gray pea soup, Reid halted.

"Another tree?" she asked.

"No, I think I spy . . . Yes! The golf cart!"

"Oh, thank heavens, salvation!"

They edged nearer, and Reid helped her onto the passenger side before bumping his way to the driver's seat. "A blindfold would improve my vision at this point."

"Is it safe to drive?"

"Safe is not the word I'd use. I'll take it slow. Ready for the world's slowest, most terrifying joyride?"

"Teleport us out of here, Thornton, and I'll be forever grateful."

"How grateful?" Although his face lay shadowed in mystery, she swore he quirked a cocky eyebrow.

"We'll talk about it later." She hedged to cover up her galloping pulse. Since that day in the bell tower, she'd longed to take him to bed, but he insisted she needed time to trust him fully. "Let's go to your place. It's miles closer than Crafters' Corner, and we're far less likely to maim anyone on the way."

"Your wish is my command, Princess."

The electric motor whirred to life, and they inched into the murk. Grunting, Reid leaned forward as if, by sheer willpower, he might part the fog.

Holding her breath, Calista strained to see the path ahead. She couldn't visualize it, but the tires bumped across the cobblestones. At least they were still on the road. They crawled along at a snail's pace, the silence broken only by their tense breathing.

A shape loomed from the gloom, and he jerked to a stop.

Calista's stomach vaulted into her throat, visions of trees or boulders or cartoon-style TNT crates flashing through her mind.

"It's just a bench," he said. "We must be near the ninth tee box."

"Terrific, so we know where we are, but no idea where we're going."

"My house is down the road about half a mile."

"Lead on, Columbus."

They set off again, this time with Calista leaning out, scanning for any sign of his lodgings. The mist thickened as they dipped down the incline. Had they somehow driven off the end of the world and floated in some weird golf cart purgatory? After an interminable amount of time, she spotted something.

"Hey, it's the fig tree." The fig her mother planted and nurtured so long ago. It stood as a marker for Calista, her touchstone. *Thanks, Mamá.*

Reid's cottage was where her mother lived when she first moved to Hobby Island after the divorce. Calista's stomach tightened, and she blinked back tears. Not that Reid would have noticed. Moisture soaked her face, and she could barely see him anyway.

More details emerged as they drove closer—a porch, windows, the vague outline of a roof. Relief flooded Calista's body as Reid pulled up close to the cottage and killed the engine. For a moment, they sat without speaking, the magnitude of their narrow escape settling over them.

With a sharp exhale, he flopped back, winded from the ordeal. "Well, that wasn't quite as harrowing as the Mermaid Cove storm, but it was close."

"Wow. That was scary." She pressed her palm to her forehead.

"C'mon, I'm soggy as a wet cracker. Let's get inside."

He got out and waited for her to scoot across the seat to join him. He took her arm, guided her up the steps to the front door, keyed the lock, and the door creaked open like an intro to a B-grade horror movie, which, given their fog-drenched adventure, felt appropriate. In the foyer, they shook water from their hair and clothes.

"Thank you for getting us here safely." She met his gaze.

His eyes softened as he took her in. "I can't take credit. My instincts kicked in, and my brain shifted to autopilot. I guess all those years caddying for Gavin paid off."

"Speaking of Gavin, how is he? I remember how kind he always was to me."

The light in Reid's eyes dimmed, and he shifted his weight from one foot to the other, looking uncomfortable. Instead of answering, he said, "Would you like to shower after our cloud walk? I can loan you a change of clothes, and we'll pop your things into the dryer."

Why did he avoid her question? Did he and Gavin have a falling-out? She'd tried bringing up Gavin before, and he'd cut her off then too. Okay, if it was a touchy subject, she'd back off, but would it cause a problem when Gavin arrived for the tournament?

*Not your problem, Dempsey. You have enough baggage of your own to tote.*

"Sure, a shower sounds blissful, but what about you?" she asked.

"There's two bathrooms. Hang on. I'll get you something to wear." He disappeared down the hall, and before Calista had time to feel weird about being there, he returned with a T-shirt and drawstring sweatpants.

"My hero," she said, only half joking as she took the clothes and squished down the hallway, leaving a trail of damp footprints behind her.

In the bathroom, she turned on the shower and let the water

heat while she undressed. A sudden image of Reid in the other bathroom, stripping down just as she was, popped into her mind. She pushed that thought aside, along with the flutter in her stomach. Steam filled the small space, and she stepped under the spray, the hot water absolute heaven on her chilled skin.

Lathering up with the new bar of soap she found on the counter, she battled not to think about Reid lathering up on the other side of the cottage. The fog was thick outside, and Crafters' Corner was miles away. Too dangerous to drive that far in this inclement weather. What if she spent the night?

A hot thrill raced through her at the thought. She'd been longing for the man's body for three weeks now. Craving him, really.

But he'd hurt her twice . . . badly. Was she honestly willing to risk her heart to him again? Right now, her body didn't give a good damn about her heart.

Calista finished showering, got out, and dried off with a towel fluffier than it had any right to be (seriously, where did Eloisa get her guest linens?). Unfolding the clothes Reid gave her, she slipped into the size large hunter-green T-shirt that proclaimed "I'd hit that" above a picture of a golf ball, and a pair of the softest gray flannel sweatpants she'd ever put on and cinched the drawstring tight to keep them from slipping down her hips.

The clothes smelled of laundry detergent and fabric softener, and the scent shot her back to the locker room where they made love for the first time on a pile of clean towels. The memory was so vivid she could almost feel the warmth of Reid's skin against hers.

Calista gulped down the lump in her throat. Now was not the time for a nostalgic breakdown. She had an ex-boyfriend-turned-maybe-something-else to face without getting misty-eyed over laundry detergent.

She borrowed the hair dryer she found in the cabinet and dried her hair, running her fingers through the damp strands. The familiar routine helped ground her, giving her a moment to collect her thoughts and steel herself. In the kitchen, she found Reid dressed in clothes similar to hers, his hair still damp as he assembled a charcuterie board.

"I'm impressed with your well-stocked larder since this is just your vacation rental," she said, watching him. "Why'd you buy all this food?"

"Since this is an employee cottage and too far from Crafters' Corner for me to pop over for takeout, I picked up cured meats and cheeses at the Chef's Chop in town because they don't go bad quickly. I've also got . . ." He pointed at the variety he'd arranged on the tray. "Fat green pimento-stuffed Spanish olives, deep purple Greek Kalamatas, black French Niçoises. Almonds, cornichons, dried figs, apricots, cherries—"

"Got any condiments or gourmet dipping sauces?"

"Mais oui, mademoiselle," he said with an exaggerated accent meant to be French, but he sounded more like a congested Pepé Le Pew. He produced a variety of condiment packets with a flourish. "We have your classic ketchup, your bold barbecue, Lebanese tahini, and for the truly adventurous, spicy honey Dijon. Four kinds of crackers and bagel and pita chips."

Calista laughed, charmed. Okay, Reid was a fun guy. Always had been. That meant nothing beyond right now, but she wasn't looking for happily ever after. All she wanted was a good time and maybe a sweet stroll down memory lane. He might not have been her most accomplished lover, not at sixteen anyway, but hands down, he'd been the most entertaining.

"Wanna eat at the table or the bar?" he asked.

"The bar is fine."

He set the charcuterie tray on the counter as she eased down on the barstool. "What'll you have to drink?"

"Whatya got?"

"Water, coffee, and a bottle of Merlot that was in the welcome basket . . ."

"What are you waiting for? Crack that bad boy open," she said. "We have a lot to celebrate. We survived an epic-level blackout fog."

He opened the wine and tippled a generous pour into two glasses, then came to sit at the bar beside her. They fell into a comfortable silence as they ate. The only sounds were the crunch of meats and cheese-laden crackers meeting their demise.

"Feeling better after our misadventure?" His eyes crinkled with amusement, and oh, that was dangerous.

"What do you mean misadventure? People would pay good money to see that fog in a haunted house."

His smile encompassed his entire face. That cheery grin made her want to do ridiculous things like compose sonnets about the ocean blue of his eyes. "You roll with the punches, Cal. It's one of the things I love most about you."

"Yes, well." Stunned by his use of the word *love*, she aimed for a supercasual tone. The cool girl. "Someone has to balance out your gung ho 'let's go golf carting in pea soup fog' energy."

His expression softened, turning serious in a way that made Calista suck in her breath. "I'm glad it was you."

"Huh?"

"That I was with you. If I had to become one with the mist, there's no one I'd rather do it with."

Dirty pool! How was she supposed to maintain her carefully constructed walls when he said sweet things like that, looking at her like she was the answer to a question he'd been asking his whole life?

"Reid . . ." She paused, unsure what she would say but feeling the need to say something. Anything to break the tension that sprung up between them.

But before she could plan a response that didn't include incoherent sputtering or, god forbid, blunt honesty, Reid leaned in. Slowly, giving her time to pull away if she wanted. As if there was a universe in which Calista Dempsey would not want to kiss Reid Thornton.

Their lips met in a kiss that started soft, hesitant like they were both afraid the other might disappear if they pressed too hard, but then Reid's hand came up to cup her cheek, and something inside Calista snapped.

She surged forward, deepening the kiss, years of longing and missed opportunities and what-ifs pouring into it. Reid responded in kind, his other hand entwined in her hair as he pulled her closer.

They fell off their stools and into each other's arms, a tangle of limbs and half-whispered endearments. Somehow, Calista's hands found their way under Reid's shirt, relearning the planes of his back, the dip of his spine. Every touch felt like homecoming and embarking on a grand journey all at once.

Reid pulled back slightly, his eyes dark and serious. "Cal," he said, voice husky in a way that did dangerous things to Calista's insides, "there's something I need to tell you before we—"

"*Shh*, no talking," she said, fearing conversation would kill the mood. She wanted him *now*!

Reid looked as if he wanted to protest, but she kissed him again, and whatever he'd been about to say was lost in a groan that she felt more than heard. After a shower of fiery kisses, she pulled back, panting.

"Protection?"

"I bought a box of condoms after that day in the bell tower."

"Why did it take you so long to tell me that?" she asked but didn't wait for an answer. "Never mind. Let's go."

Somehow, they made it to the bedroom, shedding clothes along the way like a very intimate breadcrumb trail. But at the door, fear wrapped icy fingers around her neck, and Calista wrenched away from him, unable to meet his gaze. There she stood in her bra and panties, fully exposed. She'd let her guard down with him before . . .

"Hey," Reid said, his voice so soft she could barely hear him. "Seriously, if you're not ready, you're not ready. I want you more than I can breathe, but this is too good to screw up. I'll wait for you forever if you ask me to."

Her hand rested on the doorknob. Her heart thundered. She wanted this—god, did she want this! But years of keeping people at arm's length set her fingers to trembling.

"Cal?"

At last, she lifted her head and met his concerned eyes. He was in nothing but boxer briefs, just as exposed as she was. "I want this. I want *you*. I'm just . . ."

He arched an eyebrow. "Scared?"

She nodded, swallowing hard. "Terrified, actually. Letting people in isn't exactly my strong suit."

He stepped closer but didn't touch her. "My knees are knocking too. But, Cal, I think we're worth the risk."

Calista looked up at him, seeing her vulnerability reflected in his eyes, and took a deep breath. Eyes that said, *Trust me, I promise not to shatter you this time.*

He lowered his head, inch by inch, until he was in kissing distance again. She didn't move. Not one little bit. His breath warmed her skin, and he smelled of wine and cheese.

"Calico?"

That "ico" added to her nickname completely did her in. She grabbed his face with both palms and kissed him so hard he let out a groan. At the same time, she kicked wide open the bedroom door.

*Call Frito-Lay, baby, because she was letting those chips fall where they may.*

# Chapter 26
## *Athena*

*"In the mist of our illusions, truth chimes softly. Listen closely. It calls you home to yourself."*

—*Eloisa Hobby*

A thena paced from one end of Crafters' Corner to the other, head down, book clutched to her chest, muttering under her breath.

She'd spent the past two hours after fleeing the brunch reading *It's Not You* cover to cover, and her world came crashing down around her. Calista had been right all along. Benjamin was not a golf genius as he professed. He was not a good father because he applied strict discipline. He was not the perpetual victim of others; in fact, he was the perpetrator, bullying those around him.

All the ways he'd used to bind Athena to him raced through her head, thoughts speeding like a bullet train. The times he told her that she was the only one who truly "got" him. The way he would pull her aside to whisper in her ear, "You are the best part of me" or "No one is as good a golfer except for me." How whenever she won a tournament, he was there, putting his arm around her, taking command of the mike and the media, speaking for her. Never letting her have a say in her career.

Distressed, she started walking, no destination in mind, except to outwalk her mistakes and misbeliefs, but no matter how far or fast she went, she couldn't shake her demons.

And she'd been so bent on proving she deserved her father's praise, and staying on his good side, she hadn't noticed how he'd taken over her life.

He was controlling. He was grandiose. He was entitled. He was self-important. He could only be around people he deemed important or successful. He was exploitative. He was arrogant. He was jealous. He lacked empathy. He ticked off every box for a clinical diagnosis of narcissistic personality disorder, but the label didn't matter. What caused deep pain and suffering in all who came in contact with Benjamin Dempsey was his behavior. He put himself above others, and he didn't care about anyone but himself. Not even his children.

Especially not his children.

The excuses she'd made! Defending him to Calista.

*You don't understand Daddy. He's special, talented, the best.* In actuality Athena was the one who hadn't understood Benjamin.

*He has good qualities too; why are you so focused on his flaws? It's not like we're perfect.* But all Benjamin did was berate them for their flaws, and when he did praise them, it was to take credit for their achievements.

*He's just trying to make us better. Maybe his methods are skewed, but he means well.* Except no, he did not mean well. This was projection on Athena's part. Because *she* meant well, she assumed he did, too, but he did not. He looked out for number one. Always. Forever. No matter who he stomped on to get his way.

Oh dear, oh dear. She couldn't take a deep breath. Only the top part of her lungs functioned. Her head spun. She bumped into a jacaranda tree and apologized to it. Pain shot through her hip, but she didn't feel it. People stared at her. Shamed, she swallowed the feeling whole, and it settled into the silt of her stomach, in the murky depths of childhood trauma.

All this time, she'd felt sorry for Calista. How she'd gotten locked out in the cold of their father's affection. But now she saw the truth with the clarity of a microscope. Benjamin had never loved either of them. He simply did not have the capacity for love.

Bereft, shattered, Athena didn't notice the weather changing, the humid air mixing with a cold northern breeze and spreading a misty fog over the land, damp and blinding.

But instead of seeking shelter, Athena took refuge in the vapor. She was not a person to live in her imagination like Calista. Athena was sensible, grounded, focused.

Except not today.

Crossroads. Life's biggest intersection. If she kept on her current path she would always and forever be under her father's thumb. But if she left the endless freeway of achievement, where would she go? What would she do?

Calista had been so brave, breaking free, walking away. Athena didn't know if she was that strong.

The fog formed a thick cocoon around her. She welcomed the ethereal veil separating her from the world she knew. From the father whose love always came with conditions. From the sister she pushed away in her relentless pursuit of perfection, trying to please an unpleasable man.

How had she been so blind? How had she not seen the manipulation, the constant molding of her personality to fit her father's grand plans?

*You are the best part of me*, Benjamin told her, but what he meant was, *You are the best part of me because I made you in my image.*

Athena's breath hitched, a wretched noise ripping from her throat. She swallowed it down, a habit ingrained since childhood.

Dempseys didn't cry. Dempseys didn't show weakness. Dempseys were winners, *always*.

But what did winning mean when the game itself was rigged?

She stumbled forward, the mist clinging to her skin, seeping into her bones. She should have been scared. Instead, a wild freedom pulsed through her veins. Here, in this space between what was and what could be, she didn't have to be anyone's perfect anything.

A sound whispered at the edge of hearing, faint, melodic. Wind chimes in a gentle breeze. The soft tinkling tugged at something buried deep, some long-forgotten ache. Athena followed, drawn by its haunting call.

She pushed through a curtain of misty leaves. Their cool touch against her skin felt like absolution, or her mother's fingers brushing away childhood tears.

The fog that swallowed Athena whole began to lose its grip. At first, she thought she was imagining it—a trick of hope, of desperation. But no. The white wall around her was thinning, like cotton candy dissolving on the tongue.

Light seeped in, turning the mist into a living thing. It glowed from within, pearl white and opalescent. Wind swirled, sending the mist dancing. It twirled upward in gossamer ribbons, revealing the world in teasing glimpses. A patch of emerald moss, soft as velvet. A clutch of wildflowers, their petals still heavy with dew. Each revelation was a gift, a secret shared between the island and Athena.

As the last wisps of fog retreated, curling away from her ankles, Athena felt naked. Exposed. All her carefully constructed walls were vanishing with the mist, leaving her raw and achingly alive.

Then the world just fell away.

Before her stretched a clearing.

Athena sucked in her breath, stunned. Thousands of wind chimes hung from branches, a symphony of metal, wood, and glass. Athena stood rooted, her chest heaving.

The chimes' song swelled, wrapping around her like her sister's arms used to, before golf and expectations and the weight of being Benjamin Dempsey's daughters crushed the joy from their lives.

In the clearing's center stood an ancient oak, its trunk twisted with age and secrets. It drew her, inevitable as gravity. At its base, nestled between gnarled roots, lay a hollow. A transparent lid shimmered with otherworldliness.

What was this?

Athena knelt. She reached for the lid. Warmth bloomed up her arm and settled in her chest. It felt like her mother's hugs, before she left. Like Calista's hand in hers, before the gulf between them grew too wide to cross.

"What are you?" Athena lifted the lid.

Inside lay a journal, bourbon-colored leather soft with years of handling. It smelled of secrets and memories, of hopes poured onto the page and dreams long deferred.

Athena traced the tooled vines on the cover. How many others had sat here, bleeding their hearts onto these pages? How many had found the strength to change their lives?

She opened it.

The spine cracked softly, releasing the scent of old paper and something green, something alive. Her eyes skimmed entries from strangers. Their words touched something raw within her, creating a bridge to these unknown souls who had faced their own demons in this magical place.

Then—a familiar scrawl. Looping curves, a deep forward slant.

Calista's handwriting.

Athena's heart stuttered. Her sister's words, here? It seemed impossible. And yet . . . Hands trembling, she began to read.

*Sometimes, I dream I'm shaking Athena. My hands on her shoulders, my voice hoarse from screaming, "Can't you see what he's doing to you?" But she just stares at me with those blue eyes of hers, confused and hurt, like I'm the one betraying her.*

*God, Attie. He's turning you into his mirror, and you can't even see it. Every day, you become a little more him and a little less you.*

*I want to grab your hand and run. I want to pull you away from his poison, his twisted love that's not love at all. But I can't. I've learned that the hard way. You have to want to leave. You have to see the bars of the cage before you can break free.*

*So I wait. I hope. I pray to a God I'm not sure I believe in anymore that one day, you'll open your eyes. That you'll see the truth and find the courage to walk away. And when that day comes—if it comes—I'll be here. I don't care if we're forty or sixty or ancient and gray. I don't care if we've forgotten how to talk to each other, if we've become strangers who share nothing but a last name and a history of hurt.*

*I'll be here, Attie. Waiting. Ready to help you pick up the pieces and remember who you were before he got his hands on you.*

*I love you. Always have, always will. And I'm sorry. Sorry I couldn't shield you from him. Sorry I couldn't make you see. Sorry I left you behind.*

*But I'm not sorry for hoping. For believing that one day, we'll find each other again. That we'll sit on some porch somewhere, gray-haired and wrinkled, and laugh about how we escaped.*

*We'll be free then, Attie. Free of his shadow, his expectations, his crushing transactional version of love. And maybe, just maybe, we'll remember how to be sisters again.*

The words blurred. Athena blinked, and tears splashed onto the page. She pressed a hand to her mouth, trying to hold back the sob that threatened to tear her apart.

All this time, she'd thought Calista was the one who needed saving, but they'd both been drowning, hadn't they?

The wind chimes sang, giving voice to years of unspoken pain. Of longing. Athena wept. Deep, racking sobs that shook her entire body. She mourned for the relationship she and Calista should have had. For the childhood they'd both lost. For all the years wasted, trapped in their father's toxic web.

How had it come to this?

Memories flooded back, sharp-edged and painful. Calista, wild-haired and laughing, daring Athena to climb higher in that old backyard oak tree. Calista, eyes flashing with hurt and anger, screaming that their father didn't love them, he only loved what they could do for him. Calista, packing her bags, begging Athena to come with her.

And Athena, always Athena, choosing to stay. Choosing the familiar cage over the terrifying freedom her sister offered.

"I'm sorry," she whispered to the empty clearing. To the sister who wasn't there. "I'm so sorry, Lissy."

She stood on quivering legs. The wind whipped her hair, carrying the song of the chimes. It sounded different now. Mournful. Keening. A lament for all that had been lost. All that might never be reclaimed.

Drawn to the ocean, to the setting sun, she walked to the edge of the cliff and stared down at the churning water. For a moment, she imagined letting go. Letting the sea wash away the pain. The confusion. The suffocating weight of expectations she'd carried for so long.

Who would miss her, really? Her father, now that she was no longer his perfect puppet? Calista, who she'd hurt so deeply? The golfing world, which would surely move on to the next rising star?

One step. That's all it would take to end the pain.

A gust of wind tossed her forward. Athena pinwheeled her arms, teetering on the brink. Her heart leaped into her throat. In that moment of pure animal panic, she realized—she didn't want to die. She wanted to live. To make things right. To become the person—the sister—she should have been all along.

But as she scrambled backward, her foot caught on a root. She fell hard. The impact drove the air from her lungs.

Athena lay gasping. Tears streamed down her face, mingling with the damp grass. She was alive. Broken. Humiliated. Utterly alone. But alive.

As the adrenaline faded, leaving her shaky and nauseated, a new sound cut through the foggy air.

A rhythmic thudding, growing louder. Footsteps? No, too heavy. Too . . . alien. Athena pushed herself up on her elbows, squinting.

An ostrich, its long neck swaying as it loped toward her.

She blinked, certain she must be hallucinating. But the large bird—Shushu, the island's infamous rescue ostrich—was real. She stopped just a few feet away, regarding Athena with eyes that seemed far too knowing for a mere animal.

Athena stared back, feeling stripped bare under that steady gaze. She had lost everything. Her identity. Her purpose. Her sense of self.

A laugh bubbled up, half hysterical. This was rock bottom. This was her all-is-lost moment.

But as she looked into Shushu's eyes, a strange calm settled over her. The ostrich took a step closer, then lowered itself to the ground beside Athena.

An offer. A choice. She could stay here, wallowing in her pain and confusion. Or . . .

She reached out to touch Shushu's soft feathers.

"Okay," she said, pulling herself onto the ostrich's back. "Okay, let's go."

Shushu rose, surprisingly gently, and Athena made a silent vow. She would find out. Whatever it took. However long it took. She would discover who Athena Dempsey really was—beyond the golf prodigy, beyond her father's daughter.

Even if it broke her completely.

Even if it remade her entirely.

# Chapter 27

## *Calista*

*"Golf is a game of inches. Life, as it turns out, is measured in even smaller increments."*

—*Eloisa Hobby*

Calista stood in the bedroom doorway, frozen like a Popsicle in the Arctic. The bed loomed before her, a continent of crisp white sheets and fluffy duvet. Reid perched on the mattress, looking unfairly calm for someone about to sleep with his ex.

"Cal?" His voice was soft, careful, like approaching a skittish animal. Which, fair. "We don't have to—"

"No, I want to," she blurted. *Smooth, Dempsey. A+ for enthusiasm, F- for execution.* "It's just . . ."

"A lot?"

Calista nodded, grateful and frustrated in equal measure. Where had this fear sprung from? Ten minutes ago, she'd been ready to audition for the lead role in *Hobby Island After Dark*. Now she felt sixteen again, all sweaty palms and racing thoughts.

His eyes crinkled at the corners in a tender smile, and he patted the bed beside him. "Come here. I have an idea."

She arched an eyebrow. "If you're about to suggest a game of Monopoly as foreplay, I'm out."

Reid's laughter wrapped around Calista like a favorite sweater, warm and familiar. "No board games, promise. Just . . . trust me?"

And there it was.

The million-dollar question. Did she trust him? After everything—the years, the hurt, the misunderstandings that could fill a book titled *How to Screw Up Your Love Life Royally*—could she put her heart in Reid's hands again?

The answer, terrifying in its simplicity, was *yes*.

Calista crossed the room and lowered herself onto the bed as if it might suddenly become sentient and kick her off for crimes against romance.

Reid's hand found hers, and his touch sent a jolt through her that had nothing to do with static electricity and everything to do with years of pent-up longing. "Stretch out, milady."

She side-eyed him. "If you start quoting Shakespeare, I'm leaving."

"Please. I'm more of a 'there once was a man from Nantucket' kind of guy." His infectious grin lured her in. "Ever heard of yoga nidra?"

Calista blinked. "Is that like hot yoga, but for people who'd rather nap than sweat?"

His laughter rumbled through her. "Not quite. It's a kind of guided meditation. Just humor me, okay?"

"Um." She lay down, muscles coiled, ready to hop up again if this got too weird.

Reid fussed over her, sliding a pillow under her knees and draping a blanket over her. "Comfy?"

"Uh-huh."

Reid settled beside her, close enough that she could feel his body heat. "Close your eyes," he murmured, voice low and soothing. "We'll start with a body scan."

"A what?"

"Just close your eyes, please."

Reluctantly, she closed her eyes, but not all the way, leaving a slit to peek through.

"Focus on your toes," he said, his voice honey smooth. "Wiggle them, then let them relax."

As he guided her attention through her body, Calista experienced tension she didn't even know she was carrying melt away. By the time he reached the top of her head, she felt like she was floating, anchored only by the sound of his voice, her eyes fully closed.

"Now," he said, "you'll set a sankalpa."

"A what?" She cracked one eye open.

"An intention. Something short and positive you want to manifest."

"Oh." Calista pondered and shut her eye again. World peace? A lifetime supply of ice cream? In the end, she settled on *I am worthy of love*. She repeated it in her head, feeling it resonate throughout her body.

"Got one?"

"Uh-huh."

"Good. Now focus on your breath. Don't control it, just observe."

Calista paid attention to her breathing. In . . . out. In . . . out. Until she rode the waves of her respiration, a surfer in the Zen Olympics.

"Count your breaths backward from twenty-seven. Lose count? No biggie. Just start over."

She began. Twenty-seven, twenty-six, twenty-five . . . Somewhere around eighteen, she lost track. It didn't matter. Nothing mattered except the rhythm of her breath and Reid's deep voice, a lighthouse in the fog of her mind.

"Let go of tension, thoughts, worries. Just be."

Calista felt herself sinking deeper into relaxation. Her thoughts, which had been doing the Macarena earlier, slowed to a gentle waltz. She was aware, yet not. Awake, yet not. It was like being pleasantly buzzed, minus the tequila and regrettable text messages.

"Now . . ." His voice seemed to come from everywhere and nowhere. "Imagine intense heat. Feel it on your skin, in your body."

Calista pictured standing on a sunbaked beach, heat radiating up from the sand like a giant, grainy sauna.

"Shift to intense cold. Feel the chill, the shiver."

She imagined plunging into icy water, the kind of cold that makes you question your life choices and your swimwear options.

He led her through more opposites—heavy and light, pain and pleasure. With each transition, Calista sank deeper into blissed-out relaxation.

"Now . . . recall your sankalpa and repeat it three times."

*I am worthy of love. I am worthy of love. I am worthy of love.*

"When you're ready, wiggle your fingers and toes. Take a deep breath and open your eyes."

She blinked, the dim bedroom coming into focus like a Polaroid developing. Reid watched her, his expression a mix of tenderness and something more profound that made her breath catch.

"How do you feel?" he asked.

Calista took stock. Her body lay heavy yet oddly light as if filled with helium and sandbags in equal measure. The nervousness from earlier evaporated, leaving behind a clarity that felt foreign.

"Like I just had an emotional spa day. I want to marry yoga nidra."

His smile could power a small city. "Good. That's good."

"Wow, just wow. Where did you learn that?"

"Meditation retreat in a Tibetan monastery."

"You went to Tibet?"

"For a month. I needed tools to help me deal with the fast-paced life of sports vlogging and a couple of my friends were going, so I tagged along."

"I'm impressed. Although I'm having a hard time imagining you in a monastery." Calista reached out and cupped his cheek. His stubble rasped against her palm, grounding her in this place and this time.

"I'm multifaceted," he teased. "Not just a pretty face."

"Thank you," she murmured. "For not letting me spiral into a meltdown."

He pressed a kiss into her palm that sent wild sparks racing up her arm. "Anytime, Cal. I mean it. Though next time, maybe we can try body painting with melted chocolate?"

"Don't push your luck, Thornton."

He turned on his side, tucked his hands under his cheek, and she mimicked him. They lay still, simply looking at each other. Calista marveled at how different this felt from their earlier heat. This was tender. Intimate in a way that transcended physical desire and spoke to the connection between them, a language all their own.

"Reid?"

"Hmm?"

"I'm glad it's you."

His voice went husky, his eyes shining in the dim lighting. "Me too. More than you know."

She scooted closer, and he nestled her into his arm. Her head found a perfect spot on his chest where she could hear his steady heartbeat. This moment was its own kind of perfect. Different from what she'd imagined, yes. Colored by all they'd been through. All they'd lost and found again, but exceptional in its own messy, honest way.

She couldn't go back and change the past, but maybe she could move forward into something equally beautiful. Something real, with all its complications and challenges and unexpected joys. Maybe second chances weren't just the stuff of fiction, after all.

For the first time, the thought didn't terrify her. It felt like possibility. It felt like hope. It felt like redemption for them both.

And then Reid's mouth came down on hers in the hottest of kisses, and this time, she was truly ready.

\* \* \*

After knock-her-socks-off sex—he'd learned a few things in the interim—Calista rolled over, nearly smooshing Reid. Poor guy didn't sign up to be a human pillow when he agreed to this whole rekindled romance thing, but here he was, snoring softly next to her.

She snuggled against him, curling up tight, her heart bursting with happiness. Oh, what a day this had been!

"Mmm," he murmured, voice drowsy as his arm slipped around her waist. "That was *beyond* beyond."

"Really?"

"As if you don't know how spectacular you are."

His words lit her up inside, and she let loose a giddy giggle. "Only because of *you*."

That tugged a chuckle from Reid, who looked more awake by the second. He propped himself up on one elbow, his expression relaxing into something that sent Calista's stomach cartwheeling. Damn him and his ability to look unfairly attractive at stupid o'clock in the morning.

"That yoga nidra thing . . . wow, it was like you erased a lifetime of trauma in one session."

"Wanna talk about it?" he asked, running a hand through his hair, which somehow made him look even more handsome.

"It was like I finally could let go."

"That's because you've done a boatload of healing on your own," he said. "I'm so impressed by you and how you didn't get bogged down by our misspent youth."

"Misspent youth?" Calista snorted. "More like mistreated youth, at least in my case." She paused, then added, "Hey, want to hear about the time I tried to impress Benjamin by caddying for his entire four-hour golf game in August without a water break? Spoiler alert. I passed out on the seventeenth hole, and he just stepped over me to take his shot."

"Jesus, Cal. That's . . ."

"Awful? Yeah, I know." She shrugged. A gesture that felt both casual and monumental. "But hey, it's fine. I mean, it's not fine-fine, but you know, character building and all that jazz."

His thumb traced soothing circles on the back of her hand. "You know you didn't deserve that treatment, right? Any of it."

Her chest tightened. "Yeah, well, try telling that to ten-year-old me."

At that age, she'd been convinced if she just tried hard enough, ran fast enough, smiled wide enough, her dad would actually see her.

The silence that followed was heavy, filled with all the things Calista spent years trying to bury, but now, in bed with Reid, moonlight painting the room in shades of silver and shadow, everything she worked hard to release came rushing back.

Calista's gaze drifted to the window, where the moon hung like a cosmic night-light. "You know who I can't stop thinking about?"

"Who's that?"

"Gavin."

"My Gavin?" Reid's body tensed, but maybe she was just cutting off the blood supply to his arms.

She moved, rolling from his embrace. "Weird, huh? I guess it's because he'll be here for the tournament. In my memories, he's like this background character in a video game. You know, the ones that make you go, 'Wait, why is this dude even here?'"

Reid's voice sounded strained. "Really?"

"I remember how my dad would react whenever Gavin's name came up. It was like watching a human embodiment of a Wikipedia page edited in real time. All fury and . . . I don't know, unease? Like Gavin's mere existence was a glitch in my dad's matrix or something."

He reached out to squeeze her hand. "Cal . . ."

She let out a small, humorless chuckle. "God, I wish I could understand it all, you know? It's like I'm trying to solve a Rubik's Cube, but half the stickers are missing, and someone's replaced them with emoji faces."

"Calico?"

"Yeah?" She glanced over and caught a flicker of uncertainty in his eyes.

"There's something I really do need to tell you."

"No, wait, let me finish. I need to get this all out."

Reid looked as if he was about to say something else but then bit his bottom lip. "Go on, but then we really need to talk."

She was so wrapped up in expressing her thoughts, Calista glossed right over that. "I guess that's why being here with you feels so . . . I don't know, grounding? Like, you're this weird time traveler in my life. A link to my past, but as well"—she smiled, feeling ridiculous—"a bridge to whatever comes next. You were there for so much of it—the Hunger Games: Golf Edition, my dad's 'Impossible Standards R Us' routine. But you also saw the real me. Does that make any sense?"

He took a deep breath like he was about to dive into the emotional equivalent of the Mariana Trench. "It makes sense, but Calista, there's something I *must* tell you. I should have told you before, but—"

The sound of the front door opening cut him off midsentence. Startled, they stared at each other doing their best impression of deer caught in headlights.

"Are you expecting someone?" she asked.

"No. You?"

She gasped. "Someone's breaking in!"

What followed was the least graceful scramble in human history as they tried to wrap themselves in sheets, like two mummies attempting synchronized swimming, but with more panicked whispers and accidental elbow jabs. Just as they covered themselves, the bedroom door swung open.

And there, looking like he'd stepped out of Calista's fragmented memories and into this bizarre reality show called her life, stood Gavin Gonzales.

The man loomed in the doorway. His salt-and-pepper hair was cropped short, emphasizing the sharp angles of his face that time had stressed. Deep laugh lines framed dark brown eyes the same shade as Calista's. He wore a golf shirt and khakis as if he'd just stepped off the eighteenth green despite the late hour. His startled gaze flicked between Reid and Calista.

"Gavin!" Reid clutched the top sheet against his chest.

"Calista?" Gavin's eyes widened in surprise with a twist of something Calista couldn't quite place.

She jerked her gaze to Reid, searching for answers. "Reid?"

For a moment, they all stood frozen, like the world's most awkward game of statues. The air in the room thickened with unspoken words, leaving Calista feeling like she'd shown up to a test she didn't know she had to take, and oh yeah, she was nearly naked.

"What's going on here?" she asked.

Then Reid, bless his heart and curse his timing, decided to go for gold in the Worst Moment to Drop a Truth Bomb. He gestured weakly at Gavin and blurted, "This is what I was trying to tell you. Cal, meet your biological father."

\* \* \*

*Cal, meet your biological father.*

Reid's words hung in the air, sharp as broken glass, and yet his statement made absolutely no sense. Blinking rapidly, Calista swiveled her head from Gavin to Reid and back again . . . twice.

When she snagged Gavin's gaze for the second time she saw in his face the stark truth. Gavin Gonzales *was* her father. His dark-chocolate brown eyes, the same color as her own, filled with such tenderness and regret that his desperate longing tore her right in two.

Benjamin Dempsey was not her father.

All the air left her lungs in one audible whoosh, half sob, half grunt. Her world tilted, cottage walls blurred, and Gavin—a family friend turned sudden father—swam before her eyes.

This simply couldn't be happening. Her whole life was a lie?

Everything she believed, everything she knew about herself, was built on a foundation of deceit. What was left? Who was she now?

Calista teetered on the verge of collapse. Her vision blurred. Her legs wobbled beneath her as the weight of the truth bore down on her. This couldn't be happening. How was this happening? But the expression on the two men's faces told her it was true, and there was no escape.

"Calista!" Gavin and Reid exclaimed in the same breath and surged toward her.

She crossed her arms in front of her face, forming an X, blocking them off. The bedsheet she'd wrapped around her like a toga stayed in place miraculously. "Don't touch me! Either of you!"

"Cal," Reid said, his voice beseeching. "I know you're—"

"No! You know *nothing*. Get out! Both of you." She pointed to the door, so shaken she didn't trust herself to stay standing. "Please, leave me alone!"

Gavin and Reid exchanged glances, nodded at each other, and filed out the door, shutting it softly behind them.

Calista crumpled onto the bare mattress. She curled into a fetal position, making herself small, the way she had as a child when she hid in a closet or under a bed to escape her father's tirades.

How could she have been so stupid? The signs had been there, hadn't they? The way Gavin had always been on the periphery, the way Reid had held back, not telling her the truth. She let herself believe in a fantasy, in a life that was never real.

Gavin Gonzales was her father, *not* Benjamin Dempsey.

The pieces fell into place, clicking like tumblers in a lock, and everything made sense. No going back. Calista couldn't return to the life she had known, couldn't undo the lies that had shaped her. History was gone, stripped away like the bed linens, leaving her exposed and vulnerable in the harsh light of this new reality.

The reason Benjamin had been especially cruel to her? She was the biological daughter of his greatest rival. Demetra had an affair with Gavin, and Calista was their love child. Was that why Benjamin divorced Demetra and took Calista and Athena away from their mother? To get even with her for stepping out on him?

She had questions for Gavin, a mountain of them, but she

couldn't face him right now. This revelation was too much to absorb, but she couldn't avoid it forever. She would have to face the man and confront the truth, no matter how much it hurt.

Right now, though, she needed time and her older sister's perspective. Athena would know what to do, which would help her make sense of this chaos.

*Get dressed. Get out of here.*

There was no other choice. She couldn't stay here. She must act. She uncurled herself, body aching, got to her feet, and looked around for her clothes, but she could find only her bra and panties.

Ack! She and Reid had undressed each other before entering the bedroom hours earlier.

Their tryst seemed exceptionally long ago, eons even, instead of just a few moments from cuddling with Reid to Gavin walking into the bedroom to the crashing of her entire world.

She hooked her bra in the back, then bent to scoop up her underwear and shimmied into them. When she raised her head, she caught sight of herself in the dresser mirror.

A stranger peered back at her. Staring at herself, she traced the line of her jaw, the curve of her cheekbone, the shape of her lips and twirled a strand of dark curly hair around an index finger. Gavin's features, hidden in plain sight all these years. How had she never seen it before?

Unbidden memories surfaced.

Gavin, at the edge of the eighteenth green, watching as Calista lined up her final putt. His sharp intake of breath echoing her own as the ball rolled true. "That's my—" he started to shout, then swallowed the rest, his eyes locked on her. After her loss at regionals, he found her crying behind the clubhouse and offered a quiet "You'll show them next time, kid" that soothed the sting of Benjamin's caustic criticism. Dozens of insignificant memories. The too-formal "Sincerely, Gavin" on her graduation card, the way he lingered at gatherings, nursed drinks in hand, his gaze following her.

*Go. Get out of here.*

She cracked open the door and peered out. Someone (Reid?) had folded and stacked her clothes in the hall. She snatched her shorts and T-shirt and tucked them under her arm, but before she could shut the door, the indistinct murmur of male voices reached her.

". . . should have told her sooner . . ." That was Reid.

". . . wasn't our decision to make, Demetra was adamant . . ."

". . . how do we fix this?"

*Fix this.*

As if her life were a broken toy, something they could mend with superglue. A harsh laugh bubbled up in her. If she started laughing now, she wasn't sure she could stop. Reid and Gavin were discussing her as if she were a problem to be solved rather than a person whose world had just imploded.

Calista backed into the room, shut the door, and pressed her hands to her ears, blocking out their conversation. How long had Reid known Gavin was her biological father? Weeks? Months? *Years?*

She shoved her feet into her shoes and opened the door again. In the dim hallway, Reid's and Gavin's somber voices drifted from the kitchen, still discussing her. She tiptoed as fast as she could toward the front door.

Her heart was a sledgehammer in her chest, slamming, slamming, each step throbbing to the beat of her distress. She needed to be far away from here, from this cottage, from a life ripped apart at the seams.

She reached the door, her hand on the knob. Sweet escape. Footsteps behind her. Her pulse quickened.

"Calista, are you running away from me?" Reid's voice held a mountain of hurt.

*Well, join the club, buddy.* She was in a ripe lot of pain herself. She opened the door without looking back at him and stepped out into the moonlight. The evening air hit her, carrying the scent of deep summer and ugly truths.

"Cal, please, just talk to me." He followed her into the honeysuckle darkness.

She turned. The boy she'd loved, the man she'd trusted, was now the keeper of a secret that changed everything.

"Talk?" The word tasted like dirt. "What's left to say, Reid? You've been carrying this truth, letting it fester between us. You kept this from me. How am I supposed to trust you now?"

He reached out as if to touch her, but she backed away, and he let his hand fall to his side. "Gavin asked me not to tell you. I wanted to honor his wishes, and I never meant to hurt you."

"I know. But that doesn't change the fact that you did."

"I thought I was protecting you—"

"Protecting me?" Her laugh rang out bitter in the quiet night. "You think keeping the truth from me was protecting me? All you did was shatter my trust in *you*. I can't—I can't do this, Reid."

She saw Reid's heart splinter in his eyes the moment her words landed. For a second, Calista wavered, but the chasm of unspoken truths yawned between them, too wide to bridge.

"We can work through this. Tonight, we shared something special, and you know it. Yes, this is a lot, but we can figure it out together—"

"No, Reid. It's over. *We're* over."

"Cal, please—"

"We can't. It's too late. I can't be with someone who hides things from me, who doesn't trust me enough to tell me the truth."

He stared at her, pain etched across his face. "I'm so sorry."

"I am too." She glanced away, defeated.

Silence stretched between them, thick with all the things left unsaid. Calista experienced the finality of it. The weight of the decision pressing in on her.

"I'm leaving," she said. "I need to go."

Turning, she walked to the golf car and slid into the driver's seat, the key left in the ignition.

Reid stood motionless, watching her. The moonlight cast him as a dream figure, unreal and ghostly. But this was no dream. This new development was stark reality.

"Calico," he called after her one last time, his voice threaded with hurt, but she refused to look back.

Cutting people out of her life was her superpower, after all.

# Chapter 28
## *Eloisa*

*"Life is like art—you never know what shape your creations will take, but oh, what fun it is to try!"*

—*Eloisa Hobby*

On Monday morning, following the revelation of Cantu's big secret, Eloisa Hobby stood in the clearing beneath Opportunity Ridge, her eyes fixed on the thick cable stretched three feet above the ground, threaded between jacaranda trees shedding their purple blooms.

In her hands, she gripped two large bubble wands and grinned at them like an old friend.

She dunked the wands into a small bucket filled with soapy water, took a big breath, stepped up onto the stool, boosted herself onto the tightrope, and started her walk.

Adroitly, she put one foot in front of the other, flicking bubbles into the air. They caught the sunlight filtering through the branches and turned into floating rainbows all around her.

"Ha! Take that, gravity! Eloisa's Bubble Bonanza!" She hummed. "Defying Gravity."

The bubbles drifted. Some popped against leaves with little *plink* sounds. Others floated toward the clouds. Eloisa imagined them chatting away.

"Yo, Bob," one bubble might say, "looking a bit puffy today. Too much soap in your diet?"

Footsteps snapped her from her bubble trance. She glanced down to see Reid trudge into view.

His usual confident strut was gone, replaced by the plod of a man carrying the world on his shoulders. His every-which-way hair looked as if he'd stuck his finger in an electric socket, and his untucked shirt screamed *I've given up on life and fashion.*

He stopped and stared.

She waved the wands for one last shower of bubbles and hopped off the rope. Her landing was less than graceful. She stumbled, arms windmilling, and managed to avoid face-planting into her soapy brew, even as fresh bubbles flew from the wands. She recovered with a grin and a bow, because why not?

"Hello, Reid." She plopped down on a grassy spot and crossed her legs tailor style in billowy palazzo pants that draped nicely around her ankles. "Have a seat and let's chat. Don't worry, the grass only bites during the full moon."

He didn't even laugh at her silly joke, just shuffled over and plopped down beside her. Eloisa picked up a bubble wand and started twirling it, an old habit she'd picked up somewhere between "learning to adult" and "giving up on other people's expectations."

"All right, spill it," she said. "Your face is doing more talking than an auctioneer on espresso. What's eating you?"

Reid exhaled in a whoosh. "I really messed up with Calista."

Eloisa smiled gently. *No kidding, Sherlock.* She nodded for him to continue.

"I thought keeping Gavin's secret as he asked was the right thing to do," Reid said, his hands clenching and unclenching like he was trying to strangle the air. "But I was so wrong. It's all come out, and now . . . god, Eloisa, I think I've lost her for good."

"Ah, you're afraid she won't forgive you."

Reid nodded, his hair flopping like a sad puppy's ears. The pain in his eyes was so raw it pained her heart. "I never wanted to hurt her, but now it feels like that's all I've done."

"Tell me exactly what went down."

"We were . . . you know . . . *together*."

"Oh, you mean . . ." Eloisa suppressed a knowing smile.

"Yeah." He winced. "And then Gavin showed up out of nowhere. He wasn't supposed to arrive until July first. I panicked and just blurted out that he was her real dad while we were in bed together."

"Oh dear."

"Eloisa, you should've seen her face. It was like watching someone's whole world fall apart in slow motion."

Eloisa grimaced. "Ouch! Talk about bad timing. When Gavin arrived much earlier than expected late last night, I put him up in the cottage with you because I was short on space. I had no idea Calista was with you."

"It's not your fault. I was the dunderhead."

"What happened after that? Did she and Gavin get a chance to talk?"

"She refused to speak to either of us. She just ran off. Withdrew like she always does when she's wounded. She wouldn't let me explain or anything. And now I don't know if she'll ever want to see me again. I've ruined everything."

Eloisa listened as Reid poured his heart out. She punctuated his story with the occasional bubble wand wave, because sometimes life needs a little whimsy, even in the toughest moments.

"Reid," she said when he finished, her voice kind but firm, "love isn't about hiding the hard truths. It's about facing them together, even when they suck. Even when all you want to do is hide in your blanket fort and pretend the world doesn't exist."

"I get that, but what if it's too late? I've let her down so many times."

"Oh, honey." Eloisa sighed and patted his arm. "It's never too late to be honest, but trying to protect someone from pain often backfires. It's like trying to keep a bubble safe by never letting it float. Sure, it won't pop, but it'll never really be a bubble either."

Reid blinked at her, looking like he was stuck somewhere between an existential crisis and a bubble-induced epiphany.

"Look, you messed up, we all do, but that doesn't mean you've lost Calista forever."

Hope flickered in Reid's eyes and relief spread over his face. "You really think I have a chance?"

"I do, but here's the deal. You must give her some space. Let her process all this chaos. Finding out your father isn't your biological dad, and your boyfriend was in on the secret? That's a lot to take in."

Reid looked gut-punched by his own guilt.

"When she's ready, be open, be patient, and for the love of all things bubbly, be honest. That's the only way to rebuild what's been broken."

Reid looked over at her, a small smile tugging at his lips. "How do you always know what to say to make people feel better?"

"Years of practice and a slight obsession with being helpful." Eloisa winked. "Now scoot. Go take a shower, brush your hair, and do some serious thinking. Doctor Eloisa's orders."

Reid stood, dusting off his pants. "Thanks."

"Good luck." Eloisa watched him go, her heart filled—hope, worry, and a splash of *your kids are gonna be the death of me, Demetra.*

# Chapter 29

## *Athena*

*"Sometimes, letting go doesn't mean surrender. It's about making room for something new to grow."*

—*Eloisa Hobby*

There were exactly seventy-two reasons why she shouldn't be standing on the first tee of the Hobby Island nine-hole golf course at 10:47 a.m. on a Monday morning, and she'd counted them all, but after nearly walking off a cliff the night before, numbers lost some of their comfort. Amazing how an existential crisis in a mystical forest clearing could rearrange your priorities.

The question that had driven her here was deceptively simple. Did she actually love golf, or had she just loved being good at it?

After finding her sister's journal entry, after realizing just how thoroughly their father had shaped every aspect of her life, Athena needed to know. Not the kind of knowing that comes from lying awake at 3 a.m. cataloging every wrong turn, but real knowing. The kind that only comes from picking up a club and seeing what happens when you strip away thirty-one years of parental expectations.

Three weeks ago, she would already have mapped out every shot, calculated wind resistance, and recited her father's mantras about precision and excellence in preparation for this weekend's tournament. She'd have broken down the entire course into a series of mathematical equations, factoring in everything from the dew point to the angle of the morning shadows.

Her first swing was, objectively speaking, terrible. The kind of awkward, jerky motion that would have earned her a fifteen-minute lecture on proper follow-through and the importance of maintaining the Dempsey legacy.

The ball skittered sideways, coming to rest in what her father would have deemed "amateur territory," which ranked somewhere between "utter disgrace" and "why do you hate success?" on the Benjamin Dempsey Scale of Disappointment.

Athena stared at the ball, waiting for the familiar surge of perfectionist panic. It didn't come. Instead, she felt something that took her a moment to identify.

*Relief.*

Because this horrible shot? This was hers. Not Benjamin's carefully crafted prodigy, not the golf world's reigning queen, but just Athena, making a mess of things on her own terms.

A breeze ruffled the grass, carrying with it the sound of laughter. Not the polite, golf-appropriate chuckles that usually echoed across country club courses—real laughter, the kind that bubbled from somewhere genuine and unrestrained.

Athena looked up.

Down the fairway, a man knelt beside a young girl as he showed her how to hold a club.

The girl's tongue poked out in concentration, mimicking her father's stance. The sight hit Athena like a perfectly executed drive to the solar plexus. She'd forgotten golf could look like this—joyful and utterly free of scorecards.

Her own childhood memories of the game came with a soundtrack of corrections, each swing annotated with her father's running commentary on angle, stance, grip pressure. The word *fun* had been systematically eliminated from her golfing vocabulary around the same time she'd learned to spell "championship."

She took another shot, this one marginally better, and the ball rolled to a stop not far from the pair.

"Daddy! Look at the pretty lady. She has sparkly shoes."

Athena glanced down at her golf shoes—practical, titanium-reinforced that just happened to have the tiniest hints of glitter in the leather. An impulse purchase she'd justified as "adding flair to her professional image," though really, she'd bought them because they made her think of the light catching in her mother's chandelier earrings.

The father looked up, offering an apologetic wave. "Sorry! Chloe has never met a stranger she didn't want to befriend. Especially ones with good taste in footwear."

There was something endearingly rumpled about him, like an absent-minded professor. The gold band that might have been on his left hand was absent, though the barely visible tan line on his ring finger suggested its removal wasn't recent.

Athena smiled. "I've been on the island for three weeks and I haven't seen you two around. Where have you been hiding out?"

"Oh, we're from Everly. We just came over for the day. There's a kids' golf clinic this afternoon and we wanted to get a head start."

Athena turned her attention to the girl. "Those are some impressive practice swings, Chloe."

The child beamed, brandishing her club like a magic wand capable of transforming the manicured fairway into something enchanted. "Wanna see? Daddy says I'm getting really good at the whoosh part!"

"The whoosh part *is* crucial," Athena agreed, drawn in by Chloe's enthusiasm.

"I'm Dave," he offered with an easy smile and stepped back to give his daughter room to demonstrate.

Chloe's swing was a full-body experience, the kind that would have sent Benjamin into apoplexy. Her club traced a wobbly circle in the air as she spun. The ball remained untouched, but Chloe threw her arms up in triumph anyway, as if she'd just won the Masters.

"Perfect form," Dave said, and the simple truth in his voice made Athena's throat tight. He meant it. His daughter had just turned a golf swing into a pirouette, and he was genuinely delighted.

The concept felt foreign, like trying to translate a language she'd only ever seen written down. In the Dempsey household, "perfect" had been a moving target, always just slightly out of reach, no matter how many trophies lined the shelves.

"Can you show me how you do it?" Chloe asked, turning those huge, hope-filled eyes on Athena. "Daddy says watching good players helps you learn, and you look like you're really good because your shoes are fancy." She delivered this with the absolute certainty of someone who still believed in both tooth fairies and the direct correlation between sparkly footwear and athletic ability.

Athena's spontaneous laugh surprised her. "Solid logic."

She stepped up to demonstrate but then paused. For the first time in her life, she wasn't sure how to swing a golf club. Every motion she'd ever made on a course had been calibrated, engineered for maximum scoring efficiency. How did you swing a club just for fun?

Chloe solved her dilemma by grabbing her hand. "Like this!" She tugged Athena's arm in a circle that defied several laws of physics and probably a few of golf etiquette. "You gotta feel the whoosh in your belly!"

So Athena Dempsey, top of the LPGA leaderboard for the past five years, felt the whoosh in her belly. She let her hips wiggle and when her ball sailed in a completely respectable arc toward the green, Chloe's victory dance felt more satisfying than any trophy.

"That was amazing!" Chloe bounced on her toes, her club swaying dangerously close to Dave's shins. "Did you see how far it went? It was like whoosh and then zoom and then—" She paused. "Oooh." She breathed with the reverence only children can muster for shiny things. "It's so pretty! Is that a tiny golf club?"

Huh? Athena followed Chloe's gaze and looked down at the bracelet around her wrist. The one Benjamin presented to her the day she won her first junior tournament. "Every champion needs her symbol," he'd said, fastening it around her wrist with a photographer-ready smile. She'd worn it religiously ever since, treating it as a good luck charm, a marker of belonging to the elite world Benjamin crafted for her. Now it just felt heavy, like carrying around a tiny gold-plated piece of all the expectations he placed on her shoulders.

"Here," Athena said, the word escaping before her brain could catch up with her heart. Her fingers worked at the clasp, muscle memory fighting against her sudden need to be free. "You should have it."

Chloe's eyes went saucer wide, the kind of pure wonder that adults spend their whole lives trying to recapture. "Really?" She looked up at her father, seeking permission in that universal child-to-parent way that made Athena's heart twist. Had she ever looked at Benjamin like that? With pure trust, unmarred by the fear of disappointing him? She must have, once. Surely.

Dave started to protest—the polite parent deflection of an overly generous offer—but Athena shook her head. "I insist."

The clasp opened and the bracelet slid free. The tan line beneath it looked like an accusation, a visible marker of everything she was trying to leave behind. "Every future champion needs a symbol, right?"

She managed to keep her voice steady on the word *champion*, though it tasted different now. Less like a crown and more like a costume she'd worn for too long, one that had started to chafe at the edges.

Chloe accepted the bracelet with the solemnity of a knighthood ceremony, cradling it in her small palms like it might dissolve if she breathed too hard.

Dave helped her put it on, careful and patient. The sight of the bracelet on Chloe's wrist switched something inside Athena.

"What do we say, Chloe?" Dave prompted gently.

"Thank you!" Chloe launched herself at Athena's legs, wrapping her in a fierce hug that smelled of strawberry shampoo and pure joy. "I'm gonna practice extra hard now! Can I show you my special victory dance?"

Athena found herself nodding, throat too tight for words. She watched Chloe spin and jump, the bracelet catching sunlight with each movement. No longer a symbol of perfection but a child's treasure, transformed by simple delight.

"That's really kind of you," Dave said, watching his daughter with the sort of gentle pride that made Athena's heart ache. "She'll remember this forever."

"It's my pleasure."

"Things have been rough for us since . . ." He bit off his sentence, shook his head. "Well, that doesn't matter. No need to burden you with my difficulties."

Athena lifted her shoulders. "I don't mind if it's something you need to get off your chest."

He glanced at his daughter, who was examining the bracelet in the sunlight. "We lost her mom three years ago and it's been a bit of a struggle getting back to normal."

"That must be so tough. I can't imagine."

He bobbed his head. "We're getting to a good place. This upcoming tournament for Demetra, well, it's bringing everything full circle."

Athena cocked her head. "You knew Demetra?"

"She was my wife's—Keely's—hospice nurse. Honestly, Demi was a saint. I don't know what we would have done without her."

"That's good to know," Athena whispered.

"Good to know?" Dave looked confused. "What do you mean?"

Athena's stomach dropped. She hadn't meant to say that out loud. One of those automatic responses you make when someone shares something meaningful. Except her response made no sense to someone who didn't know the whole story.

"Oh," he said, and realization dawned in his eyes, that slow-motion moment when coincidence crystallizes into connection. The same microexpression she'd seen on a dozen faces since arriving on the island, as people put together her features with her mother's, her presence with the upcoming tournament, her last name with . . . everything.

"You're one of Demetra's daughters."

"Yeah." She nodded, her throat tightening, and suddenly she wanted to be anywhere but here with this nice man and his sweet child. "You have a good day. I'm just gonna . . . um . . . go."

Then, before she burst into tears, Athena hopped into her golf cart and drove away.

# Chapter 30
## *Calista*

*"Life's hardest truths crash like waves, pulling us under, but it's in the struggle to the surface that we find our strength."*

—*Eloisa Hobby*

Yesterday, if someone had told Calista she'd be trudging across Mermaid's Cove five days before her mother's memorial golf tournament, wrestling a world-class identity crisis, she would've laughed. Then again, if someone told her Gavin Gonzales was her biological father, she would have asked for the punch line.

Funny how life worked sometimes.

She'd spent the remainder of last night roaming the island revisiting every spot she and Athena went during their stay here, putting a fine point on the ending of her time on Hobby Island—save for one destination.

Mermaid Cove.

She'd been too exhausted to tackle that without sleep. She'd stumbled into the Lavender Lark at dawn, fallen into bed, and slept for several hours. Finally, she'd gotten up, showered, changed clothes, stuffed herself on take-out fried chicken. Once fortified, she trekked to Mermaid Cove on foot because although the place was accessible by both land and sea, she didn't know how to sail. So she walked instead, even though it took much longer.

She planned a good, cathartic cry in the place where everything changed between her and Reid—damn him—before letting it all go forever. At the B&B she'd made a point to avoid her sister, because she wasn't ready to explain everything, but now, near the water, she spotted Athena walking barefoot at low tide, searching the sand for shells.

"Attie!" Calista waved, suddenly desperate to feel her sister's arms around her.

Athena's head snapped up, her face breaking into a smile that lasted approximately 0.5 seconds before morphing into concern. She rushed toward her. "Lissy? What's wrong? You look like you've seen a ghost."

Calista let out a laugh that came out more like a sob. How exactly do you drop a bombshell like this? She knew how *not* to do it. Reid Thornton's abrupt blurting a case in point.

Athena rubbed Calista's forearm. "Good grief, you're cold as ice. Here." She took off her cover-up and draped it over Calista's shoulders.

Calista met her sister's concerned eyes and offered a limp smile. It was the best she could pull off. She motioned toward the large flat rock a few feet up the beach. "Maybe we should sit."

"Is it that bad?" Athena splayed a hand to her heart.

"It's earth-shattering . . . at least to me."

Athena took her arm and guided her to the rock. It was only then Calista realized her legs were trembling. "What is? Just tell me."

"It's . . ." Calista blew out her breath.

Athena massaged her back and murmured, "Whatever it is, it'll be okay."

Calista stared down at her sister's feet dangling over the rock, covered in sand, the pink pearl of her toenail polish barely visible through the sugar-fine dusting. Her mind shot back to childhood when they'd played together on this very beach, building sand-castles and chasing baby turtles to the ocean.

Demetra had sat on this very rock, watching them, a happy smile on her face, even though her eyes had been so sad. Had she been pining for her lover?

"It's about Benjamin," Calista said. "And Gavin Gonzales."

Athena's eyebrows shot up. "Okay, that's a combo I wasn't expecting. What about them? Did they get into another 'whose golf swing is better' pissing contest?"

No point sugarcoating it. "I just found out that Benjamin is not my father."

"Wh-what?" Athena pulled back to stare at her, stunned shock in her eyes. "What do you mean?"

"Gavin is my *real* father. My biological father."

Athena let out a gasp and slapped a palm across her mouth. For a moment, the only sound was the gentle lapping of waves against the shore and the distant screech of a seagull that seemed to be saying, *What the fuuuck?*

Athena's face went through more changes than a chameleon in a yarn store—shock, disbelief, confusion, and finally, understanding.

"Oh, Lissy." Somehow those two words held a lifetime of shared secrets, sisterly love, and holy-crap-our-family-is-messier-than-a-toddler-with-fingerpaints. "When? Where? How?"

"In the middle of the night." Calista laughed, but it sounded more like a sob. "After Reid and I . . . well, never mind that. Turns out he's been sitting on this bombshell for who knows how long and when we were in the middle of, well . . . you know . . . Gavin showed up, and everything just . . . went sideways."

Before Calista could blink, Athena enveloped her in a fierce hug that smelled of sea salt and their mom's favorite perfume—the one that always made Benjamin sneeze. She buried her face in Athena's shoulder, letting the tears flow. They sat like that for what felt like hours, Athena murmuring soothing nonsense while Calista did her best impression of a sprinkler system.

When her tears slowed to sniffles, Athena took her hand and they sat side by side, facing the ocean, which seemed a lot less vast than the sea of confusion Calista was drowning in.

"I don't even know who I am anymore, Attie," Calista whispered, her throat raw. "It's like someone took the autobiography of my life and revealed it was actually fiction this whole time."

Athena was quiet for a moment, her gaze fixed on the horizon as if the answers might be skywritten in the clouds. "You're still you, Lissy. The you who can't wink without looking like you're having a stroke, who cries at those ASPCA commercials, who once ate an entire jar of pickles on a dare. This doesn't change your fundamental Calista-ness."

She nodded, desperate to believe her sister, but doubt was a persistent little gremlin, whispering *yeah, but what if it does?* in her ear.

"It explains a lot why Benjamin was so cruel to me. Do you think he knew?"

Athena shrugged. "I had an epiphany of my own yesterday. Our father—well, lucky you, now you don't have his genes—would have made a scapegoat of one of us. It's just who he is. He has to have someone to blame for his own shortcomings." Then she told Calista about Benjamin shutting down her bank accounts and credit cards.

"Oh, Attie, I'm so sorry. I was afraid this would happen."

"I do have a secret bank account of my own," Athena said. "I'm not a total fool, but it hurts, you know?"

"I do. All those years of us trying to be perfect daughters, and for what? A gold star in the 'Congratulations, You've Been Duped' category?"

Athena's expression hardened, a look Calista rarely saw on her sister. It was like watching a Teletubby go Rambo. "You always knew what he was, didn't you? A controlling demigod who cared more about his golf handicap than his kids' emotional well-being. This doesn't change that. If anything, it explains why he always treated you like you were auditioning for the role of 'Good Enough Daughter' in the world's worst play."

"You get it now," Calista said, scarcely daring to breathe. "You understand what he did to me . . . to Mom . . . wasn't really about us, but rather his own shame and insecurities. Inside he's a small person who puffs himself up by belittling others."

"I've made enough excuses for him over the years, Lissy, and I am so sorry I was blind to my part in his gaslighting and manipulation. The man's emotional capacity is smaller than a thimble, and neither one of us needs to live in his shadow any longer."

"You're breaking away?" Hope choked her up and Calista put a hand to her throat.

"I'm leaving, just as you did."

A weight lifted from her shoulders. At last! Her sister's eyes were opened. "Do you think Mamá ever planned to tell me about Gavin?"

"I think that's what this month was all about. Eloisa did say Mom had planned all these activities, that the tournament was her idea, and you know she hated golf. It was all to reveal Gavin's identity to you."

"But I still have so many questions and so few answers!"

Athena plucked a seashell from her pocket, turning it over in her hands as if it might contain a Magic 8 Ball with all the answers. "I guess we'll never know for sure why Mom did what she did. It couldn't have been easy for her."

Calista nodded, remembering how their mother would smooth things over after Benjamin's outbursts, always the peacekeeper.

"She did try to protect us the best she could, even if it wasn't good enough. She did install Cantu in our lives to watch over us."

"Yeah, well, loving two men and having to choose between them? That's not exactly a Hallmark movie scenario." Athena gave a wry smile. "Unless Hallmark's branching out into *Polyamory in Paradise*."

The idea of their serene, somewhat distant mother caught in a love triangle was mind-boggling. Like finding out her kindergarten teacher moonlighted as a Vegas showgirl.

"I wish I could talk to her about it," Calista said, a fresh wave of grief washing over her. "There's so much I want to ask, so much I need to understand. Like, was Dad always this much of a jerk, or did he level up over time? I'm assuming she felt trapped."

Athena's eyes glistened, reflecting a sorrow Calista felt in her own body. "Maybe we can corner Eloisa and wring more details out of her."

Calista leaned into her sister's side. "I'd like to understand Mamá better . . . God knows we've got enough material for a lifetime of therapy sessions."

"So . . ." Athena pursed her lips and let out a hiss. "What about Reid? How are you feeling about Mr. Secret-Keeper? On a scale of 'mildly annoyed' to 'plotting his demise,' where do you land?"

Calista tensed and toyed with a loose thread on her shorts. "I don't know. Part of me gets why he did it, but another part . . . Attie, I *trusted* him. I opened up to him in ways I *never* opened up with anyone and he was keeping this huge, life-altering secret from me. It's like finding out your favorite book has a secret chapter that changes everything."

Athena nodded and her expression was thoughtful. "I get that. But, Cal, I've seen the way Reid looks at you. It's like you personally hung the moon and stars, then threw in a few planets for good measure. Whatever his reasons for keeping this secret, I believe he truly loves you."

Calista wanted to hold on to the connection she'd felt with Reid, but the hurt and betrayal were still too raw, like a sunburn that made even the gentlest touch feel like sandpaper. "I don't know if I can trust him again. He took my heart, used it as a hacky-sack, then tried to give it back with a 'no harm, no foul' attitude."

"You don't have to decide anything right now. Give yourself time to process. Reid's a big boy, he can handle being in the doghouse for a while. Maybe we can get him one of those cone collars they put on dogs after surgery."

Calista chuckled at that. "What about you? How are you feeling about all this craziness? And don't say 'fine' or I'll push you into the ocean."

Athena blinked and looked surprised by the question. "Me? Oh, I'm peachy. Just found out my entire family history is a lie, but hey, at least it's not boring, right?"

"It's okay to have feelings about this too. It's your family being turned upside down as well. You're allowed to freak out a little. Or a lot. I won't judge."

"Don't worry about me. You're the one who just had your entire identity ripped to pieces. It's natural for you to focus on that. I'm just the supporting character in this particular episode of 'Who's Your Daddy?'"

"Still, your feelings matter too. We're in this together, okay? Whatever happens, whatever we discover, we face it as a team."

"I like the sound of that. You and me forever." Athena hooked her pinkie around Calista's.

"Me and you forever and always." She bumped her shoulder against Athena's. "Unraveling family secrets and supporting each other through existential crises since . . . well, coming to Hobby Island. We're new, but we're dedicated."

Athena cocked her head, studying something on the ground.

"What is it?" Calista turned to see the sun glinting off something gold in the sand.

"Is that your locket?" Athena asked.

"What?" Calista hopped off the rock and hurried over. She bent down, heart skipping.

It *was* the locket she'd lost. She picked it up.

"Oh my gosh," she whispered, brushing sand from the locket. She glanced back at Athena, who had come up behind her, peering over her shoulder. "I can't believe it's here. Washed up on Mermaid Cove."

They returned to the rock and Calista opened the locket. Inside was the photo of her and Athena when they were toddlers, their baby faces smiling up at her. No damage at all.

"It's a sign," Athena said. "Mamá is still looking out for us."

They sat there together, the ocean whispering its secrets, the locket clutched in Calista's hand. A piece of the past returned to them.

Athena glanced over Calista's head and squinted down the beach.

Calista turned to see a man loping toward them. "Who is it?"

Her sister slid off the rock. "Here comes your daddy. I'm gonna go back to shell collecting and give you two some alone time." She pointed a short distance away. "But I'll be right over there if you need me."

Calista sat fused, watching Gavin approach. Her pulse galloped faster with each step he took toward her, and by the time he reached the rock, her heart was pumping so much hot blood to her extremities, her mind floated dazed, and dizzied.

He stopped before her, his hands crammed deep in the pockets of his cargo shorts, shoulders slumped, eyes downcast. He looked less like a PGA legend and more like a kid who accidentally set the kitchen on fire trying to make breakfast in bed for his folks.

"You want to talk," she said. Not a question. Questions were for people whose lives hadn't been drop-kicked into a parallel universe.

"May I sit?" He waved at the spot Athena had just vacated.

Calista shrugged, her chest so twisted with emotions she couldn't wrap her tongue around words. Not that she even knew what she wanted to say.

Gavin took a tentative step forward as if approaching an unpredictable animal. "I've owed you this conversation for years, Calista. An explanation, an apology, the whole messy truth."

She studied him, wary. Regret tugged down the corners of his mouth, but his gaze never left her face. Her skin burned with the heat of his stare, but inside she was frozen solid.

He eased onto the rock but left a significant amount of space between them. Good. She wasn't ready to have him that close to her.

For a long time, neither of them said a thing. She shot a glance down the beach. Athena had walked several yards away, well out of hearing range. Drawing in a deep breath and then blowing it out slowly through clenched teeth, she turned to him.

"Let's start with why," she said.

"Wh-why?"

"Why did you leave me with *him*? Both you and Mamá knew what Benjamin was like—how he treated me."

Gavin pressed a palm to his forehead, his eyes murky with regret. He carried three decades of secrets. "God, I wanted to whisk you away, I wanted that so much, but things were so complex. Demetra and I were terrified of Benjamin and what he might do. He isn't exactly the 'let's discuss this rationally over a latte' type. Staying close seemed like the best way to protect you."

Calista let out a bitter laugh. "Protect me? Stellar job there, really. Gold star."

"You're right. I have no defense. I failed you."

"You know, I could never understand why Benjamin treated me so badly, but now it all makes sense. When did he find out I was your kid?"

Gavin lifted his shoulders in a helpless gesture. "I don't think he does know . . . not for certain, but you do look so very much like me." His voice softened along with his eyes. "The moment I met your mother, I fell head over heels, and she felt the same for me, but we were both married. We resisted the attraction for years, and then one night, she and Benjamin had a huge argument at a tournament. He kicked her out of their hotel room, and I found her sobbing in the corridor."

"You escorted her to your room and nature took its course?" she asked.

"Yes. We knew it wasn't smart, but we couldn't regret it." His voice and his eyelids lowered. "Especially when our night together ended up with you."

"You were together just that once?"

"While we were both still married, yes. Neither one of us wanted to ruin our marriages. Back then, we didn't fully understand how toxic Benjamin was. Oh, we knew he was a control freak, but we didn't grasp the extent of it until he used Demetra's depression against her to file for divorce and get full custody of you girls."

Calista's anger was a hard thing in her chest. She appreciated Gavin was in a tough spot but couldn't help resenting him.

"I tried to support your mother as best I could, but she moved to Hobby Island after the divorce and cut off all ties with me. I was married, but I stayed in your lives as much as Benjamin would allow. It helped that I lived across the street and could watch you grow up."

"All this time," she whispered, and felt her anger soften. "You were there."

"No. Not in the way I should have been, and it ate me up inside. In my grief over being unable to tell you who I was—how could I when you were so young—I pushed my wife to have a baby. She didn't want kids, and my pressuring her ended our marriage."

"Is that why you made Reid your ward when his parents were killed? To assuage your guilt over abandoning me?"

"Maybe. Who knows. I just know, next to you, Reid is the best thing that ever happened to me."

"You think my birth was a good thing?" She hated that she sounded like that desperate little girl who felt so unloved after Demetra was gone, hurt and confused over why her own father seemed to despise her.

"Calista." His gaze locked onto hers. "*You* are the best thing about me. I wanted to tell you so many times, but while you were still in Benjamin's orbit, I was simply a coward. Terrified he'd take it out on you even more. I thought about telling you after you left golf, but you moved away and seemed to want space from your old friends, your old life, and I didn't want to make things harder for you. But I can see now, those were just excuses to make myself feel better. I'm sorry."

She curled her fingernails into her palms. *This* was her father. Her real dad. He was flawed. He hadn't done right by her, but the look in his eyes left no doubt. He *loved* her.

Her breath stalled.

He reached out his hand, and she couldn't stop herself from taking it. His face dissolved into stunned disbelief and he squeezed her hand as joy washed away the disbelief. "I am so sorry I failed your mother, failed you. I was wrong. Weak. Letting fear call the shots instead of doing the right thing."

Compassion for this man welled up inside her. What good did it do to hold on to anger? The past was over. He was here now, trying . . .

"I want to make amends. It's why I'm here."

She squeezed his hand back. "Stop beating yourself up. Benjamin made me who I am, for better or worse. I'm stronger than steel because of him."

"You don't have to let me off the hook. I deserve your condemnation. I need to tell you something else." Guilt and love played tug-of-war on Gavin's face, and he dropped her hand.

Afraid what he would say might push her away?

She braced herself. "What is it?"

He gritted his teeth, winced. "When I learned you and Reid started dating, I panicked and told him to end things with you. I convinced him if Benjamin knew, he would take it out on you because he hated me, and Reid was my ward. Benjamin would have done it too. I couldn't dare risk it, so I messed around in your relationship."

Calista gave a little gasp and touched two fingers to her mouth. Reid had let her believe Benjamin was the one who'd told Reid to break things off with her. Now, to find out it was Gavin? She didn't know how to respond.

"Don't blame Reid, Calista. He was just a kid trying to protect the girl he loved, and he did love you. Still does."

"You're the reason Reid dumped me? I drowned my pillow in tears and wrote poetry that would make emo bands cringe, because of you." She turned it into a joke and added a laugh to make it less painful for them both.

Gavin looked ready to test theories about spontaneous human

combustion. "Don't let me off that easy. The leak about Benjamin's million-dollar Chevron tournament Vegas wager? That was me too. I hoped it would wake you up to who Benjamin was, and it did. You left. I was trying to help, but you know what they say about good intentions and road construction materials."

She laughed. Serious as this topic was, her father, her *real* father, had a terrific sense of humor even in the midst of accepting responsibility for some serious shit.

Gavin gave a half laugh, nervous and unsure, and he glued his gaze to Calista, taking his cues from her. She studied him closely. It was like looking into a mirror—same chocolate-brown eyes, same nose, identically shaped lips.

"And Reid knew all this and kept quiet for fifteen years? What? Did he minor in secret-keeping along with his business degree?"

"No, no." Gavin's laughter danced up the musical scale, getting higher, thinner. "Reid didn't know I was your father until Demetra died. Everything before that was just a kid caught in the cross fire of adult screwups, trying to do right by you. He caught me bawling my heart out when I heard about Demi, and I broke down, confessed. He promised he wouldn't reveal my secret, but he did tell me he was coming here to be with you."

"He came to Hobby Island for *me* and not for his vlog?"

"You believed that?"

She nodded and bit her bottom lip.

"Oh, Calista." Gavin shook his head, cupped her cheek with his palm, and gazed deeply into her eyes. "I hate how I let this happen to you. Is there any way I can repair it? I need to make amends. I want a relationship with you if you'll allow me."

*Reid.*

The name flashed in neon in her brain palace. Funny, sexy Reid, who looked at her like she was the only person on Earth.

Reid, who'd been carrying the weight of secrets that weren't even his to keep.

*Reid.*

Who she'd left standing there in the dark, shell-shocked and hurt, while she ran away to have her existential crisis.

"Calista?"

"Huh?" She shook her head. What had Gavin said?

"Do you want to have a father-daughter relationship?" He looked so terrified she'd say no.

Compassion flooded her. Keeping secrets all these years couldn't have been easy for him. Forced to watch her from afar. Her heart ached for what he'd gone through. At least she'd been blissfully ignorant.

"I'd like that," she said.

"Really?" His face lifted, gratitude a gift in his eyes.

"Yes." She bobbed her head.

Gavin looked as if he didn't know whether he should jump up and down or grab her into a tight hug. He went in, she pulled back and held up a palm, laughing. "One step at a time, *Dad.*"

"Yes, yes, yes." Sunbeams shone from his eyes, heating her with his love. "Right." He put his arms behind his back. "Slow is better. Thank you."

"I'd love to spend more time getting to know you, but there's someone I need to apologize to first."

"Reid?" Gavin—*Dad*—slid off the rock to the ground and held out his hand to help her to her feet.

"Of course Reid. Always Reid." Grinning, she took her father's hand, thrilled at the idea she'd had a good enough dad all along. "I have to go. I need to find Reid. I may have slightly overreacted. I need to fix this before he decides to join a monastery or something."

"Good. Go." He smiled and waved her off. "Go get him."

She turned to go, her brain already rehearsing what she would say to Reid.

"And Calista?"

She stopped, looked back at Gavin. "Yes?"

"I'm here. Whenever you're ready to talk more. I've got twenty-nine years of dad jokes saved up, so consider yourself warned."

"Thank you." She bobbed her head, put the locket around her neck where it belonged, and went after Reid.

# Chapter 31

## *Calista*

*"Sometimes, the greatest love story is the one where you learn to
love yourself—flaws, weird noises, and all."*

—*Eloisa Hobby*

Gavin Gonzales was her father. The truth dribbled through
her brain. Gavin. Not Benjamin Dempsey. Gavin, the man
who had loved Mamá desperately. The man who now wanted a
relationship with her.

*Calista Gonzales.*

Wow, that was gonna take some getting used to, but it made her
so happy. Grinning, Calista rushed from the beach to the cobblestone path where she parked her borrowed golf cart.

Joy knocked inside her as she sped toward the cottage where
Reid and Gavin were staying. The cottage with the fig tree her
mother had planted and nurtured all those years ago.

She fingered the locket at her throat and fought back tears,
tears of both grief and overwhelming happiness. "Oh, Mamá, I'm
so glad you were loved the way you deserved to be loved, but so
sorry you never got to be with him. I won't make the same mistake with Reid. I won't keep pushing him away the way you did
with Gavin. Thank you for the lesson."

At the cottage, she was so focused on getting to Reid, she

didn't notice Orion off to the side of the house unloading luggage from the trailer hitched to her golf cart until she was halfway up the porch. Calista supposed it was Gavin's luggage since he'd arrived so late last night, long after everyone else had gone to bed.

"Reid's not here," Orion called.

Calista jerked around to face the teenager, caught off guard. "Do you know where he went?"

"He left."

"To go where?"

Orion reached up to shift her baseball cap, moving the bill to the back of her head. "Home."

"He left the island?"

Orion shrugged. "I heard him tell Eloisa that there was nothing here for him anymore."

Calista's pulse skittered, alarmed she wasn't in time. "So he just left without saying goodbye?"

"Maybe he's Irish," Orion said.

"Huh?" Calista blinked.

"You know, an Irish exit, when someone sneaks out the door without telling anyone at the party goodbye."

"I can't believe he'd leave before the tournament," she said, indulging her hurt.

Orion's eyes narrowed. "Did you break his heart?"

"I think I might have," Calista said. "But I want to fix things."

"You better hurry." Orion consulted her watch. "The Hobby Island ferry keeps a tight schedule. It'll depart in ten minutes and it's a ten-minute drive if you take the path, but if you cut through the Majestic Meadow, you can shave off a couple of minutes. Be forewarned, though—"

"Thanks," she told the girl, jumped back into the cart, and took off, goosing the thing as fast as it would go.

Calista veered from the path, her thoughts careening as wildly as her ride, bouncing and bobbing over uneven terrain. Would she be in time to stop him from getting on that ferry?

The golf cart bottomed out, jarring her teeth. *Ouch.* She'd probably owe Eloisa a new golf cart after her mad dash through Orion's shortcut. She bumped over a divot the size of a dinner plate and her foot slipped off the accelerator. She battled to get her foot back into her flip-flop. Ack! Flip-flops probably were not the proper footwear for a dramatic romantic gesture.

*Go, go.*

She crested the rise and saw Majestic Meadow stretched out before her, a carpet of wildflowers from lupines to black-eyed Susans to Prairie Fire, but she bulleted by so fast the landscape blurred like a Monet.

Reid had brought her here for a picnic during one of their dates. They had stretched out on a blanket and smooched up a storm. The memory pinged inside her. She needed more of his kisses. More of *him.*

The shimmering ocean lay beyond, and she could see Marshmallow Landing below. The ferry was pulling up; the passengers on board looked like tiny dots and there was only one person standing on the pier, waiting to board.

Reid.

Hell-bent on reaching him in time, Calista didn't see a familiar shape sitting in the thick grass until she was almost upon it.

Suddenly, Shushu leaped up from the flowers, dooryard violets entangled in her feathers and dangling from her head as she took off running beside the golf cart.

The ostrich must have thought they were in a race. She galloped beside Calista, her long legs vibrating the ground, head thrust forward as she zoomed alongside her.

Startled laughter shot from her throat. If the racing ostrich didn't get Reid's attention, nothing would.

The ferry docked. Arriving guests disembarked. She was closer now, close enough to see Reid standing to one side, letting everyone off before he got on.

"Reid!" she yelled, but the wind snatched up the name and threw it back at her.

The commotion, however, spurred Shushu, who picked up the pace and weaved in front of the golf cart.

Terrified she would run over the ostrich, Calista trod on the brake.

The golf cart hit a large rock hidden in the grass and the cart flew, airborne. If she hadn't been utterly terrified, it would have been comical. The cart slammed to the ground, blowing out all four tires.

Jolted, she gasped as Shushu ran away squawking.

Well, dammit. Shaking her head to clear it, Calista leaped from the golf cart, abandoning it and rushing toward the landing. The ferry horn tooted as the boat turned in the water to head back to Everly. The small crowd pooling on the deck obscured her view and she couldn't find Reid on either the ferry or the wharf. Up on the hill, she was still a good hundred yards away, but she wasn't giving up hope.

Not yet.

"Reid!" she hollered, praying he'd heard her before and hadn't gotten on that ferry. "Reid Thornton!"

Heads turned in her direction.

She tried to run, but the flip-flops hindered her. She stopped to strip them off and toss them aside, sprinting full-out barefoot. Tall grass slapped against her shins, her pounding footsteps churning up the fragrance of wildflowers.

Then her toe caught in a clump of thick clover, and she stumbled, falling forward. Don't ask how, but she managed to fall headfirst into a somersault and roll wildly down the hill. She curled herself into a tight ball for protection as gravity pulled her toward the landing.

She slid to a halt and flopped onto her back, arms outstretched, peering up at the blue sky dotted with fluffy white clouds.

Was she injured? Hmm, she took inventory. Nothing hurt. Amazing, considering the tumble she'd taken.

"Calista!"

Reid's voice rang out across the meadow, and she jumped right to her feet to see him hurrying over to her.

"Are you all right?"

"I'm fine," she said, gluing her gaze to his. "Don't go." The words burst from her before she could overthink them. "Please, Reid. Don't leave."

He stared at her, eyes flared wide, mouth moving down, then up, then down again as if he was wrestling against hope. Or maybe that was just projection on her part.

"I thought . . ." he said, "after everything that happened, I figured you'd want me gone."

"No! I mean, okay maybe, for a while as my trust issues got triggered, but that's all it was. *My* issues."

"You sure you didn't hit your head when you wrecked the golf cart?" he asked.

She waved a hand. "I'm fine, or I will be as long as you stay here and work this out with me."

He came closer. "You're okay?"

"One hundred percent. Why didn't you get on the ferry?"

"How could I when the woman I love was barreling down the hill in a golf cart screaming my name." A wry grin quirked his mouth.

*The woman I love.* If he loved her, that meant this was fixable, right? A guy didn't say things like that to a woman he was breaking up with.

"You saw that, huh?" Her cheeks heated.

"I did."

"How much of it?"

"Every bit." He reached up to pluck a wildflower from her hair.

"And you still love me after I made a giant ass out of myself?" She was breathing hard, and it had nothing to do with the circus act she'd just performed and everything to do with the man standing in front of her.

"More than ever."

Her heart beat fast and frantic, so loud she could barely hear herself. "I was wrong."

This close to him, she could count the freckles across the bridge of his nose. God, she loved those freckles. "I was scared and confused, and I lashed out. That wasn't fair."

Reid's jaw tightened. "Calico, you—"

"No, let me finish." She held up a hand. "I've been doing a lot of thinking. About my mom and Gavin . . . about *us*. And I realized something."

"Yeah?" Reid asked, his voice neutral. But Calista knew him well enough to see the tension thrumming through him, like a guitar string strung too tight.

She took a deep breath. This was it. No more running, no more hiding from her feelings. "I don't want to end up like Mamá and Gavin," she said. "Always wondering what might have been. I love you, Reid. I have for years. I was just too stubborn and scared to admit it."

He didn't move, his face fixed in a neutral expression. "Say that again."

*Whee! He was gonna forgive her!*

"I love you," she repeated, stronger this time. "I love you, Reid Thornton, and I'm done running away from it."

In the next second, Reid's palms were cupping her face, and his lips were on hers. She melted against his chest, mimicking an ice cream cone in the sun, hooked her fingers in his shirt, and tugged him closer. It was messy, a little desperate and vulnerable as hell.

Applause started behind them, a singular person at first, but soon a dock full of people were clapping for them.

When they finally broke apart, both slightly breathless, Reid rested his forehead against hers. "I love you too. God, Cal, I've loved you for so long. Even when you were driving me crazy . . ."

Calista laughed, the sound watery and full of joy. "Good, because I have a feeling I'm gonna drive you crazy for a long time to come."

Reid grinned, that crooked smile that stole her breath. "I'm counting on it."

They stood there for a moment, just holding each other, the crowd behind them cheering now. Calista breathed in the familiar scent of Reid's cologne mixed with salt air, feeling more at peace than she had in . . . well, she didn't think she'd ever felt this much at peace.

"So, what do we do now?" she asked.

Reid pretended to consider, rubbing his chin and shaking his head. "Well, I suppose I could go unpack. Unless you've changed your mind and want to get rid of me after all?"

Calista swatted the air around him. "Not a chance, Thornton. You're stuck with me now."

"Good"—his smile softened—"because there's nowhere else I'd rather be than here with you."

He moved to pick up his abandoned duffel bag and then held out his palm.

Grinning, Calista clasped his hand, let it drop to her side. Holding hands. They were holding hands like when they were teens.

"Need a ride?" Cantu called out, pulling up on a six-person golf cart.

"Well, that was convenient." Calista giggled.

"Not really." Cantu grinned. "Eloisa sent me to keep an eye on you. She was worried. Hop in."

They climbed into the back, and as Cantu carted them to Reid's cottage, hope overflowed Calista's heart. It felt as if the sun had chased away all the shadows and she was bathed in light. Her head spun and her toes tingled.

*Please don't let this feeling be from a head injury.*

Worrying again. Worst-case scenario. She didn't have to do that anymore. It would take time for her to honor her anxiety for what it was, the long-term effects of toxic abuse, but she was trying.

She still had a lot to work through, trust to rebuild, a new family dynamic to navigate, but she was ready to face it all for the first time ever.

After Cantu left them at the cottage, Reid turned to her, speaking the same words that were tromping through her head. "You know this doesn't magically fix everything, right? We've still got a lot to sort through. Both of us."

"Agreed."

"Promise me, we talk things through, no matter what."

She put a hand to her heart. "No more running away, no more pushing you away when things get tough. I'm all in if you are."

"You know," Reid said, "your mom would be proud of you. For facing your fears, for giving Gavin a chance, for having the courage to walk away from golf and Benjamin."

Thinking about Demetra, she got teary-eyed. "You think so?"

"I know so. She wanted you to be happy, Cal. Even if she wasn't able to reach out to you. She loved you. She did her best even if it wasn't good enough."

"Athena and I . . . we get to break the cycle."

He leaned over, gently tugged her head to him, and kissed her crown. A caring caress. Tenderness. "Yes, you do."

Calista palmed her mouth, touched. "I wish she could be here. There's so much I want to ask her, so much I want to tell her."

Reid took her hand, squeezed it gently. "I know, but she's still with you in a way. In your smile, in your stubbornness, in the hugeness of your heart. And now you have a chance to get to know Gavin, to understand that part of yourself as well."

Hope waltzed, daring her to grab hold and hang on tight. "It's gonna be weird getting to know him as my dad. I mean, I've known him my whole life, but not like this."

Reid's kind smile promised support and encouragement. "It will take time, but you've got all the time in the world now. No more secrets, no more hiding. You can build the relationship you both want, on your own terms."

Calista tightened their entangled fingers as if hanging on to the last shred of her emotional stability. Which, if she was being honest with herself, she probably was.

"You know, I've always felt like a dolphin at a cat show," she said.

Reid's eyebrows quirked in that adorable way of his, encouraging her to go on.

"You know, sleek and smart and supposedly amazing, but completely out of place and constantly making weird noises."

His lips twitched, trying to contain his grin. "I don't think I've ever heard you make weird noises, well, unless you count last night . . ."

She laughed and nudged him with her elbow. "That's because I've been holding them in. For years. It's incredibly stressful."

His laughter joined hers. "Calista Gonzales, professional weird noise suppressor. I like it."

She rolled her eyes but couldn't help grinning at him. "Be serious."

"I am serious. About you, not the noises." His voice lowered and the air felt thick with Things Unsaid. "What's really going on in that beautiful mind of yours?"

Calista took a deep breath, steeling herself. Vulnerability, her old nemesis, knocking at the door. "I've spent so long trying to be the person everyone wanted me to be, I'm not sure I know who I am, and I'm terrified that if I figure it out, no one will like me."

Reid's hand came up to cup her face, and she resisted the urge to nuzzle into it like a touch-starved kitten. "I like that person. I more than like her, actually. Even if she makes weird dolphin noises."

"I don't deserve you."

"Probably not," he agreed cheerfully. "But you're stuck with me anyway."

She swatted at his chest, but there was no heat behind it. "Egomaniac."

"*Your* egomaniac," he said, pulling her closer.

"What did I get myself into?"

"You love me, and you know," Reid said. "So, about that golf tournament this weekend."

Calista groaned. "And here I thought we were having a moment."

"We were. Now we're having a different moment. Will you play the course?"

She paused, considering. "I suppose I have to, in honor of my mother, and to bond with Athena."

"You don't have to do anything you don't want to do, Cal."

"I think I want to."

"Good!"

"Will you vlog it?"

"Of course. I want to capture your win on camera. The Comeback Kid." His grin took up his entire face, his eyes sparkling with mischief and something deeper, something that made her heart do a little flip in her chest.

"It's just this once. To play with my real dad."

"There won't be a dry eye among my two million subscribers."

"I'm glad you're here for it."

"Correction, I'm here for *you*. C'mon, let me prove it." Smirking, he tugged her toward the porch.

And she giggled all the way to the bedroom.

# Chapter 32
## *Athena*

*"You can't control where or how others hit their balls, but you can choose how to play your own, and sometimes walking away is how you win the game."*

—*Eloisa Hobby*

The nine-hole golf course (which they would play twice for the tournament) sprawled in front of them, an expanse of serene green.

A gentle breeze rustled through the jacaranda trees, carrying with it the scent of freshly mown grass and the happy chirp of birds. The temperature, a balmy seventy-two degrees, sent fluffy clouds floating across the sky. It was the kind of morning that inspired poets to pen odes.

And Athena wanted to wail because Demetra wasn't here to see it.

The bleachers near the first tee hummed with energy as spectators took their seats. Friends, family, and a smattering of guests who had arrived for the charity event exchanged smiles and greetings. Eloisa distributed commemorative sun visors to the attendees, her bright laughter cutting through the murmuring crowd.

Near the first tee box, Reid stood a little apart from the action, his camera in hand as he narrated an intro for his vlog. Calista was by the practice green, adjusting the strap of her golf bag. She looked like her old self in a fresh polo and tailored Bermuda shorts, but the nervous energy radiating off her made her seem like a child wearing too-big clothes.

Gavin was at the tee, testing his club. He glanced up, caught Athena's gaze, and gave her a reassuring smile. His calmness lent her courage, and she smiled back.

Reid walked over to Calista, put his arm around her waist, and drew her close to whisper something in her ear. Her sister laughed out loud at whatever he'd said and Athena's affection for the man surged.

Guests mingled and golfers practiced their swings under the morning sun, the atmosphere light with camaraderie and excitement for the day ahead.

Then, suddenly, the buzz died. Conversations faltered midsentence, leaving an eerie silence in their wake. Heads turned as a golf cart pulled up near the first tee.

Athena's pulse reeled, stuttered, and for one wild second, stopped as the golf cart driver disembarked.

Benjamin Dempsey.

He strode forward with his trademark swagger, his every step exuding a sense of entitlement that made Athena's skin crawl. Dressed in a pristine polo shirt and pressed khakis, he looked like he'd stepped out of a high-end golf catalog, complete with his caddie trailing dutifully behind him, lugging an unnecessarily large and expensive bag of clubs.

Stunned by his audacity in coming here, Athena froze.

The sharp intake of breath from someone nearby mirrored Athena's own reaction. Her muscles locked, a flash of disbelief flooding her. Of course Benjamin would arrive unannounced.

Of course he'd find a way to insert himself into an event meant to honor the woman he'd spent years undermining.

"Viewers, it seems we have an unexpected guest." Reid's voice was dry as stale bread. "Benjamin Dempsey himself, a divisive figure in the golfing world. For those just joining, this tournament is a tribute to Demetra Sarris, Benjamin's ex-wife and mother of reigning LPGA champion Athena Dempsey."

Reid filmed Benjamin as he turned toward the gathered crowd, his smile as polished and insincere as a cheap trophy. "Athena, darling. And Calista, my angel."

Athena darted a look at Calista, who stood rigid, jaw hanging open, eyes vacant as if experiencing a PTSD flashback.

Reid, always quick on his feet, stepped closer to Calista, his free hand brushing her elbow in a protective gesture. He nodded at Athena and silently mouthed, *I've got her.*

"This is supposed to be a tribute to Mamá," Athena muttered under her breath. Her eyes narrowed as Benjamin scanned the crowd, soaking in the attention like a star actor on opening night. "You're not wanted."

"I was invited." He flashed a fake smile.

Eloisa had *invited* him?

Stunned, Athena turned on her heel and marched over to Eloisa.

"Hello, my dear." Eloisa beamed at her. Today, the older woman wore a marigold-orange polo shirt and matching golf skirt with a gingersnap-colored tweed golfer's cap. "Excited?"

"What is *he* doing here?" Her voice shook with barely contained anger. "Why did you let him get off the ferry?"

Tension lined Eloisa's eyes and Athena recognized her own turmoil reflected back at her. "Athena, I know this is a shock—"

"A shock? It's an ambush!" She raised her voice, drawing curious glances. She couldn't muster the energy to care. Let them look. Let them see. Maybe if enough people witnessed the truth, it would finally stick.

Eloisa rested a gentle hand on her arm. "Demetra wanted to give him a chance to make amends. For you and Calista, not for him. She believed people could change."

Athena jerked away, her laugh sharp enough to cut steel. "Change? Him? You've got to be kidding me."

How many chances had they given Benjamin over the years? How many times had hope risen, only to be crushed under the weight of his cruelty and indifference? Her stomach churned. Her mother's endless capacity for hope and forgiveness felt both inspiring and maddening in equal measure.

She glanced over her shoulder. Benjamin was chatting with a spectator, his head thrown back in laughter as if he hadn't a care in the world. Seething, she gritted her teeth.

"This isn't about forgiving him, Athena," Eloisa said, her tone brooking no argument. "It's about showing him—and yourselves—that he no longer has the power to hurt you."

"Fine." She glowered at the unflappable senior citizen. "But if he so much as looks at Calista wrong, I'm throwing him off this course myself."

Eloisa nodded, approval in her eyes. "Understood. Now, take a deep breath and remember why we're here today."

Athena closed her eyes, hauling in a massive amount of fresh air to center herself, and conjured Demetra, her laugh like summer rain, fragrant with the scent of lavender, her ability to infuse even the darkest day with possibility. *Okay, Mamá, if this is your wish, I'm here for it.*

Dot, resplendent in a lime-green visor and matching outfit, took her place at the podium near the first tee. She spun the handle of a bingo cage, releasing a numbered ball that clattered into a tray and announced the foursome pairing. "Numbers 6, 13, 22, and 17. You four are up first."

The first competitors, whose entry numbers were pinned to the backs of their shirts, moved toward the first tee box. Athena knew all of them from either the PGA or LPGA and forced a smile in greeting as they walked past.

Reid followed the foursome and got short interviews with each player.

Dot kept pulling numbers and calling them out as one after another, players teamed up. Athena moved to stand beside her sister, shoulders ironed straight, eyes locked on Benjamin. As long as neither she nor Calista got stuck with him, they'd be okay.

One after another, the players were matched up until only four were left—Gavin, Athena, Calista, and Benjamin.

Was this intentional? Athena stabbed Eloisa with a look. Unruffled, the older woman simply shrugged and held out her arms in an *it wasn't me* gesture that suggested it totally *was* her doing.

Calista made a soft noise of despair and twisted her fingers in the hem of her polo shirt, an emotional "tell" left over from childhood.

"Don't worry," Gavin said, stepping over. "I'm here."

Calista sent him a look of such gratitude and relief it broke Athena's heart.

"Well, isn't this cozy?" Benjamin strolled over, his faux nice face fixed in place, the hapless caddie loping along behind him. "Just like old times, eh, girls?"

Athena bit back a retort. She refused to let him burrow under her skin.

Reid's voice filtered through the crowd. "And there you have it, folks," he said, his phone perched on a stabilizer as he walked beside their group. "The final foursome of the day is shaping up to be one for the books. We've got PGA legend Gavin Gonzales, LPGA phenom Athena Dempsey, and Calista Dempsey, making her long-awaited return to the game. Oh, and let's not forget Benjamin Dempsey, whose, uh . . . reputation precedes him."

Athena shot him a grateful glance. Reid gave a small nod, his way of saying he had their backs. She could feel him nearby, steady as a caddie who knew when to step in and when to let the player handle the moment alone. Then again, he had been Gavin's caddie once.

After the group in front of them reached the green, their foursome gathered at the first tee. Gavin took the lead, stepping up with an easy confidence that belied the tense moment. He swung smoothly, sending the ball sailing down the fairway.

"Nice shot," Reid commented, his voice carrying just enough admiration to make it into the vlog.

Benjamin stepped up next, his movements practiced and precise. He smirked as his ball landed a few yards beyond Gavin's.

Athena suppressed an eye roll. Of course he'd have to one-up Gavin.

As she prepared to take her shot, she felt her father's gaze boring into her.

"Focus, Athena," Calista murmured, her sister's voice steadying her.

She drew in a deep breath, exhaled slowly, and swung. The satisfying crack of the club meeting the ball sent a small surge of confidence through her. The ball arced, landing right beside Benjamin's.

"Nice swing, Athena." His voice slithered into her ear, dousing her small spark of joy. "You've improved. Maybe one day you'll be a better golfer than Calista."

*Ouch.* The gloves were off. She was unaccustomed to his derision he'd mainly saved for her sister. Fine. She turned and curled her upper lip at him in a sneer. "Maybe one day you'll become a decent human being, but I'm not holding my breath."

Benjamin laughed. Darn it! She was giving him narcissistic supply like she'd read about. *Note to self, don't feed the troll.* Athena turned away.

It was Calista's turn.

"You've got this," Gavin said, his voice filled with encouragement.

Calista nodded but didn't look up. Her swing was rushed, the ball veering into the rough. She bit her lip, frustration flashing across her face.

"Don't worry about it," Athena said, stepping beside her sister. "It's just one shot."

Benjamin, however, couldn't resist. "A little rusty, aren't we?" he said with a chuckle. "You used to have a much better swing, Calista."

Reid's camera zoomed in on Benjamin, capturing the subtle cruelty in his words. "And there's the Benjamin Dempsey we've all come to know."

Gavin placed a reassuring hand on Calista's shoulder. "Shake it off, kiddo. You're here for Demetra."

Benjamin snorted and started ahead, his lackey on his heels. As they followed him down the fairway, Athena fell into step beside Calista.

"You okay?" she asked, pitching her voice low to avoid Benjamin's ears.

Her sister nodded, eyes distant, focused where past and present blurred. "I just . . . I wasn't prepared for this."

"Me neither, but we're in this together, okay? Don't let him get to you."

"Ditto," Calista said. "You've been staring at him as if you'd like to eviscerate him with your fingernails."

"Now, there's a thought." Athena steeled herself. Seventeen more holes to go, but they'd survived worse. They'd endured Benjamin, weathered the aftermath of their mother's death, persevered through long, dark nights when pain seemed endless.

They'd survive this too.

As the group moved down the fairway, Reid followed at a respectful distance, his commentary weaving between celebrating Demetra's memory and subtly highlighting Benjamin's behavior.

"Here we are at the first green," Reid said, his tone upbeat but edgy. "It's incredible to see so many people gathered to honor Demetra's legacy. But as we've seen, even on a day meant for healing, old habits die hard."

Athena glanced over her shoulder at Reid, his focus on the camera. His presence was a reminder of the world outside Hobby Island, of the millions who might see this footage and know the truth.

They all sank their putts in one shot and moved on.

Approaching the second tee, Benjamin maneuvered himself next to Calista, effectively isolating her. Athena's muscles coiled and her senses heightened.

"You know, Calista . . ." Benjamin's voice lowered, meant for her sister's ears alone. Athena strained to catch every word. "I've been thinking about you lately. You were always so much better than Athena. Smart, talented, driven. That fire inside you . . ."

Her sister's steps faltered as her head tilted toward Benjamin. The look in her eyes—desperate, long-buried need for approval bubbling up—tore Athena up inside.

"Come back to the LPGA," Benjamin coaxed, his words honeyed poison. "Come home . . ." He paused. "I've missed you, Calista. All those years apart . . . I've been lost without you. You've always been my favorite, Calista." Benjamin's voice dropped to a whisper Athena could barely make out. "I pushed you hard because you were the *real* star. Athena wasn't tough enough, but you are."

Athena snapped. She couldn't stand by and watch this happen, not again. Not after everything they'd endured. Not after how far they'd come in healing their relationship in the wake of Benjamin's relentless triangulation.

"Lissy," Athena said, moving to touch her sister's hand.

The contact jolted Calista from Benjamin's spell. She blinked as if waking up from a confusing dream.

"You know who you are," Athena said. "You don't need his validation. You don't need him at all. You were the strong one, the one who had the courage to walk away. Don't let him suck you back in."

"I-I don't . . ." Calista stammered, voice small and uncertain.

For a moment, a look of pure evil crossed her father's face, but he quickly replaced it with a mask of concern and a condescending tone. "Now, Athena, this is a private conversation between—"

"No." Athena cut him off. "There are no private conversations here. Not with you." Never again would Benjamin isolate them and pick them apart with surgical precision.

"Remember all the things he did." Athena held her sister's gaze. A lifeline thrown, praying Calista would grasp it. "Remember what we talked about."

"Love-bombing," Calista whispered.

"That's right."

Benjamin laughed but it was a sour sound. "Your sister has been pumping your head full of lies. It's not too late." He slipped an arm around Calista's shoulder. "We can start over, build something incredible together, just you and me. The way it should have been from the start."

Calista's breath hitched, audible in the hush, and when she didn't immediately move away from Benjamin's touch, Athena's stomach dropped to her feet.

Reid popped up between Calista and Benjamin. "Up to tee off we have Benjamin Dempsey. A man who's made headlines for his competitive spirit and unconventional approach to family dynamics."

Beside Athena, Gavin grunted and said in a low voice, "Reid has a way with words."

"Yeah, but let's hope his way doesn't get us all into trouble," Athena said, glancing at her sister.

Calista's focus seemed elsewhere, a tight grip on her club as she adjusted her stance.

Benjamin, meanwhile, stood off to the side, arms crossed, his gaze darting toward the crowd as if seeking validation. When none came, his jaw tightened, a flicker of irritation flashing across his face.

The next few holes passed in a blur of forced politeness and simmering tension, a real minefield tiptoe. With each swing, Benjamin's civility wore thinner and thinner. He couldn't help himself. He was gonna blow.

Athena girded herself, preparing for the battle she knew lay ahead. She had seen it play out time and time again. Before she'd read *It's Not You*, she hadn't understood the pattern. Now she did.

And with knowing came greater fear, because she could no longer make excuses and pretend in some twisted, roundabout way her father wanted what was best for them. Benjamin cared about one person and one person only.

Himself.

On the sixth hole, Benjamin whistled far too cheerfully as he approached the tee box for his shot. His usual swagger was intact.

But hypervigilant, Athena noticed a muscle tic at his jaw and the loose way he held his club.

The eyes of the crowd bored into him. He turned and bowed to the gallery, squared his shoulders, took his stance, and drew the club back in a smooth arc. The sound of contact rang out—a hollow *thwack*.

The ball sliced hard to the right, bouncing awkwardly before disappearing into a grove of trees. A murmur rippled through the crowd, and someone let out a laughing snort.

Athena winced. Laughter was the last thing Benjamin would tolerate in a moment like this.

Benjamin straightened, his face darkening as he scanned the group. "Who laughed?"

No one responded. The laughter had been knee-jerk, but it hung in the air like smoke from a fire, impossible to ignore.

Reid, standing a few paces back, kept the camera trained on Benjamin. His calm voice carried on the warm summer breeze. "A rare misstep for Benjamin Dempsey, a onetime Masters winner, known for his take-no-prisoners-approach on the course."

Athena's throat tightened and she was eleven all over again. She glanced toward Calista, who had her head down, avoiding Benjamin's glare.

Gavin stepped forward, casually clapping Benjamin on the shoulder. "Tough lie," he said, his voice even. "We've all been there."

Benjamin jerked away from Gavin's touch, his expression mean-spirited. "I don't need your commentary," he snapped. "Or your sympathy."

Athena bristled at the tone, but Gavin didn't react, his calm unshaken. "Of course," he said, stepping back. "Your ball."

Benjamin strode toward the rough, his movements stiff, the

poor caddie scrambling to keep up. Her father's muttering was low but sharp, words Athena couldn't quite make out. She exchanged a glance with Gavin, who shook his head slightly as if to say, *Let it go*.

As the next players stepped up to the tee, Athena's attention flicked to Reid.

"It's moments like these that reveal character," Reid said into the camera, his tone measured. "Golf is as much about resilience as it is about skill."

Ahead, Benjamin reemerged from the rough, his face stormy as he lined up for his recovery shot. He made no comment to the group, but the anger radiating off him was palpable.

They all made par on that hole, leaving Benjamin and Gavin tied for first place. Athena was one stroke behind. Calista lagged at one over par. Athena could tell her sister's mind simply wasn't on the game.

On the seventh hole, Benjamin pulled ahead, making up for his shanked ball, and immediately began gloating, puffing out his chest like a cocky rooster and getting digs in on Gavin, retelling the story of their head-to-head competition at the Masters where Benjamin beat him on the final hole.

Reid filmed the whole exchange, staying silent, letting his subject do all the talking.

They finished the ninth hole with Benjamin still holding a one-point lead and started the course over with the first hole becoming the tenth to mimic a full eighteen-hole golf course. The second hole—now the eleventh—was a short par three that everyone had birdied the first time. This hole was deceptive—its inviting layout masked the potential hazards of the surrounding water and strategically placed bunkers.

Benjamin got on the green in one stroke and stood aside for

Gavin to tee up. Conversations fell away as spectators leaned in closer.

Athena stole a glance at her father. His face was a careful mask, but she could see the hostility in the tight set of his jaw and the stiff way he gripped his club.

With an easy confidence, Gavin lined up his shot.

"And here's Gavin," Reid murmured for the camera. "Can he make it to the green in one shot to join his archrival?"

Gavin's swing was smooth and controlled, his follow-through graceful perfection. The wood connected with a gentle yet solid *whack*.

The ball soared high, tracing a flawless arc against the bright blue sky. All eyes followed its path as it descended onto the green, bounced twice, and rolled directly into the hole.

A collective gasp rippled through the crowd, followed by instantaneous cheers and wild applause.

"Unbelievable!" Benjamin's caddie exclaimed.

"Shut up," Benjamin snarled at the guy, who backed up with raised hands.

"A hole in one, Dad!" Calista squealed and then slapped a palm over her mouth, as if realizing too late what she'd called Gavin out loud.

Gavin tipped his cap, his smile easy and unassuming as he walked toward the green to retrieve his ball.

Reid stepped into frame, excitement in his voice as he narrated the moment. "And just like that, Gavin Gonzales delivers a flawless hole in one. Talk about rising to the occasion! This eagle shot puts Gavin in the lead!"

Athena clapped along with the crowd; she was happy for Gavin, but scared of what her father might do.

"Lucky," Benjamin muttered under his breath, the bitterness

dripping from each word. He didn't applaud, gluing his hands at his sides, his neck tendons straining.

A few heads turned his way, but he ignored them, his focus fixed on Gavin, who was now accepting congratulations and high fives from the gallery.

Athena felt a fresh prickle of unease. Benjamin's anger wasn't new to her, but this level of restraint was. Usually, he wielded his emotions like weapons, cutting down anyone in his path. This simmering was different. More dangerous.

"Guess some people can't stand not being the center of attention," Reid murmured at her elbow.

Athena let out a soft breath, her chest achy. "It's not over yet."

Benjamin spun on his heel. He wasn't looking at anyone, his eyes fixed on the bag as though it might offer him some way to claw back control. For a moment, she thought her father might explode. His face flushed red, a vein pulsing at his temple, but then, as quickly as it appeared, anger vanished behind a brittle smile. A transformation Athena had witnessed countless times— the whiplash of rage to charm in seconds.

After the twelfth hole, scores were unchanged.

"Ready for lucky thirteen?" Reid asked, turning the camera back to Benjamin. "Your chance to come roaring back, Mr. Dempsey."

"Of course." Benjamin flashed his teeth. A row of the best veneers money could buy. "We wouldn't want to hold up the game with Gavin's grandstanding. This is all about Demetra, after all."

Then *it* finally happened on the fifteenth hole.

Despite his best efforts, Benjamin hadn't been able to overtake his nemesis. Gavin was still one ahead and Athena had caught up to her father, leaving them tied. Calista was two behind them, but she didn't seem to care.

The dogleg par five demanded strategy and accuracy to birdie.

Benjamin's turn came first. He teed up. His swing was powerful but a little sloppy. He was rattled. The ball veered left, catching the edge of a sand trap.

Reid, ever composed, reported for the camera. "A tough break for Benjamin Dempsey. That trap's going to test his recovery game."

Benjamin shot Reid a glare that could curdle milk.

Athena bit her lip. Calista, who stayed rigidly at her side, darted her gaze between Benjamin and the sand trap.

Gavin's shot sailed straight down the fairway. Athena's ball landed not far behind.

Then Calista stepped up to take her turn. Athena sent her positive vibes. *Fly it to the moon, Lissy.*

Calista slammed the ball, and it shot into the air as if propelled from a cannon, flying far past Gavin's ball in yardage, so long it had to be a first for her. At least three hundred and fifty yards. Gobsmacked, Athena's jaw unhinged.

Reid let out a long, low whistle.

A cheer erupted from the crowd. Athena joined in, clapping enthusiastically as Calista's face lit up with pure, unguarded joy.

"A perfect shot," Gavin said. "That's my girl. Well done, sweetheart."

Reid, camera in hand, added, "And there you have it—Calista Dempsey, showing everyone why she's still a force to be reckoned with. Is a comeback in her future?"

Benjamin glowered at Calista, hatred in his eyes, his lip curled in a snarl. In a flash, he snatched the club from Calista's hands.

The sudden violence jolted Athena.

"You think you're so special. You ungrateful little bitch. You owe me the one million dollars you cost me!" He growled low in his throat, all pretenses gone, his face twisted in fury. He hurled Calista's club to the ground with chilling force. The metallic clang echoed across the green, and nearby players gasped and froze in shock.

"Benjamin!" Gavin's voice cracked like a whip. "Stop it!"

Benjamin was too far gone, lost in his rage. He ranted and raved, spittle flying from his mouth.

Athena leaped without thinking, planting herself between Benjamin and Calista. She felt her sister trembling behind her.

A sense of déjà vu hit Athena. They'd been here before many times. Benjamin attacking Calista or Demetra and Athena—the good girl, the golden child—stepping in to soothe him.

She could do it too. Tell him he'd been horribly wronged, that *he* was the victim, that he was the greatest golfer of all time, and everyone knew that and anyone who said otherwise was just jealous. All the greatest hits to calm his childish ego.

But no more. No more placating the monster.

He jabbed a finger at them, looking like a deranged traffic conductor on the world's worst acid trip. "You're ungrateful! You're all ungrateful!"

Athena's blood boiled hot lava. She opened her mouth, years of unsaid comebacks jostling on her tongue.

And then a gentle hand touched her shoulder. The young caddie, nodding behind her. Athena turned to see Eloisa, Cantu, and Paul arriving in a golf cart. Cantu was at the wheel. He parked while Paul got out and offered his arm to Eloisa.

The elderly woman strolled over, the picture of self-control, and picked up the damaged club, bent at an odd angle. Flanked by Cantu and Paul, she straightened. They looked like the world's most unlikely superhero team, ready to save the day armed with nothing but sensible shoes and stern expressions.

"That's enough of that behavior, Benjamin," Eloisa said, her voice steady as a surgeon's hand. "I gave you an opportunity to redeem yourself and you failed. You need to leave. *Now.*"

His head whipped around so fast Athena thought it might unscrew from his neck.

"You think you can tell me what to do, old woman?" Benjamin ground his teeth.

"You will not turn Demetra's memorial into *The Jerry Springer Show Golf Edition*." Eloisa's smile turned deadly. Cantu and Paul, hands clasped in front of them, stepped forward, a silent warning.

For the briefest of seconds, just the span of a heartbeat, something flickered in her father's eyes. Regret? Shame? Gas? But he snuffed the emotion like a candle and replaced it with his default setting. Righteous indignation. Benjamin harrumphed and tossed his head, lifted his haughty nose in the air.

As Paul motioned Benjamin to the awaiting golf cart, and Cantu blocked him from getting to the others, he let out a string of curses, saying every foul word Athena had ever heard.

"We don't tolerate that kind of language on Hobby Island." Eloisa made shooing motions. "Your luggage is waiting for you on the dock and the ferry will be along shortly."

Benjamin stormed to the golf cart and shot them all both middle fingers as Cantu and Paul whisked him away.

Athena turned to Calista. A watercolor of emotions painted her sister's face, fear bleeding into relief, anger swirling with a desperate kind of sadness.

"You okay?" Dumb question. Of course Lissy wasn't okay. None of them were.

Calista nodded, then shook her head, then laughed. It was a sound caught between hysteria and relief, like someone had crossed the wires of her emotions. "You didn't give in to him, Attie. Finally, you didn't play the peacemaker."

"I did stand up to him, didn't I?" Athena puffed out her chest, damn proud of herself.

Calista hugged her hard and then Eloisa was hugging them

both. And Gavin got in on the act and they waved in the woeful caddie who seemed grateful to be included in the group hug. Because, of course, he'd been a victim of Benjamin's abuse too.

After the hugging, as they stood there surrounded by their makeshift family, Athena felt something loosen inside her, and for the first time, she genuinely believed healing was possible. Because anything was possible as long as you had the ability to love and be loved.

# Chapter 33
## Calista

*"The heart's greatest strength lies in its capacity for understanding and forgiveness."*

—*Eloisa Hobby*

The funny thing about coming in third place (Benjamin got disqualified for poor sportsmanlike conduct, so his score didn't count) at her dead mother's charity golf tournament was that Calista couldn't have cared less where she ranked on the leaderboard. Last place would have been just fine with her.

After Benjamin was escorted off the island and they finished the tournament, Gavin took first place with Athena coming in second. Eloisa presented the trophies and announced they'd raised twenty-two thousand dollars for cancer research in Demetra's name. Then everyone else left for Crafters' Corner to take part in the Fourth of July celebration. All, that is, except Calista and Athena.

Eloisa had requested they drop by her house to discuss the dedication of Demetra's remembrance garden, set for the following day.

Reid kissed Calista goodbye at the final green. It was a long, sweet kiss filled with promises of many more kisses to come. "I'm off to edit the footage. You were incredible out there."

Calista gave him a weak smile. "I don't know about that."

"I do. You weren't just playing. You fought for something bigger than a game, and you didn't let him win." He reached out to tuck an escaping tendril of hair behind her ear and kiss her again. "Maybe we meet up at the barbecue later?"

"Plan on it."

"Perfect." He kissed her one last time and turned her over to Athena, who was waiting in a golf cart. By the time the sisters reached Eloisa's front porch, the setting sun's rays stroked the horizon an orangey purple and the scent of honeysuckle wafted on the soft ocean breeze.

Calista stared at Eloisa's front door, her fingertips hovering millimeters from the sun-bleached wood.

"You know," Athena said, "I'm fairly sure the door won't open itself. Unless Eloisa installed some kind of fancy entry system we know nothing about."

Calista shot her an amused look. "Ha ha. You're hilarious."

"I try." Athena gave a mock bow.

"Here goes nothing." Calista bounced the knocker against the door and the hard *rap rap* echoed across the island, like a starting gun for . . . what, exactly?

The door swung open, and Eloisa poked her head out, her silver hair escaping a loose bun in wisps. For once she wasn't wearing a hat and she had on an understated shift dress in a black-and-white floral design and a pair of black ballet flats.

Where was her usual color and flair?

"Is this a bad time?" Athena asked, eyeing the older woman up and down.

"No, no, of course not. I've been expecting you. Please, come inside." She motioned them over the threshold.

Eloisa led them through the cozy living area—the patchwork quilt draped over the overstuffed armchair, shelves crammed with dog-eared books, lace curtains fluttering in the open windows—to the kitchen where the scent of cinnamon and yeast bread enveloped them.

"Have a seat." Eloisa waved at the small table in the breakfast nook overlooking the ocean. "I'll put on the teakettle."

They settled in their chairs and exchanged glances. Athena raised her eyebrows and her shoulders, indicating she, too, thought something was a bit off about their normally exuberant host.

"This morning was certainly an experience, wasn't it?" Eloisa turned on the gas burner beneath the copper teakettle and took teacups from the cupboard.

"That's a word for it," Athena said.

"How are you two doing?" Eloisa arranged the cups on a tray and peered over at them.

"We're okay." Athena shifted in her seat. "How are you?"

"Fine, fine." Eloisa waved a hand, but she didn't seem fine; her brow was furrowed, and she kept battling back wisps of loose hair. "I've dealt with my fair share of Benjamins in my seven decades. It's distasteful and unsettling, but we can't allow dark forces to mess with our equilibrium and steal our joy, now can we?"

It seemed she was speaking to herself as much as to them.

The teakettle sang and Eloisa's hands shook a little as she poured the hot water into the delicate porcelain cups.

Calista stood up. "Do you need any help?"

"No, no." Eloisa forced a smile, added honey, cream, and a small wicker basket filled with various flavors of teabags, along with a plate of shortbread cookies, to a tray and carried it to the table.

They gathered around the table and made idle chitchat while they sipped tea and ate shortbread cookies. Calista and Athena shared meaningful looks. What was this visit all about?

"Well," Eloisa said at last, "I suppose you're curious about why I invited you here."

"It's not about tomorrow's dedication for Mamá's remembrance garden?" Calista asked, stirring a bit of honey into the tea she topped up with fresh hot water.

"Not exactly." Eloisa rested her hands in her lap, took a deep breath, and fixed her gaze on some point beyond them. "There's something I need to tell you. About your mother. About . . . me."

"We're listening." Calista nodded, encouraging her to continue.

Eloisa cleared her throat, looked first at Athena and then at Calista. "It's not an easy story, but it's time you knew. About how I came to be part of your mother's life. About everything."

The older woman paused, and in that moment, Calista saw someone burdened by a long-held close secret. "This is something you haven't told many people, is it?"

Eloisa shook her head. "I've never told the whole story to anyone except your mother."

"You don't have to tell us anything you don't feel comfortable sharing," Athena said.

"It's not about my comfort." Eloisa offered her a tender smile. "It's about helping you put the pieces of the past together so you can move forward into a guilt-free and loving future with each other.

"I grew up in a world of absolutes." Eloisa's voice took on a faraway quality. "Black and white. Right and wrong. My father was a fundamentalist evangelical megachurch pastor, and his word was law. Not just in the church, but in our home."

Calista leaned forward, drawn in.

"Love, in our house, was conditional on toeing the line and living his version of God's will. And harsh punishments for stepping out of line." Her voice wobbled as her eyes took on the overlay of past pain.

"That sounds rough." Athena bit her bottom lip and she, too, appeared lost in thought.

Jettisoned back to *their* childhood and Benjamin's brand of punishment? Calista wondered.

Eloisa's lips quirked in a sad smile. "It was all I knew. I never experienced real love until I was sixteen, and I met Jamie."

"Jamie?" Calista canted her head, studying her mother's oldest friend.

"Our new gardener's son," Eloisa said. "Jamie was kind. Gentle. Everything my world wasn't. And we fell deeply in love."

There was a wistfulness in her voice that made Calista's heart ache. She could picture a young Eloisa, sheltered and starved for affection, finding a connection with someone who showed her a different way of being.

"What happened?" Athena asked.

Eloisa picked up her teacup and cradled it between her palms as if doing so stabilized her. "I-I got pregnant and my parents' solution was to send me away to a home for unwed mothers and force me to give the baby up for adoption."

"They didn't!" Calista breathed, horror washing over her.

"They did. To protect the family's reputation, they said. To save my soul." She let out a bitter laugh. "Instead, it became the loneliest time of my life."

Calista reached out, covering Eloisa's hand with her own. She felt the slight tremor running through the older woman's fingers, saw the sheen of unshed tears in her eyes.

Eloisa squeezed her hand in return. "Things were different in those days. Good girls did not have babies out of wedlock, especially not when your father was a powerful preacher."

"I'm so sorry," Calista whispered.

"It gets worse before it gets better." Her mouth formed a grim line.

"We're here." Athena got up and moved to the chair on Eloisa's other side. "Whatever it is, we're here to listen, to hear you."

"The baby's birth . . . there were complications. I got septic and fell into a coma. And when I woke up . . ." Eloisa's voice broke and she had to take a few deep breaths before she could continue. "They told me my baby died and that they'd already buried her. I never even got to see my baby."

The silence that followed was heavy, charged with grief that felt as fresh as if it had happened yesterday, not decades ago.

Tears pricked at Calista's eyes, and her heart broke for the girl Eloisa had been, for all she'd endured alone.

"And then they told me, because of the illness, I would never be able to have children. I wanted to die," Eloisa whispered. "I *prayed* to die. I couldn't see any reason to go on. And then . . . then there was Demetra."

"Mamá?" Athena's voice went up in disbelief.

"Yes, your mother. You see, another girl at the home had died in childbirth, leaving behind a baby girl—Demetra—and I became her wet nurse. In caring for her even in that short time, I found . . . not healing, exactly, but a reason to keep going."

Calista saw the whole thing. Eloisa, lost and heartbroken, finding a lifeline in a tiny, helpless newborn. A bond forged in the darkest of times, but no less powerful for it. "What happened then?"

"Life went on," Eloisa said. "My parents arranged a marriage for me—a wealthy older pious man who didn't ask too many questions about my 'time away.' But I never forgot Demetra. I stayed in touch with her foster parents, watched her grow from afar."

"And our mother never knew?" Athena asked.

Eloisa shook her head. "Not until much later. After my parents died and I inherited this island. It was my chance to start over, to build a life on my own terms. And when I heard from Cantu that Demetra was struggling—with depression, with everything that happened with your father taking you away from her—I reached out. Invited her here."

"To heal," Calista murmured.

"Yes," Eloisa said. "For both of us, really. We saved each other, in a way. Became more than friends. We became family."

The weight of Eloisa's words descended over them. Calista viewed her entire childhood through a new lens, understanding for the first time the depth of the bond between Eloisa and her mother.

"There's more." Eloisa's gaze drifted to the corner of the breakfast nook.

Calista turned, noticing for the first time a small, battered trunk sitting on the floor. "What is that?"

Eloisa pushed back from the table and got to her feet, retrieved the trunk, and brought it back to the table. Athena moved the dishes so Eloisa could settle the trunk in front of them.

"Remember, Calista, I told you I had a trunk of your mother's? She left this for you both." Eloisa rested her hand on the lid. "I've been keeping it safe, waiting for the right time."

Calista and Athena exchanged a look.

"You ready for this?" Calista asked her sister.

"No, but we gotta open it."

"Together?" Calista asked, putting a hand on one of the clasp locks.

Athena nodded and placed her hand on the opposite clasp. "Together."

Simultaneously, they flipped the clasp locks open and raised the lid.

Inside, they found handwritten letters tied with faded ribbons, worn journals, and a few small packages in gift wrapping paper.

"Mamá's personal correspondence." Tears swam in Athena's eyes as she sat back hard into the chair, looking dumbfounded.

Eloisa placed a comforting hand on her sister's forearm. "Things she wrote, all those years, letters, journals full of things she couldn't say out loud. And gifts . . . unopened and marked 'return to sender.'"

"Dad," Athena said, bitterness creeping into her voice.

A lump filled Calista's throat. All those years of feeling abandoned, of not understanding why her mother hadn't tried to get them back or make contact when they were older, condensed into these brittle papers and forgotten presents.

"Why? Why didn't she tell us that *he* sent her letters and gifts back?"

Eloisa's expression softened, filled with a sadness and compassion that hurt Calista's heart. "She was afraid you'd reject her. She was ashamed of her affair with Gavin and terrified you'd judge her harshly. She let shame and fear stop her from reaching out. She regretted it so much, all the rest of her life. I know it's hard to understand, but she never had a road map for what a loving family unit looked like. Her foster parents were kind, but it wasn't the same. They had so many kids coming and going from their home."

"She tried once to reach out, didn't she?" Calista said, her memory of Demetra at Chevron shimmering in her mind. She'd been dressed in daisy yellow, standing out in the crowd, or Calista probably wouldn't even have seen her there.

"Yes," Eloisa said. "She finally felt strong enough to risk your rejection. She wanted to see her two daughters compete against each other in the most prestigious tournament in women's golf."

"So why did she run away?" Calista asked. "Why didn't she stay?"

"Because Benjamin saw her there and threatened her to stay away. He vowed to take his anger out on you, and she knew his threats weren't idle."

"Oh, Mamá!" Athena exclaimed.

"Demetra's dying wish was for me to bring you two back together, and in my devotion to her, I said yes. I was manipulative," Eloisa said. "I admit it and thank heavens your mother's plan worked. Otherwise you two might never have reconciled."

Calista met her sister's eyes.

"I love you," Athena said.

"I love you too."

They reached across the table and held hands. Then Calista reached into the trunk with trembling fingers and pulled out a letter at random. The paper felt delicate, as if it might crumble at any moment. The familiar handwriting was a gut punch. It was dated a few years after Benjamin gained custody of them.

"Read it out loud," Athena said.

Calista exhaled, cleared her throat, and started reading. "My darling girls, there's so much I wish I could tell you, so many things I want to explain. But the words never seem to come out right. How do I make you understand that staying away was the hardest thing I've ever done, but it was the only way I knew to keep you safe. How do I tell you that not a day goes by that I don't think of you, wonder about you, love you with every fiber of my being?"

Athena placed a palm over her mouth, silent tears slipping down her face.

Eloisa slipped away from the table and returned with a box of tissues.

Reading on, Calista said, "I know you must be angry. Confused. Hurt. You have every right to be, but please know that everything I've done, every choice I've made, has been out of love for you. Even if it doesn't feel that way."

Tears blurred Calista's vision, and she had to stop reading.

Athena pressed a tissue into Calista's hand and dabbed at her own eyes with another.

"There's a lot more," Eloisa said. "So much more. Letters she wrote after you left home, even when she knew you'd never read them. And these . . ." She lifted one of the gift-wrapped packages. "Presents she tried to send that got returned."

Athena took the package, addressed to her, and unwrapped it with careful fingers, taking her time. Inside was a black velvet box with a pair of pearl stud earrings inside. "She tried to send this to me, and I never knew she cared."

Calista reached for a package marked with her name. She tore away the paper, revealing a beautiful leather-bound journal. The cover was soft and pliant. Inside, the pages were blank except for a single inscription on the first page:

*For Calista, moro mou, my dreamer. May these pages hold all the hopes and wishes of your heart. Never stop reaching for the stars. All my love, always, Mamá.*

Calista hugged the journal to her chest, tears flowing now. She'd spent so long feeling disconnected from her mother, but these letters, these gifts, were tangible proof of the love that had always been there, even when she couldn't experience it.

She looked to Athena, both of them holding pieces of their mother's love. The weight of the past, the pain, the misunderstandings—

it all shifted, not disappearing, but transforming into something new. Something that held hope and healing.

"We need time," Calista said to Eloisa. "To go through all of this, to . . . process it."

Eloisa nodded. "Of course. Take all the time you need. And remember, you're not alone in this. I'm here, so are Dot, Vivian, and Clare, as well as Luna and Paul, Orion and Artie, and now Cantu, Julia, and Mateo too. Whenever you need help, we'll be here."

# Epilogue
## *Eloisa*

*"Healing isn't a destination, it's a journey."*

—*Eloisa Hobby*

*One year later . . .*

What a whirlwind this past year had been! Not just for Eloisa, but for everyone who'd been on Hobby Island during the extraordinary summer following Demetra's passing.

She still missed her dear friend with every beat of her heart, but Eloisa channeled her grief into helping others. Day by day the acute pain faded a bit more, leaving behind happy memories and deep appreciation for the loved ones who remained.

With help from Paul and Mateo, Eloisa poured her energies into growing the remembrance garden until it flourished, and Demetra's favorite flowers thrived as surely as her daughters. The tall yellow sunflowers basking in the sunlit section, so much like statuesque blond Athena, and the small amber angel kiss pansies spilling from hanging baskets, delicate but hardy, the spitting image of Calista. Along with the numerous String of Tears plants that grew between the two.

And the fig tree at the cottage where Gavin now lived year-round, filling the position Eloisa created for him as Hobby

Island's golf pro, loaded with so much fruit they'd need a community event to deal with the figs once they ripened. Demetra would be so happy the love of her life moved here.

And as for that devil Benjamin, he'd been banished from Demetra's daughters' lives as Athena and Calista erected strong boundaries and went no contact with the man who'd made everyone's life pure misery. It was a shame, really, that Benjamin had been unable to see how his egomania and insecurity kept him from loving people. Tragic.

But Eloisa didn't like to dwell on unpleasant things. She'd once gotten lost in the shadows herself and understood the only cure for darkness was to live in the light. Benjamin had never learned that lesson and probably, at this late date, never would.

Sighing, Eloisa shook off Benjamin Dempsey and the misery he caused and put a happy smile on her face, for today was a special day. The return of Demetra's daughters to Hobby Island for the dedication of their mother's remembrance garden.

Eloisa danced along the path, her red dress a burst of color against the greenery. She hummed "One Love" under her breath, Demetra's favorite song, as she tidied up—snipping a wilted bloom here, coaxing a stubborn vine there. The dress was the same one she'd worn to Demetra's memorial last year, but today it felt less like mourning and more like celebration.

Butterflies kept landing on her, making her laugh. "Do I look that much like a flower?" she wondered aloud, shooing them gently away.

Cocking one eye to the sky, Eloisa said, "Did you send them?"

She liked to think Demi was giggling in heaven, releasing a river of butterflies. She could almost feel her friend's presence, as if Demi's spirit lived on in every petal and leaf. This wasn't just a special day, it was a celebration of life itself.

Eloisa took it all in and smiled. Demetra would have loved this.

Paul and Mateo worked setting up chairs in the garden for the small ceremony. Eloisa smiled, watching them work in comfortable silence. Three times a week, Mateo took the ferry to Everly for his Narcotics Anonymous meeting, and he was so proud of his one-year chip. Eloisa was so glad she'd taken a chance on letting him move here with his parents when Cantu and Julia took over running the Lavender Lark.

"Eloisa!"

She glanced up to see Calista and Reid coming toward her, hand in hand. She rushed to greet them, wrapping first Calista and then Reid in a fierce hug. "Oh my goodness! It's so good to see you. We've missed you so much!"

"You just saw us last month, Auntie Eloisa, when we came down for Dad's birthday party." Calista laughed, the happy sound filling the garden.

"A month without your smiling faces is too long," Eloisa said resolutely. "But come, tell me all about your life in Denver before everyone else descends."

Reid grinned, his expression a mix of pride and humility. "Well, the video series has taken off in a way we didn't expect. I mean, we hoped it would resonate, but it's been overwhelming."

Eloisa raised her eyebrows, intrigued. "The series about golf and . . . ?"

"Abuse," Calista finished softly, glancing at Reid with a tender smile. "We called it *The Other Side of the Green*. It started with me sharing my story and grew from there. Women from all over started reaching out, sharing their experiences. We've even had a few pros come forward to talk about toxic coaching and family dynamics."

"Oh, that sounds healing." Eloisa pressed her palms together, sending her bracelets jangling.

"Reid's been incredible," Calista added, her voice brimming

with admiration. "He used his platform to make sure the stories reached the right audience. He's even been helping some of the women find resources."

Reid ducked his head, clearly embarrassed but pleased. "It's the least I could do. Honestly, it feels like the first time I'm using my skills for something that matters."

"My dears, that's remarkable. Demetra would be so proud of you both."

"And now we're building something even bigger," Reid said. "A nonprofit focused on mentorship and advocacy, with Athena's mentoring program as one of the cornerstones."

Calista beamed as they talked about her sister. "Athena's been amazing. Her coaching isn't just about the game; it's about helping these girls find their voices."

"We do have something big to ask of you," Reid said.

"Ask away! The answer is most likely yes!" Eloisa folded her fingers together.

Calista held out her left hand, flashing an engagement ring and giggling. Reid looked so proud he might burst.

Eloisa pounced, grabbing hold of Calista's hands. "You're engaged!"

"He proposed last night." Calista slid a sidelong glance over at Reid, happy tears in her eyes.

"We'd like to get married on Hobby Island," Reid said, wrapping his arms around Calista's waist and drawing her closer to him.

"Maybe right here in the remembrance garden," Calista said.

"Or Mermaid Cove." Reid nuzzled her ear.

"Of course, whatever you want! I'm thrilled for you both and I want to hear all about the proposal when we have time to catch our breaths," Eloisa said. "In the meantime . . ." She waved at Athena coming through the entrance.

Athena hurried over, looking like summer in a snazzy designer ensemble. There was another round of hugging and congratulations for the bride- and groom-to-be.

"So," Eloisa asked Athena, "how's the golf coaching and mentoring business going?"

Athena splayed a hand to her heart. "Leaving the LPGA was the best thing I ever did. I get so much more gratification out of watching my protégées win trophies than I ever did winning my own. Thank you, Eloisa, for all you did to wake me up."

"You woke yourself up, dear. All I did was provide the venue." Eloisa gave her a pat on the shoulder, just as proud of Athena as Athena was of her students.

The young woman looked so much more at peace since she had taken control of her own life. She'd filed a lawsuit against Benjamin to get the monies owed to her, and he was now under forensic audit for embezzling from both Athena and Calista for years.

"Not to be nosy . . ." Eloisa leaned in closer. "But are you seeing anyone? Never mind. That *was* nosy, don't answer it."

"Now that you mention it." A shy smile crossed Athena's face and she lowered her lashes. "I'm seeing the dad of one of my students, Chloe; she's adorable. His name is Dave Kipling. I met him last year right here on the island. He's been widowed for four years. He's a psychologist, go figure, but that comes in so handy. I'm learning what it means to fight fair. We like each other a lot, but we're taking it slow. There's no rush."

"He sounds yummy." Eloisa gave Athena a hug. "I'm so happy for you."

Gavin arrived next, and then Cantu, Julia, and Mateo. Right after them came Dot, Vivian, Clare, Luna, Paul, Artie, and Orion. The gang was all here.

"Let's get this party started!" Eloisa said to a chorus of whoops and hollers.

The group gathered in the heart of the garden, surrounded by the gorgeous flowers and the power of their shared love and respect for one another.

Eloisa clapped her hands together, drawing everyone's attention. "Grab a flute of sparkling cider. We're having a toast!"

She waited until everyone had gotten the drinks Luna passed out and gathered around her again. "I want to thank you all for coming today. This garden was created as a place where we can all come to remember Demetra and the good she spread in the world."

She paused, looking around at the faces of those who had become her family. "But it's more than just a remembrance. It's a celebration of life, of healing, and of the journey we've all been on together."

The guests looked at one another, smiling and happy, and Eloisa's silly old heart melted. If Demetra could only see them now!

"Flutes up." She raised her glass. "To Demetra, because of her, we're all here together."

"To Demetra!" everyone echoed and clinked their glasses. Then in unison, they all said, "To Eloisa!"

Oh dear. She was going to cry. Eloisa fanned her face and smiled and cried and it was a beautiful moment. But she couldn't be sappy and sentimental for long, she was too practical for that.

"And now, it's time we made it official." She reached into her pocket and pulled out a small pair of red-handled scissors, handing them to Calista. "Would you do the honors?"

Calista smiled, took the scissors, and moved to the ribbon that had been tied across the entrance to the labyrinth. With a quick snip, the ribbon fluttered to the ground, and a cheer went up from the small group.

"Welcome to the Demetra Sarris Remembrance Garden. May it always be a place of peace, love, and healing for everyone who visits!" Eloisa said. Okay, maybe just a *little* more schmaltzy stuff. "Time for the Labyrinth Walk."

Leading the way in her bright red outfit, Eloisa took the first step into the labyrinth, Athena right behind her, followed by Calista, Reid, Gavin, and the others. Slowly, they walked, heads down, hands clasped behind their backs, counting the steps, fully experiencing the feel of their feet on the stones, the sound of birds in the trees, the rate of their breathing, and the mind-boggling number of butterflies surrounding Eloisa.

Okay, Demi *was* releasing butterflies from heaven, case closed.

Waiting for them at the center of the labyrinth lay a feast of all Demi's favorite foods. They ate, talked, and toasted for hours and it was one of the best days ever. Then one by one, people started drifting away.

In the end, it was just Athena and Eloisa.

"You don't have to worry about me, dear. You can go on with the others. I just want to sit in the garden for a bit." Eloisa eased down on a concrete bench.

"I lingered behind for a reason," Athena said.

"Oh?" She looked up.

Athena settled down beside her. She had a white envelope in her hand. "Calista and I have been so busy, and going through our mother's correspondence has been overwhelming, that we just now got through all of it."

For some strange reason, Eloisa's pulse quickened. "Dear, that's absolutely fine. No one expected you to read it all at once."

"The reason I'm apologizing is because Calista and I just recently found this." Athena turned over the envelope. It was addressed to Eloisa, in red ink, in Demi's handwriting.

"A letter for me?" Eloisa pressed two fingers against her mouth.

Athena passed the envelope to Eloisa. "I'll give you some privacy." She gave Eloisa a hug, got to her feet, and walked away.

Blast! Why were her silly old fingers trembling? Eloisa moistened her lips and, holding her breath, opened the letter. She started reading, then gave a sudden little gasp and clutched her heart as the letter fluttered to the ground.

She tilted her head back and stared up at the clouds through the tree branches. "Dear god, Demi, this changes *everything*!"

# About the Author

LORI WILDE is the *New York Times*, *USA Today*, and *Publishers Weekly* bestselling author of more than ninety-nine works of romantic fiction. She's a three-time Romance Writers of America RITA Award finalist and has four times been nominated for the Romantic Times Reviewers' Choice Award. She has won numerous other awards as well. Her books have been translated into twenty-six languages, with more than eight million copies sold worldwide. Her breakout novel, *The First Love Cookie Club*, was made into a Hallmark movie titled *A Kismet Christmas*.

Lori is a registered nurse with a BSN and an MLA from Texas Christian University. She holds a certificate in forensics and is also a certified yoga instructor.

A sixth-generation Texan, Lori lives with her husband, Bill, in the Cutting Horse Capital of the World.

## Discover more from
# LORI WILDE

---

| The Summer That Shaped Us | The Undercover Cowboy | How the Cowboy Was Won |

---

### JUBILEE, TEXAS

A Cowboy for Christmas

The Cowboy and the Princess

The Cowboy Takes a Bride

### TWILIGHT, TEXAS

The Christmas Brides of Twilight

The Cowboy Cookie Challenge

Second Chance Christmas

The Christmas Backup Plan

The Christmas Dare

The Christmas Key

Cowboy, It's Cold Outside

A Wedding for Christmas

I'll Be Home for Christmas

Christmas at Twilight

The Valentine's Day Disaster

The Welcome Home Garden Club

The First Love Cookie Club

The True Love Quilting Club

The Sweethearts' Knitting Club

### MOONGLOW BAY

The Wedding at Moonglow Bay

The Lighthouse on Moonglow Bay

The Keepsake Sisters

The Moonglow Sisters

---

DISCOVER GREAT AUTHORS, EXCLUSIVE OFFERS, AND MORE AT HC.COM.